FRANCINE
RIVERS

THE
ATONEMENT
CHiLD

Tyndale House Publishers, Inc.
WHEATON, ILLINOIS

Visit Tyndale's exciting Web site at www.tyndale.com

Library of Congress Cataloging-In-Publication Data

Rivers, Francine., date
    The atonement child / Francine Rivers.
      p. cm.
     ISBN 0-8423-0041-4. — ISBN 0-8423-0052-X (pbk.)
     I. Title.
PS3568.I83165A95 1997
813'.54—dc21

96-40212

Printed in the United States of America

09 08 07 06 05 04 03
13 12 11 10   9   8

*To all those who live
with the anguish of abortion,
and to their families
who suffer with them
in secret and in silence.*

Come to me, all of you who are weary
and carry heavy burdens, and I will
give you rest. Take my yoke upon you.
Let me teach you, because I am humble
and gentle, and you will find rest
for your souls. For my yoke fits perfectly,
and the burden I give you is light.

MATTHEW 11:28-30

Acknowledgments

Rick, thank you for your continued support through a long and highly emotion-charged year. Without your support and encouragement, and that of our children, I would have shelved this project long ago.

To the ladies who have shared their abortion experiences with me, I am especially grateful. As far as the east is from the west, so far has Jesus removed our transgressions from us. I love you all.

Donna Cornell, you are a wonder. You and the men and women who volunteer at PCC have such open hearts. The love of Jesus shines from you as you minister daily to those facing crisis pregnancies and those suffering from the anguish of past abortions and incest. It's my prayer that your kind of ministry will spread across our nation to reach the millions of men and women who suffer in secret and in silence.

Diane Naber, thank you for sharing your excitement and wonder at the birthing process. My children are almost grown, and I'd forgotten the awesome wonder of giving birth. Those who have you as their coach are blessed indeed.

I also want to thank Lee Ezell for spending some precious time with me and sharing her experiences and thoughts. I highly recommend her book *The Missing Piece*. I also want to thank Lissa Halls Johnson for sharing the information she collected in writing her novel *No Other Choice*. May God bless both of you in your work.

Peggy, Leilani, Karen—nothing I can say will be thanks enough for your wise counsel and prayers. I could not have finished this novel without you. And Rick Hahn, thank you for your counsel and patience. How many times have I called and asked you to clarify Scripture? Or, "Tell me where it is!"? You continue to be a man after God's own heart and a blessing to our church family.

To all those at Tyndale House, thank you for your continued encouragement and support. May all we do continue to be our offering to the Lord.

It was on a cold January night when the unthinkable, unpardonable happened.

The evening had gone as usual for Dynah Carey as she served food at the Stanton Manor House, a retirement home established for Middleton's city employees. She enjoyed her work, often talking animatedly with the elderly patrons who came down from their small apartments for communal meals in the basement cafeteria. Sally Wentworth was a great cook and planned a varied menu. The only complaint Dynah had heard in five months on the job was how much food there was left over. Most of the people who lived at the Manor had come through the depression years and hated to see waste.

The rest of the diners had left for the evening, all but Mr. Packard, who was taking his time sipping his cup of decaf. "Your car still in the shop, Dynah?"

"Yes, sir. They're still waiting for a part to come in."

"Thought it was supposed to be fixed yesterday."

"I guess there was some kind of delay," she said with a shrug. She wasn't worried about it.

"Is that young man of yours going to come pick you up tonight?" he said, watching Dynah fill the saltshakers.

She smiled at him as she moved on to the next table. "Not this evening, Mr. Packard. He's teaching a Bible study."

"Maybe Sally can take you home."

"It's not far to the bus stop."

"A mile at least, and a pretty girl like you shouldn't be out on her own after dark."

"I'm always careful."

"Careful isn't always good enough these days. I've gotten so I hate reading the newspaper. Time was you could walk from one end of town to the other without worrying." He shook his head sadly. "Now the town's gotten so big you don't know anybody anymore. People coming and going all the time. You never know who's living next door. Could be Pollyanna or Son of Sam. Houses spreading all over tarnation, and no plan to the way it's sprawling. I remember when I was a boy, we knew everybody. We left our doors unlocked. Never had to be afraid. I don't know what the world's coming to these days. Makes me glad I'm almost to the end of my life. When I was growing up, we used to sit outside on the front porch and talk. Neighbors would come by and have lemonade. Those were good times. Now nobody has time for anything. They don't even build porches on houses anymore. Everybody's inside watching television and not saying much of anything to anybody."

Dynah stayed close, responding to the ache of loneliness she heard in his words and voice. He wasn't whining. He was grieving. His wife had passed away four months before. The family had gathered around him long enough for the memorial service and then scattered across the States again. His two sons lived on the West Coast, too far away to make frequent visits. His daughter lived in Indiana but called him every Sunday. Sundays were good days for Mr. Packard.

Tonight was Wednesday.

"I miss Trooper," he said quietly. He smiled wistfully. "I used to call Freda 'Trooper.'"

Mr. Packard told Dynah how he had come up with the

nickname just after World War II. He had fought in the Pacific two years before being blown off a transport. He landed in a field hospital where he spent another three months before he was shipped stateside.

"While I was away, Freda had our son and managed a part-time job. When my father got sick with cancer, she quit and stepped into his shoes to help my mother run the family grocery store. My Freda was a home-front soldier." His expression softened in memory, his eyes glistening with tears. "So I called her 'Trooper,' and it stuck."

"We have to close down, Dynah!" Sally said from behind the counter. She said it loudly enough so that poor Mr. Packard would hear. Dynah looked at his face and wanted to weep.

Taking the hint, the old man got up. "Everybody's in a hurry these days," he said with a glance toward the kitchen. Then his eyes came to rest on her again. "Good night, Dynah. You be careful out there tonight."

"I will, sir," she said with a fond smile, touching his shoulder as he passed. "Try not to worry."

Juan Garcia began putting chairs upside down on the tables. Gathering Mr. Packard's spoon, cup, and saucer, Dynah watched the old man walk stiffly across the room. His arthritis was troubling him again.

"I didn't mean to break up your little chat," Sally said as Dynah put the things into the big industrial dishwasher and pulled the door down. "Some of these old people could talk until your hair turned gray." She took her sweater from the hook on the wall. "They've got no place to go and nothing to do."

"He misses his wife," Dynah said and thought about following Mr. Packard's suggestion and asking Sally for a ride.

"I know. I miss my husband. I miss my kids. You miss your handsome fiancé." She dumped her shoulder bag onto the counter and shrugged into her sweater and parka. "And as

Scarlett O'Hara always said, 'Tomorrow is another day.'"
Picking up her bag, she said a brisk good-night and headed for
the back door.

Sally seemed in such a hurry, Dynah didn't want to impose
upon her. Besides, it wasn't that far to the bus stop, and there
were plenty of streetlights along the way. Getting her backpack
from the storage room, Dynah slipped off her rubber-soled
white shoes and pulled on her snow boots. Zipping the shoes
into the backpack, she said good night to Juan. Crossing the
dining room, she went into the lobby that opened out onto the
back parking lot. Sally had already turned the lights down for
the night. There was only the soft glow of security lights and
the bright lights behind Dynah where Juan was getting ready to
wash and wax the floors.

Pulling on her parka, Dynah went to the back door.

The idea that she needed to be concerned hadn't ever crossed
her mind before. The Manor wasn't exactly a center of crime.
The worst thing that had happened was someone's spray painting graffiti on the walls three months ago. The manager had
painted over the bubble letters and numbers by the next afternoon, and the police increased the number of times they drove
by each evening. The vandals hadn't returned.

Pushing the door open, Dynah stepped outside. The air was
crisp; the snow from last week's fall was packed hard and dingy.
Her breath puffed white in the stillness. She heard the lock click
behind her and shivered slightly. She zipped her parka up to her
neck and looked around. Maybe it was Mr. Packard's warning
that made her edgy. There was nothing else to bother her. It was
an evening like any other, no darker, no colder.

There were shadows all around, but nothing unfamiliar or
threatening as she walked down the wheelchair ramp. She took
her usual path through the back parking lot to Maple Street. It
was only a few blocks down to Main, another eight to Syca-

more, and a few more to Sixteenth where she caught the bus. It only took fifteen minutes to reach her stop at Henderson. From there it was seven blocks to the dorm.

Dynah glanced at her wristwatch. Nine-thirty. Janet Wells, her roommate, would be in the library studying late tonight. Janet always left things till the last minute and then aced every exam. Dynah smiled to herself, wishing she were that fortunate. She had to study all term long to pull grades high enough to keep her scholarship.

Relaxing as she walked, Dynah enjoyed the clear night. She had always liked this street with its turn-of-the-century houses. She could imagine people sitting on their front porches in the summertime, sipping lemonade just the way Mr. Packard remembered. Like something out of a movie. It was a life far removed from the way she had grown up on Ocean Avenue in San Francisco—and yet similar as well.

Looking back, she realized how she had been protected by her parents and cloistered in home schooling. In many ways, she had led an idyllic life with few bumps and twists in the road. Of course, there had been times when she had been curious to know what lay beyond the hedges her parents had planted around her. When she asked, they explained, and she complied. She loved and respected them too much to do otherwise.

Her mom and dad had been Christians forever. She couldn't remember a time when they hadn't been involved in the church or some community service project. Her mother sang in the choir and led Sunday morning Bible studies. Dynah had grown up surrounded by love, protected and guided every step of the way, right up to the doors of New Life College. And now it seemed her life would continue that way, with Ethan Goodson Turner at the reins.

Not that I am complaining, Lord. I am thankful, so thankful. You have blessed me with the parents I have and the man I'm going to marry. Everywhere I look, I see your blessings. The world is a beautiful place, up to the very stars in the heavens.

Lord, would you please give poor old Mr. Packard a portion of the hope and joy I feel? He needs you. And Sally, Lord. She's always fretting about something and always in a hurry. She has so little joy in her life. And Juan said tonight one of his children is sick, Father. Pedro, the little one. Juan can't afford insurance and—

A car passed slowly.

Dynah noticed a Massachusetts plate before the vehicle sped up. The red taillights were like a pair of red eyes staring back at her as the station wagon went down the street, then squealed onto Sycamore. Frowning slightly, she watched it disappear.

Odd.

Her thoughts wandered again as she walked more slowly past her favorite house. It was two doors from Sycamore, a big Victorian with a porch around the front. The lights were on behind the Nottingham lace curtains. The front door was heavy mahogany with small leaded panes of glass and stained glass at the top. The pattern was a sunburst of golds and yellows.

It would be nice to live on a shady street like this one, in a big house, complete with a trimmed lawn, a flower garden in the front, and a yard in the back with a swing and a sandbox for the children. She smiled at her dreaming. Ethan would probably be offered a church in a big city like Los Angeles or Chicago or New York. A man with his talents for preaching wouldn't end up in a small college town in the Midwest.

She couldn't believe a young man like Ethan would look twice at her, let alone fall in love and ask her to marry him. He said he knew the day he met her that God meant her to be his wife.

She wouldn't have met him at all if her parents hadn't insisted she visit New Life College. She had already decided on a college in California. When they mentioned NLC, she declined, convinced the cost and distance should eliminate it. They assured her they had planned for the first, and the second would be good for her. They wanted her to become more independent, and attending college in Illinois was a good way to accomplish that. Besides, her grades were good enough that she could receive scholarships.

Dynah smiled about it now. Her parents had never been subtle in what they wanted for her. Her mother had left pamphlets of a dozen Christian colleges scattered about the house to tweak her curiosity. Each had been opened to beautiful, idyllic places with stretches of lawn lined with manicured gardens. NLC had a quad with six majestic brick and white-columned buildings, two to the east, two to the west, one on the north and a church to the south. But what appealed most to Dynah were the wonderful young, smiling faces of the students.

There had never been any question that she would end up at a Christian college. Where better to learn how to serve the Lord than in an environment centered on Christ? Yet, the Midwest had seemed so far from home she had dismissed it.

While completing her final year of work for her high school diploma, she sent out a dozen applications and received as many acceptance letters. She narrowed it down to four possibilities, dismissing all those outside the state. Her father suggested she and her mother take a trip to southern California and see the three campuses that were there. After visiting one in San Jose, she contacted the others and made appointments with the dean of admissions to discuss programs and scholarships.

While she was gone, her father had contacted four colleges he thought "good enough" for his daughter. One was in Pennsylvania, one in Indiana, and two in Illinois. One sent a video.

Two had students call and talk with her about the campus, activities, and curriculum. The last was New Life College. They sent a catalog and an invitation to come and take a firsthand look at what they had to offer.

She thought it preposterous and a terrible waste of her parents' money, but her father insisted she go. "You have to learn to fly sometime."

It was the first time she had gone anywhere without her parents or a church group. All the arrangements had been made by the college beforehand, so she had the safety net of knowing she wouldn't be on her own long. A student would meet her at the airport and bring her to the campus where she would spend two days with a personal guide.

Dynah smiled as she remembered her reaction when she first saw Ethan with a sign bearing her name. She thought he was the most gorgeous young man she had ever seen. Her mother had told her the college would probably send a nice young man to meet her and drive her to the college. She hadn't expected someone who looked like he belonged in the movies. She was completely flustered and tongue-tied, but by the time they were halfway to the campus, he had put her so much at ease that she had shared her Ocean Avenue life with him. By the end of the trip, she knew Ethan didn't just look good, he was good. He was on fire for the Lord, ambitious for godly service, and filled with ideas about ministry.

"My father's a pastor, and his father before him," he told her. "My great-grandfather was a circuit rider for the gospel. I'm following in their footsteps."

By the time they drove beneath the brick arch to the NLC campus, she was convinced Ethan Goodson Turner would be the next Billy Graham.

Upon their arrival at the women's dorm, Ethan introduced her to Charlotte Hale, a music major from Alabama. Charlotte was vibrant and full of southern charm and hospitality. A senior graduating in June, she had already made plans to go with a mission group to Mexico and present the gospel in music and drama.

Over the next two days, every minute was taken up seeing the campus, especially the departments in which Dynah was most interested: music and education. She heard about various programs, scholarships, and activities and met dozens of people. Charlotte seemed to know everyone and introduced Dynah to them all. She met professors and students, the deans, the manager of the bookstore, and even two of the gardeners who kept up the grounds. Dynah loved every minute of her stay.

On Saturday evening, to her surprise and delight, Ethan joined them for dinner at the mess hall. She blushed when he sat down. He lingered until a girl came over and asked if he was going to an evening Bible study.

"Half the girls on campus wish they could marry him," Charlotte had remarked, watching him walk away.

"I'm not surprised," Dynah had said, remembering how embarrassed she had been for daydreaming about just that during the drive from the airport.

Charlotte had looked at her then, straight on, and smiled. "You should come back. He'll be a senior next year."

She hadn't dissembled. "Are you suggesting I join his legion of admirers?"

Charlotte laughed. She didn't say anything about Ethan after that, but it was clear she had done her best to plant a seed for thought.

They hadn't been back at the dorm fifteen minutes when Ethan called. He told Dynah he would be picking her up and taking her back to the airport. She thanked him and said she would be ready. By morning, Dynah had decided against coming back to NLC because of Ethan. If she was infatuated after a few days, she knew she would be head over heels in love if she saw him every day of the year. And NLC wasn't so big a campus that she could miss him. No, she didn't want to become one of the legion, and she held no false hopes of becoming his choice.

She smiled now, thinking of it, feeling his engagement ring on her finger with the back of her thumb. She had been so nervous on the drive back to O'Hare. She had told Ethan he could drop her off in front of the Delta terminal, but he had insisted he would accompany her inside. He parked, took her carry-on, and stayed with her. When they got inside the terminal, he stood with her in line as she got her boarding pass. Then he sat with her in the gate area. She had been so embarrassed, she wanted to crawl under the seat.

"I know I haven't seen much of the world, Ethan, but I don't need baby-sitting," she had said, trying to laugh off his concerns.

"I know that," he said quietly.

"I don't need a bodyguard, either."

He looked at her, and she felt foolish and young, too young for him. There had been such an intensity in his eyes that she had blushed.

"Come back to NLC, Dynah."

It had sounded like a command. She smiled. "Do you have to meet a quota?"

"God wants you here."

He sounded so serious, so certain, she had to ask. "How do you know?" Surely, if God wanted her at NLC, God would tell her.

"I just know, Dynah. I knew the minute I saw you."

Looking into his blue eyes, she decided not to dismiss what he said. In truth, she wanted to believe him. She wanted to see Ethan Turner again, and the thought that he wanted the same thing was heady incentive indeed.

"Will you pray about it?"

She nodded, knowing she would be doing little else.

She didn't hear one word from Ethan through spring and summer, but five minutes after she walked into the gymnasium for registration that fall, he came up to her and put his hand on her shoulder as though staking public claim to her. The first thing he did was introduce her to Joseph Guilierno, his best friend and roommate.

Joe was a surprise. He didn't appear to fit the NLC mold but looked more like the many young men she had seen around San Francisco on excursions with her parents. Tall, dark-eyed, strongly built, Joe looked street-tough and older than Ethan. Not so much in years as worldly experience.

"No wonder," Joe said cryptically and extended his hand. His fingers curved around hers firmly as he smiled. Three months later, after she was wearing an engagement ring, Joe told her that Ethan had come back to their apartment the day he picked her up at the airport and said he had met the girl he was going to marry.

"I asked him if he had consulted God, and Ethan said it was God who put it in his head."

Smiling again now as she had when Joe first told her that, Dynah reached the corner of Sixteenth. She let her mind drift along rosy avenues. Ethan had a wonderful future laid out for them. He would graduate with honors at the end of the year. Dean Abernathy was very impressed with his work and was encouraging him to go on for his master's. The dean had already arranged for Ethan to work part time at one of the local churches. Dynah would be able to finish her education as well. Ethan was adamant that she get her degree, convinced that her studies in music and youth ministry would be of great use in his ministry.

She felt so blessed. They would be equally yoked, working together for the glory of God. What more could she want?

Oh, Lord, you are so good to me. I will do anything for you. All I am, all I ever hope to be, is from you, Father. Use me as you will.

A car pulled up alongside her and slowed to her pace. Her heart jumped as she noticed it looked like the same one that had passed her on Maple Street. Her nerves tensed as the window lowered and a disembodied male voice said, "Are you going to the campus, miss?"

"Yes, I am," she said before she thought better of it.

"I can give you a lift."

"No, thank you."

"I'm going there myself. Visiting my brother. Unfortunately, I'm lost. First time in town. He lives near the main gate of the campus."

She relaxed and stepped closer. Leaning down, she pointed. "Go down a mile to Henderson and turn right. Keep going, and you'll run right into it. It's a block past the city park." She couldn't see the man's face.

"If I give you a ride, you could show me."

A strange foreboding gripped her. "No, thank you," she said politely and took a step back. She didn't want to offend the man. What excuse could she offer? She looked toward the bus stop where a woman was sitting and found an excuse. "I'm meeting a friend."

"Sure. Thanks for the directions," the man said, sounding far less friendly. The window whirred up. As he drove on down Sixteenth, she saw the car bore the same Massachusetts plates. The two red taillights stared back at her as the car passed the bus stop.

Shivering, she walked on. She recognized the waitress sitting on the bench. "Hi, Martha. How are you this evening?"

"So-so. My feet are killing me. Was someone trying to pick you up back there?"

"Not really. He was lost."

"Yeah, right. That's his story."

"He was looking for the campus."

"I hope you told him where to go."

"I gave him directions."

Martha laughed. "I'm sure you didn't give him the ones I would've given him."

They talked about their jobs until the bus arrived. Martha climbed aboard first and moved to her usual place near the back, where she could read her romance novel uninterrupted. Dynah took a seat at the front, across from the driver.

Her first day aboard, she had noticed the pins on the lapel of Charles's neat uniform jacket. When she asked what they were, he said he had one to show for each five-year period he had driven without an accident. After a few weeks of riding with him, Dynah had gone to a trophy store and had a plaque made up for him that said, "In honor of distinguished service to Middleton, Charles Booker Washington is awarded the title of Driver Emeritus." He had laughed when he opened it, but it was now proudly displayed next to the No Smoking sign at the front of the bus.

"How's things, Charlie?"

He grinned at her as he hit the button to close the door. "Pretty good now you're aboard. Missed your sunny smile last night."

"Ethan picked me up."

"He driving a Cadillac yet?"

She laughed. "No, sir. Still has his Buick." She leaned forward in the seat and rested her arms on the iron railing.

Charlie nodded. "When he gets a church, he'll get his Cad. We don't let our preachers drive anything else. Treat 'em good."

"I noticed." When she had gone to Charlie's church, she had

seen the new maroon Cadillac parked in the "Reserved for Pastor" space. She had enjoyed herself so much at the service, she pleaded with Ethan to go back with her. He had gone once, grudgingly, but had refused to attend with her again. He said the service was a little "too lively" for his tastes. He hadn't felt comfortable with the loud gospel music pouring from the choir, nor with the way the members of the congregation interjected their remarks during the pastor's sermon.

"It felt irreverent."

She hadn't shared his discomfort, though the service had been far from the kind of service to which she was accustomed. She felt the Spirit moving in that church. The members celebrated their love for Jesus and for each other. She had enjoyed the experience. Something about it had stirred her. The pastor had preached straight from the Word, and the people made sure he knew his points were sinking in. However, Dynah didn't argue with Ethan's assessment. She had learned early that he took his role as the spiritual head of their relationship to heart. She also knew he had been brought up in a conservative denomination who showed their zeal in other ways. His parents, like her mother and father, were deeply involved in community action and charities.

She and Charlie talked about all manner of things. He had been driving a Middleton city bus since before she was born and had learned a lot about human nature. He didn't mind sharing what he knew.

Tonight, Mr. Packard was on Dynah's mind.

"I know the Packards," Charlie said. "He and his wife used to get on the bus every Tuesday and ride it to the end of the line. Good people. I read she passed on. Too bad. She was a nice lady."

"Maybe I could tell him you miss seeing him."

"You do that, girl. Maybe I'll drop by and see him myself.

Between the two of us, we might get him out of his apartment and back among the living." He brought the bus close to the curb and slowed to a stop at the corner of Henderson.

"Thanks, Charlie."

"You watch yourself, girl."

"I will."

"Tell Mr. Packard I have a front seat saved for him," he said and hit the button. The doors swished closed, and he gave her a wave through the glass.

Dynah waved back and watched as the bus pulled away from the curb. Adjusting the strap of her shoulder bag, she started the walk to campus.

Henderson Avenue was a long, pretty street with old-growth maples and neat brick houses with snow-covered lawns. In the city park located a block south of the campus was a small community-center building used by students interning as youth leaders and teachers. In two years, she would be working there. The center housed a daily preschool program in the morning and youth activities through the afternoon every day of the week except Sunday, when everything in town shut down for worship services. Only a few businesses, mostly nationwide chains, stayed open.

As Dynah came abreast of the park, she paused, frowning. The car with the Massachusetts plates was there, just across the street, parked beyond a cobblestone driveway beneath a canopy of winter-bare branches. She peered at the vehicle, anxious, then noticed with relief that no one sat in the driver's seat. The man must have found his brother after all. He had said he lived not far from the campus.

A twig snapped to the right, and her nerves jumped. She turned and saw a tall dark shape moving toward her. A man.

Every instinct screamed "Run!" but surprise made her hesitate—and within a few seconds she knew she had made a terrible mistake. A couple of seconds. That's all it took for the man to have a hold on her.

■ ■ ■

Purdy Whitehall received the call at Middleton Police Department at 10:37 Wednesday evening, January 8. It had been a quiet evening with only one complaint, about a party disturbing the peace. Sergeant Don Ferguson had reported a few minutes earlier that it was nothing more than a bunch of baby boomers feeling nostalgic and singing to Elvis records.

This call was altogether different.

"Someone's screaming in the park," a woman said. "Come quick, please! Someone's screaming!"

The caller's telephone number came up on Purdy's computer screen along with the address. Henderson Avenue. Speaking with a trained calmness, she assured the woman help would be coming and put her on hold in order to dispatch a squad car to the location.

Frank Lawson was just pulling up to Ernie's Diner on Sixteenth for a badly needed coffee break when his radio crackled with the message. Muttering under his breath, he rapped the radio sharply and picked up the speaker. Depressing the button, he identified himself and his car number. "My radio's having PMS again, Purdy. Repeat the message."

"There's a disturbance at the park on Henderson Avenue, Frank. How close are you?"

"Ten blocks. I'm on my way." Putting the speaker back, he swung the squad car in a sharp U-turn and hit his flashing red lights. Few cars were on the road at this time of night, so he didn't use his siren. No use waking people up if it wasn't necessary.

As he barreled down Sixteenth, he saw a white station wagon heading west. The red taillights glowed as the car pulled to the side of the road in obedience to the law. Frank never passed it. He made a sharp left onto Henderson Avenue.

Coming to a smooth stop by the park, he grabbed his heavy flashlight, made a quick call to Purdy, and got out. He surveyed the park as he came around his squad car. His heart quickened, the hair on the back of his neck prickling.

Something was wrong. He was sure of it.

Adrenaline pumping, Frank glanced around and saw lights on in three houses near the park. A woman came out to stand on the front porch of one.

"Over there!" She came down the front steps in her bathrobe. "Over there near the activity center! Please hurry. Someone's been hurt."

"Go on back in your house, ma'am. We'll take care of it." Another squad car pulled up, and Frank saw Greg Townsend get out.

The woman fled up her steps and banged the screen door behind her, but she remained silhouetted in the doorway watching, her arms hugged around herself to ward off the cold.

Greg reached Frank. "See anything?"

"No, but it doesn't feel right. Take the path over there, and I'll come in from this side."

"Gotcha."

Frank knew every inch of this park like it was his own backyard. He brought his three small children here to play every Saturday afternoon so his wife could have a few hours respite.

There was enough light from the park lamps that he didn't need to use the flashlight, but he kept it in his left hand anyway, his right over his gun. He saw evidence of a struggle in the snow near the sidewalk that ran the length of Henderson to the NLC campus. A little further in, he found a backpack. Just beyond it was a torn parka. He walked along the edge of the pathway cautiously, eyes sweeping, ears trained for any sound out of the ordinary.

As he neared the activity center, he heard a rustling sound in the bushes nearby. Something was scrambling frantically away, like an animal clambering for a hiding place.

Instinctively he removed the loop from his gun and pulled it free of his holster. "Police! Come out onto the walkway where we can see you." He moved slightly, away from the light, so he wouldn't make himself an easy target.

The rustling stopped, and he heard another sound, soft and broken. A woman sobbing.

Oh, God. Oh, God, no. Not here. Not where I bring my kids every week.

Holstering his gun, Frank went to the bushes and drew some branches back. Training his flashlight, he saw a girl huddled beneath the canopy of leaves. Flinching back, she covered her face with her arm. Her blonde hair was tangled and damp from the snow. Frank noticed the ripped waitress uniform, the bleeding scratches on her shoulder, the fresh bloodstains on her skirt.

Anger filled him. "Easy," he said gently. Lowering the light so it wasn't straight on her, he hunkered down. She cowered from him. "I'm Sergeant Lawson, miss. I'm here to help you." He kept talking quietly, trying to give her a sense of safety.

She raised her head after a few minutes, her blue eyes wide and dilated. Her lower lip was split and bleeding, her right eye swollen from a blow. Drawing her knees up, she sat on the dirty snow and then, covering her head with her arms, she cried.

Compassion filled Frank, along with a sick rage. Whoever had done this should pay.

Greg approached from the other side of the park, his footsteps crunching in the hard snow. The girl's head came up again, eyes wide and frightened. He could see the pulse hammering in her throat.

"It's all right," he said, sensitive to her fear. He straightened and stood aside so she could see Greg. "This is Officer Townsend, miss. He was just checking the area to see if anyone's still around." He looked at Greg.

Greg shook his head and looked past him to the young girl huddled in the covering of bushes. "Rape?"

"I'm afraid so. Better call an ambulance."

"No," the girl said brokenly, covering her face again. "No, please don't." Her shoulders began to shake violently.

"You need medical assistance."

"I want to go home."

"You're going to be all right," he said firmly, hunkering down again, keeping his voice calm and low. "I'm not going to leave you alone." He glanced up at Greg. "Tell them no sirens, and lights only when they need them."

"Done," Greg said tightly and strode off toward the west side of the park where they had left the squad cars.

"Come on out, ma'am. You're safe."

She moved, scooting a little bit closer and then stopping. Sinking back, she started to cry again, her body bent over, her arms wrapped around her middle. She rocked herself slowly, head down.

A lump lodged in Frank's throat. She didn't look more than eighteen. "Was it someone you knew?" He wished he didn't have to ask questions, but every minute counted if they were going to arrest her attacker.

She shook her head slowly.

"What did he look like?"

"I don't know," she stammered. "I never saw his face." She tried to get up and uttered a gasp of pain. Frank reached out, but she drew back sharply, clearly not wanting to be touched. She sank down again, weeping.

"What's your name, miss?"

"Do I have to tell you?"

"I want to help you. I have to know your name to do it."

"Dynah Carey. I live in the dorm. My roommate's expecting me. Her name's Janet, Janet Wells. It's only two blocks. Can I go home now? Please?"

"Not yet. You need to go to the hospital first, Miss Carey. Just stay put. We'll get help for you." He hoped the ambulance crew had a woman with them.

They didn't. Two men arrived with a gurney. The older man spoke with the girl and coaxed her out of her hiding place. Frank stood close by, watching the paramedic support the shivering girl as she lay down upon the gurney. They wrapped her in warm blankets, snapped the belts around her, and wheeled her along the park pathway to Henderson Avenue. She said nothing and kept her eyes tightly closed.

Frank's mouth tightened when he saw the ambulance lights flashing. The woman who had called in the report was outside on her porch again. So were others all up and down the street. Windows were illuminated in half a dozen houses, faces peering through the curtains. Some, bolder in their curiosity, came out onto their lawns to watch what was going on. He had hoped to save the girl further embarrassment.

She was loaded quickly into the ambulance. One of the men went inside with her and closed the doors behind him. The other took the driver's seat. They pulled away from the curb and were on their way to the hospital before Frank had reached his squad car.

Greg was waiting for him. "We patrolled the other side of the park but didn't see anyone. No cars parked along this street or on the other side. Did she give you a description?"

"She said she never saw his face. I'll talk to her more as soon as the doctor's examined her."

■ ■ ■

Dynah couldn't stop shaking. She asked the nurse if she could shower but was told she would have to wait until after the doctor had seen her. The nurse helped her undress and don a white hospital gown. Shivering, Dynah watched the nurse put her torn, stained waitress uniform, undergarments, and shredded nylons into a large plastic bag. Her muddy snow boots were placed in another. Both bags were given to someone waiting outside the door.

Dynah's teeth chattered, but her chill had nothing to do with the temperature of the room, which was kept at a comfortable sixty-eight degrees. The shaking, the terrible cold, came from inside her. Even the blanket the nurse put around her did nothing to ward off the chill.

"I'll get you another blanket, Miss Carey," the nurse said and went out.

Dynah almost protested, afraid to be alone. Clutching the blanket, she sat on the edge of the examining table, wondering what she was going to wear home. The silence increased her anxiety. She wanted desperately to wash. She yearned to stand beneath a scalding spray, so she could soap and scrub every inch of her body and wash away what had happened.

Would she ever be cleansed of it? Could she wash the horror from her mind and heart? She squeezed her eyes shut, willing the images in her mind away. She was safe now. Or was she? Her eyes flew open. She'd thought she was safe before, but that had been an illusion, ripped away. Sitting on the examining table in the short, backless gown, she felt naked and as vulnerable as she had been in the park. Sick with fear, she looked from one end of the cubicle to the other for some avenue of escape. She wanted to go home. Home to her parents. Home to the house on Ocean Avenue. But what would her parents say? Perhaps locked in her dorm room, she would feel safer.

Someone rapped on the door, and she jumped. A doctor entered, the nurse who had taken her clothes just behind him. "I'm Dr. Kennon, Miss Carey. How are you feeling?"

"Fine," she said without thinking. Wasn't that what she always said in a doctor's office? She grimaced, her eyes tearing up, and he winced. When she spoke again, she hardly recognized her own voice. "Could I take a shower, please? I want to take a shower."

"In a little while." He reached into his pocket and took out a small tape recorder. Depressing the button, he set it on the counter to his right. "Now, let's take a look at that eye first." As he gently tested the bruised flesh and flashed a small light into her pupil, he told her he was recording the examination in order to help the police apprehend her attacker. He asked her if she was experiencing any dizziness. Some, she said. She was nauseated.

"Lie down, please."

The nurse assisted her, speaking softly, encouraging her to follow the doctor's instructions. Dynah trembled even more violently as he examined her scrapes and asked more questions. As she answered, she relived the nightmare in the park, seeing it from every angle. Some of the questions the doctor asked made her blush with embarrassment and pale in shame: Was she on birth control? When was her last menses? He wanted details about what had happened to her, details she was loathe to remember, let alone speak aloud.

"I don't want to talk about it."

"Everything you're telling us will help the police."

And who would help *her*?

God, where were you?

When the doctor told her to scoot her bottom to the end of

the table and put her feet in the stirrups, she didn't understand. The nurse, sensitive to her anguish, tried to explain as delicately as possible.

"The doctor needs to make sure you're not injured internally, Miss Carey. And he'll be able to collect a specimen. For evidence."

"Evidence?" she said.

The doctor explained; revulsion filled her.

Oh, God. Oh, God. Why do I have to go through this? Haven't I gone through enough already?

"I'm going to be sick." She sat up quickly. The nurse held a small basin for her and stroked her back, murmuring words of sympathy. The doctor went out to give her a few minutes to recompose herself. After a while, the nurse calmed her down enough to continue, and the doctor came back.

The nurse's eyes were filled with compassion. "It'll be over soon, dear. Hold my hand. Squeeze if you want to."

Dynah clutched it tightly, her body tense.

"Breathe, Miss Carey. That's it. Try to relax."

The doctor explained everything he was doing to her and why, but it didn't help. The physical examination was extensive, intrusive, and painful. When he finished, he apologized and then told the nurse to cut her fingernails. More evidence. The clippings were put in another small plastic bag and labeled for the police lab. The nurse took pictures of the abrasions on her shoulder and right hip, the bruises on her thighs, her throat, and her battered face.

Spirit crushed, Dynah fell silent.

Dr. Kennon looked at her sadly and said again that he was sorry.

"You can sit up now," the nurse said gently.

"I'll have admissions get all the paperwork going," Dr. Kennon said, turning toward the door.

"No!" Dynah said, heart jumping. "I want to go home!"

"I understand your feelings, but—!"

"No, you don't! How could you?" For all his assurances of wanting to make sure she was all right, she felt degraded. She had wound down to a strip of black tape on his recorder, and that would be turned over to the policeman waiting outside the door. "You don't understand!" She covered her face and cried.

"I'd like to keep you here overnight, for observation."

"No." It was all she could choke out.

"We would start you immediately on estrogen therapy."

She raised her head. "Estrogen—? Why?"

"In case conception has taken place."

Dynah felt all the warmth drain from her. She stared at him in horror as full comprehension struck. "I might . . . I might be pregnant?"

"The chances of that are extremely small, but it's better to take precautions."

If she had conceived, it was already too late.

"There may be some side effects to the estrogen. That's why I'd like to keep you here for one night, possibly two."

Dynah sat on the edge of the examining table, her eyes closed tightly. She had attended several pro-life rallies with Ethan. She knew he was talking about an abortifacient.

"No." She shook her head. "I want to go home. Please."

Dr. Kennon glanced at the nurse, and she moved to his side. They talked in hushed tones for a moment; then the doctor left the room. The nurse put the blanket around her shoulders again. Dynah clutched it tightly.

"I'm sorry you had to go through this, Miss Carey. Dr. Kennon was only trying to make things easier on you." She offered her a cup of cool water. "I know how difficult this is. If you'd rather not take the medication right now, that's fine. You can take it tomorrow."

Dynah shook her head.

"You've been through enough tonight. You can wait a few weeks. If you miss your period, you come back and have a pregnancy test. If it's positive, you can have a menstrual extraction."

Dynah didn't want to think about what the nurse was saying. Being raped was horror enough without considering the possibility she might have become pregnant.

Oh, God, you wouldn't be so cruel. Would you, Lord?

"You can take a shower now, if you'd like."

Down the hall, in a quiet room, Dynah stood beneath a hard, hot spray of water, scrubbing and scrubbing. Still feeling dirty, she sank down hopelessly in the corner of the stall and wept.

God, why? I don't understand. Why did you let this happen to me? Where were the angels that are supposed to be protecting me? What did I do to make you angry?

Someone tapped on the door, making her start.

"Are you all right, Miss Carey?"

"I'm fine," Dynah said in a choked voice, huddled beneath the hot pounding water. "I just need to stay in here for a little while longer."

"Your roommate brought you a change of clothes."

Dynah pushed herself up. "Janet's here?"

"She just arrived. She's in the waiting room. Officer Lawson is speaking with her now."

Dynah closed her eyes in relief and leaned her head back against the wall.

"I'll leave the clothes on the seat for you. Don't feel rushed, Miss Carey. Take all the time you need. I'll be right outside the door if you need anything." Dynah sensed the unspoken message. The nurse would be far enough away to give her a sense of privacy but not so far she would be left alone.

Dynah emerged from the shower and dried herself quickly.

She donned the fresh cotton underwear, a lightweight white turtleneck T-shirt, a pair of faded blue Levi's, and a cable-knit pale yellow sweater. Even after pulling on the white woolen socks and gray vinyl zip-up boots, she was still shivering. She couldn't seem to stop. The dark violence of the assault gripped her soul and wouldn't let go.

Looking in the mirror, she saw the reflection of a face she barely recognized. Raking trembling fingers through her tangled blonde hair, she tried to make a French braid. After a few minutes, she gave up. She didn't care how she looked. She just wanted to leave. She wanted to go back to her room in the dorm, bury herself beneath a mountain of heavy blankets, and never come out into the light again.

The nurse ushered Dynah to the waiting room. She saw Joe first, standing in the middle of the room, his expression filled with pain and compassion. Janet was sitting on the couch; Ethan stood near the windows. As she drew near, he turned and looked at her, his face etched with a terrible grief and anger. Janet bolted from the sofa and hugged her tightly. "Oh, Dynah," she said, crying. "Oh, Dynah, Dynah. Come on, honey. We'll take you home. You'll be OK now."

On the way out, Ethan touched her once, a brief squeeze on her bruised shoulder. She flinched, and he withdrew completely, eyes shadowed. She felt his anger and was frightened and confused by it.

Janet bundled her into the backseat of Joe's Honda. She kept her arm around Dynah, holding her close. Dynah glanced up and saw Joe looking at her in the rearview mirror. His eyes were dark, reflecting her pain.

"There's a blanket back there, Janet," he said quietly, starting the car. "Keep Dynah warm."

Ethan didn't say anything until Joe pulled out of the hospital parking lot. "We'll find the guy, Dynah. I swear. And we'll—"

Joe glanced at him sharply. "That's enough, Ethan."

"It's not enough! It's not enough by half!" Ethan's voice cracked. He turned. "What'd he look like, Dynah?"

"I don't know." She felt her mouth trembling, but she couldn't stop it. "I never saw his face. All of a sudden, he was there, a shape in the darkness. And he grabbed me."

"Leave it alone, Ethan," Joe said firmly. "The police will handle it."

"Yeah, right. They'll handle it, like they handle everything else these days." He kept looking at Dynah. "You must've seen something. Weren't you paying any attention when you walked up Henderson?"

"Leave her alone!" Janet said, angry now as well. "You act like it's her fault she got raped!"

"I didn't say that!"

As soon as Joe parked in front of the dormitory, Dynah pulled away from Janet and fumbled for the door handle. Joe got out of the car and opened the door for her. He helped her out. Contrite, Ethan caught up with them at the front door. "I'm sorry, Dynah. I didn't mean—"

"I just want to go inside." She pushed at the handle and found the door locked. Curfew had long since passed. Her heart hammered. The glass door rattled loudly as she fought to open it.

Joe put his hand over hers. "Easy. The housemother's coming, Dynah. She'll open the door. You're safe." His calm, reassuring voice and presence calmed her slightly.

Mrs. Blythe opened the door. She allowed Dynah and Janet inside. "She'll be all right now, gentlemen. Thank you. We'll look after her," she said and closed the doors again. Dynah glanced back at Ethan standing on the other side of the glass. She was thankful to hear the sound of the key turning in the lock. Mrs. Blythe turned to her in concern and put her arm around her. "I thought the hospital would keep you over-night."

"She wanted to come home," Janet answered for her, a solid presence on her other side.

"Well, that's all right, I suppose, if you're sure she'll be all right." She looked at Dynah, assessing her and grimacing in sympathy.

"I'll be all right," Dynah said, forcing a smile, wanting to allay the dorm mother's worries. She wanted to stay here, not in a strange room with strangers to care for her.

"I called the dean. I'll let him know you're here so he won't go to the hospital in the morning. He'll want to know how you're doing."

Mortified, Dynah said nothing. How many people knew what had happened to her?

"He's alerting the student body tomorrow to the danger in our community," Mrs. Blythe went on. "He assured me your name wouldn't be mentioned, dear, but it's important for everyone to be warned until this man is arrested." She pressed the top button. "Dean Abernathy wants to save you as much embarrassment as he can." She assessed Dynah's bruised face again. "I think it would be best if you stayed in your room for a few days."

"I have classes."

"I'll send word to your instructors that you have a bad case of the flu. They can send your assignments here. And Janet can bring you your meals. How does that sound?"

Dynah nodded bleakly as she stepped inside the elevator.

"I'll call your parents in the morning."

Dynah slapped her hand against the door to keep it from sliding closed. "No! Please, don't do that!"

"But they should know what happened, Dynah."

"There's nothing they can do. You'll just worry them. I want to forget it happened."

"We'll talk in the morning. You get a good night's sleep first."

"Promise me, you won't call them."

"Do you think they'd blame the school?"

"They'd be upset. I don't know what they'd do."

"Well, we'll wait and see then."

Janet stood by solicitously while Dynah got ready for bed. She asked how it all happened, and Dynah told her. She wanted to talk about everything, to pour out her anguish and fear, her feelings of shame and degradation, but at the facts, Janet grimaced in repugnance.

"I'm sorry I asked. We won't talk about it anymore. It's better you forget it happened." She pulled the blankets up and tucked them snugly around Dynah. "Put it out of your head and get some sleep." Bending down, Janet kissed her forehead. "I wish you'd called me. I would have picked you up."

Dynah felt a stab of guilt for not having done so. She should have heeded Mr. Packard's warning. She should have asked Sally Wentworth for a ride. She should have listened to Charlie and watched herself. "You said you were going to study at the library tonight."

"I didn't go. I went out with Chad for coffee instead and then came back here and studied."

Dynah didn't say anything more. She couldn't speak past the lump of pain tightening her throat. If only . . . if only . . .

"Will you be all right by yourself for a few minutes? I need to wash my face and brush my teeth."

Dynah nodded, forcing a smile as she fought back the tears that burned so hot.

Janet picked up her pink silk pajamas and her toiletry kit, then turned out the bedside lamp. Opening the door, she pressed the switch for the overhead light and sent the room into darkness. She stood silhouetted against the light from the corridor. "I won't be long, Dynah. Try to sleep. Everything will look better tomorrow." She closed the door behind her.

Turning onto her side, Dynah curled into a fetal ball, pulled the covers over her head, and sobbed.

■　■　■

The next day, Dynah called Sally Wentworth and quit her job at Stanton Manor House. Surprised, Sally asked why.

"I'm going to put more time into my studies." She ignored the feelings of guilt that tugged at her. It was true, in part. She was going to have lots of work to make up once she resumed classes.

"If you need more money, I can get you a dollar-an-hour raise."

"It's not the money, Sally. Really." She knew she would have to find some kind of job soon. She didn't have the luxury of not working at all. The scholarship took care of part of the tuition. Her parents paid the rest, as well as her dorm fees. However, there were still the expenses of clothing and books and her car. She had to pay for insurance and gas and repairs.

If her car had worked last night, maybe . . .

"Mr. Packard has been asking for you. He'll miss you, you know."

"I know," she said, her throat closing up. She thought of the old man's warning and felt the added burden of not having heeded it. "I can't help it, Sally. I just can't come back." She couldn't bring herself to even say she would come to visit.

"I guess I can understand your feelings. This isn't exactly a happy job."

"I enjoyed it."

"If that's true, you wouldn't be quitting. Are you sure there isn't more to it, Dynah? This is awful sudden."

She hesitated, then leaned her forehead against the wall. She couldn't bring herself to tell Sally the truth. It was too humiliating. And worse, she couldn't stop thinking about it. She was afraid, so afraid. Even the thought of being across town from the campus made her heart race. Ethan had gotten her car for her this morning, but what if it broke down again? What if Janet couldn't pick her up? What if Ethan was too busy? She would have to make that long walk down Maple to Main and catch the bus. She would have to walk up Henderson past the park—

No. She shook her head. She couldn't face it.

"I'm sorry, Sally." She was ashamed to quit without notice. She was sorry to leave Sally and Juan with added responsibilities. She was sorry Mr. Packard would miss her. She was sorry about everything.

"Well, I took a chance hiring a student. I should've known better. I'll have to work overtime until I can find a replacement. Don't expect a recommendation." There was a sharp click as Sally hung up.

Over the next few days, Dynah tried to pour herself into her studies, but she found it difficult. She was so tired, all she wanted to do was sleep. When she did, she was tormented by strange, vivid dreams. She couldn't concentrate.

Officer Lawson called and arranged a follow-up interview at Middleton's police station. He said he could send a squad car to pick her up, but Dynah said she would get there on her own. The last thing she wanted were rumors starting. Janet said the campus was already buzzing with the news of someone's being raped in the community park.

Ethan insisted he would drive her. When he picked her up, he said if anyone saw them at the police station, he had a plausible reason worked out. They were doing jail visitation and research. "Let me do the talking," he said.

Neither spoke after that. He seemed preoccupied, grim, and

her own thoughts were rushing headlong toward disaster. Her stomach churned. It was the first time she had left the dormitory since that night. Instead of driving out the east entrance, Ethan took his usual route straight through the front gate and down Henderson. She kept her eyes closed until he turned onto Main.

Once at the police station, Ethan waited in the lobby. Dynah endured an hour of questions about the night of the rape. She mentioned the white station wagon with the Massachusetts plates. She couldn't remember any of the numbers or letters. Officer Lawson kept going back to the man again and again, gently but persistently prodding for details about his appearance, voice, anything that might identify him. Was he tall or short? Heavyset or thin? What was he wearing? Did he have any kind of an accent?

"All I saw was a dark shape. He didn't say anything. He just . . . grabbed me."

There was nothing conclusive to connect the man driving the white station wagon with the man who had raped her.

She went home with a splitting headache that kept her vomiting half the night.

Dynah returned to her classes nine days after the attack. The first day was torturous. She had always felt comfortable around people. Now she was nervous with so many around her. Worse, her friends chose the "incident" as their primary topic of conversation.

"I wonder who it was."

"Maybe that girl from Maine. Didn't she leave school a few days ago?"

"I heard she was pregnant."

"I didn't hear that. Really?"

"What if it was her? Could you blame her for leaving? I wouldn't want to stay here if anything like that happened to me. Would you?"

"Did they catch him?"

"No. I saw a police car on Henderson yesterday. I think they're talking to all the neighbors, trying to find someone who might have seen something."

"It was in the paper yesterday that they're looking for information about the driver of a white station wagon with Massachusetts plates."

"My boyfriend doesn't think they'll catch the guy. He's probably over the border and long gone by now."

"Back in Massachusetts."

"I hope he stays there."

"I hope he has a wreck on the way."

"Doesn't it give you the willies thinking about it? I mean, can you imagine? I've been going down there every afternoon to study since I came to NLC. It sure doesn't have the same feel now, does it?"

"Where are you going, Dynah?"

She blushed, trapped by their curious looks. "To the student employment office," she said, backing away, her books clutched against her chest like a shield.

"You already have a job, don't you? At Stanton Manor House."

"I had to quit."

"I thought they paid pretty well."

"The pay is all right, but it's too far away and was eating into my study time. I'm going to see about getting a job here on campus."

Lies, lies. There were so many lies now. . . .

"There's a job open at the library. I know because I just quit. Shelving books was a bore."

She got the job, and by the end of the week, she had her work schedule. She started work on Monday.

To all outward appearances, everything was fine. If she

seemed to smile less, friends just assumed it was because she was distracted by midterms looming. Wasn't everyone?

But deep within, Dynah knew. . . . She was shattered and didn't know how to put herself together again. She lay sleepless in her dorm room, a nursery rhyme running through her mind again and again.

Humpty-Dumpty sat on a wall.
Humpty-Dumpty had a great fall.
All the King's horses and all the King's men
Couldn't put Humpty-Dumpty together again.

She wanted to talk about her feelings with Ethan, but every time she tried, he changed the subject. She felt the distance between them like a yawning chasm, growing as each week went by. They still studied together in the library between classes. They still went to dinner on Friday and the movies on Saturday and to church together on Sunday. Yet she was left yearning for what had been. She missed the tenderness and intimacy they had shared. They had always talked about everything. They still talked, but not about anything that mattered—not about what preyed constantly on her mind and heart, not about whatever was eating away at him.

Tonight, she sat in a small booth in a quiet Italian restaurant and listened to Ethan talk about his homiletics class. Over the past hour, he had gone over four different ideas he was considering for his final presentation. The waiter had given them menus, returned to take their orders, delivered Ethan's salad and veal parmesan and her side order of pasta, and left the check.

"What do you think?" he said finally, finishing the last of his dinner and looking at her over the edge of his water glass.

Dynah pushed her pasta around the plate and raised her head

slightly. "What do *you* think?" she said quietly, aching inside. She wanted to say, "What is it you really feel about what happened to me? Do you blame me, Ethan? Do you think it was my fault I was raped?" She voiced none of those questions, but he must have seen them in her eyes because his face hardened.

"Why can't you just forget about it?"

"Can you?"

"I'm trying. I'm trying to forget it ever happened."

His eyes were dark, though whether from anger or pain she couldn't tell. She knew he wanted to forget about it, but burying it wasn't helping. She didn't know what would.

"I'd like to forget, too. I would. But I can't. Every night, I dream about it." She looked down at the red checkered tablecloth, biting her lip. If she cried, it would only make things worse for him.

"Maybe you ought to get counseling."

She wondered if he realized how dispassionate he sounded, how uninvolved. Was this just her problem? Didn't it concern him as well? He was going to be her husband in a few months. Shouldn't he care about what she was feeling? What was he really telling her? She searched his face, hurt and confused. "Maybe we both need counseling."

"Maybe we need time."

"You're angry."

"Yes. I'm angry. I'd like to kill the guy. I think about what I'd like to do if I ever got my hands on him. Is that what you wanted to hear, Dynah? Sits nice with my chosen vocation, doesn't it? It tears me up every time I think about what was taken. So if you don't mind, I'd rather not have this topic as dinner conversation." He tossed his napkin on the table.

Snatching up the check, he looked at it, dropped it on the table, dug for his wallet, and extracted a twenty-dollar bill. "Let's get out of here. It doesn't look like you're interested in eating anything." He tossed the money on the table and slid out of the booth.

She didn't say anything on the drive back to campus. What could she say that would change anything? Ethan didn't tell her what was wrong, but she felt it. She saw it in his eyes sometimes, though he tried to hide it from her and from himself.

She was defiled.

Ethan pulled into a parking space near the dorm and shut off the engine. Gripping the steering wheel, he sighed heavily. "I'm sorry, Dynah. I don't like to think about it, let alone talk about it." He looked at her bleakly. "It wasn't your fault. You didn't do anything wrong. We'll just have to live with it."

"Live with it." The words reverberated in her mind. *Live with it. Live with it. We'll have to live with the monstrous reality of what happened? It will grow like a living, breathing thing between us, a crouching beast waiting to devour. . . .*

"Oh, Ethan, I wish you'd hold me and tell me everything will be all right."

He reached out then and drew her close, but she felt the difference. His touch was tentative, almost impersonal. "Will things ever be the way they were?" She didn't have to look up at him to feel his withdrawal.

"If God wants them to be."

His words were like a blow. Dynah drew back and looked up at him, stunned. "You think God was punishing me for something. You think he allowed it to happen because he wanted to teach me a lesson."

"I don't know. Maybe. Maybe not. We've always agreed there's a lesson in everything. Look, I don't know why things like this happen. Why are there wars? Why do people in Third World countries starve? I can't pretend to understand the mind of God. All I do know is God has a reason for everything he does."

Dynah looked at him, sick at heart. Ethan had always been so certain he knew what God wanted. God wanted her to come to NLC. God wanted her to be his wife. Had all that changed?

Turning away, she opened the door abruptly and got out.

"Dynah, wait a minute!" Ethan got out the other side. "Dynah, don't be like this!"

She ran up the steps and went inside the dorm before he could close his door and follow. Several girls were just coming out of the elevator when she reached it and ducked inside. She punched the button for the third floor.

Thankfully, Janet was out on another date, and she could be alone to think, to feel. She put her purse on her desk and sank down, head in her hands.

She remembered the violence of the Old Testament. It was filled with stories of adversity, slavery, and deliverance. The Israelites had wandered in the desert. Even after they entered the Promised Land, things hadn't gone smoothly. There had been wars, death, tragedy. The people were stubborn and rebellious. Prophets cried out for repentance. Israel turned away over and over again. God's people wouldn't listen. They wouldn't trust and obey. They were stiff-necked and head-strong. And God punished them in order to turn them back.

Oh, God, I trusted you. I've obeyed.

All men sin and fall short of the glory of God.

She tried to think how she had displeased the Lord. She loved him. Sometimes she thought she was born adoring him. As far back as she could remember, Jesus had been real to her. He was the Bridegroom, the Holy One, her Savior and Lord. She had been raised to feel secure and safe and protected in his love. She had been taught that his loving hand was in everything.

In everything.

Are you in this, Lord? Are you?

God is the potter. I am the clay.

She could see her mother smiling and saying, "God is molding you into the beautiful woman he wants you to be."

Oh, God, why have you crushed me? Why have you cast me into the pit? Aren't acts of violence wrought in retribution? Oh, Jesus, what did I do to displease you? Was it because I was too proud of Ethan? Was I too happy about marrying him? Was it because I didn't spend enough time with poor Mr. Packard? Was I rude to that man in the white station wagon? Haven't I prayed enough? Have I loved Ethan more than you? Is that why you've put this wall between us? Oh, Jesus, what did I do wrong? Oh, Jesus, Jesus . . .

The telephone rang. She knew it was Ethan and didn't answer.

2

Dynah saw Joe sitting comfortably at the top of the marble steps of the library, his back resting against a pillar. He smiled and stood, meeting her halfway as she came up.

"Going to work?"

"Not until six." She raised her head and searched his eyes briefly. "I thought I'd study for a while."

"It's a nice day to study outside. What do you say we go to the quad?"

She hesitated, suspicious. "Did Ethan send you?" When his mouth curved ruefully, she rushed on to explain herself. "You've always made it such a point that I'm Ethan's girl."

"You still are."

She frowned, wondering why he was waiting for her. He must have a reason. It had to be Ethan. Shifting her books, she held them tightly against her chest and waited. She wasn't sure she wanted to hear what Joe had to say. She wasn't sure she wanted to hear what Ethan might have told him about her behavior last night. "I'm not angry anymore, if that's why you're here waiting for me. You can tell Ethan I find no fault with him. He can't help how he feels."

Joe's expression changed, softening as he searched her face. He didn't avoid looking at her the way Ethan did but gazed straight into her eyes, accepting the inner turmoil and anguish that lay just beneath her surface control. He didn't hide from her pain. "Let me be a gentleman and carry your books."

Dynah allowed him to take them from her. They walked along the cobblestone road and between the political science and liberal arts buildings to the quad. The maple trees were just beginning to bud with spring leaves. Before the attack, she would have noticed and remarked about it. Now, she didn't even look up. She stayed close to Joe as they walked beneath the shade and into the sunlight again.

Joe didn't say anything, but she felt comfortable with his silence. Unlike Ethan, Joe didn't try to fill every minute with words or suppositions.

"God has a reason for everything he does."

She couldn't seem to drive that thought out of her mind.

What reason, Lord? Tell me what reason.

"This looks good," Joe said and put her books down.

Dynah looked around. He had picked a place in the open, no shade, sunlight streaming down from blue heaven. She used to love this exact spot—had come often with Janet and other friends to feel the sun beat down. Now she wished for a dark corner away from people. She felt Joe watching her, waiting. Forcing a smile, she sat down and curled her legs to one side. Joe sat resting his forearms on his raised knees. She had always felt at ease with him, which made her tension now that much more disturbing.

Picking up a textbook, she opened it. "So, what does Ethan want you to tell me?"

"He didn't send me, Dynah."

She raised her head, her eyes narrowing slightly. "Are you sure?"

"I want to sit with you and talk. I want to know how you're doing."

She lowered her head. "I'm fine."

"No, you're not. You're too pale to be fine."

"I spent the better part of two weeks in my room. Now I work at the library." She was ashamed by the edge of bitterness she could hear in her voice, the undercurrent of anger. Anger was the enemy now. Christians were supposed to be docile, accepting, obedient to God's will. . . .

Was it your will, Lord? I don't understand. Why has this happened? Why is my life turned upside down?

"How are you sleeping?"

"Fine."

"Come on, Dynah. You can talk to me."

She clenched her teeth. Why did it have to be Joe asking? Ethan should be the one to want to know. Ethan should be listening and comforting, but then Ethan was personally involved, wasn't he? He had lost the most, hadn't he?

She looked away. "I have nightmares," she said dully. Embarrassed, she looked down again. She shouldn't be exposing her feelings to Joe. "I need to study."

"OK," he said quietly and stretched out on his side. "We'll study." Propping himself up slightly, he pulled out one of his textbooks. Taking a highlighter out of his backpack, he pulled the cap off with his teeth as he read. Every now and then he ran the pen along a line of text or over a term.

Looking down at her own open textbook in her lap, Dynah tried to concentrate on the terms she needed to memorize. Midterms were coming, but she couldn't seem to get the terms to sink in. She rubbed her forehead and started over, taking one term at a time, trying again, but her mind kept wandering.

"Do you think there's a reason for everything that happens?" She felt Joe look at her. Afraid of his answer, she went on quickly. "I mean, Ethan thinks so. He thinks God must have a reason for punishing me."

"Were those his exact words?"

"Something like that. Maybe not in those words. Oh, I don't know. Maybe that's not what he meant." Maybe she hadn't heard him correctly. Maybe she was being unfair. Maybe she wasn't thinking straight about anything anymore. She rubbed her temple with trembling fingers.

"It wasn't your fault, Dynah."

"How can I know that? I should've listened to Mr. Packard. I could've asked for a ride from Sally or called Janet or waited until Ethan was finished with the Bible study. I could've—"

Joe sat up, halting her flow of words, and reached over to take her hands firmly. "Look at me."

She did, hardly able to see his face through the blur of tears.

"It was not your fault. You didn't do anything to deserve it."

"There has to be a reason."

"God didn't send that man to rape you."

"He didn't stop him, either," she said, pulling her hands free and clutching her book again. "Maybe he did send him, Joe." He didn't say anything, and she tried to explain her jumbled feelings. "Didn't God send the Assyrians to destroy Israel? Didn't the Babylonians conquer them, too? And Job. Joe, what about Job? What did he do wrong that he had to suffer that much?"

"He didn't do anything wrong, Dynah. He loved God. He honored him. That's why Satan wanted to sift him, to prove he could break Job's faith."

"So I'm being *sifted?*" She saw him wince at the quick sarcasm of her response and blushed, ashamed that she could sit right here, dead center of a Christian college, and dare criticize God. She wanted to say she wasn't like Job. She would break. Her faith could be crushed. A few words from Ethan and it was already unraveling. She closed her eyes and lowered her head. "I'm sorry."

"For what? For being hurt and angry over what happened to you? You have reason."

"God has a reason."

Maybe she just wasn't good enough to be part of his kingdom. Her heart squeezed tight, shrinking inside her with fear. "Maybe Ethan's right. I should try to forget about it. Put it behind me and go on like nothing happened." She opened her book.

"Dynah," Joe said, and the compassion in his tone made her stomach tighten in a painful knot.

"If we have to talk, Joe, let's talk about something else. Please. I don't want to talk about it. I don't want to think about it. OK?"

Joe sat silent for a moment and then nodded. "You call the shots. I just want you to know I'm around if you need me."

■　■　■

Ethan called that night and apologized. She said it wasn't his fault, though his defection hurt deeply. She said she understood, and in part she did, though she didn't want to look at it too closely. He said he didn't understand anything himself. It was all a confusing mass of emotions inside him, and he'd have to deal with them. "I never meant you should blame yourself for what happened."

"I know," she said, giving absolution, knowing it was what he wanted.

He was different the next time they went out. "Joe and I have been doing a lot of talking," he said, taking her hand between both of his. "Why don't we take a walk tonight instead of going to a movie?" It was a nice evening. They didn't say much as they wandered along the cobblestone pathways. Dynah didn't tell him the shadows made her uneasy and every night sound made her heart jump.

They passed other young couples walking hand in hand around the manicured grounds of the campus. She supposed she should feel safe in the cloistered environment, but she didn't. Not even with Ethan at her side.

He paused once and drew her close. Touching her cheek, he kissed the corner of her mouth. It was the first time he had kissed her in the weeks since the rape. He stroked her cheek and drew her into his arms.

"I still love you, Dynah."

She knew he meant for her to be comforted by his words, but she wasn't. *"Still,"* he said. He *still* loved her. Somehow, there was an unspoken *despite* in his words. I *still* love you, *despite* the fact that you're defiled. I *still* love you, *despite* the fact that you didn't stop the man. I *still* love you, *despite* the fact that you're not what you once were. . . .

She pushed the thoughts away. She couldn't believe them, not if she was going to hang on to the emotional equilibrium she strove so hard to maintain—not if she wanted to be able to look ahead to a future that was supposed to be secure.

But things had changed. The warm stirring of desire when Ethan touched her wasn't there anymore. All she felt was a cold knot of fear and revulsion in the pit of her stomach. She was no longer comfortable in his arms, but she remained there because she knew it was what he wanted, what he expected. He held her and whispered tender words into her hair. Apologies. Promises.

She remained still, fighting the turmoil inside her, the rush of blood in her ears. She shut her eyes tightly when her mind flashed back to another man's hands holding her, grabbing, hitting, yanking, tearing. Panic threatened to overwhelm her, but she couldn't tell Ethan what she was feeling without destroying this brief, tenuous moment of tenderness—and maybe destroying whatever chance they had of working things out altogether.

He let her go slowly, looking down at her. She could see he was frowning slightly. He was perplexed. She forced a smile, clinging to the pretense that everything was fine. Or would be. Someday. *Trust in the Lord. Trust in the Lord.*

"Your hand's cold," he said as they began walking again. "Let's get you something warm to drink."

They went to the student union and found a table in a back corner. A few minutes after they ordered hot cocoa, students poured in, laughing and shouting.

"Basketball team must have won," Ethan said, watching the wild antics of students marching around the room. "I forgot they were playing tonight."

Dynah saw Joe among the throng, singing a boisterous song of celebration. His gaze caught hers, and his broad grin softened into a smile. Someone shoved him from behind as more whooping students swarmed into the union, scraping chairs and filling the place with pandemonium.

Ethan leaned forward, resting his arms on the table. "Want to leave?"

"No. It's all right." She preferred the raucous noise to the dark silence. She preferred a table between her and Ethan rather than his efforts to pretend everything was the same.

Joe came over and took a chair beside her. His eyes assessed her face before his glance took in Ethan, who looked grimly uncomfortable. "You guys missed a good game."

"We weren't in the mood," Ethan said, his mouth tipping sardonically. "I take it they won."

"It was neck and neck to the end. We beat them by three points. Almost brought down the gymnasium when the buzzer sounded."

"Great," Ethan said, his tone flat.

"Hey, Joe!" Someone called from across the room. He gave them a wave and pushed his chair back. "Want to join us?" he said, looking at her and then Ethan. "We're going to have a victory bonfire."

Ethan gave a bleak laugh. "Yeah, right. Just what we need." A muscle jerked in his jaw. "Another time. We're going to sit here and talk for a while, and then I'll take Dynah back to the dorm so she can get some rest."

Joe's expression was grim. "Take it easy."

"There's nothing easy about it."

Joe didn't say anything to that, but Ethan's anger withered beneath his friend's look. Standing up, Joe put his hand on Dynah's shoulder, gave her a gentle squeeze, and left them alone.

"Sorry," Ethan said. "I should have asked you." Leaning forward, he put his hands around the mug of cocoa. "You want to go with them?"

"No."

"You want to go someplace else? Someplace where we can talk in private?"

She didn't want to be alone with Ethan. The realization hurt and roused doubts about their relationship. She was afraid to be alone with him, afraid of what he had to say about his deepest feelings. She was afraid she already knew.

She was so confused, the choir of voices in her head debating and running through a hundred painful scenarios. "No. This is fine," she said bleakly, knowing it wasn't.

He looked into his mug. "You want to talk about what happened that night?" He raised his head slightly and looked at her. "Maybe it would make things better."

Feeling a flicker of hope, she did as he asked. After all, he was the one who'd had all the counseling classes. He was the one who was going to be a pastor. Relief swept over her. Ethan was a shepherd. He would see her for what she was—a lost and wounded lamb. Drawing a steadying breath, she told him slowly about her evening at Stanton Manor House, starting with Mr. Packard's warning. She told him about her long walk down Maple to Sycamore. She told him about the man in the white car and Martha waiting at the bus stop. She told him about Charlie and the ride along Sixteenth. She had relived that night a dozen times at the police station with Officer Lawson. She could do it one more time for Ethan. Surely it would be easier with him.

It wasn't.

"I walked up Henderson. When I got to the park . . . he was just there. In the shadows. A shape."

"And?"

"He grabbed me."

His knuckles whitened around his mug. "Did you fight?"

She raised her head slowly and looked at him. Angry words poured into her head, but she held them back. Her mother had taught her not to give in to anger, not to speak rashly. Walk in the other person's shoes for a mile.

"Yes," she said simply, giving no details of how hard she had fought to get free. She hadn't stopped fighting until he dazed her with a blow to the head.

"And?"

She looked down, unable to meet his eyes. "That's all. You know the rest."

"No, I don't know the rest. What'd they do to you at the hospital? You were in that examining room a long time, Dynah. What was going on?"

She could feel the blood receding. "They were getting evidence," she said in a low, shamed voice and bit her lip, praying he wouldn't ask for details.

"Did they give you any tests while they were doing that?"

She went cold, the beginning of understanding striking her heart. Raising her head slowly, she searched his eyes.

"For venereal disease," he said in a hushed voice, though no one was close enough to hear. "You know what I'm asking. Did they test you for HIV?" He looked down at his mug and then back up at her. "Well? Did they? You've a right to know if the guy gave you some disease."

She wondered if it was her rights that worried him or something deeper, something more primeval. What he was really saying was *he* had a right to know. Tears burned. Of course, he was right. He did. "Yes. They gave me tests."

"And?"

The hospital had called a few days later. "They were negative," she said dully. For now. She'd have to be retested several times before they knew for sure she was OK. She pushed the mug away from her with trembling hands. If she tried to drink a drop of it now, she would throw up.

Ethan's voice was tight. "I wasn't trying to hurt you. I just thought . . . well, I thought we ought to get that out in the open."

"Now that it's in the open, I hope you feel better."

His face darkened. "Don't take it out on me. I didn't rape you."

Her cheeks went hot and then cold again. She stood up and fumbled with the small shoulder bag looped over the back of her chair.

"Where're you going?"

"Back to the dorm."

He uttered a word under his breath, a foul word she was sure had never before crossed his lips. He never would have said it at all if he hadn't been so overwrought by what had happened to her. So she supposed she was to blame for that as well.

She heard his chair scrape back as she headed for the doors. He caught up with her just outside and fell into step beside her. "I'm sorry," he said tersely, sounding anything but sorry. "I get mad every time I think about it."

Mad at whom, she wanted to say. She wanted to jerk free and

hit him. She wanted to scream and scream, but she kept silent because she had been brought up to be polite. If you don't have something nice to say, don't say anything at all. Don't say anything. Pretend it doesn't hurt. Especially when someone you love is doing the hurting.

She was wearing Ethan's engagement ring. The wedding was set for August seventeenth. She had already ordered her white wedding dress.

White.

For purity.

Only she wasn't pure anymore. She wasn't a virgin.

Pulling away, she walked faster, desperate to get to the dorm, to get away from him, to close herself in her room and cry.

He caught hold of her hand and pulled her to a stop. "Is this how you're going to handle everything? By running away every time you hear anything you don't like? Talk to me!"

It was a command, not a plea. All his anger aimed at her.

"I did talk to you."

"In a monotone voice. Like you were talking about something that happened to someone else. Don't you feel anything?"

"Feel?" she said stiffly, pushed by his insensitivity. "I *feel*, Ethan. I feel defiled," she said in a choked voice. "I feel ruined. I feel raped. Is that enough? Does that satisfy you?"

Ethan caught hold of her. "Dynah," he said, pulling her back against him and locking his arms around her. "Dynah," he said again and wept. Was he crying for her or himself? It didn't matter. Turning in his arms, she put her arms around him. She understood his grief, but she knew, far better than she'd ever wanted to, that some grief was too deep for tears to wash it away.

■ ■ ■

Things didn't improve over the next week.

Dynah had just finished a calming shower when Janet came

into the room. "Your mom called again," she said as she set her books down. "She asked me if I knew why you were so down in the dumps."

Dynah sat on the bed, her head wrapped in a towel and her body encased in a thick bathrobe. "What'd you tell her?"

"I didn't tell her anything."

"Thanks."

"I didn't convince her, Dynah. She knows something's wrong. Don't you think you should tell her what happened?"

Dynah sank to the bed, unwinding the damp towel from her hair. She didn't want to think about that night. She didn't want to think about the shattering effects it had had on her relationship with Ethan. He was just beginning to adjust. He was getting past it. Things were improving between them. A few more weeks, a month, maybe two, and it would be forgotten. "She'd tell my father, and then they'd both worry. And what good would come of it? It can't change what's already happened."

Janet studied her. "She knows something's wrong. She said she's thinking about flying back here and seeing you."

Dynah let the towel drop around her shoulders.

Janet came over and sat on the bed beside her, brushing the tangled hair back from Dynah's face. "Maybe Ethan could help you talk with them."

Dynah gave a soft humorless laugh and shook her head. "I'll tell them I have the flu or something." She smiled wanly. She had never lied to her parents before, but what other choice had she? They would go to pieces if they knew the truth. "It's partly true," she said, trying to excuse herself. "I've been feeling sick to my stomach for the last week."

Janet stared at her. "Oh, Dynah! You don't think . . ."

A chill crept over Dynah as she looked into Janet's horrified eyes. "Think what?" she said softly, afraid.

"That you might be pregnant?"

Dynah's heart began to pound with sickening beats. "No." She clung to that word as it hung in the air. *No! You wouldn't do that to me, would you, Lord? Oh, please, God, no.*

TRUST ME, BELOVED.

Dynah began to tremble inside. She knew. She didn't have to take a test. Something told her already that the sifting hadn't stopped. It had only just begun.

Janet stood up and began to pace. "You can't be. There's no way. They would've given you something at the hospital that night to make sure it didn't happen. A morning-after pill. Or something! They did, didn't they?"

"No."

"You were in shock, Dynah. You probably don't remember."

She remembered every single detail of that terrifying night. She hadn't been able to forget any of it. "They didn't give me anything, Janet."

"But that's criminal! Didn't they even ask?"

Dynah bit her lip, ashamed to admit the doctor had done more than ask. He had tried to convince her to have estrogen therapy. She was the one who had refused to face the devastating possibilities. It was her fault. It was all her fault.

Reaching for her Day Planner, she opened it with trembling hands, turning back the pages one by one. Two months and four days to the day of the rape. She kept going until she found the small notation two weeks before that. Clutching the planner on her lap, she stared at the date. "I guess I'd better go see the doctor."

Janet came back and sat down beside her. She took Dynah's hand between her own. "It'll be OK," she said, sounding less than convinced. "I'm sure if you are pregnant, which you probably aren't . . . I mean, you've been through so much; of course, you'd skip. That's probably what's happened. They can give you something to get you back to normal again."

Normal? Oh, God, will I ever be normal again?

Janet's hand tightened on hers. "Even if you were pregnant, they'd take care of it for you. You wouldn't have to worry about it. Nobody would even have to know. This early, it wouldn't be anything anyway, and it's not like it was your fault. So it'll be OK. Whatever happens, it'll be OK. Hang onto that, Dynah. It'll be OK."

Only it wasn't. It wasn't OK.

I'm never going to be the same, am I, Lord? Never again.

■　■　■

Dr. Kennon pulled off his rubber gloves and dropped them into a metal waste receptacle while a nurse helped Dynah sit up on the end of the examination table. The doctor glanced at the nurse and gave her a nod. She quietly left the room. Turning his back on Dynah, he turned on the water and began washing his hands while she adjusted the hospital gown to cover herself completely. Her heart thumped heavily as she awaited his verdict.

He pushed the faucet handle down with the back of his hand and yanked two paper towels from the holder. "You should've taken the estrogen therapy, Miss Carey."

Her heart sank into the pit of her stomach. He might as well have punched her the way he said the words. The implication was clear enough. She had been a fool. Her skin went clammy, yellow spots danced before her eyes.

Drying his hands, he looked at her grimly. He dropped the towels into the waste receptacle. She closed her eyes, feeling the wave of shock crest and recede, leaving her numb.

"I'm sorry," he said flatly. Assessing her face, he took her wrist lightly, checking her pulse. "Lie down for a few minutes."

"No, thank you," she said. She wanted to sit up and die.

He put her hand on her thigh and stepped back. "I'll schedule a suction curettage for later this afternoon." He took up her chart and began making notations on it as he spoke. "It won't be as easy as the pill would have been, but it won't be too bad either. The procedure won't take very long, but expect to be in recovery for about an hour afterward. I don't expect any complications. It's just a safety precaution." He flipped the chart closed and lowered it to his side as he looked at her again. "You'll need a friend to drive you home. Your fiancé, perhaps?" He had noticed the diamond solitaire she wore.

She didn't say anything.

"Miss Carey? Do you understand what I am saying to you?"

"Yes, sir," she said in a choked voice, trembling inside. Was life really so cut and dried?

He looked at her solemnly. "Can you get dressed by yourself, or would you like the nurse to help you?"

"I can manage. Thank you."

As soon as the door closed behind him, she quickly slipped down from the examination table and reached for her clothing. Dressed, she folded the hospital gown and left it on the examining table.

Dr. Kennon was speaking with a woman at the nurse's station. He handed the chart over the counter and took another. Seeing Dynah, he turned to her. "The procedure is scheduled for three o'clock. Be here about thirty minutes early."

She kept her head down as she passed the nurse who had assisted Dr. Kennon. The clerk glanced up. Dynah had already filled out the medical and personal forms. No one said anything as she kept going. The glass doors swished open before her, and she went outside.

She wanted to run. Fear caught her high in the throat, and her mind flashed back to that night in Henderson Park. Gulping in the crisp air, she hurried along the sidewalk toward the parking lot. Unlocking the door, she slid quickly into the front seat and slammed the door, locking it.

Clutching the steering wheel, she leaned forward and pressed her forehead against it. She sat for a long moment, until her heart slowed its crazy beat and she could breathe properly again.

She didn't feel safe until she drove beneath the arch of New Life College. Pulling into a parking space near the dorm, she sat for a few minutes, trying to think. Her mind was such a jumble, ruled by emotions. She felt like a rabbit being chased by a pack of hounds. She needed a hole in which to hide. A place of safety.

A tap on her window made her jump.

Joe stood looking in at her, his brow furrowed. "You OK?"

Fumbling for her shoulder bag, she opened the car door. She forced a smile and shrugged, hoping she didn't look the way she felt.

"Don't forget your keys," he said.

Blushing, she sat and leaned in to get them. She got out again and closed the car door behind her.

"You should lock it," he said, opening the door and hitting the switch before closing it again. He turned and looked at her. "You're shaking," he said softly. "What's wrong?"

"I'm pregnant," she said before she knew she was going to say it aloud. "I'm pregnant, Joe." The emotions welled up inside her like a volcano until she was sure she was going to explode. "Oh, God. What am I going to do, Joe? What am I going to do?"

Joe put his hand beneath her arm. His hand was warm and strong, offering her support. "Let's go sit down by the lake and talk about it," he said quietly, his tone filled with tenderness.

She pulled away. "I can't. I can't talk to you about it. I have to talk to Ethan first. I shouldn't've said anything." She had to calm down. People were going to notice. People were going to talk.

"He's not due back on campus until this evening."

"But I have to go back to the hospital this afternoon. I have to be there by two-thirty." As soon as she said it, she wished she hadn't. Joe knew. She didn't have to spell out what she was talking about. He understood perfectly. Ashamed, she looked away. "The doctor said—" She looked at him again beseechingly, wanting his understanding if not his approval. "I have to do it."

Joe touched her cheek tenderly. "Don't let anyone do your thinking for you, Dynah."

His words calmed her somehow, easing the turmoil within her. "What else can I do, Joe? I don't know what to do."

"Don't rush into anything."

"But the doctor said . . ."

"The doctor doesn't know everything. He doesn't know you."

She looked away. "I can't talk about it right now," she said, unable to bear his gentleness. It made everything worse, and she knew why.

"Dynah, please. Let's sit and talk."

"Why? So you can tell me what to do?"

"I won't. I promise."

"Yes, you will. You think you know better than anyone what's right and wrong, don't you? Just like Ethan. I got myself into this, didn't I? I was in the wrong place at the wrong time. I should never have walked up Henderson that night. I should have called Janet for a ride. I should've pressed the mechanic harder and gotten my car back sooner. I should have called a taxi. I should've done anything but what I did. Isn't that it? No one cares what I feel."

"Dynah . . ."

Turning away, she hurried toward the dorm. She glanced back as she went inside and saw Joe standing where she had left him.

She didn't go back to the hospital. She stayed in her room, sitting on her bed, her back against the wall, her knees pulled up against her chest. The telephone rang at four o'clock. She pressed her forehead against her knees, sure it was the doctor wanting to know why she hadn't shown up to have the procedure.

The answering machine clicked on, and she heard her mother's voice. "Dynah, honey? It's Mom. Call me. Please. I know you're busy studying, but it's been weeks since we talked. I miss you, sweetie."

Dynah leaned her head back against the wall and closed her eyes.

■　■　■

Ethan stared at her, his face white. "Are you joking? There must be some mistake."

"No," she said dully, looking down at her clenched hands. "There's no mistake. I wish there were."

"I don't believe it," he said, raking a hand back through his hair. "I don't believe this is happening! I didn't think things could get any worse."

Raising her gaze, she watched the turmoil in his face. She was afraid of what she saw, afraid of what this might mean to their relationship. Only a few days before, she thought they had reached a place of repose, accepting what had happened and moving on together. Now, she saw that wasn't so. Nothing was settled. Nothing was certain. "What are we going to do?"

Ethan looked away, a muscle working in his cheek, his eyes narrowed with anger. After a moment, he looked back at her, his expression grim. "What you have to do, I guess."

"Have the baby?"

"No!" His voice was low, his eyes blazing. "The doctor told you what you have to do."

"He was talking about abortion."

He leaned closer, looking around the restaurant to make sure they weren't overheard. "Don't you think I know that?"

"But it's wrong, Ethan. We've talked about it. We've agreed abortion is wrong."

"Of course it's wrong—when girls are using it for birth control or women are doing it because having a baby is an inconvenience or a financial burden or a guy doesn't want to take responsibility. But under these circumstances? How can it be wrong? Is it your fault you're pregnant? Am I supposed to be a father to something so despicable?"

She trembled inside. She couldn't bear to look into Ethan's eyes and see the revulsion. Had it occurred to him that what she carried was part of her, too?

"Besides," he said, his voice less harsh, more in control, "do you think that doctor would have suggested anything he didn't believe was absolutely necessary?"

"Just because it's legal doesn't mean it's right."

"It doesn't mean it's wrong, either. What about your mental health? You were raped!"

"And an abortion will make me feel better?" she said, fighting back the tears. Did he know what he was saying? Hadn't he been the one to write papers about the procedures employed? Hadn't he read it all to her, his voice ringing with righteous zeal?

"It would put a finish to what happened. It wasn't God's desire that you get pregnant."

"How do I know what God wanted? Haven't you been saying God has his hand in everything? That this is all part of his plan for me?" she asked in despair.

"You can't believe that, Dynah. Do you really think this is his best for us? God wouldn't do this."

"I didn't say he *did* it. He just didn't stop it from happening."

Ethan gripped her hands. "We've done everything right, Dynah. We've kept our relationship pure. We're serving him. This . . . this act upon you was an abomination. It was Satan trying to disrupt my plans for our future."

"But now there's a—"

"No." His hands tightened painfully around hers. "Don't even say it. Don't think it. You've got to listen to me, Dynah. There's no way God would expect you to go on with this. No way!" He leaned back, taking his hands from her, his face stony. "No way, Dynah. I don't believe that God expects it of us. I won't."

"I can't go back there, Ethan. I just can't." She covered her face, shaking. "You don't understand." The physical examination she had suffered the night of the rape had been traumatic enough. She didn't think she could stand to go through something worse. She knew what they would do to her body.

"I'll go with you. It'll be all right. I swear to you. I won't let anything happen to you."

She looked at him, wondering how he could say such a thing in the face of what he was suggesting.

"It won't take long, and then it'll all be over. We'll put it behind us."

She wrapped her arms around herself. He was in such a hurry to have it over and done with. Would it ever be over? "I'm not ready to do it."

"What do you mean, you're not ready?"

"I have to think about it."

"Think about *what?* You're not telling me you *want* it?"

Her breath caught softly at his accusation. "No, I don't want it!" Couldn't he even try to understand what she was going through? He was in such a hurry to make the decision for her, to make sure nothing interfered with his precious plans. Well, their plans had already been disrupted. Her life had been disrupted, shattered, blown to smithereens. And abortion was going to be the quick fix? For whom? The rape had been bad enough. The physical in the hospital had almost been worse. And now, she was supposed to submit to an abortion? A suction curettage. The doctor had said it the same way he might have said she needed a vaccination against some dread disease.

"I don't want it." None of it. Not the abortion. Not the child. Not the fear and heartache that were her constant companions since that cold January night.

"Then get rid of it. The longer you wait, the harder it will be to make the decision. The sooner it's done, the sooner it'll be over, and we can try to get things sorted out between us."

What things, she wanted to ask, but didn't dare. She shook inside, wondering if he loved her anymore. "Joe said not to rush into anything."

"Joe?" His head came up. "He knows you're pregnant?"

She blushed. "I'd just come back from the hospital. I was sitting in my car and he—"

"You told him?"

"You weren't due back until—"

"You told *him* before you told *me?*"

"I'm sorry. I didn't mean to, Ethan. I was just so upset."

"But I don't have the right to be, is that it?"

"I didn't say that."

"Joe isn't emotionally involved. He can play the cool head. He can have all the pat answers. He can tell you to wait and think about it." His face darkened with anger. "What right has he got to say anything?"

"He was trying to help."

"Yeah? Well, it's none of his business. It doesn't ruin his life."

She could feel the blood draining from her face.

"Who does he think he is? He has no right to speak for me."

"He didn't say it to interfere, Ethan. All he said was I should think things through before I make any kind of decision."

"Because he is against the whole idea of abortion, and you know it!"

"So were you before all this happened."

"Maybe I have a little more compassion now," he said, teeth gritted. "Look. You can't go through with it. Do you want everyone knowing what happened to you?"

He said it with such vehemence . . . and she heard a hint of what lay behind it. She saw it in his eyes as well. She lowered hers, not wanting to see more. "Joe won't say anything."

"No, he won't, but then he won't have to if you don't do something soon. Everybody'll see for themselves and come to their own conclusions. And you know what those will be."

She froze inside, seeing where his true concern lay. Was he worrying about her reputation or his own? Beyond hurt, anger stirred. "Then maybe we should tell the truth. Isn't that always the best policy?"

He gave a bleak laugh, toying with his silverware. "People would still come up with their own conclusions. We're engaged. With the world the way it is, you know what they'd think."

So there it was, in the open. "Maybe we could blow up pictures from the police files and post them around campus. Then everyone would know you didn't do anything wrong."

His hand stopped shoving the fork around. "I don't deserve that remark."

"And I deserve what you're suggesting?" Her eyes filled with hot tears. She slid along the seat, meaning to leave the booth, but he caught hold of her wrist.

"We have to settle this," he said fiercely.

"You mean you want me to do what you're telling me to do. Well, I'm going to take Joe's advice and not rush into anything."

"I know you're scared, Dynah."

"I wonder if you know anything. I wonder if you can even guess at what I feel. Let go of me."

"No way. I've got to make you understand. It'll get worse if you—"

"I didn't say I wouldn't do it, did I?"

"Keep your voice down," he said, his eyes flickering.

"God forbid your reputation might be soiled."

"I didn't say that!"

"Didn't you? Isn't that what's really worrying you?"

"You're not being fair."

"Fair? Has anything been fair? Is what I'm going through fair?" She glared at him through her tears. "I have a right to think about it. It's my body, isn't it? My life. We do live in a free country last I heard. I'm supposed to have a *choice.*" Jerking her wrist free, she slid from the booth.

Crossing the restaurant quickly, she stepped past a couple entering and went out the door. It was still light outside, the days lengthening now that spring had arrived. Spring with all its promises.

Broken promises.

Broken dreams.

She went into the Jewel-Osco supermarket half a block away, knowing Ethan wouldn't look for her there. More likely, he would drive along the street heading back for NLC, thinking he could pick her up somewhere along the way. And he'd expect her to apologize for her emotional outburst.

Well, she wouldn't apologize.

She didn't want to talk to him anymore this evening. She had enough money in her purse that she could call a cab.

Wandering aimlessly through the aisles of canned goods, produce, dairy products, and meats, she tried to think through her situation. Truth was, she wanted out of it. She didn't want to be pregnant. She didn't want to face the months ahead with people staring and asking questions. She didn't want her life in upheaval. She didn't want the pain and grief and shame and ultimate sorrow.

What sort of thing was growing inside her? Should it be allowed to live, considering the way it had come into being? Rape. What sort of conception was that? Did it count? Her head ached thinking about it.

"Can I help you find something, miss?"

She glanced up and saw a man wearing a store work coat. Her face flooded with heat. He smiled slightly, a troubled look in his eyes. "Miss?"

How long had she been wandering the aisles of the store? He probably thought she was a shoplifter. "No, I . . ." She shrugged. "Aspirin. Do you have any aspirin?"

"Aisle 10-B, bottom shelf."

After making her small purchase, she went outside. There was a public telephone outside on the brick wall. She opened the book to the yellow pages and looked for a cab company. The line was busy. Resting her forehead against the cold steel, she fought the prick of tears. The last person she wanted to call was Ethan. She didn't want to go through it all again. She didn't want to look across a booth and see his revulsion and hear how ashamed he was of what she'd let happen. As if she'd had a choice. She punched her own number and prayed.

"Janet, if you're there, please pick up."

"I'm here. What's up?"

"I need a ride, Jan. Can you pick me up?"

"Where are you?"

"At Jewel-Osco. On the corner of Talbot and Sixteenth."

"Give me fifteen minutes." The telephone clicked.

Dynah sat on the bench out front. A moment later, an elderly lady in a nice dress sat next to her, a wire pull cart with a bag of groceries sitting in front of her. She smiled and then folded her hands in her lap and sat waiting in silence. The old lady reminded Dynah painfully of elegant Mrs. Packard and made her wonder how Mr. Packard was doing. It would be nice to go visit the old gentleman, but if she did, he would ask where she had been and why she had quit her job. And what could she tell him?

Janet's white Camaro pulled into the parking lot.

"Ethan called a few minutes before you did," she said as Dynah slid into the front seat. "He sounded pretty upset. He said you walked out on him at a restaurant and he didn't know where you were."

"I suppose I should call him," Dynah said. It wasn't right to let him worry.

"I already did," Janet said, pulling out onto the main street again. "He wanted to pick you up, but I told him you called me and I didn't think you'd be too happy if he showed up."

"Thanks, Jan."

"I'll warn you, though. He'll probably be sitting on the dorm steps."

"Could we . . . ?"

"We can go to the Copper Pot. How's that sound? I need a break from studying, anyway."

"Thanks."

Janet turned south. Dynah sat silent, watching stores and houses whiz by. Neither said anything for the better part of a mile.

Janet glanced at her. "What happened, anyway?"

Dynah leaned her head back against the seat. "I'm pregnant."

"I was afraid of that," Janet said softly. "And what did he say? You should have it?"

Dynah turned her head and stared at her.

Janet glanced at her again, her eyes snapping with anger. "He did, didn't he? Sanctimonious jerk."

"No, he didn't."

"He broke up with you?"

Dynah turned her head and stared out the front window. "No," she said dully, wondering if that would be the next thing to happen. She knew that Ethan was having difficulty dealing with what had happened to her, and the bottom line was that he didn't have to deal with it. He could just walk away. She stared down at the diamond solitaire she wore. Tears blurring her eyes, she twisted it around and around on her finger, wondering if she could bear to lose him. She would die if she did. She was sure of it.

Janet frowned, giving her another quick glance. "Dynah, you OK?"

She gave her a wan smile. "I'll be fine," she said, clinging to those words. *Oh, God, will I be? What am I going to do?*

Janet pulled into the Copper Pot parking lot. "Busy tonight," she said, taking the keys from the ignition and dropping them into her purse.

Though the place was crowded, they were quickly seated in a booth near the back, right beside the doors to the kitchen. Janet ordered two coffees before the waitress even handed them the menus. "I'm starving," she said and began reading the selections. "To heck with my diet."

Dynah stared at the laminated menu. She and Ethan were supposed to have had dinner together tonight. Instead, they had sat arguing in that nice restaurant, never looking at the menus. She could still see the look on his face when she had told him she was pregnant. Horror. Revulsion.

"Dynah?"

She glanced up and saw that the waitress had returned and was ready to take her order. "A bowl of soup, please," she said, putting the menu aside. The last thing she cared about was eating anything, but if she didn't order something, Janet would be uncomfortable.

"What kind would you like? Split pea, minestrone, beef barley, chicken noodle, or potato?"

Dynah shrugged. "Beef barley, I guess."

"The minestrone is out of this world."

"All right. Minestrone."

"What kind of bread would you like with it?" the waitress said, pen still poised. "Rye, wheat, white, sour dough, or corn bread."

"Wheat, I suppose."

"The corn bread is great," Janet said.

"Corn bread then," Dynah said with a weak smile. She could always give it to Janet.

Janet closed her menu and handed it to the waitress. "I'll have the hamburger deluxe with everything, fries instead of potato salad, and coleslaw. And I'd like a piece of chocolate-cream pie first." She grinned. "If I wait, I might not have room for it later on."

The waitress laughed. "I'll bring it right away."

Janet rested her arms on the table and leaned forward. "You don't have to do what Ethan tells you, Dynah. It's your decision."

"He wants me to have an abortion."

Janet's eyes flickered. "But I thought. . . ." She frowned. "Well, then, what's the problem?"

"I don't know if I should."

"Of course you should," Janet said quietly, her voice low and gentle. "What else can you do?"

"Have the baby, I guess."

"And then what? Who'd want a baby conceived that way? You'd be stuck with it for the rest of your life. It's not fair,

Dynah. It's not right, either. Why should you have to suffer for what someone did to you? You've never done anything to deserve this."

"I'm not sure what's right anymore."

Janet leaned closer, filled with sympathy. "I don't know of anyone who'd look down on you for having an abortion under these circumstances, Dynah, even at NLC. Except maybe a few radical fundamentalists who don't matter anyway. Like a dean or chairman of the board or something. And they don't have to know. Nobody has to know."

"I'd know."

Janet bit her lip and frowned. She didn't say anything for a moment. "You also know the circumstances that this baby was made in. What sort of beginning is that for a life?"

Dynah cringed inwardly at the memory. It was still so raw, she focused instead on what had happened that morning. "I was so scared when the doctor told me. He said it without the least feeling, Jan. He wanted me to be back at the hospital by two-thirty. He didn't even ask if it was what I wanted."

"Maybe he was trying to make it easy for you."

"How can something like that be easy?" Eyes swimming with tears, she looked at Janet. "I've been against abortion since I first knew what it was, and now I'm supposed to have one? How can I?"

"What did Ethan say about it?"

She looked down at the place mat. "He said he'd take me back to the hospital and stay with me."

Janet sat back, surprised and showing it. "Well, that's something. I didn't think he'd be so understanding."

Understanding. The word reverberated in Dynah's mind. She wished she could understand so many things. Why it happened. Why, against all the odds, she should get pregnant. Why nobody seemed to want to hear how she really felt. She couldn't

understand anything anymore, least of all the arbitrary emotions that churned within her now. Fear uppermost. Guilt.
Anguish. Despair. Anger. All tumbling over each other and
churning inside her.

It would have been better if I'd died that night.

The thought stood stark in the silence between her and Janet.
It would have been easier.

The waitress returned with Janet's pie and Dynah's soup.
Odd that the smell of food didn't turn her stomach. In fact, she
was suddenly terribly hungry.

Another reminder of her condition, she supposed, wanting to
weep.

Janet smiled at her. "You want to say the blessing?"

Thank you, God. For what?

Knowing Janet had never been comfortable with praying
aloud, Dynah nodded. The words came easily to her, out of
years of habit. "Thank you, Lord, for the food we are about to
receive, and may we be truly thankful. Amen."

Oh, God, she thought, her heart crying out to him, her hands
clenched beneath the table, out of Janet's sight. *Oh, God, help me.
Help me! Take this burden from me. Let it be a false test result. If
not, let me miscarry. Just let it be over. It's more than I can bear.*

"Good, isn't it?" Janet remarked, tucking into her meal with
her usual gusto.

Dynah ate in silence while a chorus of voices inside her head
carried on a screaming debate. Those on the side of abortion
were the loudest, the most logical, the most appealing to her
bruised and battered spirit. And yet there was another voice,
quiet, calm, almost imperceptible, that said NO, THERE'S
ANOTHER WAY.

The anger that stirred in her was focused upon that voice,
aimed against it, for she knew Whose voice it was. She recognized it. She had been listening to it all her life.

What way? What way that isn't unbearable? What way that won't bring shame upon me? What way that's not fraught with complications and years of heartache? It's not fair! It's not right!

BE STILL, BELOVED.

Why should I be still? I've been still and quiet and complacent all my life! And what has it gotten me but this grief? I have loved you from my first breath. And you do this to me. Why did you let this happen?

Ethan's words drowned out the quiet voice in her head. *"This can't be God's best for us."* Surely he was right. Surely Ethan knew better than she. He was closer to God, wasn't he? His father was a pastor, his grandfather, and back another generation. He had studied the Bible from the time he could read. He was going to preach the Word. He would shepherd his own flock in the next few years.

It makes a nice picture, doesn't it, Lord? Me standing beside him holding the hand of a child begotten by rape? A pastor's wife is supposed to be above reproach. I am a reproach! We saved ourselves for one another so that we could enter this marriage pure. Instead, I have this thing growing inside me, this creature put there by someone whose face I never even saw!

"Your mom called again," Janet said, finishing off her pie and pushing the plate to one side. "There was a message on the answering machine when I got back."

"I know. I was there when she called."

"Why didn't you pick up?"

"I couldn't." She shook her head, unable to give any solid reasons. The waitress delivered Janet's meal, and they finished eating in silence.

"I've heard it's not so bad," Janet said. "They give you something for the pain, and the actual procedure only takes about fifteen to twenty minutes. Then you rest for a while afterward. When you walk out of the hospital, you can put the whole thing behind you. It'll all be over and done with."

Fifteen to twenty minutes sounded like a lifetime to Dynah. The rape hadn't taken so long, and she hadn't been able to forget that in two long months.

■ ■ ■

It was late by the time they returned. Ethan wasn't waiting at the dorm, but he'd left a message: "I'm praying for you. I know you'll do the right thing after you think it over. Love, Ethan." She knew what his prayers involved. In truth, they were probably not much different from her own.

Janet returned to her studies. Dynah opened her own books and tried to concentrate. She'd barely passed the English exam and knew her grades were falling. She'd lose her scholarship if she didn't get her mind focused soon.

Another reason for having it over and done with.

She had to make a decision. *"The longer you wait, the harder it will be."*

"I'm done in," Janet said, snapping a book shut and stacking it with the others on her desk. "I can only cram in so much biology at a time." She gathered her toiletries and headed out the door. When she returned, face scrubbed, teeth brushed, and short hair brushed, she bid Dynah good night and went to bed. She was asleep almost immediately.

Dynah sat on her bed with her back against the wall, still reading, still trying to get the information into her head. She stared at the printed page feeling a hopeless lethargy grip her. What was the use of any of it? None of it made sense to her, and what did seemed useless information.

Lord, is it all right with you if I do this? There isn't a word about it in the Bible. I've looked. But surely you wouldn't want such a child. . . .

The telephone rang, startling her from her prayer. Her heart jumped, racing in apprehension. With Janet asleep, she had no choice but to answer.

"It's Joe."

Relief filled her until she looked at the clock and saw it was past midnight. "Is something wrong?"

"I don't know. Are you OK?"

"I . . ." She started to lie and then closed her eyes and leaned her head back. "Not really."

"Wanna talk about it?"

She smiled wanly at the tenderness in his tone and closed her eyes. "That's all I've done most of today. Talk and talk and talk about it. It doesn't do any good."

Joe didn't say anything for a moment. "I care about you, Dynah. I want you to know that."

Her throat closed up. She would have given almost anything to hear the same tone in Ethan's voice. Instead, she'd faced his anger and disgust, his demands that she do what he thought best. Best for whom? Best for what?

Is it best, Lord? Is this your best? This rotten miserable mess?

"I care about what happens to you."

She could hear tears in his voice and struggled against her own. "I don't know what to do, Joe."

"Don't do anything you'll regret," he said gently.

He didn't have to say what he meant. "Ethan said he thinks I should have the abortion."

"I know what he says. That doesn't mean you have to have one."

"And if I don't? What then, Joe? Will he still love me? Ethan says this isn't God's best for us. He said God wouldn't expect me to have it."

"Ethan isn't God, Dynah. No matter how much you love him, he isn't God."

"So what are you saying, Joe? That I have to have it. Is that it? Ethan said that's what you'd say."

"Hang up on him," Janet muttered, rolling over and pulling the pillow over her head.

"I don't want to see you hurt more than you already are," Joe said gently. "I care about you."

Her eyes burned. "I know what you care about, Joe. Saving the unborn." She pressed the off button and threw the telephone into the dirty-clothes hamper. Hugging her knees against her chest, she put her head down. The telephone rang again.

Rage burst inside her, unreasoning and focused. On Joe. On his principles, his values, his morals, his strong foundation in Christ Jesus. All of which she had shared not so long ago and which now filled her with unspeakable confusion and anguish, guilt and despair. Joe with that old question, unspoken but emblazoned nonetheless: What would Jesus want you to do?

Jumping up, she pushed the portable telephone deep into the clothes. Snatching up her pillow, she pressed it down into the hamper, muffling the insistent ringing. When it didn't stop, she grabbed her towel and went out the door.

Standing in the shower, she put her face into the stream of warm water, trying to drown the thoughts that rang in her head as insistently as the telephone had in her dorm room. She wished she had listened to the doctor. She wished she had gone back at two-thirty this afternoon. She wished it were all over and done with and she wouldn't have to think about it anymore.

She started to cry, deep wrenching sobs, and wrapped her arms around herself, the water pouring down over her in a baptism of pain. Would it ever be over? Would nothing ever be the same? And if she chose abortion, could she ever feel clean again?

■ ■ ■

Dynah called home the next morning. She knew she had put off speaking with her parents for far too long. The longer she waited, the harder it would be.

Her mom answered. "Oh, Dynah. Thank God. We've been worried sick about you."

The sound of her mother's voice made Dynah want to weep again. She wished she were home and could fall into her mother's arms—but how could she without spilling her insides and the awful news with it? So she kept her voice warm and tightly controlled and said she was sorry. She said she hadn't been feeling well. She said she hadn't called because she didn't want to worry them. She said she was so busy with classes and tests. And there was Ethan, making his demands of her. You know how men can be, Mom. It was all true. She was sorry. About everything. She was pressured. She didn't feel well. Past exhaustion. Desperate. Despairing. And gripped by morning sickness.

"Are you sure you're all right, Dynah? You don't sound like yourself."

"I'm fine. Really, Mom. Everything's fine." *Oh, God, oh, God, oh, God*.

"Dynah," her mother said in that gentle tone she always used when trying to draw her out, "you can tell me anything. You know that."

"I know, Mom. Haven't I always?" This was exactly why she had put off calling for so long. Her mother always knew when something was wrong. She had some second sense about her daughter. Maternal radar, she jokingly called it. But it was no joking matter, not this time.

"Are your classes going well?"

"Classes are going well." Classes would go well with or without her presence.

"Ethan?"

"Healthy." Biting her lip, she hesitated and then went on. "He's still on the dean's list. He's teaching Bible studies two nights a week."

"Does that bother you?"

"Bother me? Why should it?"

"I suppose his activities cut into your time together."

"We still have time together. Every afternoon. Most evenings."

"Are you having any second thoughts about getting married so young?"

"No." Was Ethan having second thoughts? Second, third, and fourth thoughts?

"Dynah," her mother said, her tone hesitant, even cautious, "are you and Ethan . . . well, are you getting a little more involved than you intended?"

Dynah frowned, wondering what she was talking about. "We're engaged, Mom. We'll be married in August."

"Yes, and with our blessings."

"You like Ethan, don't you?" They had met him only once. They had flown back for that express purpose the moment she told them she was in love with a young man on campus.

"Your father and I like him very much. It's just that . . . well, I guess we're feeling protective."

Protective. The word jarred.

She had always felt protected, safe. Her mother and father had watched over her and loved her so well she had never had reason to be afraid. Now her life seemed permeated with fear. Fear of what happened. Fear of what she carried. Fear of what to do. Fear of the future and all its unknown pain and anguish. Unending fear. It stretched out ahead of her, a lifetime of it.

"Ethan's a healthy young man," her mother said. "Your father and I haven't forgotten what it's like to be young and very much in love. Sometimes, well, sometimes spending so much time together can cause . . . temptation."

Dynah knew her mother was testing, gently probing, trying to draw out reasons for her long silence. It was a moment before she understood what her mother was trying to say. She thought they were sleeping together. Shocked and hurt, Dynah closed her eyes. "Oh, Mom . . ."

"Honey," her mother said, distressed. "I didn't mean to upset you more than you already are. If that's what's wrong, you can stop it."

"It's not."

"It's not?"

"No." Ethan couldn't even bring himself to kiss her the way he used to.

"I know something's wrong. I assumed . . . I'm sorry I assumed. Oh, honey, you've always called us every other week, and we've been playing telephone tag for over a month. Your letters haven't said very much. We love you. If you and Ethan have gone . . . well, gone further than you intended, we can understand."

Dynah sniffled, wiping her nose with the back of her hand and staring at the wall. "We haven't."

"Dynah, I—"

"We haven't, Mom."

"OK," her mother said slowly.

She sounded so unconvinced, Dynah felt driven. "I swear before God Almighty I have not slept with Ethan. It's nothing like that." *It's a hundred times worse.*

"I'm sorry, honey. I didn't mean to assume the worst."

The worst. Her mother couldn't even imagine the worst. Thank God. Dynah didn't dare even think what her mother would feel if she told her she had been raped, let alone tell her the awful news that she was pregnant. It would shatter her parents. It would destroy all their dreams for her.

But how could she not tell them? How could she hide what happened from them and spare them hurt? She was going home in June, spending the summer with them before she married Ethan in August.

In August she would be in her seventh month of pregnancy if she went through with it.

Horrified, she imagined herself standing before Ethan's father, resplendent in his pastoral robes, as he officiated at their marriage. And behind them, a church filled with relatives and friends all wishing them well.

Oh, God! Oh, God, I couldn't bear it.

And it came to her with cold clarity. She didn't have to bear it. Her parents didn't have to know. Nobody had to know. If she did exactly what Ethan wanted, she could protect her parents and his from knowing how truly terrible the world is.

"You and Ethan both have a strong set of values," her mother said. "Purity is a precious gift to give one another on your wedding night."

Purity.

Smashed and broken.

What gift would she have to give Ethan when she married him? A body scraped clean of a rapist's begat?

Scraped clean but still ruined. She saw it in his eyes. Her parents and his need never know, but he always would.

"What's the matter, honey?" her mother said. "Please trust me."

"Oh, Mom. The pressure, the pressure's so awful."

"What sort of pressure do you mean?"

"Everything," she said dismally. She couldn't unburden herself and burden her mother instead. What good would it do? It wouldn't change anything. It wouldn't make her forget the rape. It wouldn't make this thing inside her disappear. There was only one way to do that. "I don't know if I'm going to make it, Mom."

"Of course, you'll make it. You have everything it takes, honey."

"You don't understand." How could she? And Dynah couldn't explain.

"You've always expected so much of yourself. You've expected to do everything exactly right. Sometimes life gets in the way, honey. Sometimes you just have to do what's necessary."

"Necessary."

"Prioritize. Remember how we used to talk about the ant that ate the elephant?"

Abortion first, then everything would fall neatly into place. Once it was over, she could get back to doing what she was supposed to be doing, finishing a year of college, keeping her grades up so she'd still have her scholarship next year, finishing plans for her wedding, looking ahead to a bright, happy future.

"Set your mind on getting through what you have to do," her mother said.

"I guess," Dynah said, rubbing her temple. She supposed that was what she would have to do. Set her mind on having the abortion. Set her mind on getting through it. Set her mind on going on with her life. Set her mind on keeping what she had done a secret forever.

"You can do it," her mother said gently. "I know you can. Sometimes when you break things down into small pieces, they're easier to handle than looking at the thing as a whole."

Dynah's eyes filled with hot tears.

"Have you spoken with a counselor, honey?"

She had spoken with the doctor and Ethan and Janet and Joe. Did they count as counselors? "No. Not really."

"I always go to Pastor Dan when things seem to get squirrelly," her mother said with a soft laugh. "Sometimes an objective eye can help bring things into focus."

She couldn't go to the dean or the pastor of the church where

Ethan taught Bible study. Maybe Charlie's pastor. No. Charlie did a lot of volunteer work at the church. He might see her there. He'd want to know why she hadn't been on the bus. She'd have to find another church, another pastor, someone who didn't know her or Ethan. Maybe she could go into Chicago.

"Why don't you come home for Easter? We can send you plane tickets."

"I don't know if I can, Mom. I doubt the library will give me the time off."

"Library? I thought you were working at Stanton Manor House."

Heat flooded Dynah's cheeks as she realized her blunder. "I quit."

"Quit? That's not like you."

"It was a long bus ride, Mom, and the hours weren't that good, and—"

"Bus? Is your car acting up again?"

Closing her eyes, Dynah wished she hadn't said anything about the bus. "A little, but it's fixed now." The car had a new fuel pump and battery, but it was going to need new tires soon. That would use up most of what she'd saved.

How much did an abortion cost? The doctor had said nothing about it, but she was sure he wasn't going to do the procedure gratis. Would her insurance cover it?

She couldn't use her insurance. If she did, the statements would be sent to her parents. That's how they knew she had been x-rayed in October when the campus doctor suspected she had walking pneumonia. She could just see her mother's face when she opened the mail and found a statement from the insurance company saying her daughter had had an abortion.

"Well, I can't imagine a Christian college keeping their library open on Easter," her mother was saying.

"They don't. Not for that weekend. But I still can't come home, Mom. Ethan's expecting me to go to Missouri with him." She calculated how far along she would be by then if she didn't go through with the abortion. Not quite four months, probably not far enough along to show, but her mother would know in an instant. She noticed everything.

What if Ethan's parents were the same way? What would Ethan say if asked? "Yes, Father, she's pregnant, but I assure you it wasn't of my doing. She got herself raped when she walked by Henderson Park one night."

Would they believe it? Or would they, like others, make assumptions about how far her relationship with Ethan had gone?

Like her mother and father had assumed . . .

His reputation would be compromised.

"You went back on December 27 so you could be with his family for the New Year, Dynah. I think Ethan can spare your company for Easter. We'd like to see you."

"I'll talk to him about it, Mom."

"We miss you, honey."

"I miss you, too," Dynah said, her throat closing up.

Silence.

"You're sure you're OK, honey?"

"I'm sure. I've gotta go, Mom. I'm . . . I'm late for class."

"We love you, Dynah."

"I love you, too. Bye."

Dynah stood in the middle of her dorm room, the portable telephone clutched in her hand, feeling as though her last connection with safety and understanding had been broken.

Joe leaned back in his chair and stretched out his legs beneath the table. He'd been studying for two hours, preparing a paper due in his linguistics class. He could have done the work better in his apartment. Ethan was off on another of his good works. He could have turned up his music and used his computer. Instead, he had opted for the library.

Because of Dynah.

He saw her come in, her shoulder bag laden with books. She was pale and wan but smiled when someone said hi to her on the way out. She opened the gate and went behind the counter. Depositing her things in a cabinet against the back wall, she set to work immediately, sorting books and arranging them in Dewey-decimal order on a push cart. Her supervisor spoke with her for a moment. Dynah blushed, nodded, and set back to work.

Joe watched and waited, willing her to look up and see him. When she did, he saw the unease in her expression. Immediately he understood: She'd felt someone staring at her and was frightened. He hadn't thought of that possibility. When she spotted him, relief flickered, along with a smile to meet his own. But only briefly. Another look came into her blue eyes, and she lowered her gaze from his.

Leaning forward slowly, he looked down at the book in front of him dismally.

"I know what you care about, Joe. Saving the unborn."

She didn't know the half of it.

Raking one hand back through his hair, he picked up his pen and made a couple of notes. He read a few more lines.

"Do you mind?" someone snarled from across the table, and he realized he was tapping his pen.

"Sorry," he muttered, tossing it onto a stack of notes. Dynah wheeled her cart through the gate and headed down the aisle, disappearing behind several high metal shelves of books.

Scraping his chair back, Joe encountered another annoyed look from the guy across from him. He raised his hands. "Sorry," he muttered again and set the chair back carefully before following Dynah.

There were so many uptight people. Even on this campus, where he expected stress to be in small, measured, healthy amounts. If anything, he found it more intense. Everyone wanted to be the best. Best student. Best servant. Best Christian. They got caught up in it, pressing and pushing until they forgot whom it was they were trying to please.

Like Ethan.

Dynah was leaning down over the cart, her long, blonde French braid swinging gently. She glanced his way and then focused her attention on the books again. Selecting one, she turned and reached up, pushing a book aside and sliding the one she held into its proper place.

She stood there for a long moment, her hand still resting on the shelf. "I haven't done it yet," she said in a flat tone. She glanced at him, eyes flashing briefly.

Joe winced.

Turning her back on him, Dynah took hold of the cart and wheeled it down the aisle. Pausing, she looked up and then wheeled it back a few feet, shelving two more books. She had to concentrate. She had to get it right.

Joe followed. "Shelve that issue, would you, please?" he said softly. "I'm concerned about you."

She shoved another book into place, looked at it, pulled it out, pushed a book to one side, and shoved it in again. He saw her hand tremble slightly as she ran her finger over the letters and numbers, rereading· them to make sure she had put the book in the right place.

Leaning against the metal shelf, he pushed his hands into his pockets. "Did you see Ethan this morning?"

"No. We talked on the phone. He said he'd be busy today. He's got classes and work. And he has to prepare for the Bible study tonight at Community Church."

Joe knew she was making excuses for Ethan. She was isolating herself against the hurt. Anger stirred. Frenetic activity seemed to be Ethan's forte. And safety valve. When he didn't want to face something, he served, mightily, as for the Lord. But not really. It was easier to teach God's Word than to live it.

Pushing his hands into his pockets, Joe admonished himself. He had no right to criticize, even in the privacy of his mind. *Sorry, Lord. He's yours, I know. And he's doing the best he can. But I wish he'd open his eyes and take a good look at Dynah and see what's happening to her.*

Joe felt caught between two people he loved. He'd spent hours over the past few months listening to Ethan vent his anger and disappointment and disillusionment.

"I'd like to kill him!" Ethan had said again last night, crying at the power of his rage. "I'd like to hunt that animal down and kill him with my bare hands for what he did."

Joe hadn't felt it would be productive to say he shared the same feelings. When he'd seen Dynah's face that dark January night, the wounded, demolished look in her eyes, emotions he had thought long washed away with his rebirth in Christ returned full force. Heat like the fires of hell surged through his blood. His heart pounded. He shook with the power of anger, a killing, bloodthirsty wrath. It was the kind of emotion he used to feel when he was a teenager running with a rough crowd in Los Angeles.

Civilization was a thin veneer.

God knew.

Maybe Christianity was the same way.

He'd wondered about that a lot over the past weeks as he struggled with his own feelings, facing some he hadn't dared face before.

"I still love her," Ethan said, tormented. "I mean, I look at her, and she's so beautiful, but I can't . . . I can't . . ." He shook his head. "She looks the same. She's still Dynah, but every time I touch her, I get this sick feeling, Joe. I know what happened isn't her fault. I know it in my head. But it doesn't help. I mean, what if she has AIDS?"

Dynah's pregnancy added new dimensions to Ethan's confusion, while focusing his anger. With the rapist gone and little chance of his being apprehended, there was only one person on whom to focus his wrath: the child Dynah carried.

"It's not a child," Ethan had erupted in rage last night. "Don't tell me it is! This thing she carries is an abomination before God. It's a sucking parasite! The sooner she gets rid of it, the better."

Joe wondered if his roommate had shared those feelings with Dynah. Ethan had always been perceptive and sensitive to others' feelings, careful in how he dealt with people. Was he being careful with Dynah?

It didn't look like it.

Dynah glanced back at Joe. He looked so grim, that muscle working in his jaw again. Was he angry with her, too? Ethan was. He said she was vacillating. She said she couldn't help it. When she told him this morning that she was going to seek counseling before making any kind of decision, he'd slammed the telephone down in her ear. Oh, he'd called back a few minutes later to apologize. She knew because she stood listening as his voice was recorded on the answering machine. "Dynah, look, I'm sorry. Pick up. Please. I know you're there, Dy. You're being unreasonable. I've been under a lot of pressure lately. Can't you try to understand how I feel? I can understand how you'd like to think things through, but we've been over and over this. You're just making the whole thing worse for both of us."

She'd left the room before he finished.

Sometimes she wondered if she knew him at all.

"Never marry a man until you've seen how he handles getting a flat tire," her aunt had joked once.

Some flat tire, Lord.

And now here was Joe, looking grim. She knew what side he'd be coming from. He was as adamant against abortion as Ethan was now for it. The only thing she didn't know was where she fit into the equation.

She pushed the cart farther down the aisle, shelving books carefully, afraid she'd make a mistake. "Go away, Joe. I don't want to talk to you."

When he did, Dynah went on shelving books, gripped by guilt. She shouldn't have been so rude to him. He had never said or done anything to warrant it. When she finished shelving all the books on the cart, she wheeled it back down the long aisle between the stacks of shelves. Joe was still sitting at the same table, books and papers spread out around him. He looked up when she paused at his table. "I'm sorry, Joe."

"You don't have to apologize."

She shrugged, throat tight.

The student across the table, appearing somewhat resigned and disgruntled, gathered up his books and papers, shoved them into his backpack, and departed to a cubby near the windows. Dynah blushed and wheeled her cart into the work area.

Mrs. Talbot asked her to go out again and pick up texts that had been left on the study tables. Wheeling the cart out again, she carried out the chore, saving Joe's table for last. Embarrassed, she spoke softly without meeting his gaze. "I'm going to talk to the pastor at Community," she said in a hushed tone, putting two books on the cart.

"Sounds like a good idea. When're you going to see him?"

"Sometime this week." Whenever she could gather enough courage to do so. She wished she didn't sound so ambivalent.

"Want some company?"

Surprised, she looked at him and almost said yes. Hesitating, she frowned slightly. She'd asked Ethan to go with her, but he refused. What problems would she create between Joe and Ethan if she said yes. "No, that's all right. I think it'd be better if I went on my own."

"You're sure?" Joe said, sensing her concerns. Sure, Ethan would be mad, maybe even jealous, but he didn't care about that right now. Dynah was more important. Sooner or later, Ethan would come to his senses and see that.

"I'm sure, but thanks."

She was far from sure several days later when she walked through the doors of Community Church and asked to see the pastor. The secretary was polite and asked no questions. She said Pastor Whitehall was with someone at the moment but would be finished shortly. Could she wait? Dynah said she could and took the seat offered, her stomach knotted.

The door of the pastor's office opened and a distinguished-looking man in a dark gray three-piece business suit came out holding a polished black briefcase. He nodded to the secretary and noticed Dynah. He smiled slightly and looked back briefly at the man standing in the office doorway. Dynah felt some current in that look, some silent message being passed.

"Miss . . . Miss? I'm so sorry. I didn't get your name," the secretary said.

"Jones," Dynah said, blushing and lowering her eyes. "Mary Jones."

"Miss Jones, this is Pastor Tom Whitehall. Pastor, this is Mary Jones. She asked if she could speak with you."

"Didn't I have another appointment? One at the hospital?"

The secretary looked momentarily confused and flustered. She glanced at her calendar and back at him. "No, sir. Not unless I forgot to write it down."

Dynah looked up at him.

The pastor met her eyes and frowned slightly, looking disturbed and faintly annoyed. "I guess I have some time then. Come on in."

Self-conscious, Dynah sat in a wing chair before a big oak desk and avoided looking into the man's eyes. She looked at his desk instead. It was strewn with texts and papers. Behind it were shelves lining the entire office. One shelf held nothing but various versions of the Bible. Theology books and commentaries lined several shelves, and she noticed a plethora of counseling texts. Interspersed throughout the shelves were family photographs and memorabilia from mission trips to Southeast Asia, Africa, and Mexico.

"What can I do for you, Miss Jones?" Pastor Whitehall asked, sitting down in the swivel chair behind his desk. Mary Jones! She might as well have said her name was Jane Doe.

Dynah's heart drummed, and she pressed her damp palms against her skirt. She sensed his reticence, but it had taken her five days to get the courage to come here, and she didn't dare leave now. She knew if she did, she wouldn't have the courage to come back. "I need some advice."

Tom Whitehall leaned back slowly and assessed her. She was a beautiful girl and clearly a troubled one. He could see the dark shadows beneath her blue eyes, the wariness in her expression. He could guess what was the matter. It was probably the same problem most young women like her brought into his office, and the last thing he needed to face today, right after the attorney had left.

Jack Hughes's look had been clear enough. Community Church was in deep trouble because of a lawsuit over a young girl who had received counsel and then gone out a week later and killed herself. The court seemed to be leaning toward the parents' viewpoint. They claimed he'd given counsel when he was untrained to offer it, and his blundering attempts to help had caused the girl to go over the edge. He had no doctorate in psychology, and therefore had no right to offer counsel to a troubled girl.

It made Tom sick with grief every time he thought about Mara. Stricken with guilt, he went back over everything he had said to her, trying to find something that might have put her over the edge. She had been a deeply troubled girl, estranged from her physically abusive parents, promiscuous, newly clean from drugs. He thought she was doing better. He thought she was seeing some glimmer of hope. Then the news had come that she'd committed suicide. And now the lawsuit. His stomach churned, burning.

He looked at Mary Jones and wondered if he was being set up by Mara's parents or their slick attorney. Community was a big church. Jack said all concerned figured it had deep pockets. "What sort of advice were you looking for, Miss Jones?" he said cautiously.

"Of a delicate nature," she said, afraid she was going to cry.

Weaving her fingers together, she let her breath out slowly, trying to relax and regain some control over her emotions. "In January I was raped in Henderson Park."

The information came like a punch in his stomach. One look into her eyes and he believed her, and that made everything worse. *Father, I'm not equipped for this. My training doesn't cover it. I'm not a psychologist. I'm a minister.* "I'm sorry," he said, filled with compassion and despair. "Has the man been arrested?"

"No. I never saw his face."

All manner of things came to his mind, things he could say to her to offer comfort, but he held them back, analyzing each and casting it aside. It could be misconstrued as counseling, and he wasn't licensed for that. Jack's look had been a pointed reminder and warning.

She saw the compassion in his expression and gathered enough courage to say the rest. "I found out recently that I'm pregnant."

Tom's heart sank.

"Please. I need to know if abortion is all right under these circumstances," she said softly.

He looked into her eyes and saw her fear and confusion, her anguish. He wanted to weep. He knew the answer to that question in his heart. He knew the answer by all he had studied over the years in the Word. But he couldn't bring himself to give a one word answer to such a loaded question. It was dangerous. A court would see what he had to tell her as judgmental, harsh, and intolerant. His convictions weren't politically correct, and he didn't know who this girl was, what her background was, where she was going from here. Maybe she'd be like Mara and check herself into a hotel room, swallow a bottle of pills, and leave a note saying how sorry she was to disappoint everyone.

His throat closed up tight thinking about Mara, so desperately unhappy. How could she have done such a thing? She couldn't possibly have known the mess she would leave behind. Would Community survive the lawsuit and scandal? Would he?

Dynah looked up at him again and waited, praying she would receive divine guidance from this man of God. She needed it so desperately.

"It's legal," he said simply.

His words dropped into the silence, filling both of them with a feeling of hopelessness.

"I know that," Dynah said, searching his face. "I need to know if God will understand."

"God understands everything." He grimaced inwardly. The patness of those words were like a placebo offered for a mortal wound, but what else could he say? He looked away from the pain in her eyes.

"You know what I'm asking you, Reverend Whitehall. Please. Tell me the truth."

Tom looked at her again, ashamed. He had to be honest with her. He had to make her understand and forgive him. Leaning forward, he clasped his hands on the desk in front of him. "Yes, I know what you're asking, Miss Jones, but I can't answer you. I'm not trained to counsel someone, and this church is under attack because I did just that."

"Every pastor is a counselor."

"Not according to laws of the land. I took several classes in college, but that was years ago."

"But . . ." She glanced up at his shelves.

"Yes. I've read volumes since then, but that doesn't count for anything without certification and documentation. I'm not licensed, Miss Jones. I'm being sued, and so is this church, because I gave advice to a young girl and she went out and she took her own life. I can't afford to risk further trouble for my church. I don't know you or your circumstances, and I'm not going to hazard to guess and give advice. We've worked too hard and long to build this place to have it all come tumbling down."

For her. He didn't say it, but she understood. She was a stranger to him. Why should he risk anything? But she had to try. "I'm your sister in Christ."

"Then I suggest you speak with the pastor of your own church. He'll help you."

She lowered her eyes. "He's in California," she said dismally. And even if she were there, or he here, she couldn't talk to him. Pastor Dan saw her as her parents did: unsullied, angelic. What would he think if he found out she was ruined and carried a child of shame?

Neither said anything for a long moment. Dynah made one last try. "Would you advise me according to Scripture? Could you do that much?"

Tom hesitated, thinking over what Jack had said to him. If she were a member of his church, things might be different. "I can tell you that the word *abortion* is never mentioned in the Bible," he said flatly.

Dynah saw he didn't want to say anything more than that. He would if she pressed hard enough, but that would be unfair and unkind to him. "Well, thank for your time," she said, standing slowly and fumbling with her shoulder bag.

Everything inside him rebelled. He wanted to tell her to stay, that he'd help, but he'd done that with Mara, and what had come of that? "I'm sorry," he said bleakly. "I'm so sorry."

"So am I."

"I wish I could be of more help. Really. I—"

"It's all right, Pastor Whitehall. I understand." And she did, but it didn't help much.

Standing outside, Dynah looked at the sky clouding up and

knew exactly how that girl had felt when she'd decided to take her life.

■ ■ ■

Joe called but got Janet instead of Dynah. "Do you know where she is?"

"She didn't say, Joe. She's probably with Ethan."

"Ethan's in a conference with Dean Abernathy."

"What's the urgency?"

"I don't know, Jan. I just have this gut feeling, and I can't shake it."

"What sort of feeling?"

"That we need to find her. Fast."

"You aren't thinking . . . She wouldn't do anything to herself, Joe. You know she wouldn't."

"I hope not."

"Dynah wouldn't even think about it."

"Maybe not. Any ideas where she might go to be alone?"

"You're serious."

"Yes, I'm serious!"

"Did you try the library? Well, then, what about the lake? She likes to walk by the lake. No? We hang out at the Copper Pot sometimes. Not there. How about the Tadish's Coffee Shoppe or the downtown book store, the one on Sixteenth and Webster. I'm running out of ideas, Joe. You've looked everywhere I know of to look."

"Think!"

There was a long silence, and then Janet said tentatively, "Well, there's one other place she used to go before she started going out with Ethan, but it's a long shot. She hasn't been there since the first part of this year."

"Where?"

"The prairie reserve. The one that's a couple of miles from the freeway. Do you know the one I mean?"

"Yeah, I know." The last descendant of a pioneering family had willed it to the county ten years before. Every spring the land was splashed with vibrant yellows, oranges, and blues as the coreopsis, black-eyed Susans, cornflowers, and buttercups came into bloom. Right now it would seem a place of desolation. "Thanks." Joe hung up. Digging his keys from his pocket, he left the phone booth outside the downtown bookstore and headed for his car. He knew the reserve all right. He had gone there numerous times himself. It was a great place to be alone to think and pray. Or die.

Yanking his car door open, he slid in. The tires squealed as he barreled out of the space onto the main street. He made a U-turn in the first side street he came to and headed west.

All he could think about were the acres and acres of prairie. *God, help me find her. God, don't let her do anything stupid.*

■ ■ ■

Dynah wandered along the trail near a pond left from the melting snows of winter. The sky was crystalline blue, the air cool. She filled her lungs with it and held it for a moment before letting it out slowly. Two bluebirds flitted overhead, dipping and swirling in a joyful dance to the hint of spring.

It was midweek, midafternoon, the ides of March. Caesar died on such a day. Five days short of the first day of spring. Pausing, Dynah looked around and saw no one. Relieved, she walked on, more briskly now, heading for the cottonwoods and honey locusts. She stepped from stone to stone across the creek and followed the trail past a thicket of hackberry and willow trees. Just beyond it, she left the trail and walked across the grassy expanse toward a grove of old sycamores.

She sat down and looked out over the expanses. It was quiet here, so quiet, so colorless.

Reaching into the pocket of her down parka, she pulled out

a small bottle of pills and looked at it. The directions had said to take no more than six tablets a day. There were fifty in the small plastic bottle.

Uncapping it, she spilled the red pills into her palm. Antihistamines were the strongest drug she could think of to buy over the counter. These looked like the red hots her father liked to buy when he took her to the movies. She remembered sitting through *The Lion King* with him last summer and discussing the subtle theological message over a late dinner at the wharf. She had always loved spending time with her father. One of the things she missed most when she moved to Illinois and started college was her once-a-month date with Daddy. Unlike Mom, he wasn't comfortable on a telephone.

Would Daddy understand?

She veered away from that thought. "God understands everything," the pastor had said.

Will you understand this, Lord? Do you understand anything? She looked up at the clear blue heavens. *I don't even know if you exist anymore.*

A soft breeze caressed the tendrils of hair around her face. *I don't know what else to do, Jesus. What else can I do?*

■ ■ ■

Dynah's car was the only one in the prairie reserve parking area. Joe found her keys in the ignition and her purse still sitting on the front seat. "Jesus," he said softly. "Oh, Jesus." Retrieving the keys and her purse, he tossed them into the trunk of his car for safekeeping. If she tried to take off, he didn't want her able to get far.

You know where she is, Lord. You're the one who brought me here. Show me where she is.

He strode along the trail, looking around for any sight of her. What was she wearing? He'd only caught a glimpse of her this morning. She had been wearing a straight denim skirt, lace-up black ankle boots, a white sweater, and a dark blue parka.

Jumping the creek, he ran along the trail beside it. The stream snaked toward the west. He followed it for half a mile before he stopped, feeling sure she hadn't gone that way. Looking back the way he had come, he saw four sycamores standing like sentinels to the north. And there she was.

Joe found her sitting among them, her arms wrapped around her raised knees, her head down so he couldn't see her face.

Catching his breath, he sat down beside her. She had something clenched in her fist. He took the bottle from her. It was empty. His heart drummed fast and hard. "Oh, Jesus. Dynah . . ." How long would it take him to get her to a hospital and have her stomach pumped? Time enough?

"It's all right, Joe."

"It's not all right." He came to his feet. Grasping her arm, he hauled her up with him. Uttering a soft cry, her other hand opened, spilling red pills all over the ground around her feet. "Oh, no!" She yanked free, going down on her knees.

"Leave them."

"No!" She brushed several together and started to pick them up.

Joe caught her arm and pulled her back. "You think I'm going to stand by and let you take those things?"

She jerked loose. "I can't leave them! The birds'll think they're berries." She fought loose and scrambled for them.

Joe watched her on her hands and knees gathering pills. He read the label grimly and hunkered down to help her look. He felt calmer—at least he no longer wanted to shake her teeth out of her head. Uncapping the bottle, he held out his hand. "Give 'em to me."

She did as he asked. "Count them, Joe."

"Forty-two."

"Eight more," she said, searching. "I have to find them. I have to find them."

They searched the grass for twenty minutes before they found the last pill and capped it securely inside the bottle. Dynah held out her hand to take it from him. "No way," Joe said, tucking it in deeply into the front pocket of his Levi's.

"I'll throw them away. I promise."

"I'll do it for you."

She let her breath out slowly and sat down again. "Thanks for your vote of confidence."

"Should I feel confident? I find you up here with a bottle of pills in your hand!"

"I didn't do it, did I?"

"Don't push me, lady. You scared the life out of me!"

She glared up at him. "I'm still breathing. I'm still pregnant!" Lowering her chin, she looked away.

The words knocked the anger out of him. He stared down at the top of her head. Was that all she thought he cared about? A lot she knew.

Sitting down beside her, he let his breath out slowly and set his own feelings aside. He rested his forearms on his raised knees. "What changed your mind?" he said gently.

"Not the baby." Turning her head, she looked at him, straight on, eyes glittering. "I don't care about it. In fact, I hate it!"

He heard the challenge, knew what she expected him to say. Well, he wasn't going to give her that kind of assistance.

Dynah waited. "Well?"

"I heard you."

She searched Joe's face and saw no condemnation or anger. Ashamed, she looked away and blinked back tears. "I couldn't swallow them. Satisfied? I kept wondering what my mother and father would think when they found out I was dead." She shook her head. "I talked to Mom a few days ago. She knows something's wrong. If I . . . if I . . . well, killed myself . . . she'd find some way to blame herself. She'd want to know why. It'd all come out. And Ethan. How would he feel? And Janet. What would she think?" She looked at him. "And you."

He told the blunt truth. "I wouldn't get over it. Not ever."

She saw he meant it. Somehow, it eased the anguish inside her, the feeling of being alone. "Oh, Joe, every which way I look, there's no way out, is there?"

"Maybe there doesn't have to be." He knew it wasn't what she needed to hear the moment the words were out of his mouth.

"Don't you dare tell me there's a reason! Don't tell me God was in this, because if he was, I'll hate him for it. I'll hate him just like I hate the man who raped me!" She buried her head in her arms.

Someday he'd learn to keep his mouth shut and not feel impelled, like Job's friends, to say something.

The problem was, he believed God had a reason for everything, and Dynah knew that. Life experience had taught him God was close and personal. He and Ethan had had frequent discussions on the subject and agreed. It was easy to accept God's sovereignty when everything was going great, when life was a bed of roses. Seeing God's hand in this kind of grief was something else again.

It was testing his faith.

Was it obliterating hers?

"I want out," Dynah said, not raising her head. "Oh, God, I want out. Can you understand, Joe?"

"Yeah, I can understand," he said grimly, "but killing yourself isn't the answer."

"And the other?" she said tentatively, unable to say *baby*.

She didn't have to say it. He knew exactly what she meant.

"What did the pastor of Community tell you?" he asked, hedging for time, trying to think of what the Lord wanted him to say.

"It's legal."

Joe clenched his teeth, his blood going hot. What a cop-out that was.

"But you wouldn't approve of me, would you?"

"My feelings about you wouldn't change."

She raised her head and looked at him. "Are you saying you'd approve?"

"No. That's not what I'm saying." She looked so confused, and he didn't know how to make it any clearer without telling her everything. And he couldn't do that. Not now. Not under these circumstances. "I want to help you, Dynah. Any way I can. Tell me how."

Her mouth curved sadly. "I wish I knew, Joe. Things can't be undone. They just are." She looked away, staring off across the fields toward the freeway. "Maybe God will be merciful, and I'll miscarry."

Joe didn't say anything to that, but he was thankful she didn't ask him to pray for it.

Dynah sensed his dilemma. Ashamed, she closed her eyes. She didn't want to think about it anymore. She didn't want to talk about anything. Her feelings were so jumbled. "It's nice here, isn't it?" That was innocuous enough.

Joe could feel the tension in her, the rigid self-control she was exerting. For his sake. He'd feel better if she let it out. "Reminds me of Antelope Valley. Ever been there?"

"No."

"Doesn't look like this, but it has the same feel. Desolate. And then spring hits, and everywhere you look are splashes of colors. Poppies, lupins, Indian paintbrush. When I was growing up, my mom'd drive my brother and sisters and me out there every May. I went every year until I turned thirteen."

"What happened then?"

"I started running with the gang." His mouth tipped wryly. "Going to see spring flowers wasn't cool."

A light breeze moved past them, reminding them both that winter wasn't that long ago. There was still a bite in the air. "Did you ever go back?" Dynah asked, still looking out across the rolling fields of crushed winter grass. Sprigs of green were just beginning to push from beneath the dark surface.

"First place I went after being baptized. I even took a picnic and invited a couple of my old buddies to go with me."

"Did they?"

"Yeah," he said, grinning, "but they thought I'd gone completely nuts. Crazy for Jesus."

She turned her head toward him, smiling sadly. "You still are, aren't you?"

"Convicted. Redeemed. On a mission. But it's not like it was in the beginning. That emotional high. Feeling on fire. There's effort, day by day, one-foot-in-front-of-the-other effort. And trust. That's been hardest for me. Trusting God. Walking in faith that he knows better than I do what's good for me."

Her eyes filled with tears.

Joe's heart squeezed tight at the look in her eyes. He hadn't meant to hurt her. Reaching out, he gently tucked a tendril of blonde hair behind her ear. "The Lord hasn't abandoned you, Dynah."

"I know that, Joe. His hand is heavy upon me."

Joe moved closer and put his arm around her shoulders, drawing her against him. Comforted, she leaned into him. The silence between them was companionable rather than lonely. Dynah remembered how the prairie reserve looked in September, the tall grasses dry and moving like the sea.

"I miss the ocean," she said wistfully. "That's the one thing I've never gotten over. Not being able to see the ocean. I miss the smell of the sea, and the sun on the sand. Watching the gulls flock and the pelicans dive. I used to go out to the beach whenever I could. Mom and Dad liked to go up the coast at least once a year. Highway 1. When I was a little girl, I used to wish I could live in Mendocino. Or Fort Bragg. It's so beautiful there, the redwoods behind you, the ocean stretching as far as you can see, and the fog rolling in like a gray blanket."

The wind came up again, and she shivered.

Joe noticed. "What do you say we go someplace and have something to eat?" In another hour, it would be sunset. He stood and held out his hand to her.

Dynah didn't want to go back. Ethan would be waiting. Ethan with his solutions and demands. Ethan with his righteousness and anger. Ethan with his conditional love. She wanted to stay here in the quiet remoteness and think about other things, anything but Ethan and what he expected her to do.

"I'll be all right, Joe. You don't have to stand guard over me."

He hunkered down and tipped her chin up. "You wanna stay, we'll stay."

She took his hand in both of hers and looked into his eyes. "I want to stay awhile longer, Joe, but I don't want to talk."

"OK." Straightening, he walked away. Stopping beneath the biggest sycamore, he shoved his hands into his pockets. His right encountered the bottle of pills. She needed to be alone. He could understand that. What she didn't need was isolation.

She didn't move until the sun was setting. Then she stood and watched the horizon change color. Putting aside her situation and the turmoil, she drank in the beauty. It didn't last long enough. The oranges and yellows melted away in the encroaching darkness. The North Star appeared like a tiny spot of light in the heavens. Joe joined her. She felt his hand lightly push her French braid back over her shoulder.

"You ready now?"

"I guess so." She couldn't stay here forever. She had to go back and face whatever came.

They walked back along the trail together. Joe took her hand when they reached the creek. "Careful," he said, his fingers closing firmly over hers. He lifted her the last foot and set her on firm ground. When they reached the parking area, she dug in her pocket for her keys.

"Oh, no."

"They're in my trunk," Joe said, unlocking it.

She blushed. "I guess I wasn't thinking. . . ."

He held her purse out to her. "I locked them up for safekeeping."

She knew better than that. What would she have done if he hadn't arrived when he did? She hugged him, her arms tight around his waist, her cheek against his chest. "Thanks, Joe."

He held her close, his hand cupping the back of her head. He heard her soft shuddering sigh and then felt her withdrawal.

Joe followed her back to NLC. He sat in his car, the motor running, and watched her go up the dorm steps and inside. He waited a few minutes longer and then headed for his apartment. Ethan had left a message on the answering machine that he was helping at a youth rally in Wheaton.

Taking the bottle of pills from his pocket, Joe uncapped them and dumped them down the garbage disposal. Turning the water on full force, he hit the switch. When the harsh grinding sound changed to a steady hum, he flicked the switch and tossed the empty bottle into the trash under the sink.

Slouching into a worn chair, he raked his hands through his hair and held his head. "Jesus," he said softly. "Jesus."

■　■　■

"Miss Carey, Dean Abernathy would like to see you in his office at your earliest convenience," said the pleasant female voice.

Dynah clutched the telephone tightly. "Did he say what it was about?"

"I'm sorry, no. All he said was it's important. Do you have free time this morning?"

A sick dread swept over her, a premonition. Her grades had dropped in the past three months, and she knew her scholarship was at stake. "I can see him between ten and eleven if that's all right."

"He has an appointment at ten, but it shouldn't take long. Why don't you come to his office at ten-fifteen?"

She couldn't concentrate during her British novel course. She had finished reading Dickens's *Bleak House* but didn't participate in the discussion about the characters or story line.

What would her parents think if she lost her scholarship? She was counting on it to get her through. She couldn't very well ask her parents for financial support after she married Ethan, and she and Ethan together couldn't make enough to pay the tuition and fees.

"Miss Carey," the professor said when the class was dismissed and students began filing out. As they did so, they picked up their graded midterm exams on a table near the door. "May I speak with you a moment, please?"

Heart sinking, Dynah noticed the blue essay notebook in his hand and knew it was her midterm. Nodding, she took a swift glance at her watch as she gathered her books. She had twenty minutes before her appointment with Dean Abernathy.

"Sit down," Professor Provost said, nodding to a desk in the front row. As she did so, he took a chair and turned it, sitting down in front of her. He handed her the exam without a word. She felt the blood running out of her face as she stared at the circled F on the front, then felt it flood back hot with shame. Her eyes pricked.

"I'm sorry."

"I'm not looking for an apology, Miss Carey. I'm looking for an explanation."

"I guess I didn't study hard enough."

"The results of that exam show you didn't study at all."

"I'm sorry," she said again softly, keeping her head down.

"I had you in class last year. I know what kind of work you're capable of doing. You're one of the brightest students I've had. You had a solid A in this course. Then you stopped participating."

She shook her head, her throat closed up tight, the exam clutched in her hands. All she could see was the red letter, solid evidence of her failure.

"I'm aware you're getting married in August, Miss Carey, but that doesn't mean you have to toss your education to the wind."

"That's not what I'm doing, sir."

"No? Well, I've seen it happen before. A bright student with a scholarship and great potential arrives; she meets the man of her dreams, gets engaged, and her education flies right out the window. I'm not against matrimony, mind you, or a woman wanting to be a wife and mother. What I am against is waste. God has given you gifts, Miss Carey, special gifts. It's your responsibility to make the most of them."

"I'll try, sir," she said, feeling acutely his disappointment in her. "I'll try harder."

"Don't try, Miss Carey. Do it. You have the rest of the semester to bring that grade up. I hope you won't disappoint me." He stood up and slid the chair back toward his desk. "You're dismissed."

Dynah stood outside the classroom doorway, her stomach twisted in a hard knot. Trembling, she glanced at her wristwatch again. Shifting her book bag, she headed down the corridor and out of the brick building. She stood between the marble columns, looking out at the quad.

She was five minutes late getting to the dean's office. He looked annoyed despite her apology. "Sit down, please, Miss Carey," he said, indicating a wingback chair in front of his massive mahogany desk. As she set her book bag down and took the proffered chair, he pressed the intercom button and told his secretary that he wasn't to be disturbed. Dynah waited, her heart drumming with foreboding.

Dean Abernathy took his seat and leaned forward, arms resting on his desk, his fingers tapping together lightly. "This is difficult," he said grimly, his brows knit.

"I know my grades have fallen, Dean Abernathy. I'm hoping to change that since changing jobs. I have more time to study now."

"I didn't call you here to discuss your grades, Miss Carey," he said solemnly, "but your condition."

Her head came up, eyes wide.

"It's come to my attention recently—" he lowered his hands—"that you're pregnant."

Her face went hot with humiliation.

"I know the circumstances," he said quickly, raising his hands slightly to appease any distress she might have. "And I'm much aggrieved about it. But we still need to face the possible ramifications."

Ramifications? Shutting her eyes, she lowered her head. "Who told you?"

"Ethan," he said grimly. "I assure you, he didn't volunteer the information easily. He didn't want to tell me, but it came out during our appointment yesterday morning. I'd noticed a drop in his performance and wanted to find out what was the matter. He's been at the top of his class since entering NLC. A number of men on the board of trustees have been watching his progress with great interest, as have I. I think Ethan will be one of our most persuasive preachers one day. If nothing distracts his focus, he will continue to do well. When I asked him what had happened to his concentration, he made excuses. That isn't like him, and they didn't satisfy. I pressed." He sighed heavily. "I'm almost sorry now he told me, because it's put me in a painfully awkward position."

She clasped her hands tightly; the room felt cold and filled with shadows.

"He's very distressed about what happened to you," Dean Abernathy said with sympathy. "As I'm sure you are as well, Dynah. And I'm sympathetic, believe me I am."

She raised her head and looked at him, sensing what was to come.

"Unfortunately I can't change the rules, and they are very clear. Any young woman found to be pregnant is immediately removed from enrollment at NLC. I've little choice in the matter, unless you want me to go before the board of trustees and tell all the details of what's happened to you."

"No."

"I didn't think so. You've suffered enough humiliation already."

"Am I being expelled?" she said weakly, crushed at the unfairness of it.

"That's the last thing I'd call it, Dynah, but you can't stay on here unless you agree to publicly expose what's happened. Unless you're able to do that, I'll have to ask you to withdraw from school. I won't have any choice in the matter."

What was he saying? That she would have to stand before a general assembly and tell everyone she was raped? Then people might feel some compassion for her condition.

And how many would feel as Ethan did, that what she carried was an abomination?

"Please try to understand," he went on gently, leaning forward. "If only a few of your closest friends know of the circumstances of your pregnancy, what's going to be the common assumption on this campus? That you and Ethan have committed fornication, and NLC has condoned it by allowing you to remain as a student here. Can you see the potential problems? All manner of difficulties could arise from it. We don't want people to get the wrong message."

No, of course not. She understood. They might be titillated. Then they might commit a sin, and it would be her fault. "What about Ethan?" Would he be asked to leave as well? It would destroy him.

"Ethan's not to blame for this. I'm going to work with him over the next two months. I've taken personal interest in his career since he was a sophomore, and I don't want to see his opportunities diminished by this tragedy. He's agreed to see one of our campus counselors on a biweekly basis, and I think that will help. We'll do everything we can to help him get his studies back on track again."

It wasn't what she was asking, but it answered questions she hadn't even thought to ask. The disparity struck her heart. Ethan's not to blame for this. Was she?

"Ethan wants me to have an abortion, Dean Abernathy," she said before she thought better of it, reacting from hurt and self-preservation. Ethan, the chosen one, righteous and blameless before the Lord.

"Yes, I know."

When Dean Abernathy said no more, Dynah searched his face. She saw something in his expression that filled her with confusion.

"NLC doesn't condone abortion," Dean Abernathy said slowly, choosing his words carefully. "I understand why Ethan feels as he does. I imagine I would feel the same way under the circumstances. You and Ethan are both well aware of our stand on this issue, though the hard cases are seldom discussed."

He leaned back, as though withdrawing from her as far as

possible. "We can hope, however. Sometimes God and nature are merciful in these matters." He hesitated and then continued, looking straight at her. "If you were to miscarry, no one would ever know what happened."

Unless Ethan decided to tell them, came the unbidden thought.

"Should I pray I miscarry?" She wondered if Dean Abernathy was aware of the subtle pressures he was bringing to bear upon her. If she wasn't pregnant, she could stay; if she was, she had to leave. And if she came to him and informed him the pregnancy was over, he wouldn't ask how it happened. And no one need ever know what happened to her.

"God knows the desires of our heart."

She frowned, confused and heartsick. Was he saying that abortion was the easier and most reasonable way but if she chose it, he didn't want to know about it? As long as she was unpregnant, she could continue as before?

Ethan. His concerns were focused on Ethan. He was worried about how all this affected Ethan's schooling and Ethan's career and Ethan's service to the Lord. It was Ethan's future that mattered. Not hers.

I'm expendable.

Lowering her head, she clasped her hands. She wasn't being fair. It wasn't that she didn't matter at all; it was that she mattered less. She didn't have the gifts Ethan did, gifts that might expand the kingdom and bring people to the Lord. She was just an ordinary girl. Nothing special.

"Pray as your heart leads you, Dynah," Dean Abernathy said. She met his gaze and saw sympathy there, but resignation as well. She understood. He felt he had no choice. He had to think of what was best for the majority. He had to think of NLC's reputation. "And may God's will be done."

A platitude to salve her wounds. He couldn't possibly know how much those words hurt her.

When Dean Abernathy stood, Dynah knew the interview was over. Gathering her book bag, she stood as well. He approached with all the appearance of a concerned father, but she felt his hand on her back, firmly guiding her to the door. "Let me know what you decide," he said, opening it for her. "I'll hold you in my daily prayers."

"Thank you," she said, giving the appropriate rote response. She already knew what she was going to do.

■　　■　　■

Ethan was waiting for her in the student union, a theology book open in front of him, a Styrofoam cup of herbal tea beside his notes. He was so intent upon his studies that he didn't notice her until she was standing beside the table. His eyes flickered, faint color stealing into his face as he stood and drew back a chair for her. "Do you want some tea?"

"No, thank you."

"Why don't you put your book bag down?"

"I'm not staying long." Beneath the edge of the table, she worked at the ring on her finger. As soon as it slipped off, she set it on the table between them.

Ethan stared at it and then looked at her. "What're you doing?"

"I'm breaking our engagement." She hadn't expected to see the shock or wounded look in his eyes, nor the relief mingled with hurt. He was as confused as she was, but she knew what she was doing was best for them both.

"Dynah, I'm sorry I told Dean Abernathy. I was upset. Can't you try to understand and forgive me? When he told me what was at stake, I—"

"It's not something you can hide forever, Ethan," she said, absolving him yet again of guilt.

Everyone receives absolution but me, God.

Ethan covered the ring with his hand and tucked it quickly into his blazer pocket out of sight. "I'll keep it until you're ready to take it back."

"I won't take it back."

"Can't we work this out?"

"No, we can't, Ethan. The only way things would work is if I was willing to do what you want me to do. And I'm not." She shook her head, looking down at her bare hand. Her throat closed hot and tight. She hadn't known him well enough, or maybe she had. Maybe she had just expected too much of him.

If she stayed any longer, she would make matters worse by crying and giving everyone around them something to wonder and talk about and him more cause for embarrassment. Shifting her book bag, she stepped back.

"Stay, Dynah. Please. Talk to me."

It was too late for talk. "There's no point. Nothing's going to change."

"What're you going to do?"

"I'm going home."

■　■　■

One phone call to Dean Abernathy and a few hours to pack her things was all the time it took to end her life at NLC. She knew she should call Joe and say good-bye, but she took the easy way out and wrote a note to him instead. She put it in an envelope and stamped it. She'd drop it in the mailbox on her way out of town.

"If my mom calls, don't tell her anything. I'll be home in a week, and they'll know all about it then. Promise?"

"I promise," Janet said grimly. "Are you sure you're doing the right thing? Couldn't you think about—"

"No."

"It would all be so much easier if you—"

"No, it wouldn't. Jan, even if I do have an abortion, it's not going to change my feelings. Ethan and I are through."

"He loves you, Dynah. I know he does. It'd work out. It would."

At what cost? "I love him, too, but it's not enough. It's just not."

"Why?"

"Because I don't trust him anymore. And if you can't trust someone, you can't build any kind of lasting relationship with them." *Like God,* she thought, aching inside. She didn't trust him anymore either.

Closing her suitcase, she locked it and swung it off the bed onto the floor. "I've got to go." She wanted to be as far away from NLC by nightfall as she could be.

Oh, God, what are my parents going to say when they hear? What am I going to tell them?

She would have time enough to think about that on the long drive home to California.

■　■　■

"What do you mean she's gone?" Joe said, wanting to shake Ethan out of his self-centered lethargy. "Gone where?"

"Home. Just leave me alone, would you please? I'm upset enough already without you coming at me about it." And he had a presentation to prepare, the most important presentation of the year. He couldn't afford to go on obsessing about Dynah and her problems.

"What about school? Spring break is in a few weeks. She can't afford to leave—"

"She quit."

"Quit?" Joe watched the color seep into Ethan's face. Eyes narrowing, he frowned. "Why?"

"How should I know?"

"You know something!" Joe's anger heated his blood. "What made her quit? Or should I ask who?"

Ethan glared, furious. "Don't look at me! Nothing made Dynah do anything. She wouldn't listen to reason. She wouldn't listen to anybody. She decided this for herself, along with a few other choice things along the way. She gave my ring back. Did you know that? Just tossed it on the table in the student union in front of everybody, like it meant nothing to her. I called her this morning, and Janet said she left. Yesterday! Just packed up and split! That's how much she cares."

Joe's hand clenched. The sheen of tears in Ethan's eyes was the only thing that kept him from knocking him across the apartment kitchen.

Slamming out of the apartment, he drove to the dorm and called Janet from the lobby. Pacing, he raked his hand through his hair. He was going to have to get it cut again soon. NLC had rules about hair going past the collar. NLC had rules about everything. He frowned, wondering if the rules had anything to do with what was going on. No way! They wouldn't be that heartless. Not if they knew the whole story. He saw the elevator doors open and headed for Janet. "What happened?"

"Dean Abernathy spoke with her."

"Great. What'd he say to her? Her grades were dropping and her scholarship's at risk?"

"No. He was concerned about Ethan's performance. Unfortunately, during the interview yesterday, Ethan told Dean Abernathy that Dynah's pregnant."

"Did he tell him the circumstances?"

"Yes, but it didn't make much difference."

"What do you mean it didn't make much difference?"

She told him the rest.

Joe stood for a moment, the heat pouring through him, his heart pounding. They were heartless.

"I tried to talk her out of leaving, Joe, but she'd made up her mind."

"How upset was she?" Was she going to stop somewhere along the highway and buy another bottle of pills?

"She seemed OK. She packed most of her stuff in boxes and labeled them. I'm supposed to ship them UPS in a week. She figured she would be home by then."

"What route's she taking?"

"Oh, Joe, you'd never catch up with her. Don't be crazy. Besides, she didn't say. I-80, I would guess. I hope that stupid car of hers makes it. She promised to call me every night and let me know that she's safe."

"Did she?"

"She made it to Des Moines last night. She called about ten-fifteen. She's probably halfway across Nebraska by now."

"Call me the minute you hear from her again." He strode across the lobby and punched the glass-door handles with the heels of his hand and flung the doors open. Going down the steps, he headed across the campus. People moved out of his way and watched him pass.

He marched up the steps of the administration building, banged the door open, and strode down the corridor toward the dean's offices.

"May I help you?"

"I want to see Dean Abernathy."

"Do you have an appointment?"

"No. Buzz him. Joe Guilierno. Tell him it's important."

"I beg your pardon," she said with raised brows. "You're being rather impudent."

"Forget it. I'll tell him myself." He stepped around her desk and headed for the door.

"Just a minute!" she said, rising. "You can't go in there!"

Joe banged the door open and strode into the dean's office.

Dean Abernathy was sitting behind his desk going over some papers. Startled, he glanced up, annoyed at the interruption. He had a board meeting tonight and wanted to go over his request for more funds for the sociology department. And there was going to be a discussion on adding a psychology course. "What's going on?"

"I'm sorry, Dean," the secretary said, flustered. "He wouldn't listen. He just—"

"Dynah," Joe said. "Dynah Carey."

Dean Abernathy's heart sank. Removing his glasses, he stood. "It's all right, Mrs. Halverson. You may go. Close the door behind you." He dropped his glasses on the desk and looked at Joe wearily. "I know that you and Ethan are friends."

"Dynah is a friend of mine, too."

"All well and good," the dean said, raising his hand in hopes of silencing the torrent he was sure Joe Guilierno wanted to get off his chest. These hot-blooded Italians. "But I have no intention of discussing Dynah Carey with you or anyone else."

"Fine. I'll just reenact what went on in here day before yesterday, and you tell if I'm right or not. I hope to God I'm wrong."

"I said—"

"You summoned Ethan because you were concerned about his lack of concentration over the past few months. Right? He told you Dynah was raped. Then he spilled his guts and said she's pregnant."

"Now, see here—"

"So you summoned her and informed her of the rules and regulations about unwed pregnancies on NLC. People might get the wrong idea about how she got pregnant. Right?"

"How dare you talk to me in this manner!"

"She ought to go public to save Ethan's reputation and hers.

Right? Of course, if she was too ashamed and traumatized to do that, well, she'd have to leave."

Heat flooded Dean Abernathy's face. "That's enough, Mr. Guilierno."

"Besides," Joe went on, temper at full steam, "even if the truth did come out, there's always the chance students might choose to think she and Ethan made up some story to cover fornication."

"Get out of here!"

"You sanctimonious, pharisaical—"

"If you continue with this attitude, I'll have to take disciplinary action against you!"

"Do it! Go ahead! I'd like nothing better than to go before the board of directors and tell them what happened in here. I wonder if they'd all share your narrow-minded, self-righteous view of how to handle the situation."

"Get out of my office! Now!"

"I'll get out of your office. I'll even get off your campus! But first, I want you to know what you did." He walked to the edge of the desk and jabbed a finger at him. "You aborted her."

"What are you talking about? I did no such thing."

"No? Well, you think about it. Think long and hard, Dean Abernathy. God gave you the perfect opportunity to show Dynah compassion, and what did you do? You scraped her out of your neat, perfect little world and dumped her in the trash."

Dean Abernathy's eyes flickered, his face paling.

Joe saw the words had sunk deep. "Yeah," he said, filled with sorrow, "that's what you did, you and a lot of other people who ought to know better." Turning, he headed for the door. Pausing, he looked back. "The purpose of NLC is to train up godly men and women so they can bring the light of Christ into every walk of life. Isn't that so?"

"Yes."

"Well, you tell me how we can do that, Dean. Tell me how on God's green earth we can dare offer salvation to a dying world when we're so busy shooting our own wounded." He walked out, slamming the door behind him.

Striding out of the building, Joe wondered what he could do to help Dynah now. He didn't know where she was, and even if he did, he couldn't get to her fast enough. Somewhere in the middle of Nebraska. *Jesus, God, please watch over her. Put angels over and around her. Keep her safe. Give her your peace in all this. Don't let her lose hope.* He closed his eyes, grief washing over him. *Don't let us lose hope, Lord. No matter how hopelessly we fail.*

■ ■ ■

Janet called each evening right after she spoke with Dynah.

"She made it to Grand Island, Nebraska."

"She's in Cheyenne, Wyoming."

"She's staying at some little dump in Salt Lake City, Joe. I could hear noise coming through her walls."

"She's in Wells, Nevada. She was calling from a pay phone in a truck stop across the street."

Joe kept praying. *Lord, please keep her car running. Father, don't let her break down someplace in the desert. Jesus, let her feel your presence. Keep her safe.*

"She's in Reno. She sounded really tired, Joe. She said she should be home by tomorrow afternoon. She promised to call as soon as she gets there."

"Let me know as soon as you hear anything."

Janet paused. "How's Ethan doing?"

Joe stared at the wall grimly. "He aced his presentation."

■ ■ ■

Dynah pulled up in front of the house on Ocean Avenue at two o'clock the following afternoon. She had been unable to sleep the night before and had departed Reno at seven. She had made two stops, one for gas in Sacramento and another for something to eat at a Denny's in Vacaville.

Exhausted, she unlocked the front door and entered the house. Her parents were seldom home this time of day. Dad would be in his downtown office working, and Mom would most likely be grocery shopping, reorganizing the clothing closet at the church, or visiting one of the parishioners shut into their homes by age or infirmity.

"Now that you're off on your own, there's no use in me sitting around doing nothing," she'd said the last time Dynah came home.

Setting her suitcases down, Dynah picked up the phone and punched in a number. She counted the rings on the other end. One, two, three, four. The answering machine came on. "Hi! This is Janet. I'm sorry, but I can't come to the phone right now. Please leave a message and your number at the sound of the beep, and I'll get back to you as soon as I can. Bye!"

"I'm home, Jan. Everything's fine. Thanks." Setting the receiver back in its cradle, she picked up her suitcases and headed for the stairs.

Her room was exactly the way she left it. The full-size bed was covered with a sunflower-patterned comforter and white-and-yellow pillows with eyelet lace trims. Priscilla curtains covered the windows; a long pale green cushion adorned the window seat. A high white shelf held a zoo of stuffed animals, which she had collected since she was a baby, while the bookshelves were filled with children's classics and Precious Moments figurines her mother and father had given her for each birthday and Christmas. A picture of her and Ethan standing on the shore of Lake Michigan sat on top of the white French-provincial dresser. It had been taken the day after he asked her to marry him. Joe had snapped the picture. He must have sent an enlargement to her parents.

Setting her suitcases down, Dynah picked up the ornate brass frame and looked at Ethan. He was smiling, his arm around her shoulders, looking proud and confident and happy. Their entire relationship flashed before her mind like a reel of film speeded up. The man of her dreams. Her knight in shining armor. Remembering the way Ethan had looked the last time she saw him, she closed her eyes. She had seen hurt and anger in his eyes in that unguarded moment. And she had seen something else, something that had torn her heart. Relief.

Oh, Lord, Lord, what have you done to me?

I HAVE TORN THAT I MIGHT HEAL.

Are you really so cruel and arbitrary? Inflicting wounds and then healing? For what? Why?

Opening her eyes, she stared at Ethan's smiling face, his hand firm upon her shoulder as though she was some kind of trophy he had won. He seemed to mock her. As God was mocking her.

"I thought you loved me. What a joke!"

Turning the frame around, she pried back the metal holders and opened it. She removed the picture and tossed the empty frame on the bed. Turning the picture around, she looked at Ethan as she tore the picture in half, then into fourths and eighths as she walked into her bathroom. Opening the commode, she dumped the pieces into the bowl of water and flushed.

She let out her breath slowly, as though she had been holding it for months. It was over, finished. She could put *finis* to that part of her life.

Now, for the rest.

Dynah went back into her bedroom and began unpacking her suitcases.

4

Hannah Carey had had strong premonitions for months that something was wrong with her daughter. She had been praying unceasingly for Dynah since January. It had started when she awakened in the middle of the night. She hadn't been dreaming, or if she had, she couldn't remember what it was about. All she knew was that something had happened, something awful. She had called Dynah the next day, but Janet reassured her all was well and Dynah was fine. The few conversations she had had with her daughter over the past months had convinced her both were untrue.

Now she knew her premonitions were founded in something concrete. Dynah's little blue Toyota with the NLC sticker in the back window was parked in front of the house, and it was a week too early for spring break.

"Dynah?" Hannah said, entering the kitchen from the garage. Dumping her purse on the counter, she headed through the archway into the family room. "Dynah!"

"Mom!"

Glancing up, Hannah saw her daughter running along the corridor and down the stairs. "Oh, baby," she said, filled with joy at the sight of her. Laughing, she held her arms open as Dynah flew into them the way she had as a child. *Thank God! Oh, thank you, God.*

"Oh, Mom," Dynah said, clinging to her mother as she had when she was a little girl and had been hurt. "I had to come home. I had to. I've missed you and Daddy so much."

"We've missed you, too," Hannah said, crying happily, stroking the blonde hair back. She had missed her more than she could, or should, express. The hardest thing she had ever had to do was let Dynah go. That day when she and Douglas had put their daughter on the flight to Chicago had been almost unbearable.

"You gave her to the Lord before she was ever born, Hannah," Douglas had said when she cried all the way home from the airport. "Don't you think you can trust God to take care of her now that she's a young woman?"

"I've been so worried about you, honey." Drawing back, Hannah tried to search her daughter's face. "You're home a week earlier than we'd hoped. And in your car. We were going to wire money so you could fly."

"Can we sit down, Mom?"

There it was again, that feeling she couldn't shake. A sick dread filled Hannah. "Have you eaten? Come on into the kitchen, and I'll fix you something."

"I'm not very hungry."

"Some milk. I made cookies yesterday." Tollhouse. Dynah's favorite. It had been a kind of therapy to fix them. Something to do to kill time while waiting for Dynah to come home. And now she was home, and the worry didn't ease. It grew.

Dynah laughed bleakly. "OK," she said, though Hannah sensed it was more to soothe her mother than because she wanted anything to eat.

Hannah took six cookies from the ceramic bear and arranged them on a pretty china plate. She poured a tall glass of milk and brought both to the kitchenette table in the bay window overlooking the street.

"It's so good to have you home again," she said, going back to the cupboard to take down the tin of flavored coffee. She filled a coffee cup with water and put it in the microwave, tapping in the numbers and pushing start. She glanced back and saw Dynah toying with one of the cookies. "We've been counting the days." She noticed the dark shadows beneath Dynah's blue eyes, the pallor of her skin. Her hair was limp, as though she hadn't shampooed it for days. Her face was thinner, with lines of strain around her mouth.

Oh, God, what's happened to my baby?

"Daddy's in Los Angeles until tomorrow night," Hannah went on, spooning instant coffee into the cup of steaming water. "He goes about once a month now." She brought her coffee over and sat down at the table with her daughter. As Hannah watched Dynah eat one cookie, she noticed something else.

Heart sinking, she put her hands around the cup, trying to keep calm. Her daughter's lower lip quivered slightly, and Hannah found herself fighting tears of empathy.

"You can talk to me, honey. You can talk to me about anything."

"It's so hard."

Life was hard. Grueling. Heartbreaking. She could see how hurt her daughter was, and already she was creating scenarios in her mind. *Jesus, I thought everything was going so smoothly. I thought her life was all laid out like a beautiful mosaic glorifying you.* "It's about Ethan, isn't it?"

"Partly." Dynah sniffed.

Hannah took a hankie from her sweater sleeve. She had gotten in the habit of tucking one into a pocket or sleeve or waistband since Dynah was a baby. Douglas always teased her about it. Old habits were hard to break.

"Thanks," Dynah mumbled, smiling in self-deprecation and blowing her nose softly. "The engagement's off, Mom."

"I gathered that," Hannah said gently. "No ring."

"I gave it back to him."

Thank God it hadn't been the other way around. She had prayed her daughter would never feel that kind of rejection. "You must have had a good reason." Was another girl involved? Or was it his relentless ambition? Douglas had noticed that when they met Ethan. "He's on fire all right, but sometimes that kind of fire can burn churches down."

"No, Mom. I just . . . I just didn't trust him anymore."

Something tightened inside Hannah. "Did he try to do something to you?"

Dynah's eyes came up. "No, Mom."

Hannah knew she was pressing and lowered her head, staring into the black coffee. "I'm sorry. Of course, he wouldn't." Questions poured through her mind, one tumbling on top of another, rousing anger with them. Not at Dynah. Ethan must have done something to her daughter. Dynah had been head over heels in love with him last summer. Why would she break the engagement?

"I don't know how to tell you this."

Hannah reached across the small table and took her daughter's hand, fear curling like a snake in the pit of her belly. "I love you, honey. Nothing you can tell me will alter that. Nothing." Dynah's hand gripped hers, hanging on as if it were a lifeline.

"It happened in January," she began slowly. "I'd just finished work at Stanton Manor House. My car was in the shop, so I was walking to the bus stop. A car, a white car with Massachusetts plates, pulled up beside me. . . ."

Hannah listened, her heart beating faster and faster as Dynah told what had happened. Tears came, flooding her eyes and pouring down her cheeks. *Oh, God, where were you? Where were you when this was happening?* Dynah's fingers kept tightening as though she were afraid her mother would pull away from her. When Dynah finished telling about the ordeal at the hospital and the questioning at the police station, she stopped.

Hannah felt her trembling. "I love you," she said softly. "I love you so much. I'm sorry this happened to you."

Dynah looked up at her mother's stricken face, saw the tears running down her cheeks and the compassion in her eyes. It was easier to go on after that. "Ethan and I started having problems. He didn't see me in the same way, Mom. Not for a while, anyway. Joe helped him a lot. He'd talk to him about his feelings, and he'd talk to me."

"Joe?"

"Joe Guilierno. Ethan's roommate. He's from Los Angeles. A senior. He's the exact opposite of Ethan in everything. Dark hair and eyes, tainted background. He came to the Lord in his late teens. He said someone dragged him to Victory Outreach, and he's never been the same since. If it weren't for Joe, I'd . . ." She shook her head, remembering how close she had come to swallowing all those pills.

Hannah wondered if Joe was the reason Dynah had broken her engagement to Ethan.

"But Joe couldn't fix everything." Dynah let out her breath slowly. "I'm pregnant, Mom."

"Oh, God." Hannah shut her eyes, feeling the hard punch of those words. "Oh, no . . ."

"Ethan was called into the dean's office because he wasn't doing as well in school. He was so stressed out over me and what I was going to do about the pregnancy. He told the dean, and then the dean called me in. I was given choices. I couldn't face any of them, Mom. I just couldn't. I could understand his point. I understood Ethan's, too, but it didn't help me very much. I gave the ring back to Ethan right after talking with the dean, and then I quit school."

"You quit school?" Hannah saw the cost of that in Dynah's eyes. Another dream crushed.

"I had to, Mom. I couldn't stay there."

"Honey, they don't stone people anymore."

"Oh, yes, they do." They just didn't *kill* the one they judged anymore. They left them broken and wounded.

Hannah clasped both of her daughter's hands. "We'll get through this, honey. Your dad and I love you very, very much. We'll help you."

Dynah started to cry, deep wrenching sobs of relief. She heard the scrape of her mother's chair and then felt her mother's arms firm around her. Her mother cried with her, holding her and stroking her and saying over and over that it would be all right. Everything would be all right. She was home now. She was safe. They would take care of her.

The long days of travel caught up with her. The stress that had held her in a vise for so many days dissolved in the warmth of her mother's embrace. She leaned into her, hanging on, grateful to have expunged her burdens, grateful her mother would now shoulder them.

"You're done in," Hannah said after a long while. "Come on, honey. Let's get you into a hot shower. I'll fix you something to eat. After that, you can go to bed and sleep as long as you want."

As those things were being done, Hannah stilled the wild beat of her heart, silenced the screams inside her, capped the volcanic pain that threatened to erupt and pour out like hot lava destroying everything in its path.

When Dynah was safely tucked into bed and asleep, Hannah Carey went into her closet and knelt.

Oh, God! Oh, God in heaven, why do you still hate me so much? Will you never, ever forget what I did?

She wept. For herself. And for her atonement child, who slept in the room down the hall.

■   ■   ■

"She made it, Joe. There was a message on my answering machine. She got there about one-thirty in the afternoon."

Thank you, Jesus! "How'd she sound?"

"Tired."

Smiling, Joe leaned back into the worn overstuffed chair he'd bought at a thrift store and nestled the portable phone between his ear and his shoulder. "Oh, man, I'm feeling good right now."

"Me, too. I've been worried sick about her. How's Ethan?"

"Plugging along. I think it's beginning to sink in what's really happened. He was crying into his beer last night."

"I didn't know he drank."

"Root beer."

Janet laughed. "Do you think he'll call?"

Joe leaned his head back. "I think he will."

"Got a pen and some paper? I'll give you her number, in case Ethan needs it."

Joe got up and headed for his desk. Rummaging around, he found a Bic and some ruled paper. "OK, shoot."

She read off the Careys' telephone number and asked him to repeat it. "You got it. First time. You'd make a great secretary, Joe." She laughed and then added blithely, "Say hi when you talk to her, would you, Joe? Tell her I love her too."

"Brat. I'll call her in a couple days, after she's had a chance to rest and settle in."

"You mean after Ethan's had first shot, don't you?"

"You have an evening class," he said, smiling ruefully. "Get going." He punched the off button and dropped the portable phone onto the desk.

Joe wrote the number onto a sheet of clean paper along with a note: "Dynah made it home safely. Got there about 1:30 P.M.

today." He stuck it to the front of the refrigerator with a magnet.

Breathing a prayer of thanksgiving and relief, he raked his hands back through his disheveled hair. He took a shower, a long hot shower. Tossing the towel in the direction of a plastic laundry basket, Joe went into his bedroom, flopped down onto his twin mattress, and dragged the blankets over him.

Joe Guilierno slept soundly for the first time in a week.

▪ ▪ ▪

Hannah sat in the darkened living room, her daughter asleep upstairs. So far Dynah had slept twelve straight hours; she, on the other hand, had tossed and turned all night.

She had thought she had cried enough to last a lifetime when she was nineteen. Now she realized she'd had no clue what grief was. She hadn't known how deep it could go or how long it could last and that there were ramifications she had never suspected.

Sometimes when she read her Bible, she envied the Israelites. They could wear sackcloth and ashes. They could wail and scream. They could prostrate themselves before the Lord God.

Oh, she had done that, numerous times in the years following that fateful one. She had even lain flat on the floor of the Presbyterian church in which she had been reared, begging for God's forgiveness, begging him for a child to replace the one she had sacrificed. That's how she saw it now: a sacrifice of fear. A sacrifice to protect her honor. Honor nonexistent. A mask she wore for the sake of her parents and friends.

But God knew.

And it seemed God would never forget.

Oh, Lord, why do you have to take it out on Dynah? It was my sin. What I did was of my doing. I know it! Oh, God, don't you think I know it yet? You're not being fair! Dynah's loved you since she was old enough to utter the name Jesus. *She's never walked away from you like I did. Oh, Lord, why does she have to suffer too?*

She flashed back, remembering the trailer parked beside a garbage dump miles out in the desert. She remembered the pain and humiliation, the sick fear and shame. And she remembered what the doctor had said to her when it was all done.

"You were a little further along than you thought. Do you want to see it?"

"No." She just wanted to leave, to get as far away from that trailer and him and what she had done as she could. And even after she had, she couldn't stop wondering.

What had he done with the child he had scraped from her womb? What had happened to it?

All the while, in her heart she knew. And grieved. Silently. Without anyone knowing. How else could a mother mourn her aborted child? She couldn't share her grief with loved ones; they would never have understood. Not the birth. Not the death. She couldn't even allow herself to express it for fear someone might ask the cause of her weeping. And so it became like a dark hole, bottomless, threatening to drag her down.

Most of the time she could manage to forget. Or make herself forget by steel resolve and abject necessity. She had been good at that.

Now the old pain came welling up from the grave of buried dreams. Her relationship with Jerry had disintegrated with her pregnancy. Jerry had been angry and disbelieving. He wasn't ready to get married. He was going to finish college. If he wasn't ready for a wife, he sure wasn't ready for a kid. She could do what she wanted about it. It was her problem anyway, since she hadn't had the courage to go to a doctor and get a prescription for birth control. She should have taken the necessary precautions. He thought she had. How could she be so stupid? "Don't come crying to me now that you've gotten yourself in trouble," he'd said. He was out of it. Out of the situation. Out of her life.

A student loan paid for the abortion. She told the people at the administration office she needed the money for books and tuition. Lies. All lies. One upon another, a mountain of them. She finished school, moved to San Francisco, got a good job, paid off the loan, dated any man who asked her out, partied too hard, and didn't allow anyone too close. Her life had been frenetic, packed full, overflowing. When she came home to her little apartment near the beach, usually after working late, she had the television going or the radio on or music playing on the stereo. When work didn't answer the restlessness in her, she took up watercolor painting. She tried sculpture. She dabbled in the occult. She studied Buddhism and Taoism and New Age universal brotherhood and practiced a little of all of it. She took classes in gourmet cooking and yoga and music appreciation and world history. She attended plays and concerts, lectures and public rallies. She took aerobics and exercise class and jogged along the macadam pathway that ran the length of the beach. Anything to keep her mind occupied. Anything to keep the quiet voice at bay.

And nothing helped for long.

Until she met Douglas Odell Carey.

Douglas said he loved her the first time he laid eyes on her. She was running to catch the bus on Market Street. He left his car in the garage the next afternoon and stood at the same bus stop, hoping to see her again. When she arrived, he followed her onto the bus and sat next to her, striking up a conversation. For five days he rode the bus and tested the waters before he asked her out. Of course, she said yes. Why not? They'd laughed together later when he'd admitted he got off the bus two stops after she did so he could flag a taxi back to the garage where his car was parked.

She liked him from the beginning. She fell in love with him after three dates. He was a good kisser and lit the fire she thought had gone out of her forever. He was good at everything he did. He tackled life the way a football player tackles an opponent: grappling him, wrestling him down. Douglas, the powerful. Douglas, her savior. Douglas, the man from the dark waters, or so his name meant. So apropos. Still waters run deep. She had almost drowned in the beginning. Deep hurts, deep longings, deep feelings, deep convictions.

When she lost their first baby, the rough, vibrant weave of their relationship began to unravel. In a moment of weakness and grieving, she came clean and told Douglas about the other child, Jerry's child. Douglas held her and cried with her, and she thought he understood. He did in his head, but his heart was haunted by her relationship with another man. Her despair reminded him piercingly that she had loved someone else, loved him enough to go that far. What if she'd loved this other man more? What if she still loved him?

He struggled to get past it all. He worked through it intellectually, reasoning and justifying and excusing. But logic didn't dissolve his feelings of hurt and betrayal. It wasn't rational. He admitted to her he knew it wasn't. Not in today's world, where anything goes and there is no black and white or right and wrong. But there it was, like a wound he couldn't stop tearing open. It would begin to heal, and he'd rip away the scab. Someone else had been in her life, and that someone had taken her innocence and destroyed her ability to trust. And poor Douglas was stuck with what was left. Oh, he forgave her. Countless times. Or so he told her. But after a while, she just stopped believing him. Forgiveness meant forgetting, didn't it? But she'd see that look in his eyes, and the monster would come to dwell in their living room again. Even when they pretended it wasn't there, it was there. Silent. Putrid. Corrupting. Destroying.

Paradoxically, Douglas hated Jerry. He even said to her once that he'd like to find him and beat the living daylights out of him for what he had done to her. It didn't seem to occur to Douglas that had things been different, had Jerry been different, she would never have met him on the bus and married him.

But then maybe that was part of it too. Or so she thought in her own confusion and pain and self-recrimination. Maybe Douglas wished things had happened differently so he wouldn't have to suffer with her for something she had done before she ever knew him.

All of it haunted Hannah.

And drove her.

After losing their second child, she and Douglas went to church. It was an act of desperation. "We've tried everything else. We might as well try God," he said that morning when they backed out of the garage. On the way home, Douglas said he knew what had been missing in their marriage. Jesus. That's what they needed to fix themselves. So they began going to church regularly. They joined a Bible study. They joined the choir. Their relationship improved, but the ghosts were still there, occupying the house. Occupying their lives.

Then everything changed for Douglas. After one private meeting with the pastor, he never mentioned Jerry or the lost child again. Even when she brought it up, Douglas refused to discuss it. "All that's over and done with, Hannah. What happened then has nothing to do with you and me. I love you. That's all that matters."

The words were meant to comfort, but they didn't. It wasn't finished for her. Swallowing her shame enough to ask questions, she learned from her doctor that abortions sometimes did cause problems in later pregnancies. And then he said the abortifacients her general practitioner had prescribed, and which she had taken for seven years, might also have compounded the difficulties she was having in conceiving and carrying a child to term. She had never heard the word before that day. *Abortifacient.* He had to explain that the birth-control pills she had been using weren't made to prevent conception but to abort early pregnancies.

And then she knew.

God hated her for what she had done.

There are six things the Lord hates—no, seven things he detests: haughty eyes, a lying tongue, hands that kill the inno-cent, a heart that plots evil, feet that race to do wrong, a false witness who pours out lies, a person who sows discord among brothers.

Hadn't she done all of that? She had been too proud to seek help. She had sought a way out, any way out, and then had lied to get the money for an abortion, sacrificing her unborn child. And since then, she had lied to herself and others. She could remember saying in countless office conversations that she thought women should have the right to have an abortion, even while her heart cried out against it. Oh, she had been politically correct. That was so important these days. She had been astute, glib, tolerant in the world's eyes. Sowing seeds of destruction.

Why had she done it? To hide her shame? to pretend the past couldn't harm her? to avoid condemnation?

And what had she accomplished? She was ashamed, hurting, and condemned anyway. She could make a hundred excuses for herself—and did—but none mattered. None helped heal the secret pain within her because her own blood cried out against her.

You can't run away from God!

Jonah had tried, and look how far he got.

It was there, always there, staring her in the face. Trumpets on the walls of the holy city. She was on the outside looking up at the stones that protected those inside.

God was punishing her.

And why shouldn't he? She had taken from him, and now he would take back from her. How many before the score is even? How many, Lord?

Mea culpa. Mea culpa!

Finally, in desperation, she went before the Lord and gave herself to him to do with as he wanted, promising that whatever issued from her womb would belong to him. If God would grant her a child, she promised to raise up him or her to love Jesus above all else.

And Dynah was born. Blessed Dynah, the joy of her life. She could finally breathe again. She could kneel and drink the living water beside the streams. She could slake her desert thirst. Praise God! She was forgiven.

At least, that was what she'd thought. Until now. Now it seemed God had just been biding his time until he found a more painful way of punishing her.

If this is the way it has to be, Lord, so be it.

Hannah leaned her head back and looked up through eyes blurred with tears at the stained-glass window of a dove flying above a turbulent sea. *Oh, Lord, will I never be at peace? Better I had never tasted the joy of redemption than to have it stripped from me like this.*

She was going to have to walk the sorrow road with Dynah and go through it all over again. All she could see ahead were two women in Ramah weeping for their children because they were no more.

■　■　■

"Smells good," Ethan said, taking the chair near the window and stretching his long legs out beneath the small kitchenette table.

Joe put a plate with eight strips of crispy bacon on the table. Turning back to the stove, he removed the frying pan and scraped scrambled eggs onto two plates. He set one down in front of Ethan. Before sitting down himself, he ran water into the frying pan. "You want some coffee?"

"Yeah. Why not? I could use a jolt of caffeine this morning to get going."

Joe took another mug from the cabinet.

"I'll do the honors," Ethan said when Joe joined him.

Joe bowed his head and listened to his roommate's fulsome eloquence. His words dripped with sincerity, adoration, and gratitude.

"Did you call Dynah yet?"

The muscles tightened on Ethan's face, and his eyes flickered to Joe briefly before he picked up his fork. "I called her."

Joe raised his brows slightly.

Ethan ate two bites of egg before saying more. "OK. I said I was sorry about how things turned out. I wished her well."

"That's it? She went home. So you can write her off?"

His head came up again, blue eyes flashing with anger. "That's a lousy way of putting it!"

"It's true, isn't it?" Joe said, hanging onto his cool with difficulty.

"What was I supposed to do? Chase after her? Beg her to come back? Dean Abernathy's the one who gave her the options, not me! Blame him."

"What options?" Joe shot back.

Ethan's face reddened. "Look! She gave the ring back. I didn't ask for it."

"Didn't you? Seems to me you asked for more than you got."

"And you'd like to give me what I deserve, right? Well, go ahead. Take your best shot!" He scraped his chair back and stood.

Leaning back in his chair, Joe considered it, but one long, hard look at his friend's face erased the anger. Ethan knew only too well what part he'd played in Dynah's flight. Joe didn't say anything more. He'd said more than enough already. Who did he think he was to judge and condemn?

Ethan sat down slowly. "It's over, Joe. Leave well enough alone."

Joe knew that wasn't true. It wasn't over. Never would be. Ethan was going to remember every time he faced a similar situation. And, as a pastor, he was going to face things like this time and again over the years to come.

"You weren't there," Ethan said quietly. "You didn't see the look on her face. You didn't hear her voice."

"She's hurt."

"And you think I'm not? It doesn't do any good to mourn over what might have been."

They ate breakfast in silence. When they finished, Ethan took Joe's plate and stacked it on his own. "I'll wash." He stood and went to the sink, putting in the plug and running hot water.

Joe sat staring at his coffee mug. He read the inscription emblazoned in red: "Seize the Day." Everything clicked. Like a light going on in his head. "I've decided against taking the job in Chicago."

"Get a better offer?"

"No. I think it's time I do what I've been talking about for the past four years. Round out my education." He smiled faintly. *Fool! Fool! What chance do you have?* "I got the OK from Cal a month ago." *Divine providence?* "I've held off making a decision." *Wishful thinking.*

"Cal Berkeley?" Ethan put the dishes in the frying pan and ran water over them. "That'll be culture shock."

"Yeah," Joe said, holding his mug up. "This Galilean is heading for Corinth to do a little fishing."

It didn't hurt that Berkeley was just across the bay from San Francisco.

■ ■ ■

Douglas arrived at SFO at three-forty. He'd learned long ago to carry his luggage on board rather than tempt the fates or baggage handlers. He walked down the long corridor among the throng of passengers deplaning or rushing for their flights. Passing the security station, he took the stairs. Some of the passengers who had hurried off the aircraft ahead of him were crowding around the turnstiles. All their rushing was for naught. He'd be in his car and out of the parking garage before the metal monster started moving and vomiting their luggage.

Slowing his pace, Douglas stepped onto the moving walk-way. He set his rolling suitcase to one side so others in a hurry could walk past it without difficulty. He stood thinking over his past few days in Los Angeles, mentally checking off what he'd been sent to accomplish. He couldn't shake the feeling of unease. He'd made all his contacts, presented the proposal. The amended, signed contract was in his briefcase. There'd be a bonus coming from it. So why this premonition of disaster?

He hadn't slept well last night. Something had been eating at him, rousing the old dreams of mayhem. Why?

His jaw stiffened. Why? He knew why. He just didn't want to go through it again.

He'd called Hannah as he always did when he was away. Every evening like clockwork. He liked hearing the sound of her voice just before turning in for the night. She used to accuse him of checking up on her. In the beginning, when they were mired in problems, that might have been partly true. He'd needed to know she was there waiting for him. He'd wanted to remind her he loved her more than anyone else. More than that other guy who'd used and abandoned her.

But that reason had been set aside long ago. They'd rebuilt the foundations and remodeled the dwelling of their relationship. They trusted one another now.

Or so he thought.

They'd been married twenty-seven years. She ought to be secure by now. So should he.

His heart still did a flip when he looked at her. The curve of her body, her eyes, the way she moved. There were times when he'd get the same jolt he did the first time he saw her running to catch the city bus. Yet, even after twenty-seven years, there were times when he wondered if she loved him, really loved him. Or if she'd just made do.

Maybe that was it. Maybe it was how much he loved her that left him feeling vulnerable, out in the open with the guns raised and taking aim.

Most of the time, he knew she loved him. She did everything right to prove she did. She'd shown him in a hundred different little ways. Then there would be a flicker of doubt raised by something inconsequential. Something indefinable. He'd feel it in something she'd say, or her tone, see it in a look in her eyes, sense it in the distance she put between them, a stretch of no-man's-land he had never quite been able to cross. Life with Hannah was a minefield.

Like last night.

They'd talked, but they hadn't said anything. She was distracted.

And he knew. She was thinking about it again.

It had been so long, he'd forgotten what it felt like to be shut out.

The punch. The shock. The fear-arousing anger. His heart was already pumping with it. He had to push it down, reason it out of existence. Pastor Dan had said to leave it alone. To forget the past. Forgiveness meant never bringing the issue up again. Not even thinking about it. It meant burying what happened so deep it was gone.

Jesus, I've tried. I've really tried.

What's more, he thought he'd done it. Now, here it was again, like cracked macadam, the weeds coming up fast and furious, breaking through to the surface.

Picking up his suitcase, Douglas strode along the walkway, stepped off the end and headed for the elevators. He was in a hurry to get home.

His Buick Riviera was parked on the third level. Pressing the small remote, he shut off the car alarm, opened the trunk, and deposited his suitcase and briefcase. Slamming it, he thumbed the remote to unlock his car door.

What had been going on at home while he was in Los Angeles? Had she been watching some depressing movie that reminded her of the past? Had a friend cried on her shoulder? Had the issue come up in another sermon? Why couldn't people stop talking about abortion? Why did it have to be in the papers every other day? Why couldn't everyone shut up about it?

But he knew well enough any number of things could have roused the old pain in her.

He drove up to the pay booth and handed the attendant the parking stub. His stomach clenched with impatience; his fingers drummed the steering wheel. Three days equals sixty bucks, he wanted to say, but the man still had to punch the numbers into the computer and wait for the screen to flash. When it did, Doug was ready with a hundred-dollar bill. It would've been cheaper to take a taxi to the airport, but he'd been in a hurry. He got forty in change and a receipt for tax purposes. Tossing both onto the passenger seat, he drove beneath the rising steel arm that had blocked his exit and gunned it down the ramp.

Weaving his car into the traffic leaving the airport, he

reached the right lane. As soon as he was on the freeway heading north to San Francisco, he picked up speed, turned on the radio, opened the console, and fed a CD into the player.

Sixties music blasted. *Come on, Baby, Light My Fire....*

Hannah had lost her taste for it years ago, preferring Christian contemporary, classical, and a host of other music styles, including the New Age instrumentals. He liked Elvis, Ricky Nelson, the Doors, the Eagles, and a dozen others from the same era. He knew every song by heart and loved them all. He wasn't sure why. Maybe they reminded him of a more innocent time in his life, a time before reality took hold. Or maybe they reminded him of the things he'd survived. Drinking and partying in high school. Joining the Marines as soon as he turned eighteen. Going to Vietnam. Seeing friends die. Coming back to flag burnings and accusations. It still ate at him. All of it.

He veered away from those thoughts. He'd schooled himself to stay clear of them, clear of the bitterness they roused. Still, like thousands of other men who'd fought to save something they couldn't put words around, he'd felt cheated.

Life hadn't made sense in those days.

It had all made sense when he saw Hannah. Not once in the early hiatus days had he suspected the battle fatigue she suffered. With a frustrated sigh, he pushed the thoughts of the past away. He stared out the car window, seeking a distraction. Nineteenth Avenue traffic was backed up.

He turned the volume down on the radio and let his mind mull over business transactions and possibilities. It was a habit of long practice, a survival technique. When emotions got too high, better to pour them into something where they were useful. Channel the energy into business, and something productive might develop; pour emotions into a relationship, and you got a range fire.

He'd worked out his next week's schedule by the time he got home.

Tapping the remote to open the garage door, he noticed the Toyota parked in front of the house, NLC sticker in the window. Dynah! Joy swept over him. His little princess was home. And then it hit him, a tidal wave of cold misgiving.

Oh, Jesus.

She wasn't due home for another week. Something was wrong.

Hannah was in the kitchen cutting up peeled potatoes and putting them in a pot to boil. She smiled, picking up a towel to dry her hands as she came to him. "Welcome home," she said, kissing him lightly on the cheek. "You look tired."

"I didn't sleep well last night." He put his things down by the back door, then moved to her. Slipping his hand beneath her hair, he tipped her chin. "I don't sleep well when you're not next to me." He kissed her full on the mouth.

She broke off the kiss and smiled at him. "I was just getting dinner started," she said, withdrawing. "You must be hungry."

The kitchen was small enough that she couldn't go far. Douglas slid his hand down her hip. "Starving." She moved slightly, a small hitch of tension that told him to back off. Annoyed and covering it, he leaned his hip against the kitchen counter. "I saw Dynah's car out front. Where is she?"

"Sleeping. She arrived yesterday afternoon, exhausted. She went to bed and hasn't gotten up yet. I thought it best to let her sleep as long as she needs."

His muscles tensed, preparing for a blow. It would no doubt be low and dirty. "What's happened, Hannah?"

"She and Ethan broke up." Hannah took the pot of potatoes and put it beneath the faucet. "That's not the worst of it." She set the pot on the stove and turned it on. "She's . . ." She hesitated, tense. Lifting her head, she looked at him. Her eyes flickered. "She's quit school." She turned away again before Douglas could get a feel for what else was going on. He knew there was more. He could feel it in the pit of his stomach. He watched her gather the potato peelings and put them in the trash bin under the sink.

"Why'd they break up?"

"She didn't want to talk about it. She's pretty upset." She turned on the tap to rinse her hands.

"Obviously," he said dryly. "She'd hardly quit school and drive twenty-five-hundred miles over a minor tiff." He gave a sardonic laugh. "Well, I guess we're going to save ourselves ten thousand dollars on a wedding." He couldn't believe he said it. Sarcasm, cutting deep and drawing blood.

Hannah turned her head and looked up at him, eyes blazing. Slapping off the tap, she snatched up the towel. He'd seen that look before. It wasn't annoyance. It was something deep and violent.

Anger pumped through him in immediate, conditioned response. Not for any particular reason but because of a multitude all tangled together in a mass of confusion, wrath, and frustration. "I'm going to take my things upstairs," he said before she opened her mouth. He retrieved his suitcases. He needed his hands full, or he was going to break something.

"I hope you won't say something like that to Dynah."

Douglas turned, furious. "What do you think? That I want to hurt my daughter worse than she's been hurt?"

No. He just wanted to hurt *her*.

"She broke it off with him, Douglas. Not the other way around."

"Then she must have had a good reason," he said coldly. "Better she gets out of it now than marries him and finds out she's made the biggest mistake of her life." He saw her wince, felt it through his whole body, and knew what he'd done. He hadn't meant it the way she took it, but there it was. Fallout from another war. With another man. He could say he loved her, but it wouldn't help. Not right then. Maybe later, after she'd had time alone in the kitchen to lick old wounds.

Douglas didn't want to stand and watch.

He moved upstairs quickly. Shouldering the upstairs bedroom door open, he slammed his briefcase on top of the dresser. Slinging his suitcase on the bed, he uttered a soft curse. It took him all of five minutes to unpack as he launched two suits into a chair for the cleaners, dumped underwear and socks into the laundry basket, and heaved the shaving case under the sink.

Cursing under his breath, he dragged a hand back through his hair. He'd forgotten what it felt like to have an adrenaline rush. Guns firing. Duck before you get your head blown off. He needed to cool off. Shrugging out of his suit coat, he headed into the bathroom.

■　■　■

Hannah heard the shower go on upstairs. She stood at the sink, staring into the small backyard, her eyes blurred with tears. She had known the minute he walked in the door that he was ready for a fight. She could see it in his eyes. Primed and loaded for battle. All he needed was a target, and she had always been a good one.

His trip must not have gone well. Maybe the meeting hadn't accomplished all he'd hoped. Maybe the plane had been late. Maybe someone had been rude to him at the airport. Maybe traffic was bad on the way home. It could be any number of reasons, small or large.

What was she supposed to do? Wait for a good day to tell him what was going on?

Oh, God, how am I going to tell him the rest? I can't face it, Lord. I can't.

She was shaking, her stomach clenched in a knot. She had to get control, or he was going to know something was wrong. She prayed Dynah would sleep through the night. Douglas would be off to work by six-thirty tomorrow morning, and she and Dynah would have the day to talk about options.

Options?

Abortion. That's what she was going to have to talk about. What other way was there out of this terrible mess? Maybe Douglas didn't have to know at all. Maybe she and Dynah would just handle the problem themselves and save a lot of heartache.

The telephone rang. Taking a deep breath, she exhaled slowly, calming herself. "Hello?" *God, don't let it be someone from the church. I don't want anyone knowing something's wrong.*

"Hannah."

"Oh, Mom," she sighed in relief. Stretching the cord, she sat down at the dinette table. "I'm glad you called."

"What's wrong, honey?"

"Dynah's home. The wedding's off. She's quit school. A lot of things . . ." She rubbed her forehead. "Oh, Mom, we're in such a mess." If anyone in the world would understand, it was her mother. Over the past few years, since her father died, Hannah had learned more than she wanted to know about her mother's capacity for understanding. She was beginning to understand how much a woman could survive. And hide.

"What's Doug have to say about it?"

"Not much. He just got home from L.A. He's upstairs taking a shower. I haven't told you the half of it, Mom." She shut her eyes, clutching the telephone like a lifeline. "Dynah was raped. In January. She's pregnant."

"Oh, Lord of mercy . . ."

"No mercy in it," Hannah said brokenly. "I can't tell Doug.

Oh, God, Mom, I can't tell him. He'll go ballistic." And it'd stir up the past again, bring it boiling to the surface. That terrified her almost more than Dynah's situation. She'd have to live through it all again, like a terrible recurring nightmare. When would it end?

God, why won't you forgive me?

"You can't not tell him, honey. He's going to know."

"Maybe he doesn't have to know." Silence met that statement. "What else can we do, Mom?"

"You can slow down and think it over."

"I am thinking. That's all I'm doing. Thinking and thinking."

"What does Dynah want to do?"

"I don't know. She's been asleep since she arrived yesterday afternoon. She was so tired. She looked sick when she got here. I'm worried about her."

"And no wonder," Evie Daniels said quietly. Though she was a state away, her only connection by telephone, she felt her daughter's anguish as acutely as if it were her own. And wasn't it? How could something so vile, so unthinkable, happen to her precious granddaughter? *God, answer me that. Why Dynah?*

We've got to fix this and fix it fast. "Would you like me to come down, honey?"

"Could you, Mom?" She needed an ally.

Evie hesitated, remembering why she had called Hannah in the first place. The last thing she wanted to do was add another burden to her daughter's already heavy load. "I have an appointment tomorrow morning. As soon as that's finished, I'll be on my way."

Hannah could hear the urgency in her mother's tone. Grants Pass, Oregon, was a long drive away from San Francisco. Eight hours at least. And Mom was not young. *God, don't let anything happen to my mother. Please.* "Don't rush. Stop over somewhere if you need to rest."

"I'm always careful," Evie said, smiling faintly. In the last few years, her daughter's conversations with her had taken on a certain maternal tone. Roles were shifting. Well, she wasn't ready to roll over and play dead yet. "I'll see you in a couple of days, honey. Tell Dynah I love her very much."

"I will, Mom."

Evie heard the anguish in her daughter's choked voice. "I love you, too, honey. Everything will work out."

"I wish I could believe that."

"Believe it. Hang on to it with both hands. And please, wait on any decisions. Promise me."

"We'll wait. I love you, Mom." With a soft sigh of relief, Hannah laid the phone in the cradle. Her mother was coming. Thank God.

■ ■ ■

Evie heard the soft click as her daughter hung up the telephone. She held her own receiver a moment longer before putting it gently back in the cradle. She sat for a long moment in her recliner, the television droning *Entertainment Tonight*. Standing up, she crossed the room and punched the power button. The room fell into silence. Sighing, she walked over to the cathedral windows and looked out over Applegate Valley. The view always gave her a sense of peace. Dusk had arrived, and a single star shone in the heavens. Soon it would be dark. Not like the dark of the city, where the streetlights and headlights and building lights obscured the brilliance. The heavens looked different in the country. More startling. Crisp. Clear. Closer.

In the beginning, those stars had made her feel small and alone when she and Frank had moved here eighteen years ago and built this A-frame house. It had been more Frank's dream than her own. She would have preferred staying in East Bay Area, close to Hannah and Greg and their families. Frank had said it made no sense to try to live where their children and grandchildren lived. Young families—families just starting out—moved. And moved they had. Greg went to Texas fourteen years ago, then to Georgia, and most recently to Illinois. His three children were almost grown, and she hardly knew them. She and Frank would have had to be gypsies to keep up with them.

Only Hannah had sunk roots. In San Francisco.

Sodom and Gomorrah, Frank had called it. He had always preferred having Hannah and Douglas and Dynah come up to the pristine environment of the Applegate Valley rather than making the long drive south. His health had given ready excuse.

Frank, I miss you. I thought the ache would have diminished by now, but it hasn't. Five years and I still cry for you.

She remembered the last week of his life in Medford Hospital. And their last conversation. He'd said he was sorry. He hadn't needed to explain. She'd known immediately what he was talking about. It still hurt to think about it, to realize it had haunted him all those years, just as it had haunted her. She had never realized. Maybe if she had, they could have talked about it together. They might have been able to help one another climb the mountain of grief that had stood between them.

Oh, Lord, the ramifications of our sin. If we could but see beforehand. Or admit it afterward.

COME TO ME, ALL OF YOU WHO ARE WEARY AND CARRY HEAVY BURDENS, AND I WILL GIVE YOU REST.

I've turned to you a thousand times, Lord. Over and over again. And still it's there, an ache deep inside me. What would I do without you, Lord? Still, I don't understand. What I did all those years ago had nothing to do with Hannah. And yet she suffered. And now Dynah will suffer too. Oh, Lord God, it's like a curse that runs down through the family, the sins of the mother visited upon her children. Why did it start, Lord? Oh, Jesus, how do we stop it?

The telephone rang. It was Gladys McGill, her neighbor, checking up on her. Shortly after Frank died, George McGill had been diagnosed with Alzheimer's. She and Gladys had consoled one another. They took turns calling one another. She called Gladys in the morning; Gladys called her in the early evening.

"Did you tell Hannah about the doctor's diagnosis?"

"It slipped my mind."

"Slipped your mind! What do you mean, it slipped your mind?"

"Blame it on hardening of the arteries and senile dementia."

"Evie Daniels, you know you have to make some decisions about chemotherapy."

"I don't have to be in a hurry."

"The longer you wait—"

"Hannah has problems enough without me adding to them."

"Hannah's going to be mad as a wet hen when she finds out, and you know it! Remember how she felt when you and Frank kept his heart condition a secret?"

"I remember. I'm going down tomorrow afternoon. I promise, I'll find a way to work it into a casual conversation." Her words were met with a pause.

"Trouble?" Gladys said quietly.

"In spades."

"I'm sorry."

"Pray for us, would you, Glad?"

"Unceasingly. As I always do. How long will you be gone?"

Evie heard the wistfulness in her dear friend's voice. "A week. Ten days. I'm not sure. I may be bringing Dynah back with me." She didn't say any more than that, and Gladys didn't ask any questions. God bless her. "I'm worried about you, Glad."

"Don't be. I'll be fine."

"I'll call the Brigade to check up on you while I'm gone," she said as lightly as possible. "The Brigade" was made up of Evie, Gladys, and three other women their age who had bonded together over the last years. All but one of their group were widows, hence their self-appointed name: The Widow's Brigade. Evie knew Gladys could be forgetful about taking her heart medication, and she also knew the Brigade would watch her like hawks.

"Fine, but it's probably not necessary. Florence called me yesterday. Talked for almost an hour. You forget how many lonely little old widow ladies are living up here in the woods. I couldn't be left alone if I tried."

Evie laughed.

"Call me when you get to San Francisco," Gladys said in a commanding tone. "And drink lots of tea on the way so you won't fall asleep at the wheel."

"If I drink lots of tea, I'll be making a lot of stops."

"All the better. You should get out and stretch those arthritic old bones of yours."

"Thanks for the advice, you old coot."

Gladys laughed. "I love you. Be careful."

"I love you, too. Lock your doors!"

Evie sighed. *Sometimes I wonder about your timing, Lord.* She decided her own bad news could wait.

5

Dynah roused from a deep sleep and saw her father sitting on the edge of her bed. "Hi, princess," he said, brushing the hair back from her forehead.

"Daddy . . ." She sat up and reached for him, needing to feel the solidness of him, the sense of security she'd always felt in his arms.

Douglas drew his daughter into his arms, holding her firmly against his heart. "I love you, baby," he said, choked with emotion. How long since she'd reached for him like this? He'd like to use Ethan Goodson Turner as a punching bag. Either that or thank him for giving his daughter back to him.

"You aren't disappointed in me, are you, Daddy?"

"Disappointed?" Douglas kissed the top of her head. "How could I be disappointed? There are other colleges and other young men smarter than Ethan Turner."

Dynah shivered slightly. Shutting her eyes tightly, she breathed in the scent of her father. Old Spice, Colgate, and a crisply ironed business shirt and newly dry-cleaned suit. He was on his way to work. "Did Mom talk to you?" she said cautiously.

"Briefly. Last night when I got home."

Dynah drew back slowly and looked at him, her heart thumping. He was smiling, at ease, his eyes filled with compassion.

"It's not the end of the world, Dynah."

She couldn't speak.

"I know it feels that way right now, but things will look differently in a few weeks. Give it time."

In a few weeks, she would be showing her pregnancy.

"Oh, Daddy . . ." She saw her mother standing in the open doorway. She was wearing her long bathrobe. Dynah could see the tension in her body and the swift shake of her head in warning.

"What's the matter, honey?" Douglas said.

Dynah looked at her father and saw something in his eyes that held her silent. "Nothing." She lowered her head. "It just hurts to trust someone and have them let you down."

"I know, honey. Life hurts. We'll talk about it tonight." Dynah looked up at her father as he rose. "Do you have to go?"

"I'll make it a short day." He touched her face lightly, bending down to kiss her cheek again. "You've still got me, princess. What do you say we go to dinner and take in a movie the way we used to? Just the two of us."

Her eyes filled with tears. Dinner and a movie wouldn't fix what was wrong with her, but it might ease the way for him. If her mother couldn't tell him the truth, she was going to have to do it. "I'd like that, Daddy." Maybe for one last evening she could pretend she was a child again, pretend her father could protect her from everything.

As he headed for the door, Dynah snuggled down into her covers, drawing them up until they almost covered her head. She met her mother's eyes briefly and turned away.

Hannah followed Douglas down the stairs. She hadn't slept well the night before. She never did after they argued. Her throat ached as she watched him pick up his suitcase and keys. Pulling her bathrobe more tightly closed, she wrapped her arms around herself, feeling cold. "Douglas . . ."

His knuckles whitened on the handle of the briefcase. "Everything'll be all right," he said as though uttering the words aloud would make it so. "We'll talk things over tonight." He kissed her cheek. "I love you."

"I love you, too." More than he'd ever believe. *Lord, why does it have to be this way?*

"I'll call you later."

She stood in the family room and listened to the garage door open and close. Depressed, she started back upstairs. She wanted to go back to bed and never get up again. As she came abreast of Dynah's door, she glanced in and saw her daughter sitting on the edge of her bed, a multicolored granny-square afghan wrapped around her shoulders. She glanced up, eyes bleak.

"You didn't tell him, did you?"

Hannah paused in the doorway. She shook her head. "No, I didn't. He was tired last night. I thought it'd be better to wait." When Dynah said nothing, she went on, wanting to make amends, wanting her daughter to understand. But how could she when she didn't know everything and Hannah couldn't tell her? "Why don't we both take long, hot showers and get dressed. I'll fix waffles, and we'll talk about it. How does that sound?"

Dynah was silent.

"We'll work things out, honey."

When Hannah came downstairs an hour later, Dynah was there waiting, dressed in gray leggings and a pale blue tunic sweater, her long blonde hair woven into a loose french braid. She'd already made the coffee and was holding a half-empty cup before her.

"Hungry?" Hannah said, smiling and opening cabinets. She needed to be busy, her hands full, doing something, anything.

"Is he going to be mad, Mom? Is that why you didn't tell him?"

"Not at you." She set waffle ingredients on the kitchen counter and reached for one of the nesting bowls. Opening a drawer, she took out a whisk. "It's going to be a shock, that's all." That wasn't the half of it, but what could she say?

Dynah watched her mother work. She wished she would sit down and look at her. She wished she would be still and listen. Even when the waffles were finished and served, her mother had trouble sitting and eating. She had to get up again, pour more coffee, offer orange juice. Dynah supposed she and her mother dealt with catastrophe in different ways. Her mother moved, a bundle of energy, while she sat immobilized.

Finally, when the dishes were rinsed and put in the dishwasher, her mother had no choice but to sit. Folding her hands, she looked at her daughter. Dynah saw the lines of exhaustion around her mother's eyes and felt guilty. Maybe coming home was a bad idea.

"Have you thought very much about what you want to do?"

Dynah lowered her eyes. "Yes. No. I don't know. I'm so confused, Mom."

Hannah took a deep breath, exhaling it slowly before she spoke. "You have options."

Dynah raised her head and stared at her mother. She blinked.

"Dynah, there isn't a soul who'd speak against you if you decided to have an abortion. Under these circumstances, who would dare?" She saw the shock on her daughter's face and added quickly. "I'm not saying you *should* have an abortion. I'm not saying that at all."

"Aren't you?"

"No. I'm not." The words sounded feeble.

"You've always said how wrong it is."

"When it's used for convenience or birth control or a way of getting out of responsibility, yes, it's wrong. None of those reasons apply in this situation, Dynah. You didn't bring this upon yourself. You didn't make a choice."

"God's in control, isn't he? Haven't you and Daddy always said that?"

With a shudder, Hannah looked down into her coffee mug.

"This is where Ethan and I ran into trouble, Mom. He said God couldn't want this for us and I should have an abortion. When I couldn't, everything unraveled."

"Things might have changed, given time."

Dynah shook her head. "I don't think so. I had a lot of time to think on the drive back. Even if I'd gone through with an abortion, it wouldn't have made a difference."

"Why?"

"Because Ethan didn't love me anymore." She raised tear-washed eyes to her mother. "In his eyes, I'm defiled."

"That's not fair!"

"It doesn't have to be fair. It just is."

"It isn't your fault, Dynah."

"I know that, Mom. If I've come to accept anything over the past months, it's that. But circumstances don't bear much weight with human emotions. I don't want you to be angry with Ethan. He couldn't help himself."

Bitter anger filled Hannah as she thought of another time, another man. "How can you make excuses for him? He could've helped you. Instead, he tossed you to the wolves. I can't forgive him for that, and neither should you."

It was the first time Dynah had heard her mother speak this way. Seventy times seven, she had always said before—and now everything was different? Her words rang with rancor.

"It doesn't matter anymore," Dynah said quietly. "Ethan's no longer involved. My decision can't be based on him."

Hannah forced herself to calm down. She had a hundred names for Ethan and what he had done or failed to do, but

Dynah was right. They were on their own. Wasn't that the way it always was? "What do you want to do, honey?"

Dynah smiled bleakly, eyes shadowed. "I want to have someone else decide for me. I want the whole situation taken out of my hands. I want it over." She shook her head. "Sometimes I think it's all a bad dream and I'll wake up and it will be over."

Hannah understood. Hadn't she felt the same way? And even when she'd thought it was finally over, it wasn't. It never would be.

God never forgets. He just lulls you into believing he has, and then the blow comes from where you least expect it.

Dynah.

Oh, God, why Dynah?

"I don't know what to tell you, honey. I don't know what to say except I'm sorry, so sorry this happened to you." *Why didn't you just take me when she was born, Lord? Then the score would be even, wouldn't it? Why didn't you? Is it because you like to make people suffer? Does it please you to torment us?*

"Don't cry, Mom," Dynah said, reaching across the table to take her hand. "Please don't cry."

Hannah grasped her daughter's hands and struggled for control. "I love you, honey. You can't possibly know how much I love you or how precious you are to me." *But you know, don't you, Lord? And that's why you've used my daughter. What better way to punish me?* "I know abortion is a horrible thing, Dynah. I know. And I know how I've spoken against it. Only what other way is there for you to get your life back?"

Dynah removed her hands slowly. "I can't do it, Mom."

"Even if I go with you? I'll stand by you. I promise. I'll be right there in the room with you every minute." *Even if it kills me.*

"I can't."

"Why?"

"Because God hasn't released me."

Hannah felt the punch against her heart and put her hand there, pressing. "What do you mean?"

"I've laid it all before him, and he hasn't given me an answer. I keep praying, but he won't talk to me. So I have to wait. I have to wait on him."

"Every day you wait will make it more difficult."

"I know, but I can't help it, Mom."

Hannah stared at her daughter helplessly. *Oh, God, what are you doing to us? What are you doing?*

■ ■ ■

Douglas called later in the day. He had barely two words for Hannah before informing her he had made reservations at Allioto's Restaurant. For him and Dynah. Though she felt rejected, Hannah said she thought it was a nice idea. Dynah had always loved going there from the time she was a child. She'd always delighted in watching the small fishing boats come in and out of the dock. Douglas said they would walk pier 39 and shop and then take in a movie, something PG and lighthearted to lift his daughter's flagging spirits.

He didn't need to say the rest. She understood. Her feelings didn't matter. She could sit home by herself and be miserable. She didn't have to drag him down into that pit with her. Not again. He didn't ask what was bothering her. He didn't want to know. Or maybe he thought he did. He always thought he could read her mind, but he didn't know the half of it.

Hannah made Dynah promise not to say anything to her father about the pregnancy. "Make this a special evening. Put this whole thing out of your mind for a few days. Let me talk to him about it first."

Confidence chipped away, Dynah gave in, afraid. Her

mother wouldn't argue so strongly if she wasn't convinced something horrible was going to happen when she told her father the truth. So Dynah remained silent. She would pretend to have a wonderful time. She would make small talk and act as though a nice Crab Louie and a Harrison Ford movie were all she needed to cheer her up and make her forget.

■　■　■

"Just like old times, isn't it, princess?"

Douglas watched his daughter's wan face closely as she smiled at him and nodded. He wanted to believe her, wanted to be convinced, but he knew his daughter almost as well as he knew himself. She was flesh of his flesh, blood of his blood. And something was wrong, terribly wrong. He could feel it. Something was bothering her. No, *bothering* wasn't strong enough. She was plagued. He saw it in her eyes, felt it in his gut, and no amount of avoidance on her part, or his, made it any better. It was there, like a growing cancer eating away at their relationship, making them strangers to one another.

Hannah knew what was wrong, he was sure of it. She'd probably known two minutes after being with Dynah. She'd known the night he called from Los Angeles. She'd known last night. And this morning. And she was keeping it secret.

Why couldn't she tell him? Did she think anything could destroy his love for Dynah? But there it was again. Hannah's distrust. And now its seed was planted and growing in his daughter.

Douglas held in his anger until Dynah was in bed. Asleep, he thought.

"When are you going to tell me what's going on around here?" he said, proud of the calm he managed as he spoke quietly through his teeth.

Hannah's gaze rested on his face, and he could swear she looked nearly panicked. "Promise me you'll stay calm."

"I am calm." On the surface. Like a thin layer of blackened stone covering molten lava.

Hannah sat down on the far end of the couch, her hands clasped nervously. He wondered how long it would take her to get it out. It didn't take long at all.

"Dynah's pregnant."

A fissure opened. "Ethan?"

"No. Not Ethan." She let out her breath slowly and looked at him, shattered. "She was raped."

"*Raped?*" He couldn't take it in. He thought of Dynah, pretty, blue-eyed Dynah, his little angel. Who would want to hurt a girl like her? "When?"

"January."

"How did it happen?"

She told him every detail Dynah had related to her. The car in the garage undergoing repairs. The cold night. The bus ride and walk up Henderson Avenue. The man in the white car with Massachusetts license plates. The park.

"Jesus," Douglas said brokenly. "Jesus. God!" Leaning forward, he covered his face.

"She doesn't want an abortion, Douglas."

His head came up. "Well, she's going to have to have one whether she likes it or not."

Hannah stared at him, and he saw the disbelief in her eyes. "What are you saying? She has no choice?"

"You tell me what choice she has!" he said, angry, wanting to lash out. If the man who'd done this to his daughter were to suddenly appear in the room, he'd kill him. With pleasure. Slowly. As painfully as possible. Ways flashed in his head, a dozen of them, each more horrific and satisfying than the next.

"It'll be difficult," Hannah said slowly, as though trying to sort through all the ramifications at once.

"Not as difficult as if she doesn't do it. Think about it," he said.

"It's all I've been thinking about!"

"Who's going to want a girl who had a baby by some . . . some unknown assailant?"

"It's not her fault!"

"I didn't say it was!" Getting up, he paced, too agitated to sit. He wanted to break something, smash it beyond recognition.

"But she has to suffer for it?"

"Should I?"

"What's this got to do with you?"

"Who do you think will have to take responsibility if she does decide to have it? Me! How's she going to finish school or get a job with a baby? You're going to be baby-sitting. You like that idea? You want to give up all your community work? I'm going to be paying the bills. Well, no thanks. I'm retiring in a few years. I'm not going to spend the rest of my life taking responsibility for a child forced on my daughter by rape. And neither is she!" He glared at her. "It might be different if it had been someone she loved."

The barb struck deep. "You're angry at me, aren't you?" Hannah said, and he saw her tremble. "It always comes back to that."

"Because you make it that way."

"She doesn't want an abortion!"

"So what's she going to do?"

"She doesn't know what she wants to do, Doug."

"Then help her figure it out! You know more about handling these situations than I do."

She flinched as though from a blow.

Douglas ignored her reaction, riding on his wrath. "Do you think she really wants this child? You're out of your mind if you do. You just told me she never even saw the man's face. What if he was black? What if he had AIDS? What sort of human being is it going to be? Who in their right mind would want it?"

"Lower your voice. She's upstairs."

He came closer, leaning down, jaw jutting. "If she refuses to have an abortion, people might even start wondering if it *was* rape. Have you thought of that? They might start thinking she and Ethan Turner went a little further than they intended."

He saw the jab hit home, watched it sink deep, twisting. Old wounds were ripped open, and she was bleeding again. "No, they won't. Not about Dynah."

"Yeah, right. Haven't you listened to the hens in our own church? They'd think it. They'd delight in thinking it. Especially about Dynah. She can kiss her reputation good-bye."

Hannah watched him pace. "Are you worried about Dynah's reputation or your own?"

He stopped and turned his head, glaring at her. "What're you talking about?"

Her eyes were cold. "Try this on for size. People would look at you as the father of an unwed mother."

He clenched his fist. "Is that what you think worries me? Don't you dare compare me to your father. I'm nothing like him. You didn't even trust him enough to tell him, not up to the day he died."

"From where I sit you look the same. I should never have told you. All I did was give you a weapon! Why do you think I'm the one telling you instead of Dynah?"

"Because you got in the way!"

"Yes! I did! Because I knew what would happen! Because I can take it better than she can! I've had practice! Plenty of it!" He saw the tears come to her eyes—accompanied by rage. "I know what you think. I know how you feel. Don't you think I know? I've lived with it for twenty-seven years!"

Douglas glared at her, cold with wrath. "Oh, no, you don't, Hannah. You're not dumping that horse manure on my doorstep again. You were living with it long before I ever came on the scene. You want to blame somebody? Fine. But don't blame me."

She let out her breath slowly. "This isn't doing any good," she said quietly, but it was clear how shaken she was. It always shook her to get this close to it. She wanted to retreat—he was sure of it—but she couldn't. Because this time she was fighting for Dynah. Her daughter.

His teeth clenched. *Their* daughter.

"We have to help Dynah," she said brokenly. "I don't want to watch it happen all over again. I can't—" Hunching over, she covered her face.

Douglas stared down at his wife and felt bereft. Why did he always come out feeling in the wrong, as though he were to blame? He'd had nothing to do with what had happened to her or what she'd done. Still, it made no difference. He remembered Hannah's asking him once if he would have taken her out a second time if she'd had an illegitimate child in tow. He had said, "Probably." It hadn't been the answer she needed, and amendments had never been enough to alter the damage done. She couldn't forget. Or she chose not to.

"I can't deal with it, Hannah. I'm not going to—"

"Daddy . . ."

Douglas turned, his face going hot when he saw his daughter standing in the archway, a quilt wrapped around her. Her eyes were puffed and red from weeping. She looked at him beseechingly and then at her mother sitting hunched over on the couch.

"I'll go," she said in a choked voice. "I promise I'll talk to someone at one of those clinics. I—" She shook her head, her eyes spilling over with tears, her mouth trembling. She clutched the quilt more tightly. "Only please, don't yell at Mom anymore. It's not her fault. It's not yours, either. I never meant to be a burden. . . ." Turning, she fled up the stairs.

Feeling sick with shame, Douglas stood silent in his family room.

Hannah stood up and walked slowly across the room without looking at him. He wanted to say he was sorry, but for what? For hating the man who had raped his daughter? For not wanting to see this pregnancy ruin her life? Granted, his emotions had gotten out of hand, and the past had reared its ugly head again, but was that entirely his fault? Maybe if Hannah had led into the news about Dynah instead of hitting him square in the heart. . . . He felt set up for the fall. A convenient scapegoat for all her problems.

Douglas put his hand on her arm before she could pass. "Tell her I love her."

"Take your hand off me."

The coldness of her words struck him full in the gut. He gripped her harder, wanting to hold on to her, wishing just once she'd understand how he felt about all of it. "I love her as much as you do."

Raising her head, Hannah glared at him. Jerking free, she walked away from him and went up the stairs.

■ ■ ■

Douglas didn't leave early for work the next morning. Even after a long, hot shower, he felt like he was suffering from a hangover. Dressed for work, he sat at the breakfast-nook table overlooking the small backyard flower garden, while Hannah, with the air of a martyr, stood at the stove scrambling his eggs. He hadn't expected her to come downstairs and fix breakfast for him. He almost wished she hadn't. He would have felt better if she'd stayed in bed with the covers pulled up over her head, the way they'd been when he went into the shower. Instead, he had to look at her rigid back and feel the glacial air in the room.

"What time did you finally come to bed?" he said, sipping his coffee, the *Wall Street Journal* still sitting unopened beside his place mat. He had no stomach for news this morning.

"Two." She scraped the eggs onto a plate, put the frying pan into the sink, and delivered his meal to him without so much as a glance. His toast popped up. Returning to the counter, she buttered both slices, put them on a small plate, and delivered them along with a metal carrier containing three small porcelain pots of strawberry, grape, and plum jam. He could have his choice.

Douglas bowed his head, as was his habit, and said a silent prayer. Rote words: *Thank you for the food, Lord, and the hands that have prepared it.* When he finished, he looked at her bleakly. *God, help us! Help us! What good does going to church do if it all comes back to this?*

Hannah recognized the bruised expression. Regret. Weariness. She was sorry, too, but what good had it ever done?

He looked at the bare space before his wife. "You going to eat?"

"No." She always felt sick to her stomach after a fight. It took a few days to climb out of the pit of depression; the lingering aftereffects were like a conditioned response. She always wondered what she'd done to start it, what she'd said to bring on the deluge, what she could do to mend her armor now that the demons were loose again.

Douglas let out his breath softly. So, she was going to play it that way. Fine. Annoyed, he ate in silence, refusing to feel guilty.

Hannah sat quiet, swallowing resentment with her coffee, stomach churning. She knew what was ahead. Things would get worse before they got better. Assuming, of course, that they would get better.

It was Douglas who broke first. His temper was quick to life and death, unlike her endless grudges.

"How's Dynah?"

"She'll be fine." The words came out stiffly. *Don't worry about it. We'll solve the problem, Douglas. You don't have to dirty your hands.* Unable to sit still, she got up, gathered his dishes and went to the sink, anger choking her. It came up from deep down inside her, hot and black, deadly.

"Is she OK with what she has to do? After you talked with her, I mean?"

"She's not OK with it, but she'll talk to the doctor. And I didn't tell her about what happened to me, if that's what you meant."

"Why not? Don't you think it's time?"

A chill swept over her. "I didn't see the point." And she'd been afraid, afraid of what her daughter would think of her, afraid of losing her respect, losing her love.

"It might help her to know you've been through it."

Misery loves company, was that it? "I can't."

"You didn't have any more choice about it than she does."

She gripped the edge of the sink. "Why do you always see it that way the day after an argument?"

"I wasn't the one throwing blame last night. You hurt me, too."

They'd become good at that over the years, hurting each other in ways that were subtle and swift. Coming to Christ had brought an idyll. For a time. Now, it had begun again. Somehow, it was more devastating the second time around. She was less prepared.

She stared down into the sink at the dirty dishes and frying pan. "I don't want her to know. Can you understand that,

Douglas? Or at least try. I don't want anyone to know. I wish to God I'd never told you."

Douglas rose and came to her, drawing her back against him, locking his arms around her even when she tensed and resisted. "We'll get through it. We're a family, Hannah. It won't be like it was for you. We'll help her get through it."

Hannah closed her eyes, unable to express the anguish inside her, unable even to define it. *Get through it,* Douglas said. As if it were possible. And had they? In twenty-seven years of marriage, were they over it yet?

"We have to help her do what's best for her," Douglas said.

What's best . . .

The words whirred in her head like locusts eating away at her conscience. How many times had she rationalized and justified her own abortion? What else could she have done? Had the child? Put it up for adoption? Kept it? And what ramifications would there have been for her life and those she loved? How would her parents have dealt with it? Would her father have loved her? Not likely.

So she'd done it and adjusted. Or so she had thought.

Oh, God, how many times had she thought it was over and then something would happen to bring it to the surface again?

"We have to help her make the right decision, Hannah."

"I don't know if she's ready." *God, I don't know if I am. My daughter, oh, Lord, my daughter.*

Douglas knew her inner turmoil. Hadn't he lived with it all these years whether she was willing to acknowledge it or not? "I don't want to hurt you more, honey. You know I don't."

She braced herself inwardly. "Say what you're thinking, Douglas."

He sighed heavily, his arms loosening around her. "It's not the same situation as what you went through, Hannah. This isn't a matter of Dynah's loving the wrong guy and being abandoned. Our daughter had no say in what happened to her."

"I know that."

"She needn't feel guilty about taking care of the problem."

Did he know his daughter at all? Had he considered how they'd reared her? Even under these circumstances, could Dynah turn and walk away from those principles and not suffer for it? Was she strong enough?

"I don't know if she can do it, Douglas."

"She can if you're with her every step of the way."

The burden seemed more than she could bear. "And you?" Hannah turned and looked up at him. "Where will you be?"

"Right here," he said, touching her face tenderly. *God, give me the strength to get through this. Help me instill the strength in her that she needs so she can help Dynah.*

But even as he said the prayer, he wondered why he felt sick inside and filled with so much sorrow.

6

James Wyatt sat on the sunny patio of his Mill Valley house, trying to fight off his deepening depression. He was never quite sure what had brought on the downward cycle, the sense of despair he couldn't seem to shake. He fought it with reason and activity and positive thinking, and yet hadn't been able to obliterate it or cure it. It sapped his energy.

"Would you like coffee, Dr. Wyatt?" Juanita Hernandez asked in heavily accented English as she held the pot ready.

"Thank you, Juanita," he said, giving her a nod. "Just leave the pot. Are the children up yet?" He knew his wife was out for a run.

"*Si, Señor doctor.*" She stopped, looking mildly dismayed. "Excuse me," she said slowly, concentrating. "I mean to say, yes, Dr. Wyatt. Your children are awake."

James smiled at her. "You're doing very well with your English, Juanita."

She nodded politely, smiling back shyly. "Missus Wyatt is a good teacher."

The side gate clicked, setting off a beep from the alarm system. When it was immediately shut off, Jim knew it was his wife, Cynthia, returning from her morning jog. She appeared, their Rottweiler beside her. She unsnapped the dog's leash from the collar, and the animal dashed excitedly toward Jim. "Easy, Arnold," he said, laughing, half annoyed and half pleased that the animal was so happy to see him. Scratching the dog's head and patting his back, he watched Cynthia walk toward him. She was wearing a sleeveless white T-shirt and pale blue jogging shorts. She was still the most beautiful woman he had ever seen. Smiling at him, she pulled off her headband and shook out her damp auburn hair. "Good morning!"

Admiring her tanned legs and trim figure, James smiled back, lifting his cup of coffee in salutation. "Did you have a good run?"

"Wonderful!" She sank into the chair opposite and let her breath out. "Some orange juice, please, Juanita, and a towel. I'm drenched."

"Yes, madam."

James noted the beads of healthy sweat on Cynthia's face and collarbones. Her hazel eyes caught his and probed gently. "I wish you would have come with me this morning."

"Maybe tomorrow. I didn't feel much like running this morning." He picked up his newspaper. "Juanita's doing very well with her English."

"She's quite bright," Cynthia said, clearly not fooled by his swift change of subject. "I'm glad you agreed to hire her. She's made things so much easier on me, and the children adore her. She's teaching them Spanish."

"That's nice."

He hid behind the newspaper, hoping she wouldn't notice he was mired in his dark thoughts. Still, how could she help but notice? She loved him. She was sensitive to his mood swings, and he had realized some time ago that she recognized the pattern.

"Are you working at the clinic today?"

"It's Tuesday," he said briskly, folding the paper inside out.

Nothing new in the international section. Federal budget battles. Unrest in splintered Russia. Middle East conflicts. The usual grit that ground ideals down into paths of compromise and complacency. Or that roused violence.

Don't do it, Cynth, he thought. *Don't bring it up again. Don't try to talk me out of this.* He loved his wife, adored her, but what good came of such debates between them? The last time she'd suggested Jim stop working at the clinic, they'd ended up in a distressing quarrel. He'd reminded her that the money he'd made over the past four years working at the clinic had paid off the student loans he had needed to get through medical school. With that money paid back, they had been able to save enough from the practice to make the down payment on this beautiful house in Mill Valley. She'd told him money wasn't the issue and the house wasn't the most important thing, but he'd asked her if she'd rather rear their children in the city.

Subterfuge. All of it. For all of their vehemence, they'd never addressed the real issue. And that was what he didn't want to discuss.

He'd told her, of course. She understood the real reason that drove him to do what he did. And rightfully so. He'd explained five years ago when he'd first talked with her about working at the clinic. She'd admired his decision and promised to support him in whatever he did. Hadn't she always?

Oddly enough, something had changed after that. He wasn't sure what it was, but there had been a subtle shift inside him, a giving way that affected their relationship.

Not that they weren't happy. She'd told him often enough that she couldn't be happier. He did his best to be loving, tender, thoughtful, hardworking, devoted to his family, devoted to his practice. He was a man of deep feelings and principles, determined to give the best care he could to all his patients.

Yet sometimes he saw a look in her eyes, a troubled expression . . . as though she wondered if he were happy with her. He knew why the doubts came, realized there were weeks when he wouldn't make love to her. But there were other times, too, when he would have a ravenous need, almost as though the act of love itself might drive away whatever tormented him.

"Why don't we go away this weekend?"

He sighed. She probably thought a change of scene might curb the tide of his depression and take his mind off his worries. Well, why not? Alan Keller could stand in at the practice. Jim had covered for him last weekend.

"Good idea. Where do you suggest?"

"How about Carmel? It's been two months since we were there. Or we could go back up to Calistoga. That bed-and-breakfast was nice."

He turned another page and reached the regional news. "Fine."

"Or we could stay here, have your mother pick up the children and keep them for a night, rent a couple of romantic movies, turn up the heat in the spa, stock some champagne."

"Whatever," he said, his eyes focused on a small article at the bottom of the page. A young woman had been found dead in her San Francisco apartment. A preliminary investigation had dismissed foul play and considered the possibility of suicide. Although no note was found, friends had reported that she had been despondent over the past few days. The coroner would make a determination.

James didn't recognize the young woman's name, but he knew the face. He had performed an abortion on her six days ago.

A chill swept over him.

Stop it! he chided himself. *It has nothing to do with you.* Odds were good that it didn't. She'd probably had a host of problems that seemed overwhelming. He'd solved one for her, but he couldn't solve everything. How could he in the few minutes he had with her? Fifteen. That's all it took to do the procedure. And she hadn't said much of anything, had she? He tried to remember.

"It hurts. Oh, God, it hurts. They said it wouldn't."

Had that been her or some other girl? No matter how gentle he tried to be, it remained a common complaint. He soothed his patients as best he could by telling them it would soon be over. Sometimes he wondered if it was the sound of the machine that tensed up their bodies and worsened the pain.

Sometimes he could hear that horrible sucking sound in his dreams.

Grotesque.

Unforgettable.

And necessary if he was to get the job done.

"Jim?"

Blinking, he glanced up sharply and found his wife staring at him with a frown of concern.

"What's wrong?"

"Nothing," he said quickly. "Just the same lousy news every day." He folded the newspaper so the story was hidden inside and tossed it onto the cement. He didn't want it on the table. He didn't want it anywhere near him. Forcing a smile, he picked up his coffee cup and took a sip. "Now, what were you saying?"

Juanita delivered breakfast—poached eggs, more freshly squeezed orange juice, and newly baked bran muffins, all served elegantly on Lenox china. He wasn't hungry, but he forced himself to eat. He needed the calories to get through the day, and he didn't want to worry Cynthia.

He might have been able to keep the facade in place had his two children not come racing happily into the backyard, eager for kisses and hugs from Mommy and Daddy. He was eager to dispense both, shocked at the degree of pain that shot through him as he watched them scamper off with Arnold.

Cynthia laughed at their antics. Patricia, aptly nicknamed Cricket, hopped excitedly around with the dog while her brother, Todd, ran for the tennis ball. As soon as he had it in his hand, he heaved it across the lawn, sending the dog into a frenzied chase. "Arnold, fetch!" He hadn't needed to utter the command.

Love swelled inside James as he watched his children. With love came affliction. His heart ached, fairly throbbed, with some unreasoning anguish. He listened to the laughter and watched his children play, bright spots of joy in his own backyard . . . and felt a smothering grief he couldn't dispel and didn't understand. He was oppressed with it.

"What's wrong, Jim?" Cynthia said, and he glanced at her, surprised to discover there were tears in his eyes.

"Nothing," he said again, because he couldn't put words to it. Sometimes beauty did that to him. He remembered feeling this way when Cynthia said she'd marry him. Overwhelmed with gratitude, amazed by his good luck.

Pushing his chair back, he stood. "I'd better get on the road. I'm going to be late as it is." The Golden Gate Bridge would be backed up with traffic.

Walking with him, Cynthia looped her arm through his and smiled up at him playfully. "You could always wait another hour and avoid the traffic. I need to take my shower. Want to wash my back?"

He laughed, giving no response. Dropping his arm, he put his hand lightly at her waist so she would enter the house ahead of him.

She crossed the family room with its cathedral ceiling and wall bookshelves and fireplace. Picking up his sports jacket, she held it so he could shrug into it. Coming around in front of him, she straightened the lapels and ran her hands down over his jacket. She looked up at him tenderly. "You're very handsome, Dr. Wyatt."

He made a noncommittal sound.

Reaching up, Cynthia touched his cheek, drawing his attention. "I love you, Jim. You know that, don't you?"

Jim searched her eyes briefly and then leaned down, kissing her firmly on the mouth. "I know." Straightening, he smiled ruefully. "God only knows why."

"Because you care so much," she said.

He prayed it was the truth, that anyone who knew him for ten minutes would realize he wasn't what those pro-lifers said in the anonymous letters they found in the mail all too frequently. One had come yesterday. Some Christian zealot quoting Scripture, on fire for God, ready and eager to burn someone. The letter was now ashes in the fireplace. He hadn't told Cynthia about it and didn't intend to. She would only worry. Twice before, he had received death threats. This letter had been mild by comparison, just the usual vitriolic words and rhetorical questions meant to shame and intimidate.

Still, it amazed him. It always did—almost as much as it amazed him to see Cynthia's anger. How could people who claimed to live a life in the name of love and Jesus be so heartless in their condemnation and judgment, she'd asked? "Have they ever once thought to walk in your shoes? They don't even try to understand what makes a man like you do what you feel you have to do. Besides, if abortion isn't right, why is it legal? Why is the government paying for it?"

He'd had no answers for her. Then or now.

He watched her turn to pick up his black leather medical bag. It was heavy, yet less than his burdened heart. Unfairly so. He cared so much. He knew what happened when someone wasn't there to help. Thank God Cynthia understood that.

From the beginning, she had supported him in his work, just as she had supported him financially those last few years of medical training. They'd been lean and hard, years of sacrifice. She told him that's when she'd seen how much he cared, through the long hours he studied and worked, the patients he tended, the grief he felt when he lost someone, no matter how hopeless the case. She knew his anguish and convictions. She knew his dreams. She knew his heart. And she loved him for all of it.

That was what kept him going. His wife. His family. Their love . . .

She held the bag out to him and wished him well in the day ahead.

Jim took it. "I've a couple patients to see at the hospital. Then I'll be at the office for a couple of hours. I don't expect to be at the clinic until one."

She knew he was telling her he would be late coming home. "Should I hold dinner?"

"No." He wouldn't be hungry. Leaning down, he kissed her lightly. "I don't know what I'd do without you, Cyn."

"Work yourself to death," she said with a loving smile. She drew his head down again, kissing him firmly. "I'll be waiting for you."

■   ■   ■

Elizabeth Chambers pressed the intercom. "How many?"

"Twelve."

If the wait was too long, one or two clients would probably ask for their money back and leave. "Any sign of Dr. Wyatt?"

"Not yet."

Elizabeth clenched her teeth to keep from venting her anger. Dr. Franklin had already left for the day, or she would have pressed for him to stay an hour longer. Dr. Wyatt's tardiness was becoming habitual. Maybe she should increase his cut. She had little doubt that would bring him running to the clinic in a timely manner. Unfortunately, right now, she had to deal with the problem.

"Call his practice. See if there's been some emergency."

"Jim always calls if—"

"I said call him."

"Yes, Ms. Chambers."

"And tell Brenda I want to talk to her." Lifting her finger from the intercom, she cut off any excuse that might be forthcoming. Picking up her pencil, Elizabeth tapped it repeatedly for a moment and then tossed it onto the desk in annoyance. *Now* means now, not five minutes from now. Flipping the ledger closed, she opened her desk drawer, dropped the ledger in, and slammed the drawer shut.

What a day! Sometimes she wondered why she kept on with this miserable, stinking job. If the money weren't so good, she would have been gone long ago. She was sick to death of dealing with other people's problems, problems they made for themselves and she had to help clean up. Most of the money went to the corporation that owned the facility, though their names were nowhere to be seen. They wanted to stay squeaky clean in some elegant high-rise.

Her head was aching already, and it was only a little after one. It would be pounding by three. She wished she could have a martini. Or a shot of tequila. That would be nice. Anything to deaden the throbbing in her temples.

She couldn't depend on anyone. She had to oversee everything herself because she couldn't trust people to do what they said they would do. Dr. James Wyatt for one. He'd say he'd be at the clinic at one, then stroll in at one-thirty. Or others did more than they were told, like Brenda, who answered questions with facts that scared clients right out the front door. Two this morning. Six hundred dollars gone. Stupid girl!

Hearing the tentative tap on the door, Elizabeth controlled her temper. "Come in," she called, smiling coolly as Brenda entered. She gestured for Brenda to sit in the chair near the desk. Elizabeth looked her over, admiring her neat appearance. Brenda was an attractive young black woman, a nursing student from the University of California San Francisco who had come to inquire about working at the clinic four months ago. She had said she wanted to help women. Elizabeth had recognized her sincerity and knew it would be useful. She had also recognized her need: money to finish her education.

Sitting forward in her leather chair, Elizabeth rested one hand lightly over her other on the burgundy ink-blotter. "Phyllis said two of our clients left this morning after speaking with you."

Elizabeth raised her brows when Brenda sat silent. "Is it true?"

"Yes, they did," Brenda said, trying not to sound defensive. Phyllis had been furious when the second girl left, and demanded to know what she was doing to "drive them away." Brenda had told her she wasn't doing anything to drive anyone away, but Phyllis had been less than convinced. She hoped for a fair hearing with Elizabeth, who had always been cordial and firmly on the side of women's rights. Surely she would understand. "They asked me specific questions."

"About the procedure."

"Yes."

"And you answered."

"Yes."

"In detail."

"As few as possible, but they—"

Elizabeth held up her hands to stay the stream of self-defense. "You've been through our training," she said coolly, holding her anger under tight rein. Exploding at the girl would do no good, and it might leave her thinking that Elizabeth didn't care about these women too. Of course she cared! "You know what's appropriate and what's not, Brenda. The women who come here for our help are in a very delicate emotional state. They don't need facts. They need careful and gentle guidance. They want us to help them make the right decision."

"I understand all that," Brenda said, clearly distressed, "but the patient who came in this morning was in tears. She wasn't sure what she wanted when she came into the examination room."

"And so you decided for her," Elizabeth said quietly, furious.

"Of course not. I just answered her questions."

"What sort of questions?"

"About fetal development. She said she was almost four months along. She asked if the baby had a heartbeat and brain waves. A friend had told her it did, but she didn't know for sure. So she asked me, and I told her the truth."

"And made her feel ashamed," Elizabeth said angrily.

"That wasn't my intention."

"Perhaps not, but it was the direct result of your interference. So what have you caused? Did you help her? Was her boyfriend out there in the waiting room supporting her? Is he going to marry her? Is he even still in the picture? Is her family going to support her? How old was she? Fourteen? Fifteen? What happens to her now that you've told her the truth?"

"She left before we could talk about any of that," Brenda said miserably.

"Yes, she left. Scared to death because of you. Brenda, dear, there's a reason we train you as we do. I thought you understood."

"I do understand, but a woman has a right to an informed decision."

"She wasn't a woman! She was a child! A child in trouble and needing a way out, and we offered those services to her! Now what's she going to do?" It would do no good whatsoever to tell Brenda that even the Supreme Court agreed that a woman didn't need to know very much and, in fact, agreed that the less they knew the better.

Seeing Brenda's shock at the outburst, Elizabeth sat back, forcing her anger under control. She let out her breath slowly, trying to calm down. "If that girl had wanted the sort of information you gave her, don't you think she would have gone to a Pregnancy Counseling Center rather than come to us?"

"I don't know. She was very confused. She didn't know what to do. . . ."

"All the more reason for you to counsel her appropriately."

Her telephone rang. Annoyed, Elizabeth picked up the receiver. "Not now, Phyllis. I'm in conference."

"It's Mr. Ord again."

The heat of anger burst like a rush of adrenaline. Mr. Ord was her daughter's principal. Kip was probably in trouble. Again. How many times did she have to go through this before her daughter grew up? "Ask him to hold for just a moment." She slammed the receiver down and looked at Brenda. "I have to be blunt this time, Brenda. We've covered this ground before, and I don't like going over and over things so important. So here it is. You either do things the way we trained you to do them, or you leave. Is that understood?"

"Yes, ma'am."

Elizabeth recognized the sparkle in Brenda's eyes, the zeal to help women in trouble. "I know it's difficult," she said, taking a more soothing track. She didn't want to have to look for another nurse. They were getting harder and harder to find. "Brenda, I know how much you care, and that's the quality that made me hire you in the first place. But you have to stifle your own personal feelings and think of what's best for these young girls. Put yourself in their position. How are they ever going to manage raising a child at this time in their lives? Pregnancy is a disaster for them, for their families, for everyone. We can help. We do help."

Brenda sighed heavily. "I know. I'm sorry."

"Fine," Elizabeth said, curbing her impatience. "You can go back to work. Just don't let it happen again."

As soon as Brenda closed the door behind her, Elizabeth picked up the telephone again and punched the buttons, forcing a pleasantness to her tone as she spoke. "Hello, Mr. Ord. What can I do for you?"

"I've had to suspend your daughter for drunkenness, Ms. Chambers."

"I beg your pardon?"

"I said I've just had to suspend your daughter for drunkenness."

"Drunkenness? There must be some mistake."

"No mistake, Ms. Chambers. She reeks of beer. Mrs. Cavendish brought her to the office a few minutes ago after Kip vomited in the classroom. She's on a crying jag in the nurse's office as we speak."

"I don't know what you're talking about. Kip doesn't drink. And who is this Mrs. Cavendish, anyway?"

"Mrs. Cavendish is your daughter's English teacher," he said stiffly.

"Oh," she said, face hot, resentment swelling. "I forgot." And no wonder. This was the third private school Kip had gone to in the past two years. How was she supposed to keep track of all the teachers' names? Oh, why was her daughter doing this to her again? She'd been out of control since she turned thirteen. Did Kip think word wouldn't spread? She'd end up right back in a public school again, and then what chance would she have to be anything? She'd be lucky to learn to read and write!

"Your daughter needs counseling, Ms. Chambers."

"She's *had* counseling." Psychiatrists and psychologists were always good at finding someone to blame. Mother. Father. Society. That was what was wrong with Kip. The girl was always blaming everyone else for her problems rather than dealing with them herself! What good did it do? Well, she was sick of it, sick of her own daughter.

"I'm sorry she's caused problems. I'll have someone pick her up." She'd call her ex-husband and tell him he could have his new wife pick her up. Bitterness mixed with resentment. Her ex was always so quick to tell her she was a lousy mother. Well, let's see how well he would deal with Kip!

"That won't be necessary, Ms. Chambers."

"If it wasn't necessary, why have you wasted time with this call?"

"Kip has made some accusations."

Elizabeth froze. "I beg your pardon?"

"Accusations—"

"Yes. I heard you. What sort of accusations has she made?"

"She said you've struck her, not once but several times."

"That's not true!" She had disciplined her, sent her to her room, even shouted at her on occasion when pushed beyond the limit. But she'd never struck her daughter. Not in the way he meant. "I have never abused my daughter, Mr. Ord, and I resent your accusation."

"I didn't accuse you, Ms. Chambers. Your daughter did."

A seething rage filled Elizabeth. Of all the ingratitude! She'd done everything she could to make things right for Kip, and look where it got her. "Fine, Mr. Ord. You tell my daughter she can call the youth authority. Do that for me, will you? If I'm such a lousy mother, perhaps she'll be happier in a foster home!" She slammed down the telephone.

Someone tapped at the door.

"What is it?"

Phyllis stuck her head in and grimaced. "Sorry to disturb you. I just wanted to let you know Dr. Wyatt's here."

"Good," she said and glanced at her watch. Twenty-five minutes late. That was six hundred dollars down the drain! Add that to the two clients Brenda had lost, and she had a twelve-hundred-dollar loss for the day.

What she wouldn't give for another Dr. Franklin. Someone quick and efficient. Of course, he had his weaknesses, too. Only yesterday, a young girl had become hysterical when Dr. Franklin began the procedure. He'd told her to shut up. He'd already begun, and it was too late to stop. He told her she should have thought things through before she walked in the door.

Shuddering, Elizabeth stood. She had been forced to speak with him about it. He had been less than pleased at being called to account by a mere director, but she could not allow such insensitivity to pass. She understood he had been upset, but treated in that manner, the girl would tell others in her same situation to go elsewhere. She would seek help at another clinic if she found herself in the same situation again.

And usually there was a next time. These young girls didn't learn by their mistakes. In fact, they often went right out and got themselves pregnant again within a few months. Clinic statistics bore the evidence. Though they dispensed birth control to the girls before they left, the girls either didn't bother taking it or took it inconsistently, increasing their chances of getting pregnant again. It was disheartening, often downright irritating. However, it was also profitable, and his behavior had been, quite frankly, bad for business.

Elizabeth's mouth curved into a cynical half smile. She knew exactly which buttons to push to get Dr. Franklin working properly. His bedside manner this morning had been kindly, even soothing.

Now, for Dr. James Wyatt.

■ ■ ■

Jim entered the supply room, removed his sport coat, and donned a blue paper overshirt from the shelf. He put his arms in it so it tied at the back.

"I hope nothing was wrong at your office this morning, Jim." A voice spoke from the doorway. He glanced at Elizabeth.

"A walk-in."

"Emergency?"

He sensed the frigid anger behind her sedate smile.

"Two of our clients left this morning."

"This was her third pregnancy. Two have ended in miscarriages. It takes time to admit a patient to the hospital for observation." He didn't know why he was explaining himself.

"I imagine your staff could have handled the details."

"Possibly, but I take a personal interest when one of my patients is upset."

She bristled. *"Two* of your patients were in great distress. Here. The wait frightened them away."

"Or maybe they thought better of having an abortion," he said rigidly, knowing that response would not go over well.

He was right. Her eyes flashed with growing anger. "Perhaps," she said smoothly, then stepped into the room. "Here's your check." She held out it out to him. He frowned. He was bothered by the money side of his work at the clinic, and usually she considered that, giving him his pay in an envelope. Apparently she felt like reminding him he was no better than anyone else, maybe worse for his pretentiousness. He drew pay for his part in the business just like she did, just like Dr. Franklin, just like Phyllis and Brenda and half a dozen others.

Heat flooded Jim's face. He looked at her and felt a muscle jerking in his cheek. He wanted to tell her to stuff that check where the sun didn't shine, but he held his tongue. Establishing a practice was expensive. Malpractice insurance was a killer. What choice did he have? "I'll pick it up later."

"I'll just tuck it into your sport coat, how's that?" she said, mockery clear in her tones.

"I said I'll pick it up later." He stepped past her and went out. He walked down the hallway to the first room and took the chart off the door rack. It was a brief form with the barest minimum of facts about the waiting patient. Stapled to it was a signed consent. He read everything. Sighing, he entered the room, scarcely glancing at the young girl on the table.

"Is it going to hurt?"

"As little as possible," he said, smiling at her with what encouragement he could offer.

She talked as he made swift preparations, fast words pouring out in her fear. He tried to put her at ease. She fell silent through the procedure, tensed up at the pain. One of the "nurses" took the basin from the room.

When it was over, Jim stripped off his gloves and discarded them in the wastebasket. Everything had gone smoothly and swiftly. He was good at what he did. Thorough. Elizabeth always encouraged him to finish the procedure and move on to the next room, leaving one of the counselors to give instructions afterward, but he couldn't. Not today. He lingered, concerned, and spoke gently to the silent girl. He wanted to say something to make it easier on her, but he hadn't the words.

"You'll be all right," he said, patting her arm.

Turning her head slightly, she looked up at him.

Looking into her eyes, Jim hurt. Worse, he remembered the newspaper article he had read that morning.

■　■　■

Dynah sat terrified in the clinic waiting room. Half a dozen girls sat in the chairs around the room, all with their backs against the wall. Dynah's mother sat beside her. She supposed she should be thankful for that, noting the others were by themselves. Yet she was torn. Was she doing the right thing? Was this the only way out?

No one said anything.

No one made eye contact.

Her heart thumped wildly every time the door opened and another number was called. Each seat that was vacated was filled with another girl or woman who entered. All strangers. All closed into their private anguish. She was afraid she was going to be sick.

"Mom, I don't know if I can do this," she whispered, trembling.

Hannah heard the fear in her daughter's voice and took her hand, holding it on her lap between both of hers. "Shhh. It'll be all right. I'll be with you the whole time."

"I just don't know. . . ."

"I won't force you, honey. I promise you. We'll talk to the counselor first, and then we'll see what's to be done."

Dynah looked into her mother's eyes and could say no more. She looked down, not wanting her mother to see how afraid she was. She was so afraid she had caused a breach in her parent's marriage.

"I suppose it's the only way. I don't know what else to do." *Oh, God, oh, God, oh, God, is this what I'm supposed to do? If it's right, then why do I feel this churning inside me and this gut-wrenching fear? I can't see my way out of this mess I'm in. It wasn't my fault, Lord. Why did it happen? Why?*

Dynah fought down the tears she knew would only add to her mother's distress.

Hannah felt her daughter's torment and shared it. "It'll be all right," she said again, clinging to the hollow words, wanting to believe them. Her daughter wouldn't be alone the way she had been. She would have her mother to stand beside her, to hold her hand through it all and love her afterward. It would all turn out right in the end. Dynah wouldn't hurt the way she had.

The way she still did. . . .

The door opened again, and a middle-aged woman in white stood in the doorway. "Twenty-eight."

"That's us," Hannah said softly, rising, her daughter's hand firmly in her own.

They were ushered into an examination room and joined there by a young black nurse who introduced herself as Brenda. Brenda read through the form Dynah had filled out, rechecking the data.

Dynah asked her several questions and received vague responses. Though the young woman seemed increasingly uncomfortable, Dynah felt she had to persist. "I need to know, Brenda. Won't you please tell me the truth?"

The young nurse stared at her as though caught in a dilemma. She remained silent for a moment, then shook her head. "I think you might feel better about the procedure if you both spoke with the director. Ms. Chambers will be able to reassure you. Would you like to speak with her?"

"Please," Dynah said.

■　■　■

Brenda went straight to Elizabeth. "I have a young girl and her mother who'd like to speak with you."

"I haven't the time for this," Elizabeth said, rubbing her temples.

"They've asked to speak with you," Brenda persisted. "They have some questions they want answered." Elizabeth raised her head and glared at Brenda, who spread her hands. "I'm sorry, Ms. Chambers, but they're adamant. I'm afraid they'll leave if you don't talk with them."

"How far along?"

"Four and a half months."

Second trimester. That meant more money. "What did you observe about them?"

"The girl seems to be having difficulty accepting abortion as her only option."

"And the mother?"

"Supportive. She's holding her hand and telling her everything will be all right."

Good. That would make it easier. "All right. I'll speak with them, but give me ten minutes. I have a call I need to make first."

As soon as Brenda closed the door, Elizabeth punched the autodial for her ex-husband's office. His secretary didn't want to put her through. "I don't care if he is in a meeting! You tell him it's an emergency concerning his daughter. Remind him her name is Kip."

He came on within seconds, angry and wanting to know what had happened. She told him what the principal had said.

"So pick her up! Why bother me with it?"

"Because she's made some absurd accusation that I'm abusing her!"

"Are you?"

"Of course not! We were married ten years. You should know me better than that."

"No, you're right. You never threw a fist, but you threw words like grenades."

She clenched her teeth, retaining tenuous control.

"Look," he said impatiently, "I haven't got time for this. You're going to have to sort it out yourself, Liz. Today's meeting is important. We were in a break, or I wouldn't have been able to talk to you."

Why should she be surprised? He'd never cared enough to

help her before. Why had she assumed he would jump in now? Even if it involved his own daughter. "What about your new wife? Can she help?" she said, trying to keep the edge of sarcasm from her voice and failing.

"Leslie hasn't got the time either. She's packing."

"Oh," she said with cloying sweetness, "is she leaving you, too?"

"No. We're taking a second honeymoon. She flies to Hawaii tomorrow to get our time-share ready. I'm meeting her in Maui on Saturday."

Second honeymoon. How nice. Her honeymoon had been spent in married housing on the UC Davis campus. She'd spent three years putting him through college. He had never even taken her to Monterey during their ten-year marriage. She had sacrificed a great deal to help him attain his dreams. He had been too busy clawing his way to the top. Now that he was there, he could do as he pleased and forget his responsibilities toward her. A time-share in Maui and a vacation. And where was she? Asking him would do no good.

"Leslie could take Kip with her. I could send someone to the house to pack her things."

"I don't think that's a good idea, Liz. Kip needs to face her problems, not run away from them."

"You mean the way you do."

He gave an unpleasant laugh. "Same old Liz."

"She's our daughter, Brian. We both worked and planned and sacrificed to have her. I don't know what to do about—"

"Look," he said harshly, cutting her off, "this is going nowhere, as usual. You wanted custody of Kip. You got it. You wanted everything your way. You got it. Now you complain. Tough. You hear that, Liz? The court took your side. You got Kip and the exorbitant child support you demanded. I had to fight tooth and nail to get two lousy weekends a month to see my daughter! Seven years you've had it your way, and now you wonder why you've got problems. Well, don't think I'm going to step in now and fix the mess you've made. Fix it yourself!"

Click.

Hurt and angry, Elizabeth slammed the telephone down. She sat for a moment fuming and then punched in the number for the private school. By the time she was passed from the school secretary to the principal's secretary to the principal, her temper was ragged, though controlled.

"I'm sorry, Mr. Ord, but Kip's father won't pick her up. He's busy getting ready for a vacation in Hawaii." She couldn't keep the bitter edge from her voice. What she resented most were the tears that burned her eyes. She thought she'd gotten over the pain of their shattered relationship. It hurt to be used and discarded.

As furious as she was at Kip, the thought of her daughter being taken away from her tore at her heart. Why was Kip doing this to her? Why was she so rebellious and hateful? She had provided her daughter with everything she needed. She had shown she loved her by giving her everything she wanted. She had coddled, nurtured, and counseled. Last year, when Kip had such a crush on that senior football player, hadn't Elizabeth put her on birth control so she didn't have to worry about getting pregnant? Hadn't she even purchased condoms for the boy so Kip wouldn't have to worry about contracting AIDS? Not once had she tried to stop Kip from trying to find happiness. And this is the thanks she got for understanding! It wasn't her fault the boy had dumped Kip or that a succession of other boys had come and gone since.

"She's recanted her story." Mr. Ord's quiet words broke into her frustrated thoughts.

"That's nice, considering it wasn't true in the first place."

"She seems very distressed and confused, Ms. Chambers."

"You said she's drunk."

"It's more than that."

Elizabeth glanced at her watch. She didn't have time for this. Brenda would be tapping on the door in a few minutes. If Kip thought she had problems, she ought to spend the day counseling girls in a family planning clinic. "I know that, Mr. Ord. I'm doing the best I can. Can I send someone to pick her up? One of my staff. I could have her brought here to my office."

"There's no urgency at the moment, Ms. Chambers. Kip's asleep right now in the nurse's office. An hour or two won't be a problem."

She felt his hesitance but decided not to question it. "Good. I'll be there by three."

"I'd like you to talk with the school counselor."

"Fine. I'll do that. And thank you, Mr. Ord." She hung up before he could say more. With one problem settled, she felt better able to face the next.

Moments later Brenda ushered in the mother and her daughter. Smiling warmly, Elizabeth sat at her desk, her hands folded on the blotter, and surveyed them with what she hoped was a friendly demeanor. She noted the mother's diamond studs immediately. Although her wedding ring was a simple gold band, on her other hand was a ring clustered with diamonds. Elizabeth noted other signs of affluence. French-manicured nails. An expensive watch. Designer pants and jacket. Italian shoes. The casual cut of her hair cost money to maintain.

The daughter was blonde, blue-eyed, and lovely, the kind of girl who could make it as a model. She wore an ankle-length floral skirt, a loose-fitting, hip length white sweater over a pale apricot turtleneck. Fashionable clothing to hide an unwanted pregnancy.

Elizabeth noticed something else in her swift appraisal of the girl, which brought understanding and pity. Around the slender neck was a gold chain and simple cross. *There's the problem,* Elizabeth thought, aware of the burden of guilt that religion could bring upon a girl.

"I'm Ms. Chambers, the director of this facility. Won't you sit down, please?" she said, indicating the two comfortable chairs. Reassuring a Christian it was her legal right to have an abortion was not the way to set this girl's mind at ease, if that was her dilemma. The depth of her faith and conviction came into play, though Elizabeth doubted either were insurmountable. The girl was here, after all. The first and greatest step had already been overcome. She had come through the door for help.

Now she would need to help them overcome the foolishness they'd probably been taught. Odds were good they'd been given the usual fundamentalist Christian hyperbole. Thankfully, she wasn't in such spiritual bondage. She attended a progressive neighborhood community church where others shared her convictions and applauded her work. She had learned there that Satan was a myth, the Bible a collection of stories with symbolic rather than literal meaning, and hell didn't even exist. It was a concept dreamed up by religious leaders wanting to keep their flock under control. Fear was a strong motivation for being "good." Now she was free of all that. She believed in God, and her god was merciful and loving and understanding. He made all men perfect, and no one was left out of heaven.

Elizabeth had learned something else over the years too. It was always best to respond to religion rather than avoid it.

"I see you're a Christian," she said, directing her words to the girl. She smiled. "So am I."

■ ■ ■

Hannah relaxed, letting out her breath softly. If the woman was a Christian, she would understand how difficult this was. She would also tell the truth.

Surprised, Dynah didn't know what to say. The attractive woman sitting behind the desk was far from what she had expected. She had been led to believe everyone who worked in an abortion clinic was some kind of monster. She supposed it was foolish and childish to think they would look that way as well.

The director smiled again. "Brenda said you had some concerns. I want to set your mind at rest. I assure you, the procedure is quite simple and quick. You'll feel very little discomfort. We'll want to keep you here about an hour afterward. Your mother can stay with you, of course. Within a few days, this will all be behind you, and you won't even have to think about it again."

Hannah pressed her back into the chair, her stomach clenching. Simple? Quick? Little pain? Easily forgotten? Apparently a lot had changed. "Do you use some sort of anesthetic?"

"No, unless your daughter requests it. That's an additional expense, of course. One hundred dollars." She looked Dynah over once again. "You're not far enough along to need that sort of assistance."

Hannah had only been two months along, but she remembered the excruciating pain quite clearly. "I'd like Dynah to have something."

"As you wish. If money's no problem, we can give Dynah something before the procedure and something to take home afterward."

Hannah didn't care about the money. "I don't want Dynah to feel anything."

"Fine. We'll see to that."

Dynah's heart took a hard gallop when she saw Ms. Chambers reach out to press a button on the telephone. "I'm still not sure I want to do this."

The director paused, then took her hand away from the

intercom. She leaned forward, resting her arms on the desk. "The longer you wait, the more difficult it will be on you and the more costly to your mother. I know this is a difficult decision, Dynah, but sometimes we have to do what's necessary."

"Have you ever had an abortion?" Dynah said before she thought better of such a personal query.

Ms. Chambers leaned back slightly, studying her, an odd look in her eyes. Clearly she had not expected such a question—nor was she pleased by it. Dynah blushed. "I don't mean to be so personal," she said, seeing how the woman's eyes narrowed in self-defense. She wondered how she had dared blurt out such an intrusive question. "I'm sorry. I just need to talk with someone who knows what it's like."

Hannah looked at her daughter.

The director's features relaxed. "So what you're hoping for is reassurance from someone who has been through an abortion. Then, yes, if it will be of help to you to know this, I had an abortion when I was twenty-four." Her mouth curved sadly. "I was putting my husband through college. We were poor, so poor we could barely make the rent. A baby was out of the question. Fortunately, I had a husband who supported me in my decision."

"And later?" Dynah said softly.

"Later?" the director said, perplexed.

"Did you have any complications? Miscarriages? That sort of thing?"

The woman's smile was filled with pity. "I see you've been misinformed. I assure you there are no ill effects from having an abortion. You won't have any problem getting pregnant again when the time is right and you're ready."

Hannah lowered her head, wondering if she was the only one who had suffered infertility, miscarriages, and years of depression. Was she the only one who dreamed about the child she aborted?

Ms. Chambers seemed to sense Hannah's distress and responded to it. "Sometimes we have to make very difficult decisions. Had I not terminated my pregnancy, my husband wouldn't have finished his education. He wouldn't have been able to provide for us in the way he has." She turned the picture on her desk to add to her arguments. "As you can see, I have a lovely daughter. Her name is Kip. My husband and I planned for her. She's been a wonderful blessing to both of us."

Dynah looked at the picture. In it was a man, handsome and well dressed, standing behind the woman who sat before her now, and a young girl. His hands rested on their shoulders, and they were all smiling, happy.

It would seem life could be built upon a foundation of death.

Dynah began to tremble inside for no reason she could fathom.

She felt trapped, with her mother on one side, her father behind her, Ethan and Janet and Dean Abernathy all around her, pushing and pressing her toward this end. And now, here sat this woman who had gone through it, her life intact, saying it would make for a better future.

And still she wasn't convinced.

Ms. Chambers studied her for a moment, then seemed to make a decision. "Why don't you and your mother talk it over?" She stood and came around the desk. "We have a room where you can have some privacy."

Brenda opened the door for them.

The director put her arm around Dynah as she ushered her toward the corridor. "I know how scary this is for you. I've been through it. It's difficult to put our families ahead of ourselves. Someone will be with you every moment, Dynah. I promise you. You're not alone. We're here to help you."

■   ■   ■

Brenda took charge of them and led them down the corridor. She glanced back once and saw Elizabeth still standing in the doorway, watching. She could read her expression as clearly as if she had spoken: *Do you see, Brenda? That's how it's done. Don't botch it!*

"Just press this button when you're ready."

Hannah glanced at the young woman and nodded bleakly. "Thank you." She hoped Dynah would come around quickly so they could get it done and get out of this place. She felt oppressed and sick to her stomach. She prayed God would give her the strength to get through this. *Lord, for my daughter's sake, help me!* She looked at Dynah, who was lowering herself into the straight-backed chair and staring down at her clasped hands. "So, do you feel better, having talked with Ms. Chambers?"

Dynah raised her head. "She didn't answer any of my questions, Mom."

"Of course she did."

"What are they going to do to my body, Mother? Did she tell us? And she said everything would be fine. How can she know? There's a risk with any medical procedure, no matter how simple." Her eyes welled and spilled over. "I'm scared. Oh, Mom, I'm so scared." She looked down again, closing her eyes against the pain she saw in her mother's expression.

"I'll be with you."

"I know, but . . ."

"But what, honey?"

"What about the Lord?"

"Oh, baby," Hannah said, biting her lip to keep from crying. She moved her chair close and embraced her daughter. She had prayed for this child, and God had given Dynah to her. She had given the child back when Dynah was a nursing infant, promising to raise her daughter up to love the Lord above all else.

And doesn't she, Jesus? She loves you. She sang her own made-up hymns of praise to you when she was three. I never had to remind her to say her prayers. She was eager to spend time with you, always thinking of others. Do you remember how she stood on the beach and raised her hands to you? In front of hundreds of people, without the least embarrassment. Why do you do this to her, Lord? Why have you shredded her life and deserted us?

Hannah stroked her weeping child. "I won't forsake you," she said, grieving, sure God had done so to both of them. "I love you, Dynah. You're my life. I won't let anything happen to you."

"I'm not ready, Mom. Can you understand?"

"I understand." Had she been ready? Was anyone ever ready to abort her child? Choice, everyone said. It was a woman's choice! What choice had she had? What choice had Dynah? "Honey, I understand. Believe me, I do."

Dynah shook her head hopelessly. "How can you? I want to leave, Mom."

"Dynah . . ."

"I'm not ready. Please."

Hannah saw her fear and felt it as her own. Her feelings were so ambivalent. She was so torn. What was she supposed to do? Would Doug understand if Dynah didn't have the abortion? Would he support her in that decision? No, he wouldn't. He'd made his feelings clear enough.

What was she going to do?

Oh, God, why do I have to be the one to sit in this room? Why do I have to be the one to press my daughter to this end? Because I did it? Doug's the one making the demands this time. Let him push, like Jerry pushed. They think it's so easy. Oh,

God, it's not. They say they understand. Oh, God, I don't. I never did. I never will. Is there something wrong with me that I can't give my baby up? That I can't forget? And now I have to bring Dynah into the wretched circle? She's your child! Have you forgotten you gave her to me? Why have you abandoned us?

"Mom," Dynah said, trembling, seeing how upset her mother was. She didn't want to make everything so difficult. "Can't we go? I need a little more time. Please."

Hannah could see Dynah's confusion, her fear, but she didn't want to have to go through this again. She had already paid the money. Why couldn't they just get it done now and go? "Dynah—"

"I don't know what I want, Mom. I just know I'm not ready to do this. Not today."

Hannah was torn. She would have to face Doug. She would have to take the brunt of his anger. As though she were the rapist! As though she were the one who had gotten them all into this mess! How was she going to help her daughter without turning her own life into a living hell?

"Please, Mom." Covering her face, Dynah cried.

"All right, honey. We'll go. We'll talk about it some more." And come back to face this misery all over again.

Could they leave without being seen? What if that young nurse was standing outside the door? Did they have to explain? She rose slowly and took Dynah's hand.

As they came out into the corridor, the young black nurse was waiting. She moved, obstructing their path down the corridor. "Are you ready now?"

"I'm afraid not," Hannah said, embarrassed.

"Oh," Brenda said, frowning slightly. What could she say now to allay the girl's anxiety? She could see she was intent on leaving despite her mother's support. Brenda couldn't think of anything to say to make her go through with it. Because of that, she knew she would be in trouble again. Elizabeth would cast blame. It wouldn't matter that she was the one who had spoken to them. "Would you like to speak with Ms. Chambers again?"

"Well . . ."

"No," Dynah said when her mother glanced at her.

A door opened across the hall, startling them both. A doctor came out and put a medical chart in a rack to the right of the door.

Hannah stared at him. "Jim? Jim Wyatt?"

■ ■ ■

Jim turned at hearing his name and looked at the elegantly dressed woman before him. Heat poured into his face.

"It is you," she said, amazed and oddly relieved.

He smiled bleakly. "It's been a long time, Hannah." He looked at the young woman with her.

"This is my daughter, Dynah."

Jim held out his hand to Dynah. She was pale, her hand icy, and she was pregnant. She looked close to tears and ready to flee. "I knew your mother in college. She was my sister's roommate." Was this girl going to be his last abortion for the day? Worse, was Hannah going to be standing in the room with her and watch him at work?

Hannah watched his face; he looked embarrassed and uncomfortable. He was acutely aware of their surroundings and not exactly happy to see her. He saw the question in her eyes as she looked up at him: How had he come to work in a place like this?

Jim felt ashamed, though he couldn't think of any reason why he should be. "It appears you're leaving," he said somewhat stiffly. Yes, he worked here. And they had come for his services, hadn't they?

"Dynah's uncertain."

"It's a big decision."

"She has a lot of questions."

"Mom? Let's go. Please." Dynah took a step toward the exit.

Hannah looked at him, appeal in her eyes. "Maybe you could help, Jim. Could we talk to you about . . . well, about all this. Procedures. Risks. Everything." He stared at her, aware that she believed he would be honest—and that he would help lay Dynah's fears to rest.

He glanced at Brenda, but she merely looked down at the file in her hands, offering no help. He could understand her dilemma. Policy. He didn't agree with it either, but Elizabeth had a way of driving the point home.

As though right on cue, Elizabeth came out of her office and stopped to look at them. Her eyes narrowed. Sometimes she acted almost territorial. Annoyed, Jim stared back at her. He was well aware of her views. Elizabeth was convinced women didn't need to know about the pain and possible risks. She said that sort of information only added needlessly to their trauma.

He didn't happen to agree. He thought women had the right to know the truth. But then, his feelings didn't matter. The Supreme Court upheld Elizabeth's viewpoint, not his. In most cases, no questions were asked, and he didn't have a problem. In a few cases they were, and he offered vague reassurances. With some, he wanted to tell them all the details right down to what happened to the fetus.

Why should he have to bear the burden of what they were doing? Why did he have to be the one to hold the result of their decision in his hands? Why did he have to stare the truth in the face every day he worked in this grim place?

The girl he had just helped had been in here six months ago. When he recognized her, he'd had to stuff his feelings down and stifle the angry words that threatened to pour out. He'd had to remind himself it wasn't his right to judge her.

She wasn't the first to come back for another abortion, and this wasn't the first time he'd felt such anger growing in him. Like a corrosive agent, it ate away any compassion he felt.

Why didn't these girls use the birth control given to them? Why didn't they listen to Elizabeth's admonitions or pay attention to the sex education classes taught in every grade school through high school all across the country? Every year the numbers increased.

Business was booming.

What a way to make a living.

He felt sick and hopeless in the face of it. And trapped by his own principles and reasons for being here.

Hannah's daughter looked up at him, and he thought of his sister. Beautiful. Frightened. Desperately confused. Carolyn had been about this girl's age when she died.

Why did Hannah's daughter have to come here? Why couldn't she have gone to another clinic across the city or bay or in another state? Why did it have to be him?

"Jim," Hannah said softly, as though sensing his turmoil, "we need your help."

And there it was.

He looked at Hannah and her daughter and knew he couldn't turn away from them. They wouldn't be here if they had any other choice.

"I'll meet you for coffee, and we'll talk about it."

Brenda glanced at him, surprised.

He ignored her. He would answer their questions. He couldn't do it here, in a professional capacity, but elsewhere, in a casual setting, he could talk freely. They didn't look comfortable in this antiseptic hallway, the sound of muffled crying coming from the room behind him, and Elizabeth Chambers looking at them as though they lacked the guts to do what they had to do. In another minute, she would intervene and apply just the right measure of pressure to break down their resistance.

"I have two hours before I make my rounds at the hospital," he said briskly and suggested a cafe with high-walled booths where they would have privacy. "I can meet you there in thirty minutes."

Relief swept Hannah's face. "Thank you, Jim. Thank you so much." She put her arm around Dynah as they headed down the corridor.

Jim walked with them, knowing if he didn't, they would have to contend with Elizabeth. As it was, she moved to the front counter where they would have to talk with her before leaving anyway.

"They want time to think it over," he told her as he reached the counter. "Phyllis, return their money."

Phyllis glanced at Elizabeth.

Jim raised his brow in challenge. "I've assured these ladies we aren't in the business of coercing women into having abortions."

"Of course not," Elizabeth said indignantly, eyes glittering. "Do as he says, Phyllis." She watched the money returned.

Hannah stuffed the uncounted bills into her purse and opened the door, ushering Dynah out.

■ ■ ■

Angry, Elizabeth looked up at Jim. "What did you say to them?"

"Nothing."

"Nothing? They practically ran out of here."

Ignoring her, he picked up another chart and headed down the corridor.

Fuming, Elizabeth glared after him. Who did he think he was? God? He needed to be knocked off that high horse of his. He might be a doctor, but she ran this place. He answered to her.

"Phyllis, give me the envelope in his box." When it was in her hand, she turned. "Jim, you forgot something."

Turning, he looked at her. "What?"

She walked toward him with measured steps, opening the envelope as she did so. Eyes glacial, she held out his check. "This," she said.

A muscle jerked in his cheek.

Elizabeth smiled sardonically. "Don't you want it? You earned it."

He took it. Folding it, he stuffed it into his pocket.

Elizabeth gauged his expression. "Back to business, Doctor." Satisfied with the look on his face, she turned and walked away.

7

Dynah sat in the booth sipping 7UP, feeling off balance and out of place. Her mother seemed to have forgotten the reason for this coffee klatch as she reminisced with Dr. James Wyatt. On the drive to the cafe, she had said that he was the brother of a dear friend of hers who had died and that his presence had obliterated all her fears about Dynah's care.

"James Wyatt would never do anything to harm you—or anyone," she'd said. "He couldn't. It isn't in his nature to do so, not if he's the man I remember him to be."

As Dynah studied him surreptitiously, he seemed all her mother thought of him.

"It's been so many years, Jim," Hannah said.

He smiled. "A lot of water under the bridge." Away from the clinic, he could breathe easier. "How's Jerry?"

Dynah glanced at her mother curiously, a bit surprised to see a quick blush coloring her cheeks. "I don't know," she answered. "I haven't seen him in years. I married a man I met here in the city. Douglas Carey."

"Good Scots name."

"He's a wonderful man." She looked pointedly at his wedding band. "And you?"

"Her name's Cynthia. Fifteen happy years. She helped put me through medical school."

"Do you live here in the city?"

"No. Cynthia and I have a place in Mill Valley. We wanted the children to grow up as close to the country as they could. We're a few minutes from the beach."

"How many children do you have?"

"Two." He looked at Dynah. "Much younger than Dynah. We got a late start."

"Dynah's my only child." Dynah smiled slightly when her mother reached out to touch her hand gently, pride shining in her eyes. "We should get our families together."

Dynah shrank at the thought even as her mother said it.

"Sounds good."

"We could have a picnic at the beach or somewhere in Golden Gate Park."

Jim glanced at Dynah and saw how rigidly she sat, shoulders hunched, eyes downcast, her thumb rubbing up and down on the frosty glass. "Why don't we forgo reunion plans until a later time," he said gently.

Dynah watched her mother glance at her again, then reach out to put a comforting hand lightly on her wrist. "I'm sorry, honey. It's just that seeing Jim after all these years was such a surprise. A pleasant one," she hastened to add.

What sort of friends had her mother had? Dynah wondered. And who was Jerry?

"You can ask Jim anything, honey. He'll be honest with you."

Jim hoped she wouldn't be too inquisitive. The last thing he wanted to do was discuss graphic details of what went on at the clinic.

Dynah raised her eyes and looked between her mother and Jim Wyatt. How did one begin such a terrible conversation?

Should she dance around the edges or cut straight to the heart of it?

She wished her mother would start, but she just waited quietly, watching Dynah with such an expression of sadness that Dynah wanted to cry. Her mother must have sensed her struggle, for she patted her hand. "It's all right, honey."

"Is it?" Dynah asked softly. Despite her mother's assurances, she wasn't sure she could trust this man. Could she entrust her life to him?

Lord, is he trustworthy?

Her mother turned back to the doctor, who also waited in silence. "She was raped, Jim. She's had an awful time since. Her engagement's been broken. She's had to leave college. Her life is in complete turmoil. Her father feels . . . well, we feel abortion is the best answer."

Oh, Jesus, Jim thought, bereft.

He couldn't get that other girl out of his head.

"How far along?"

"It happened in early January."

Second trimester. The girl was too far along for a menstrual extraction or suction curettage. "Too bad you didn't arrive at your decision sooner."

Dynah's head came up. She hadn't said she had made a decision, but he went on.

"Didn't the examining doctor offer you a morning-after pill?"

"Yes. I refused."

He looked at the cross around her neck and decided not to pursue her reasons. Best not to get into religious territory. It only muddied the waters. "Even a couple of months afterward, it would've been a simple procedure, about fifteen minutes and that's it. Second trimester abortions are a little more difficult." He looked at Dynah, trying to think of gentle ways to say it.

"I'd give you an injection of prostaglandin to induce contractions and expel the tissue." He left it at that. If she needed to know the grim details of how the hormone was injected and where and what it did to the fetus, she would have to ask. Time enough to know when it was being done.

"The risk is minimal," Jim continued, seeing her pallor and wanting to reassure her. In the five years he'd been performing abortions, he had kept to the first-trimester abortions, leaving the late-terms to Dr. Franklin. Since Dynah was the daughter of a good friend, he'd make an exception this time. He'd see her through it and stand beside her in recovery to make sure she was fine.

The newspaper article about the dead girl flashed into his mind.

Why should he think of that now? Why couldn't he get it out of his head?

And why was Hannah looking at him like that?

He focused his attention on Dynah. She was the one in need of help. "I'd take good care of you. I'll be as careful with you as if you were my own daughter." Even as he said it, his heart shuddered.

"What about later?" Hannah said quietly.

"She'd remain in recovery for an hour or two. I'd keep a close watch on her."

"I mean . . . *later.*"

"I've only had a few clients come back with complications, all of which were usually minor and easily solved with drugs." His mouth curved grimly. Unfortunately, most who came back were pregnant again, usually within a few months. His expression softened as he looked at Dynah. "I don't want you to worry about anything, Dynah. It's not as difficult as you've probably heard."

Again he saw Hannah glance at him, as though she wanted

to say something. But she stayed silent, a troubled expression on her face.

Dynah knew her mother had already made up her mind. She'd wanted to ask questions and now felt constrained about doing so. Her mother was tense and nearly in tears, and prolonging the conversation would make it harder for her. Yet Dynah found herself floundering. What she knew in her head and heart warred with what this man was saying.

Her mother spoke up, as though wanting to avoid talking about any more details. "How did you become involved in all this, Jim?"

"Carolyn," Jim said.

"Carolyn?" Dynah's mother said, clearly surprised. At Dynah's questioning glance, her mother explained. "Carolyn was Jim's sister. She was one of my best friends in the sorority." She smiled. "We were both freshmen, so we learned the ropes together. Carolyn was beautiful, wild about Janis Joplin and Jimi Hendrix, and enjoying her first taste of real freedom. Knowing her was like watching a fireworks display. Glorious and beautiful while it lasted."

"While it lasted?"

Her mother nodded at the question. "She died. Over spring break. Everyone was stunned. I . . . well, it was devastating to lose her." She looked at Dr. Wyatt with a slight frown. "But I don't understand. You told me she died of a ruptured appendix."

"She died of sepsis following an illegal abortion."

"Oh, Jim." Dynah heard the tears in her mother's voice.

"Some woman did it. How Carolyn found out about her, I'll never know. My parents had no idea. Mom said Carolyn went shopping one afternoon and came home pale and weak. She went to bed. She kept saying she'd be fine, but she kept getting worse. By the time they took her into emergency, it was too late."

His eyes filled, remembering his younger sister. She'd had everything going for her. "It's remembering how Carolyn died that keeps me going."

Hannah sat silent.

Jim looked at Dynah. "Things are different now. It's legal. You can have the best medical care. It's a simple procedure, done by a doctor in a sterile environment with the proper equipment; there's little risk. Within a few days, you'll be fine."

Dynah felt his determination, but as casual and easy as Dr. Wyatt made it sound, she couldn't think about it without a visceral response. She couldn't think it through without horror.

Suddenly, she felt a fluttering sensation in her abdomen, and she froze. She waited, and felt it again. A stirring of life. Her heart raced madly.

"Are you all right, honey?" her mother said, touching her again.

Dynah wanted to scream, *No! I can feel the baby moving!*

Oh, God, how can I be all right under these circumstances? Can I concentrate on the rape that produced this child and go through with an abortion? And if I do, can I walk away unscathed?

"Dynah?"

She looked at her mother and saw the hope that lay there. Her mother wanted it over and done with. She didn't want to have to deal with the problem. She didn't want to have to do battle with Daddy over the moral implications or alternatives. In their minds, there was no alternative.

Dynah envisioned herself in a narrow chute, like some poor cow being herded along, everyone she loved standing around and above her with electric prods, stinging her and moving her in one direction. Toward death. Not hers. But death nonetheless.

She felt movement again, and she could imagine small arms and legs flailing. How much worse would it be when this man injected the deadly hormone? Would she feel the child's death throes?

God, how can I live with that? God, Jesus, where are you when I need you?

"Will you please excuse me?" she said, shaking. "I need to go to the ladies' room." Any excuse would do. She had to get out of the booth and away.

"Are you all right, honey? You don't look well."

"I'm a little nauseated. I'll be fine, Mom. I just need to use the bathroom." It was all she could do to wait until her mother slipped from the booth and helped her out.

■   ■   ■

Hannah watched her daughter for a moment as she hurried away before sitting down again. She frowned.

"She's not sure," she said, almost apologetically. "I've always taught her it was wrong, and now this happens. I keep telling her it's not her fault. If anyone has a good reason for having an abortion, she does." It would be so much easier on everyone if she'd just get it done. Then they could put it behind them.

"It's not something to rush into," Jim said.

Hannah thought it ironic that he would be the one to say that.

"She's a beautiful girl, Hannah."

"Yes, she is, isn't she? And she's *good*. She's been such a joy. Never a worry." She shook her head, pressing her lips together, fighting tears. Life wasn't fair.

"Sorry I mentioned Jerry. I thought it was a sure thing."

"So did I." She gave a bleak laugh and lowered her head, her hands around her coffee mug. She was so confused, the old pain churning again. Memories drowning her in misery. When Jim had told Dynah that she wouldn't suffer any long-term aftereffects, she'd wanted to believe him. Maybe she was one of the rare cases who had had problems for years afterward. She'd wanted to say something, to ask questions . . . but she couldn't. Not with Dynah sitting beside her. What would her daughter think of her if she knew she'd had an abortion? Would Dynah lose all respect for her? Of course she would. She simply wouldn't understand. How could she?

She thought again of Jim's sister, Carolyn. Her death had made Hannah realize her own mortality. She and two other girls had driven to Pasadena for the funeral. It was after that trip that she had given in to Jerry's wishes. They'd been in his apartment, the news of Vietnam blaring reports about the offensive in Hue when she'd given herself to him. The world was winding down, blowing up around them. She'd wanted to grasp every second of happiness she could.

And everything had turned to ashes anyway.

"Actually, I could have ended up like Carolyn," she said before thinking better of it. She hesitated and then went on, seeing no reason to hide anything anymore. Not from Jim.

She raised her head to see how he took the revelation. Nothing in his expression said he condemned or judged her. Why not tell him? If anyone could understand, surely Jim would. Douglas never really had. He refused to talk about it, and she couldn't get past it.

"I heard about that woman in Los Angeles," she said softly. "One of the girls in the sorority house gave me her name. I was going to go to her, but Jerry found a doctor just outside Reno. I guess I should be thankful."

Jim didn't say anything. He just reached over and took her hand.

It was enough.

"One of my friends drove me to the doctor's house. As soon as she left, he drove me out into the desert. I thought he was going to do it there at his house, but he said no. The Catholic church had people watching him, and he said he needed to be careful. I don't remember how long he drove. An hour, maybe more. It seemed like forever. We were way out in the desert. I didn't have any idea where I was, but I didn't care. I just wanted it over."

She looked down, not saying anything for a moment, pressing the pain down so she could tell him the rest. "There was a garbage dump with a high fence. He had a trailer parked there, all set up like a hospital examining room. The table with stirrups, instruments, everything. It was clean."

He squeezed her hand. "You were lucky."

She raised her head. "Was I?"

Jim looked into her tear-washed eyes and saw her anguish. For a moment it was as though he shared a measure of the bitter brew—and felt poisoned.

She smiled sadly. "Everything was done properly. The right equipment, a sterile environment. Just like you were saying to Dynah. But it wasn't all right, Jim."

"What do you mean?"

"I couldn't have children. When Doug and I got married, I wanted a baby more than anything, maybe to atone for what I'd done. Or just because it was always a part of what I wanted. Every time I got pregnant, I miscarried. My gynecologist said it was because of the abortion. Dynah was a miracle." Tears slipped down her cheeks. "You told my daughter everything would be fine in a few days. Maybe, God willing, that's the way it'll be. But you know what, Jim? There's more to it than the physical part. It's been twenty-nine years, and I'm still not over it."

Jim felt his chest tighten. He couldn't speak. He looked into Hannah's eyes and knew he had seen that same despair in countless other women.

She drew back slightly, withdrawing her hand from his and digging in her purse for a Kleenex. "Sorry," she muttered.

He started to say something, but just then the waitress approached. "The young lady asked me to give you this." She handed the note to Hannah and left.

Hannah opened it quickly and read. She sighed heavily. "Dynah went home by taxi. She says she's fine and not to worry." Folding it, she held it tightly in her hand. "She's always concerned about everyone else. Even now." She shook her head, struggling to contain her emotions. She looked up at him, eyes fierce. "I don't want my daughter to go through what I did, Jim."

"I swear she won't."

"How can you swear that?"

"I'm a doctor. I know what I'm doing. You're going to have to trust me."

What else could she do? "I'd sooner trust you than anyone else, I guess. I know how much you care. I remember how you used to spend your weekends volunteering at the local hospital."

"I swore I'd never let another girl end up like Carolyn if it was within my power to help." Since that 1973 decision, helping had been made easy.

She studied him, sensing something behind the vehemence. And it occurred to her what it might be. "Did you know Carolyn was pregnant?"

He pushed his coffee cup away. "Yes."

"She asked for your help, didn't she?"

He looked at her, guilt-ridden, unable to answer. Carolyn had come to him, desperate and pleading. He worked in a hospital. He had access to tools and drugs. He knew anatomy. He was her brother! He had to help her!

And still he refused.

They'd argued. She'd accused him of being judgmental and self-righteous. He'd told her she was selfish and hedonistic. She should have thought of the consequences *before* she started screwing around. He was tired of being big brother and fishing her out of the soup she made. He wasn't going to jeopardize his future by performing an illegal abortion or helping convince some doctor it was psychologically necessary. It was time she grew up!

Instead, Carolyn died.

A part of him had gone down into the grave with his sister. What was left had been trying to purge the guilt ever since.

When abortion became legal, he lost all his excuses for not getting involved, not helping others like Carolyn. He discussed it with Cynthia, half hoping she would support him in anything he decided. She understood his feelings. She applauded his compassion. And the money was good. It seemed a God-sent gift to get them out from under the huge debts he'd accumulated from medical school and internship and residency. They could have a nice home where the children could grow up in safety.

Oh, God! Is any place safe anymore?

Hannah saw the torment written on his face and was sorry she'd opened old wounds. "I'm sorry, Jim. I'm so sorry."

"It was a long time ago," he said, wishing the pain weren't so fresh. "Let's get back to Dynah. You know, she might feel easier about the procedure if I performed it in a hospital setting. What do you think?"

"Possibly."

"General, for example. They have all the necessary equipment. They handle abortions all the time."

"A hospital will be more expensive."

"Don't worry about it. I'll write it up so insurance handles the cost."

■ ■ ■

The mailman hailed Dynah as she was walking up the front steps. She turned and smiled in greeting, accepting the bundle of mail he gave her. He tipped his cap and wished her a nice day before heading down the walkway again.

Slipping the rubber band off, she flipped through the envelopes, half hoping Ethan had written her. She found a letter addressed to her with no return address. It wasn't from Ethan.

Unlocking the door, she put the mail on the table in the entry hall and tore open the envelope. It was a brief note from Joe. He wanted to know how she was doing. Did she know she could call him anytime? He cared about her. He was making plans to come west right after graduation and hoped she wouldn't mind his looking her up. "Hang around June 15. I'll be on your doorstep." He was praying for her.

She tucked the note back into its envelope. Joe hadn't mentioned Ethan. She couldn't help wondering at the oversight. But then, Ethan and Joe were best friends. She wondered if Ethan was picking up his life and dating again. Girls were always around him. Easy pickings. Lots of picture-perfect virgin girls looking for a good godly husband.

It hurt too much to think of all the possibilities. Someday he would marry someone pretty, unsoiled, and supportive. Someone he could mold into the wife he wanted.

And what about me, Lord? What kind of future am I going to have?

"Dynah?"

Startled, she glanced up. "Grandma!" Smiling through her tears, she went into her grandmother's arms. She had noticed a car out front when the taxi pulled up but hadn't bothered to give it more than a cursory glance. Had she done so, she would have noticed the Oregon license plates and known.

"I got here about an hour ago. Good thing your mother gave me a key last year, or I would've had to hunt up a rest room at a gas station."

"I didn't know you were coming."

"Of course, I'd come. The minute I heard you were home and why, nothing could keep me away."

Dynah withdrew and looked at her, heat flooding her cheeks. "Mom called you?"

"Actually, I called her. I knew something was wrong and pressed her." Evie touched her granddaughter's cheek, seeing more than the child wanted to reveal. "It will be all right. That's why I came."

Grandma, come to save the day. Dynah could feel trouble coming from all directions.

She smiled wanly. "She shouldn't have told you."

"Why not? Family should hold together at a time like this." She put her arm around Dynah's waist "Let's talk in the family room. I just started a pot of coffee. Have you eaten?"

"I'm not very hungry."

"I can mix up some tuna for a sandwich. You've always liked my tuna. Or is your stomach queasy?"

"A little."

"Your mom always keeps chicken soup on hand. I'll fix some of that instead. Why don't you sit at the breakfast table, and we'll talk while I get things together. Where's your mom?"

"We ran into an old friend of hers. They're having coffee together." They were probably talking about what they were going to do about *her* problem. She sat down and stared at the envelope between her hands. She should write a note back to Joe and tell him that everything was fine and he needn't worry. If she called and told him so, he'd know she was lying. She didn't want word getting back to Ethan that her life was in ashes.

"Is the letter from Ethan?"

"No." Her throat tightened. "Just a friend." She forced a smile, trying to achieve an atmosphere of normalcy. "So how's everything in Oregon, Grandma? Are you and Gladys still chumming around together?"

Evie closed the pantry door, a can of Campbell's soup in her hand. "We keep tabs on each other. As a matter of fact, I called her just before you got home. She was already thinking I'd died in a rest stop or been hijacked somewhere. She can be an old worrywart at times." She opened a cabinet and then another until she found the mugs and silverware. "Your mom's been reorganizing again."

"She takes after you." Dynah listened to the whir of the electric can opener. "Are you still involved in your church?"

"President of the women's club," she said, pouring the chicken soup into a bowl and adding tap water. "It's the last time I'm going to do it." She stirred the soup, put the bowl into the microwave, and tapped in three minutes.

"That's what you said a few years back."

"I mean it this time. They need new blood. I've run out of juice." *And time.*

Dynah looked at her, studying her intently. Grandma was like a sprite, always moving, always finding something to do. A bundle of energy. Obsessively organized. Dynah adored her. She watched now as her grandmother drummed her fingers on the counter, waiting for the microwave to shut off. She looked older, a little thinner, more gray in her hair.

"Are you feeling all right, Grandma?"

Evie cast her a quick glance, surprised by the question. She'd forgotten how intuitive Dynah was. She noticed people, cared about them. "I'm fine." *Ping.* She opened the microwave and took out the steaming mug of soup. "If you discount the arthritis, rheumatism, constipation, fading eyesight, and ingrown toenails, I'm in the pink of health."

Dynah laughed.

Evie set the mug down in front of Dynah and took a seat.

"Drink your soup." She patted her hand. "You have to take good care of yourself, Dynah. You have someone else to think about now."

■ ■ ■

Hannah saw her mother's car the moment she pulled into the driveway. Torn between relief and frustration, she punched the garage door opener and drove into the carport. She came in through the kitchen and saw her mother rinsing dishes. "Where's Dynah?"

"She went upstairs to take a nap." Her mother put the mug into the dishwasher. "She looks worn out."

"And no wonder." Hannah put her purse on the counter and put her arms around her mother, hugging her close. "Oh, Mom," she sighed. "I'm glad you came."

Evie held her daughter close, rubbing her back. She'd seen the shadows under her eyes the moment Hannah came in the door. She always had a bruised look when things weren't going well. It was a good bet Hannah wasn't sleeping. "What time does Doug come home?"

"Around six." Hannah let go of her mother slowly. "How about a glass of wine?"

"It wouldn't hurt."

Hannah took two glasses from the cupboard and a bottle of chilled Oregon blackberry wine from the back of the refrigerator. She caught her mother's smile. "Yes, it's the same bottle you brought down at Christmas. I've been hoarding it."

"I should've thought to bring a couple more."

"Do you want to turn me into a lush?"

"I doubt there's much chance of that."

They went into the family room. Hannah set her glass down and turned on the gas fireplace. There was nothing like flickering firelight to give one the feeling of home. And right now, she was desperate for any kind of comfort. "Have you un-packed?"

"Not yet. I left my things in the car. I'll bring them in later." She watched Hannah rub her forehead. "What's happened since we talked?"

"Nothing. Dynah hasn't made a decision yet. I took her to a clinic this afternoon. . . ."

"What sort of clinic?"

"You *know* what sort of clinic, Mother." Did she have to spell it out?

"I hope you're not pushing her into having an abortion."

"I'm not pushing. Doug's pushing."

"It's not his decision."

"Tell *him* that! Dynah's his daughter. She lives in his house. He pays the bills. He's the one who'll have to keep working if she has this child. And why should she, Mother? She was *raped*. What sort of human being could she be carrying?"

"You know what abortion is."

"Don't say it, Mother."

"You've been through it yourself."

"I don't want to talk about it! I've had an awful day, and it's going to be a worse evening. All I want is to have this glass of wine and a nice comfortable visit. Can we do that? *Please?*"

Evie sighed heavily and said nothing more. Time enough when Doug got home. She intended to say what she had to say. She hoped to God they'd listen.

■　■　■

Dynah awakened once when her mother came in to ask if she'd like to come down to dinner. Tired and depressed, she declined. "I'll eat later, Mom."

"OK, honey," Hannah said, readjusting the covers and lean-ing down to kiss her.

When Hannah came downstairs, her mother was putting serving dishes on the dining-room table while Doug sat in the family room watching the news. He had changed into his worn Levi's, polo shirt, and sneakers. Even in his relaxed pose, she sensed he was coiled and ready to strike at the first provocation. They'd exchanged only a few words upon his arrival home.

"Did you take care of it?" he had said.

"I tried."

"Did you invite your mother?"

"Sort of."

He gave her a narrow-eyed look that said he didn't believe her. A muscle jerked in his jaw, and he rose, stepped past her, and went upstairs with his briefcase.

From the look of him now, she figured he hadn't removed his armor.

Choruses of bitter voices jabbered in her head, dredging up the hurts from the past. Every hurtful word he'd ever spoken was played again, fast-forward. Self-pity filled her, bringing along with it a boiling anger that steamed away love, patience, gentleness. Self-restraint hung by a thread.

They sat down at the dining-room table together and ate the spicy meatloaf, mashed potatoes, and carrots Hannah had fixed. Doug liked things hot. She watched him douse his meatloaf with Tabasco sauce and felt her temperature rising. He hadn't even bothered to taste the meal before he doctored it up.

Evie was saddened by what she saw happening between Hannah and Doug. She remembered their being like this in the early years of their marriage. Stony silences. Tension. She used to wonder if it was her and Frank who weren't welcome. It wasn't until later, when Hannah told her the whole story about Jerry, that she began to understand what was tearing at her daughter's marriage.

Well, she had her own secrets. Maybe unveiling them would help these two come to terms with their past—and their future. . . .

Or was she just going to be opening Pandora's box?

Doug finished quickly and excused himself. Hannah fumed as she heard the television go on again. A boxing match this time. A suitably violent sport. Too bad hockey wasn't on tonight. Or he could pull out one of those god-awful war movies he loved to watch so much. He said they were cathartic. What was so cathartic about seeing blood and mayhem?

She stacked the dishes noisily and carried them into the kitchen. "I can handle it, Mom. Go sit down and relax."

Evie itched to do something, anything. So she picked up a sponge and went back in to wipe the table, rearrange the flowers in the center, and push all the chairs into place.

They all sat in the family room together, separate islands with their own hurricanes. Doug stared at the television. Hannah sat fidgeting. Evie dug into her travel sewing basket and pulled out a pillowcase she was embroidering. A Christmas present for someone.

No one talked about what was on their minds. The issue could have been a pink elephant in the middle of the room, trumpeting and leaving scat about, and they would pretend they didn't notice. They'd tiptoe around it and try not to arouse it.

"We need to talk," Hannah said finally.

Doug stared at her. "We talked already."

"We haven't talked at all."

He glanced pointedly at Evie.

"Mom knows everything."

"I should've guessed. No insult to you, Evie, but this is *our* business."

Evie anchored the needle and lowered the project to her lap. Hannah grimaced, feeling the tension mounting in the room.

Pompeii must have felt like this just before Vesuvius erupted. No matter what she said, Doug was going to blow. Better she take the blast than her mother.

"We have to talk about it."

His gaze turned on her. "What more is there to say?"

She let out her breath. It was just like him to dump the whole thing in her lap. Fix it, Hannah. Don't bother me with it. "I spoke with a doctor today." She didn't dare tell him she knew Jim Wyatt from college days. Doug would make all kinds of assumptions. He'd probably think she'd slept with him, too. "He said he can admit Dynah to General and do the procedure there. She'd stay overnight for observation."

"When?"

"Tomorrow afternoon."

"So, it's settled. What do you want from me?"

She began to shake. She wanted to scream at him and pound on him. Instead, she clung to her self-control. "Dynah has to say yes. I can't drag her there."

He looked at her then, eyes fiery. "I didn't *say* drag her, did I? Did I ever say that? No. I told you to help her through this."

"Meaning it's up to me to convince her."

"You know more about it than I do."

Oh, God, here we go again.

Doug turned his head away, staring at the television.

Hannah sat silent, wallowing in her pain, filling her cup with resentment. Sometimes she almost hated him.

Evie looked between them and wanted to weep. She wondered if she was somehow to blame, planting that tiny seed all those years ago, never guessing the consequences in generations to come. She had thought Hannah was too young to know anything, but maybe she'd absorbed it somehow, taken it into herself, and kept the sorrow growing.

She dumped her handwork heedlessly in her travel basket,

quietly got up, walked across the room, and turned the television off.

"Mother!"

"What're you doing?" Doug said, furious.

She didn't mind being the target. Better they were united against her than fighting one another. "Don't let Dynah have an abortion," she said simply, ready to do battle.

"Mother," Hannah said, sure she would launch into a diatribe about the unborn.

Evie saw Doug's eyes narrow and the muscle in his jaw jump. "Please hear me out," she said and returned to her seat. She strove to stay calm though she wanted to burst out loud and say she was older and wiser and knew more than both of them put together.

"Dynah's situation has nothing to do with how you or anyone else thinks," Doug said pointedly, eyes fierce.

"You know how I feel about the issue, Doug, but you don't know why."

"It doesn't matter."

"She's my granddaughter, and I love her."

"She's my daughter, and you think I don't?"

"I know you love her. You love her more than your own life. All I ask is that you hear me out." She sat forward, her hands clasped tightly in her lap, and bowed her head. This was going to be harder than she expected. "I've carried this around in my heart for years, and now it seems I have to tell you whether I want to or not."

Doug looked from her to Hannah and clenched his teeth. He was struggling to maintain control, that much was clear. He let out his breath, as though loosening his muscles through an act of will.

Good. At least he was trying. Evie knew her son-in-law admired her spunk, but she also knew that didn't mean her opinion mattered on whether Dynah should have an abortion or not. She was fairly sure Doug thought he knew what she was going to say. He was well aware she belonged to a fundamentalist church. Her Bible was sitting beside the swivel rocker right now looking frayed and ragged around the edges, half a dozen ribbons sticking out of it—which he probably figured marked all the suitable passages for the upcoming sermon he expected. But the last thing she was going to do was preach.

After the first few years Doug and her daughter had been married, she had learned to stay out of their affairs. It had been harder for Frank, a retired executive who was used to running the show. Evie was aware that distance and poor health had saved Doug from having to tell his father-in-law to back off. She was sure it hadn't been easy for Doug and that it probably hurt knowing it had taken fifteen years to convince Frank he was sticking with Hannah through the long haul. Another residue from the past. Frank had seen his daughter hurt before and hadn't wanted to see it happen again.

Noting Doug's closed expression, she wondered if he would hear a word she said. Whatever the case, she had to take the risk. "Before Frank and I were married, I had tuberculosis."

"We know that, Mom—"

"And I relapsed after you were born," Evie went on, seeing she was going to have to plow ahead and override Hannah's desire to avoid the uncomfortable and Doug's antipathy to the truth. "The doctor wanted me to go into a sanatorium, but Frank insisted I remain home. He wanted me close, and I wanted that more than anything, too. You were three, Hannah, your brother six, and I didn't want to be away from you for months on end.

"Your father had a hospital bed brought in. We didn't let you come into the bedroom. Granny would hold you in her arms at the door, and you'd say good morning and good night to me. Sometimes we'd let you sit in a chair in the doorway so we could talk. You broke my heart, Hannah. You'd ask me over and over why you couldn't come in and cuddle with me that way you used to do. You didn't understand what TB or infection meant." She looked at her grown daughter, knowing she had felt rejected despite the reassurances. "It was so hard not to hold you and kiss you."

Her throat closed, remembering how much it had hurt to turn her children away. Even knowing her own mother was there to scoop them up and nurture them hadn't eased the pain of those months of separation. And what damage had it done in the years following?

She knew she was digressing. She could see by Hannah and Doug's expressions that they had no idea where she was going with all this. She had to gather her wits and courage.

Oh, Lord, help me!

She thought she knew how she would say it. Hadn't she planned every word on the long drive south from Oregon? Now that the time had come, she couldn't remember a single word of the speech she had prepared.

She took a deep breath and let it out slowly. "I became pregnant."

"Daddy told me," Hannah said, wanting to spare her mother, afraid of where all this was going and what Doug's response would be.

Evie struggled past the tears that threatened. Odd how time never healed some wounds. "Yes, I remember. On the night of your first miscarriage, your dad told you we'd lost one, too. He told you that because he wanted you both to know we understood and grieved with you. But the thing is—," Evie said, looking from Hannah to Doug—"I didn't miscarry. I had a therapeutic abortion."

Doug stared at her, clearly stunned; the look on her daughter's face was indecipherable.

Evie rushed to fill the shocked silence, wanting to get it all said and done. "You see, the doctor told your father I wouldn't survive another child. Frank believed him. I told him I was well enough to carry the baby to term, but I couldn't convince him. He was afraid my health would decline and he'd end up a widower rearing three small children by himself. He said he didn't want to risk losing me. God forgive me, I went along with his decision. I allowed the doctor to admit me to the hospital, cosigned the papers with your father, and went through with it."

She looked at Hannah through her tears. "I was five months along. The baby was a boy. Your brother would be forty-six had he lived."

Doug stared at her, then shook his head. "You did what you had to do, Evie. Frank was right."

"No, he wasn't, Doug. And worse, he knew it, though he never said so aloud. It might have helped both of us to talk about it. All the years we were together, we never spoke of it. I was angry and hurt for several years afterward, and he just wanted to forget. For a while, I didn't know if we'd stay married. You'll remember that time, Hannah. You were about six when things leveled off. Granny moved home, and we sold that house and started building another. Gradually, we buried thoughts of what we had done and went on with our lives."

Evie watched Doug glance at Hannah to see how she was taking this new information. She was pale, her eyes glistening with tears.

"Some things can't be buried, no matter how hard or how long you try." She looked at Doug. "Frank spoke of it before he died. He never got over it any more than I did." She broke off, fighting the tears that threatened to overcome her.

Hannah couldn't utter a word, her throat hot and tight.

It was a moment before Evie could continue to speak. "You prayed for Dynah to be born, and God gave her to you. You have both raised her up before the Lord. You know her tender heart as well as I. Do you honestly think she could have an abortion and not suffer for it for the rest of her life?"

Doug clenched his hands. "She's strong."

"She'll be broken."

"She's already been broken! She'll be broken even more if she goes on with this. She doesn't even know what the man looked like, for God's sake."

"And you think to undo one act of violence upon her with another?"

He didn't speak for a moment, again clearly striving to control his temper. "It won't be that way. We'll make sure. It'll be legal and safe."

Hannah flinched inwardly, feeling the darts.

Evie felt the anger coming up inside her and smothered the flame with cold reason. "My abortion was *legal*. It was *safe*. It was performed in a hospital by a medical doctor with several nurses in attendance. And I will tell you this, Douglas. It was an act of violation and violence upon me such as I will *never* forget. And I'm a lot harder and stronger than Dynah."

"You think giving birth to a rapist's child isn't going to cause worse trauma?"

"Childbirth is natural."

"Natural! The child she's carrying is anything *but* natural."

"So your answer is to sacrifice the child for what the father did?"

Doug's blazing eyes met hers. "I don't give a rat's scat about the child! And I'm not getting into a philosophical or theological discussion with you. It's decided. She's going to have an abortion, and that's the way it's going to be. We're not going to let our daughter ruin her life by having some crack baby. And that's all there is to it!"

Evie looked at her daughter, appealing for an ally.

"Doug . . . ," Hannah said.

He glared at her, and Evie saw he felt betrayed. "I said *no*. You took her to the clinic today. Why didn't you get it done then instead of dragging this thing out longer?"

"Because she couldn't decide if that's what she wanted or not!"

"You should have helped her! You should have made it easy for her! You've been through it."

"And she's still not over it," Evie said, furious that after all these years he dared throw that in Hannah's face again. "Don't you *get* it yet? What does it take to make you understand?" Would he never be man enough to forgive her? Hannah had been a good wife, faithful and loving. How long did she have to do penance for a sin committed before she knew Douglas Carey existed?

Doug turned his growing fury toward her. "Stay out of this! It's none of your business!"

"I'm *making* it my business! Dynah's my granddaughter, and I've a mind to go upstairs right now, pack her things, and get her out of this house!"

He half rose from his chair. "You can pack. And you *can* get out. But you're not taking my daughter."

"Stop it!" Pale and rigid, Hannah made fists against her temples. "Just *stop it*. Both of you!" Hunching forward, she wept.

■ ■ ■

Dynah sat on the stairs, her head pressed against her knees, listening to the people she loved most in the world tearing one another apart.

Over her.

She hadn't known about her mother. Now that she did, she felt doubly forsaken. How could her mother take her hand and encourage her to have an abortion when she had suffered so?

They were quieter now, having already ripped open their most vulnerable spots. Dynah could hear their voices, still tense and angry, though more restrained. Probably worried they would awaken her.

Oh, God, I never wanted this to happen!

She could hear her father dictating what she should do, her grandmother arguing with him, her mother, usually the peacemaker, lashing out at both of them in her own pain.

Dynah raised her head, tears streaming down her cheeks. She couldn't stay here. If she did, she would come between all of them. Anything she did would hurt someone. If she aborted the child, her grandmother would be hurt. If she didn't, her father would cast her out. In either case, her mother would suffer, caught between the two, confused and full of anguish.

God, what do I do? Do I buy another bottle of pills? Do I jump off the Golden Gate Bridge?

She thought of Joe. *"I wouldn't get over it. Not ever."* She could see his face, intent, sincere.

Her parents wouldn't get over it either. Or her grandmother. No matter how miserable she was, she couldn't take the easy way out. She loved them too much.

So, what else is there, Lord? What do I do?

A whisper came, a Scripture she'd learned long ago drifting into her mind: "'COME OUT FROM THEM AND BE SEPARATE,' SAYS THE LORD."

As the angry voices droned below her, she knew she had to leave, even if she didn't know where to go and how to get by. *Come out from them and be separate.*

She had to get out of here.

■　■　■

True to his word, Joe Guilierno was on the doorstep early in the afternoon of June 15. It was Saturday.

His heart thumped crazily as he rang the doorbell. He heard someone approaching and took a deep breath, hoping it would be Dynah. It wasn't. When the door opened, he faced Dynah's mother. It was easy to tell, they looked so much alike.

"Hello, Mrs. Carey, I'm Joe. Joe Guilierno. A friend of Dynah's. She's expecting me."

Hannah was surprised by his appearance. She remembered Dynah speaking of him. *"He's nothing like Ethan, Mom. He's just a nice guy."*

Hannah had to agree Joe Guilierno wasn't anything like Ethan. He was taller, broader, darker, rougher. He didn't wear slacks, a button-down shirt, coordinated tie and sports jacket, or have a neat haircut. He was wearing faded Levi's, a white T-shirt, and a black leather jacket. His hair was curling over his collar. She wondered vaguely how he'd gotten away with that at NLC. He smiled slightly, as though he knew what she was thinking, and she blushed. "I'm sorry." So this was the young man who sent a letter a week. The envelopes were stacked on Dynah's bedside table, unopened. "Won't you come in, Joe?"

"How is she?" he said, stepping into the foyer and glancing up the stairs, hoping to see Dynah.

"She's not here."

"Oh," he said, not bothering to cover his disappointment. "Do you expect her back soon?" Maybe she was avoiding him. Ideas of why she might want to do that flooded his mind. Had she had an abortion?

"I don't know."

He looked at her, frowning slightly, waiting.

"She left three weeks ago, Joe. In the middle of the night. We don't know where she is." She glanced away from his intense scrutiny. "Why don't you come into the family room? Doug is here. I'm sure he will want to meet you, too."

Joe followed Dynah's mother into the family room and saw a man he recognized as Dynah's father sitting in an easy chair staring at the television set. A baseball game was blaring. Someone had just hit a grand slam, but the man registered no interest.

"Doug? This is Joe, Joe Guilierno. A friend of Dynah's."

Doug looked up at the young man, as surprised by his appearance as Hannah had been. He reminded Doug of the guy on the TV show about immortals and swordplay. Tough. Ready for anything. He rose and extended his hand. Joe Guilierno's handshake was hard and firm, his eyes direct. Doug nodded once. "Nice to meet you, Joe. Have a seat."

"I'll get some coffee," Hannah said and headed for the kitchen.

Doug sank into his easy chair again, at a loss for words. He glanced at the television set.

"I take it you're not an A's fan," Joe said with a half smile, the TV announcer talking over the replay of the grand slam.

"I have season tickets," Doug said flatly. He picked up the remote control and punched a button. The room fell into silence.

Doug looked at the young man sitting on his couch and studied him again. Joe Guilierno had an air of confidence about him. He didn't sit uneasy but was relaxed, open, clearly concerned. "Dynah mentioned you," Doug said. He couldn't remember the context.

"I roomed with Ethan."

"Oh, that's right. You're the ex–gang member from Los Angeles, aren't you?"

Joe laughed, an easy sound at once admitting guilt and showing redemption. "Yes, sir."

"What brings you to San Francisco?"

"Dynah," Joe said frankly. Mr. and Mrs. Carey might as well know where he was coming from. "I graduated on the ninth and headed for California the next morning. I'm going to be taking some postgraduate courses at Berkeley."

"Berkeley," Doug said, impressed. "It's a little different from NLC."

"Like walking out of a hothouse and falling into the compost pile."

Doug smiled. He liked this young man. There was something about him that eased his mind. And heart. "I have a feeling you'll stay on the right track."

"With God's help. Now, about Dynah. Mrs. Carey said you don't know where she is. Are the police doing anything about it?"

"Nothing."

"Nothing?"

Hannah came back into the room with a tray. Joe glanced at her and smiled. She smiled back. She didn't know why, but she trusted him. "Dynah left us a note explaining why she felt she had to leave." She leaned down with the tray so Joe could take a mug of coffee and sugar or cream if he wanted. He took his coffee black with a murmured thanks.

"And she's twenty," Doug added grimly. "That makes her an adult."

"If you don't mind my asking, sir, what did her letter say?"

Hannah glanced at Doug.

"Go ahead and show him."

She set the tray down on the coffee table and took a single sheet of folded paper from her skirt pocket. She handed it to Joe. It was worn from reading.

Dear Mom and Dad and Granny,

I love you all very much, and I can't bear to hear you fighting over me. It's best if I leave. I need to make my decisions. When I do, the responsibility will rest on my head and no one else's. I promise I'll be careful wherever I go. Please try not to worry. I'm a big girl. I can take care of myself.

Please, please love one another. I can't bear to think that what's happened to me will tear you all apart. I'd rather die than have that happen.

I'll call you when I'm settled.

Dynah

Joe folded the note slowly and handed it back to Hannah. "Has she called?"

Hannah took the note. "Once," she said bleakly, tucking it safely into her skirt pocket again. "Doug and I were in church. She left a message on the answering machine. I'll let you hear it."

Joe rose and followed her into the kitchen. She pressed a button.

Joe heard Dynah's voice, quiet, tense, anything but all right: "I know you're both in church right now, and I'm sorry to call like this. I'm just not ready to hear what you have to say about what I've done."

Oh, God, Joe thought. *She did it.*

He heard Dynah sigh. She sounded tired, depressed. "I just wanted to let you know . . . I'm fine. I'm going to be OK."

She didn't say anything for a minute. Joe heard three cars pass in the background. He figured she was in a telephone booth somewhere.

"I'm sorry I left the way I did," she said softly, her voice choked, "but it's better this way." She was silent again. He could feel the heaviness of her heart through the wires. "I love you. I love you very, very much."

Click.

"That's all," Hannah said hoarsely. She listened to it several times a day, just to hear the sound of her daughter's voice.

Hannah's mother had gone home to Oregon after a week. Most of the time she had stayed she had spent upstairs in the guest room, weeping and praying for Dynah.

Each one of them felt to blame for Dynah's flight, though none of them had changed their opinion about what she should do. Evie was still adamantly against Dynah's having an abortion. Doug was as strong in his conviction that it was the only course to take. And Hannah was torn between the two, trusting Jim Wyatt more than husband or mother.

Joe stayed for two hours, Hannah sitting beside him, showing him albums of Dynah, from newborn to young womanhood. "These were taken at Pigeon Point. . . . These were taken at Dillon Beach. . . . These were taken at Mendocino. . . . That was at Fort Bragg. . . ." Page after page he turned, seeing Dynah's face, seeing her grow, his heart aching for her.

God, protect her. Keep her in the palm of your hand. Put a hedge around her. Send your angels to watch over her.

"This one was taken last summer," Hannah said.

Joe looked down at Dynah standing with Ethan, his arm around her shoulders. He looked proud and proprietary.

The perfect couple.

Until real life got in the way.

It hadn't taken Ethan long to find another picture-perfect girl. Mary looked a lot like Dynah—tall, slender, blonde, blue-eyed. Not as pretty, but she was a virgin and proud of it.

Joe had been torn between anger and relief when Ethan introduced him to Mary at the student union. Though Ethan had only taken her out twice at the time, the writing on the wall was plain. Block letters, bold faced. *Matrimony*. Ethan was ripe, and Mary was ready.

"God's timing is so perfect," Ethan had said, and Joe had wanted to hit him.

It was nothing against Mary. She was a beautiful girl and a committed Christian, but Joe couldn't help wondering how deep Ethan's love went and how quickly the flame would die at the first hint of trouble. Maybe the two of them would be lucky and live in a church all their lives, doors locked, stained glass over all the windows. They'd better not have many parishioners. Real people disappoint and disillusion.

Joe had done the only thing he could do. He wished them both well, packed up, and headed west.

"And Christmas," Hannah said, breaking into his grim thoughts. He gazed down at a picture of Dynah setting the table, and another of her decorating the tree with two friends from church. She was laughing, happy, eyes bright, so beautiful it hurt.

Where would she go, Lord? God, you helped me find her once. Help me find her again.

He remembered something Dynah had said at the prairie reserve.

"Mind if I look at those albums again?"

"Of course not." Hannah handed him three albums from the coffee table.

Joe paged through each one slowly, studying the scenes around Dynah this time.

And he knew where he was going to start looking.

■　■　■

Dynah awakened in the run-down motel on Highway 1, north of Fort Bragg. She had spent most of the night tossing and turning, wondering what she was going to do about a job. The area was depressed, with 17 percent unemployment. People with more qualifications than she had were out pounding the pavement. She didn't qualify for unemployment benefits. The clerk said she was sorry, but there were no jobs available. Those that opened up would go to locals receiving unemployment checks. The lady suggested she apply for welfare, but Dynah was too ashamed to follow through on that idea. She had spent her life listening to her father talking about people who had no pride and took advantage of the system. She didn't want to be someone "sucking up the hard-earned dollars of those who worked for a living." Her father said that was why California was in such a financial mess. He said there were always jobs to be had somewhere if one wanted one.

Where, Daddy? I've been looking for two weeks. I've talked to every business owner in Mendocino, including at all the bed-and-breakfasts.

She could make beds and clean houses, but most people said they were having to handle it themselves to save costs. She had been pounding the pavement in Fort Bragg for the past few days and was having no better luck.

Now she found herself down to her last ten dollars, and her car was running on fumes.

At least she had paid for this room through Friday. Two more days.

Lord, I need your help. I've been asking and asking. Do you want me to go home? You know what's waiting for me there if I do. What am I going to do?

The baby moved. She put her hands lightly over her swollen abdomen, her heart leaping with an odd mingling of joy and terror. Realization struck. She took her hands away quickly and sat up, pushing her hair back from her face. She wouldn't be in all this trouble if not for the baby she was carrying.

Guilt gripped her as she stood and went into the bathroom.

She stood in the shower for a long time, letting the warm water wash over her. It couldn't wash away her fear or despair.

I've just enough money to fill up my car. I could drive south toward Jenner and go right off that high cliff into the ocean. It would look like an accident. No one would feel to blame.

Turning the water up hotter, she tried to ward off the chill. Her skin was pink when she finally stepped out of the tub and dried herself. She caught a glimpse of herself in the long mirror on the door and stopped. Frowning, she lowered the towel and looked at her body. In another month, she wouldn't be able to hide her condition at all.

Who was going to hire an unwed girl in the advanced stages of pregnancy?

Dressing in an ankle-length flowered skirt and pale yellow tunic sweater, Dynah sat on the edge of her bed and picked up her Bible. She had been reading the Psalms, taking what comfort she could in David's anguish and frustration. More than half the songs were written when he was depressed or running from enemies or suffering from the sin he had allowed to come into his own life.

Oh, Lord, sometimes I know how David feels. Where are you when I need you? Why do you seem so far away? Why are you so silent? I can count my blessings from morning to night. I can remember all the things you've done for me from the time I was a little child. I remember and I cry out to you, and you're nowhere to be found.

I have lost my joy.

The only hope I have is the salvation you've given me through Jesus.

And the only way I can be with you is to die.

She remembered Joe again. How would he feel if she drove off that cliff a few miles north of Jenner? Would he think it was an accident? No. Would her parents believe it? Never.

Weary, she put her Bible back on the nightstand, put on her socks and shoes, and went out to try to find work again.

Deciding it would be more economical to walk, she parked her car on the north end of Fort Bragg. She would have breakfast at Maryann's Cafe. It looked inexpensive. Then she would knock on every door and ask for work until she reached the bridge at the far end of town. Then she'd come back up the other side doing the same thing. She had already applied at the larger stores and businesses and would pass by them.

She opened the door of the cafe. A bell jangled just above her head, announcing her entrance. Small empty tables lined the front windows. One old man sat at the counter. The place smelled of Chinese food.

A young woman came out from the back room. She was young, thin, had short black hair, and was dressed in faded Levi's and a T-shirt that said Hard Rock Cafe San Francisco. She took a menu from one of the counter racks and swept her hand about the empty room. "Take your pick."

Dynah hesitated, wishing she had chosen another place to eat. Maybe people in Fort Bragg knew something about this place that she didn't. Maybe the health department had just been here and threatened to shut them down. Maybe the last people who had eaten here were suffering from food poisoning. Chinese food for breakfast?

"It's good food," the waitress said. "I can swear by it. And it's cheap."

Too embarrassed to turn around and leave, Dynah gave her a tentative smile and chose a seat by one of the front windows so she could watch the cars go by.

The waitress put the menu down in front of her. "The American breakfast includes two eggs, sausage or bacon, hash browns, and toast for $2.99. Includes coffee and juice, orange or tomato."

"That sounds fine," Dynah said, not bothering to look at the menu. "Orange, please."

"Cream with your coffee?"

"Please. Do you have decaf?"

"I can brew a pot."

"Oh, don't trouble yourself."

"No trouble." She glanced down over Dynah. "Caffeine isn't good for you."

As the waitress walked away, Dynah glanced at the board with the day's luncheon specials, blushing and hoping the old man at the counter hadn't overheard the remark. He was looking at her. When he lost interest, she glanced around again, noting a chalkboard with luncheon selections. Mongolian beef, sweet-and-sour pork, and fried rice for $3.49. Other selections included broccoli and beef, egg drop soup, chow mein, and cashew chicken. The last item on the board was an American hamburger with french fries and cole slaw for $4.99.

She could hear two men behind the partition to the kitchen arguing in Chinese.

The waitress brought a tray back to Dynah. She set down a tumbler of ice water, a glass of orange juice, and a small pitcher of cream. "Fresh. The cow's out back. Just kidding. Coffee will be ready in two minutes."

Dynah could hear the hiss of something hitting the grill as the two men continued arguing.

Oh, Lord, what made me choose this place? Why didn't I walk a few more blocks and find one that had cars around it and people inside?

The coffee was good. Better than good.

When breakfast arrived, Dynah was amazed. Everything was fresh and delicious and prepared perfectly. The waitress kept her mug full and offered her a second glass of juice, no charge. "Everything fine?"

"Everything's wonderful," Dynah said, unable to understand why the place wasn't packed. She finally decided to ask.

"Because it's Maryann's."

"I beg your pardon?"

"You're not from around here, are you?"

Dynah shook her head.

"Well, Maryann owned this place for thirty years. Everybody in Fort Bragg knows and loves her. Well, she retired. No family to take over the business. Nobody around here had money enough to buy it. So, along comes my boss. A boat person. Not the sort out of Noyo Harbor, you know. I don't mean a fisherman. I mean one of those Vietnamese who came to the United States. He's a good guy. Not that anybody's given him much of a chance. A *gook*. That's what some people call him. Won't do business with a gook, you know. A lot of angry vets up here, out of work and looking for someone to blame. Charlie makes a good target."

"Charlie?"

She smiled slightly. "He Americanized his name. It hasn't helped, but at least I don't have to try to pronounce his Vietnamese one." She laughed. "He's cool. Worked hard for ten years to save enough to buy this little dump, and it looks like it's going to go bust. It's not fair." She shrugged, looking disheartened. "But that's the way the cookie crumbles, you know?"

"I guess."

"Bad part is I'm leaving for San Francisco today. My husband got a job down there. First job he's had in a year of looking. He found us a place. Charlie's in a fit back there with Ho Chi Minh. His brother. That's not his name. Just what I call him sometimes. Really bugs him. But he can get his dander up. Listen to him. Criminy! He notified the unemployment office two weeks ago when I gave my notice, and not one person has bothered to apply. He's royally ticked and ready to go declare war. Lotta good it'll do him."

Dynah blinked. "I need a job."

"You don't say! Really?"

"Yes. *Really.*"

"Well, I'll warn you, the pay's not great. Minimum wage. Hardly any tips. Gotta have customers to get tips, right?" She jerked her head toward the old man at the counter. "Harvey will leave you a quarter. He's a nice old man. A quarter for the coffee and a quarter tip. Every morning of the week. Comes in at eight. You can set your clock by him."

"I've been looking for work for two weeks. I'd just about given up hope."

"When would you like to start?"

Dynah gave a soft laugh. "How about right now?"

The waitress turned around. "Hey, Charlie. I've got a live one!" She grinned at Dynah. "He won't know what that means. He's still working on his English. You sit tight. I'll go tell him. My name's Susan, by the way."

"I'm Dynah. Dynah Carey."

Susan left the coffeepot on the table. Charlie came out thirty seconds after Susan went back. A small, wiry man with black hair and a gold-capped tooth in front, he shook her hand. The man behind the partition called out something, and Charlie called something back. It sounded like the cook was running a spoon back and forth on some pots and pans.

Susan rolled her eyes. "They get a little excited, you know? You'll get used to them."

Dynah was feeling good, really good for the first time in weeks. Minimum wage wasn't much, but it was enough to keep body and soul together.

"You come at right time, Dynah Carey," Charlie said. "If you not come today, tomorrow *I* be waiting tables, and then nobody come. Not even Harvey."

Harvey laughed. Unabashed, he turned on his stool and

looked straight at them. He didn't care if they knew he was listening. "She's pretty enough to bring you some customers, Charlie."

"What's wrong with me?" Susan said, hands on her hips. "Am I chopped liver or something?"

"You're cute, too, honey. Mouthy, but cute."

"We glad to make your acquaintance," Charlie said, pumping Dynah's hand.

"I'll show Dynah the ropes," Susan said.

"Ropes?" Charlie gave her a blank look and glanced around. "What ropes?"

Susan grinned at Dynah and patted Charlie's shoulder. "Never mind, Charlie. I'll train her. All right? Don't you worry about anything."

Charlie took Dynah's tab. "Meal free. Three squares a day. Very good for you and baby."

Dynah blushed.

Charlie headed back to the kitchen.

"Don't worry about it," Susan said gently. "You're in good company."

■ ■ ■

Joe drove all through Mendocino looking for Dynah's car. He spotted several of the same make, year, and model, but they were the wrong color and bore no fish symbol on the back or NLC sticker in the window. He parked and walked the streets crowded with summer tourists, asking business owners if she'd come in looking for work. Several remembered her but didn't know if she'd stayed in the area.

He camped at Salt Point and went to church in Mendocino on Sunday morning. It was a small, quaint church with a high-steepled New England design, the oldest on the West Coast, a historical landmark.

Dynah wasn't in attendance.

Since there was no other Christian church in the town, he figured she must have attended services elsewhere, probably up the coast at Fort Bragg.

He drove north and had a hamburger at McDonald's.

Maybe she headed home.

He found a pay phone and called the Careys.

"No, she's not here, Joe. She called again this morning while we were gone," Dynah's mother told him. "She sounded better this time, Joe. She found a place to live. She didn't say where. She said she has a job, but not what. She didn't leave a number. She wasn't on the line very long."

■ ■ ■

Dynah enjoyed her new job. The first few days were slow, and Harvey was the only regular. He came in every morning at eight, just as Susan had said he would. Dynah kept his coffee replenished while he read his newspaper. Sometimes he chatted with her about his years in the lumbering trade. From eight-thirty until just past ten, tourists came into the cafe, pausing in their scenic drive south, and Dynah was kept busy taking orders and serving. The tips were good. People tended to be generous to a pregnant waitress, especially one as young as she was.

As to lodgings, Dynah stayed where she was, content in the small motel above Highway 1. The manager was kind enough to hold winter rates for her on the agreement that Dynah would do her own housekeeping and handle a portion of the laundry. Each evening, following a long day of waiting tables, Dynah would tend the washing machine and dryer. Propping her feet up to ease the swelling, she would read her Bible while waiting for the wash cycle to end or the dryer to shut off. She usually finished her share of the workload by ten and went to bed immediately afterward.

Sunday was her only full day off. Exhausted, she attended the later services of a different church each week. Parishioners were friendly and curious. She didn't feel like talking about her circumstances and usually sat in the back where she could leave quietly and unobserved as soon as the worship services ended. Sometimes she departed before the pastor or priest made the walk to the door to give their blessings to attendees.

She didn't know what to do about the baby. All she knew was the problem wouldn't go away. Each day made it grow larger.

She was confused about everything. She hadn't been to see a doctor since the first weeks of pregnancy. Since she wasn't on welfare, she didn't think she was eligible for a free clinic, even if there was one in Fort Bragg. She didn't have the money for doctors visits, let alone a hospital delivery.

What was she going to do when the baby came? Have it in her motel room without assistance? Then what? Leave the baby on a church doorstep in the hope that someone might take it in, no questions asked?

God, what am I going to do?

She lay on the bed in her motel room night after night, staring at the ceiling, worrying about the future. The long hours on her feet working took a toll on her. Tonight she had fallen asleep in the laundry, the hum and roll of the dryer mesmerizing. Her back ached. Her feet and ankles were swollen. Her head ached.

A long hot shower helped ease her sore muscles. Climbing wearily into bed, she tucked an extra pillow between her knees to ease the ache in her lower back. Closing her eyes, she drifted off to sleep—only to find herself back in the clinic, Ms. Chambers blocking her way out. Her mother was at her side, holding her hand, drawing her toward an examining room where Dr. Wyatt waited. He was wearing a white coat and pulling on rubber gloves.

"It'll only take a few minutes, and it'll be all over."

Dynah could hear the sound of a machine in the background, like water being sucked down a drain. Someone was screaming. Was she the only one who heard it? How could they all stand and look so calm when someone was crying out like that?

"It's not so bad," Dr. Wyatt said.

"I don't want to do it!"

Ms. Chambers glared at her in contempt. "Don't be such a coward! I did it. Why shouldn't you have to do it, too?"

"You can't come home," her mother said. "Daddy won't let you."

"I can't do it!" Dynah broke free and ran into the corridor.

Ethan was sitting in a chair, his head in his hands. He looked up at her, his face streaked with tears. "You should've been my wife, but you're not good enough anymore."

Turning away, she saw her father standing at the counter. "I told you to get rid of it. It's a monster, and I won't have it in my house."

Crying, she ran down the hall, trying to find a way out. All the doors were locked. The hall turned to the right and then the left and the right again, growing narrower. She saw the door at the end and raced to it, pushing it open. Another door was on the other side, and Janet was standing in front of it.

"I don't see why you're making such an issue of it, Dynah. If anyone has the right, you do. Besides, it's no big thing. Everybody's doing it."

Dynah pushed past her to the door. When she opened it, she fell headlong into Dean Abernathy's office. He was in the process of shuffling stacks of papers on his desk. As she tumbled to the floor, he stopped and stared down at her. "She's in here! She's in here!"

She could hear the sound of running feet coming closer and closer, and she clambered to her feet.

Dean Abernathy stood and came around his desk.

Dynah sat up abruptly, bathed in perspiration, her heart pounding. Trembling, she drew the blankets more tightly around her and listened.

The room was dark and quiet, the digital alarm clock on the bedside table reading 3:45.

How long, Oh Lord? How long will you forsake me? I'm alone. I'm afraid. I don't know what to do. How is it I felt your presence all my life and now you are nowhere to be found? Was my relationship with you an illusion? Were the stories of you merely fairy tales told to me by my father and mother? Where is your protection? Where is your mercy?

Unable to sleep, she got up at five and showered again. It was Sunday, but she didn't feel like attending church. Instead, she drove down the coast to Mendocino.

She parked on Kasten Street in front of the bakery. Hungry, she purchased a freshly baked apple fritter and a tall Styrofoam cup of steaming French roast coffee laced with cream. Wandering along Main Street, she paused to admire the Kelley House, a Victorian restored by citizens of the community and made into a museum. It wouldn't open for hours yet. Across the street was Jerome B. Ford House, a state museum. Beyond were the trails along the cliffs overlooking Portuguese Beach. She walked the meandering path through the grasses to the Point.

A lumber mill had stood here a hundred years ago when Mendocino was a bustling community made up of seafaring men from New England, Scandinavia, Portugal, China, and the Azores. Immigrants had flooded California during the gold rush. By the 1880s, mining and whaling had diminished, but the wave still came, bringing farmers, fishermen, and loggers.

She stood at the edge of the Point watching the waves crash on the rocks, white spray bursting into the air, foam swirling, the cool mist stinging her cheeks. She drew her jacket more closely around her, awed by the power of the sea.

O Lord God, who is like you? You are almighty, creator of heaven and earth. Your faithfulness surrounds me. You rule the swelling sea. When its waves rise, only you can still them.

Closing her eyes, she lifted her face, feeling the salt wind caress her. Opening her arms, she opened her heart to the Lord as well. And then she could hear his voice again. Oh, God, oh, God.

Oh, Father, I have treasured your Word in my heart so that I might not sin against you—but now I see I haven't heeded that Word. That's why I've been so distressed. That's why I've received no answer to my prayers. Oh, God, all this time I've been asking your permission to end the life of this child. I've asked you to take it from me. I've asked for your approval of sin. Forgive me, Lord. My God, you have never forsaken me. I'm the one who turned away from you.

Jesus, forgive me. Oh, Father, I long for you. Sometimes I wish you were here in body. Sometimes I wish I could feel your arms around me, holding me.

Oh, Father, open my eyes, that I may behold the wonderful things you have done for me. Set my feet upon the rock, Lord. Anchor me in your love. My faith is weak, as I am weak. You alone are my strength and shield. You alone, Lord. You alone.

■ ■ ■

Joe found her car and parked beside it. It was early yet, stores closed, streets empty. Only a few restaurants and cafes were open. The doorbell jangled as he entered the bakery. The waitress said a girl who fit the description he gave had come in and purchased an apple fritter and coffee an hour ago.

Borrowing a pen, he wrote a quick note on a napkin. "Hold tight. I'm looking for you. Joe." He stuck it under the windshield wiper of Dynah's car and started off. He hadn't gone twenty feet when he came back. Popping open her hood, he pulled out the rotor and pocketed it. He wasn't taking any chances.

Walking briskly along Main Street, he passed a dozen people out taking morning strolls. Across the street were the Mendocino headlands and the cliffs overlooking Big River, the Bay, and the grand Pacific for as far as the eye could see. Several pairs of joggers were running the trails. Then Joe stopped, narrowing his eyes.

Someone was out there, standing on the far point looking at the Pacific Ocean. Long blonde hair twirled in the wind.

"Yes!" Joe said under his breath. Thanking God, he crossed the street and strode toward her. When he came closer, he slowed, watching how she wrapped her arms around herself as the wind came up, her ankle-length flowered skirt fluttering around her slender legs. She was wearing hiking boots and thick socks.

As though feeling his presence, she turned. Joe watched her eyes widen in surprise. He smiled, walking toward her.

"Joe," she said, clearly unable to believe she was really seeing him.

He stopped in front of her, drinking in the sight of her. Her cheeks were wind-stung pink, her blue eyes solemn. She had lost the hunted look.

"Hi," he said. When her arms loosened about herself, he put his arms around her, his heart taking a flip when he felt her hands slide around his back, returning the embrace. He felt the fullness of her body and thanked God again. She hadn't given in after all. Praise God!

Dynah leaned into him, savoring his warmth, feeling his hand lightly cup the back of her head, moving down over her back in a comforting caress. "What are you doing here, Joe?"

"You broke a date. The fifteenth. Remember?"

She withdrew. "Oh. I forgot. I'm sorry."

He smiled, tucking a strand of blonde hair behind her ear. "I forgive you."

"How did you find me?"

"You talked about this area at the prairie reserve, remember? And your mom showed me the family albums. I started at Dillon Beach and worked my way north."

"Oh, Joe. All that trouble . . ."

"No trouble." He tipped her chin up playfully. "You look good, Dynah. Real good."

Blushing, she laughed self-consciously. "Growing by the day," she said and opened her coat.

"You're doing the right thing."

She closed the coat around her again to ward off the cool wind. "Don't credit me with anything, Joe. I haven't been able to make up my mind up to this point."

"And now?"

"I'll go through with it, whatever it takes."

They walked along the cliff trail and down the beach. The sun was up, clouds clearing, the wind a whisper over the sand where the Big River met Mendocino Bay. The day warmed.

Dynah removed her coat and sat down on it. She took off her hiking boots and socks and stretched her legs out in front of her, pulling her skirt up so that her knees and calves took the sunshine.

"You look tired," Joe said.

"I haven't been sleeping very well."

And no wonder, he thought, having to make it all on her own. "Have you seen a doctor?"

She shook her head. "Not since leaving school."

"We'll get you an appointment."

She looked at him. "We?" She smiled faintly. "Are you going to take care of me, Joe? Are you going to solve all my problems?"

"You think I've been looking for you just to say hi and 'bye? I'll stand by you."

She searched his eyes. "I know we're friends, Joe, but there's more, isn't there? Why does it matter so much to you that I have this baby?"

Joe had known she'd ask him someday, just as he'd known he'd have to answer. At least in part. The rest in time, God willing.

"I got a girl pregnant when I was seventeen. She had an abortion."

She closed her eyes and raised her knees, drawing her skirt down like a silken tent, wrapping her arms around her legs. "Did you love her?"

He looked out at the waves crashing on the rocks across the bay. "No." Sighing, he lowered his head and closed his eyes. "Sex was the big thing with me in those days. . . ." He glanced at Dynah, relieved to see she didn't look disgusted.

"I'm listening, Joe."

He didn't like talking about his past, but she needed to know. "It was a gang thing, making conquests. The guys considered an illegitimate baby a trophy. Children were a physical proof of manhood." He shook his head in disgust. "I bought into the whole mentality until Teresa got pregnant. Then reality struck. Hard."

He spoke slowly. "She didn't want to have the baby. She was afraid her parents would kick her out. My mother said she'd take her in. She even offered to adopt the baby. Teresa said she'd think about it and let me know. She called me two days later and told me she'd had an abortion."

His dark eyes filled with tears. "It still gets me in the gut sometimes. I've heard all the rhetoric about it being her body, her choice, and I understand all that. The trouble is, you can't reason away some things. You can't alter human nature. That baby was mine, too, part of my flesh and blood. When Teresa aborted my child, it was like she killed part of me."

"Did you hate her for it?"

"Yeah, I hated her. For a long time." His mouth tipped in self-contempt. "Not that anyone knew how I felt. I was a cool dude in those days. Nothing fazed me. It was easier blaming her than facing my part in the fiasco."

Looking away, he let out his breath. He rested his forearms on his raised knees and was quiet for a long time. "Teresa and I didn't last a month after she had the abortion. We were both angry. When we broke up, she got involved with another guy in the gang. Four months later, she was pregnant again. She had another abortion."

Agitated, he stood up and moved a little away from her. He stared out over the rippling water. "Last time I was home, I looked her up. I wanted to make amends for my part in what happened. She's living in Watts. She has two children by different fathers. She's drinking, using dope, and living on welfare. Her life's a mess."

"Not everyone who has an abortion ends up like that, Joe."

"No—" he turned to look at her—"but sometimes I wonder if there aren't a lot of people out there like me. Playing it cool. Acting like nothing fazes them. Pretending it doesn't matter. All the while dying inside."

Dynah thought of her mother and grandmother. How many others suffered in silence, too ashamed and too afraid to speak about their pain? The world wouldn't let them grieve for children they had aborted. How could they when the rhetoric said there was no child? How does one grieve what doesn't exist? No one wanted to admit the truth. Even those who never had part in a decision of life and death suffered. Like her father.

She remembered a speaker at NLC saying one-and-a-half million babies were aborted every year. His focus had been on the children lost. Now, she wondered how many mothers cried in anguish over their decision. How many fathers felt as helpless and angry as Joe? What of the men and women who married them later and lived in the shadow of death? What of their children? What of the generations to come?

The weight of such grief and guilt was overwhelming.

And it occurred to her, maybe that was why everyone said it didn't exist. Not the child. Not the guilt. Not the consequences.

"One decision can permeate your entire life," Joe said grimly. Your family. Your community. Your nation.

"God can forgive anything."

Joe's mouth tipped in a half smile. "I know he's forgiven me, and I'm grateful. What happened is a big part of the reason I came to Christ. Letting go of it is something else."

She scooped a handful of sand and let it sift through her fingers. "Are you atoning, Joe? Is that why you're so set on helping me have this baby?" Was his assistance aimed at purging himself of guilt?

Joe came back and hunkered down beside her. He tipped her chin, waiting until she looked him straight in the eyes. "I don't want to see you hurt any more than you've been hurt already."

"Life hurts. You can't get away from it."

"Yeah." He brushed his knuckles lightly against her cheek. "It does." Some got hurt more than others.

She rose and walked down to the water, standing close enough that the waves lapped her feet and dampened the hem of her skirt. Joe removed his boots and socks and joined her, standing at her side, not saying anything.

Dynah looked up at the blue skies. "You know the strange part? I don't hate the man who raped me. I see him as a child of wrath who didn't know any better. Oh, he hurt me. He hurt me more than he'll ever know, but it was mostly physical." Her eyes filled. "It's the others, Joe. It's the ones who should've known better and still bought into the lies. Those are the ones who've hurt me most. Ethan. Janet. Dean Abernathy. Pastor Whitehall. My own mother and father. They never meant to betray me, but they did."

She looked up at him, tears slipping down her cheeks. "I had to get out, Joe. I had to get away. Can you understand that?" Her eyes glistened. "It'd been so long since I felt close to the Lord. I couldn't hear him anymore. I couldn't feel him close to me. I even began to doubt he existed. I felt forsaken."

"And now?"

She took a shuddering breath and released it, her body relaxing. She looked oddly at peace. "I think I did what he wanted me to do. 'Come out from them and be separate,' he said. Not just in a physical sense, by running away, but by seeing things through his eyes, understanding the truth. I have to be separate in my way of thinking and not let my emotions rule. Oh, and they have ruled, Joe. They've ruled for months. I've let myself be kept in turmoil, stumbling every which way I turn."

"And no wonder."

"Don't make excuses for me. The world's too good at that."

There was a new steadiness in her he had never seen before. It suited her.

"I knew the truth, Joe. I've always known. It's as though God put it in me from the moment I was conceived. I was just too afraid to live it out."

Taking his hand, she squeezed it lightly and smiled up at him. "I'm not afraid anymore. I'm going to have this child. Beyond that, I'll wait and see what the Lord wills."

Withdrawing her hand, she turned away, lifting her face to the sunshine. Closing her eyes, she felt the warmth. Inhaling the scent of sea and pine, warm sand and fresh air, she felt more alive than she had ever felt before.

Joe watched her, thanking God for the change in her. She had not allowed anyone to take anything away from her.

Dynah laughed. "Oh, Joe, it's amazing," she said, feeling movement inside her womb. She ran her hands down slowly over her body. She lowered her head, waiting, and felt it again. She smiled. "It's a miracle when you think about it," she said softly. "The night I was raped, the doctor told me the chances of my getting pregnant were almost nil. And yet, it happened. There must be some purpose, some reason only God knows, for this child to be born."

Joe drank in the beauty of her, watching the wonder in her expression, the way her hands moved like a caress over the unborn child.

She looked up at him. "All things work together for the good of those who love God and are called according to his purpose for them. Isn't that true, Joe?"

"That's what Scripture says."

She smiled, eyes shining with gentle humor at his solemnity. "A noble utterance." Even he wasn't fully convinced. He was still caught up in the unfairness of what had happened to her.

God never promised life would be fair. He offered a simple choice: justice or grace.

I choose your grace, Lord. Thanks be to God. You are my Lord, the lover of my soul.

"I know it won't be easy. I'm weak. Day in and day out, it's going to be a battle to keep the faith and wait to see what the Lord has planned. But what other alternative is there but death? I choose life. I choose to believe God's Word. I choose to believe in his presence and his promises. I choose to have this child. I choose to believe that God is the Father of the fatherless."

She put her hands over the unborn child, her gesture protective and tender. "However this child was conceived, God will be the Father. My baby won't enter the world unloved or unwanted. If I can't feel a full measure of joy, I know the Lord will."

Joe stroked the tendrils of blonde hair back from her face. "So be it."

Surrendering to impulse, Dynah stepped close and slipped her arms around his waist, hugging him hard. "I am so blessed to have you as a friend," she said in a choked voice. Afraid she'd embarrassed him, she withdrew quickly and walked away.

Joe closed his eyes, his pulse hammering. *Oh, God, God, you know my heart. Forgive me. I ask too much.*

Dynah picked up her coat and shook the sand from it. "What do you say I treat you to lunch?" she said, slipping her arms into the sleeves. She picked up his jacket. "I know a place at Noyo Harbor where they serve wonderful clam chowder."

He walked up the beach toward her. "You're on." Taking his jacket, he flipped it over one shoulder and fell into step beside her.

"They're such beggars," Dynah said, looking out the restaurant window and smiling as she watched the sea lions pop up and bark near a fishing boat. "Mom and Dad and I stayed at the Harbor Lite a few years ago. They barked all through the night."

"Doesn't look like they're getting much."

"I think they manage more than their share. Look how big that one is."

The waitress delivered two bowls of steaming clam chowder. At Dynah's request, Joe said grace. "Hmmmm," Joe said after his first spoonful. "It's as good as you said it'd be."

They ate in companionable silence, enjoying the view of Noyo Bridge, the sea beyond, and the fishing boats moored along the river.

Dynah tore off a piece of sourdough French bread and began to butter it. "How's Ethan?"

Joe had known the question would come up sooner or later. "He's OK."

"Just OK? Did he lose his class standing?" She knew how hard he had worked to be the best.

"No. He graduated with honors. Dean Abernathy asked him to give the commencement speech. It was a good one. He based

it on Timothy and retaining the standard Christ has given us."
Grimacing at the edge to his voice, he dipped his spoon into the
chowder again, hoping she'd leave the subject of Ethan alone.

Dynah sensed something in his silence. She knew Joe was
withholding something. Lowering her eyes, she continued eating her chowder. She had the baby to think about now. She
couldn't afford to lose her appetite. She would finish her meal
before she asked any more questions.

Joe finished first and sipped his coffee. He knew she was
distracted, and he knew why. *What am I going to tell her, Lord?
That Ethan waited three weeks before finding another prospec-
tive bride? How's that going to make Dynah feel? Don't let her
ask about him, God. Please.*

Dabbing her lips, Dynah put the napkin on the table. She
leaned back slightly and looked at him. "Go ahead and tell
me."

He put his mug of coffee down slowly. "Tell you what?"

"Don't play dumb."

He looked away, staring out over the water of the Noyo
River. *Jesus! Hasn't she been hurt enough?* "He's going out with
someone."

Dynah sat quietly, waiting for the pain to come. She expected
it to arrive in waves, pressing her down beneath the onslaught
until she drowned. It didn't happen. The news didn't hurt as
much as she'd expected. In fact, it barely hurt at all. Other
concerns rose instead. "Is she a Christian?"

Joe looked at her, studying her intently. No tears. "Yes."

"Is she nice?"

"Yes."

"Pretty?"

"Yes."

She saw the darkening in his eyes. "Don't be angry for me,
Joe. It's all right."

"Is it?"

She smiled. "It was bound to happen. Girls were always vying for Ethan's attention. You know that better than I do. I was always amazed he chose me."

"I was amazed he let you go."

She was touched by his quick defense. "Thank you, Joe."

The waitress came with the check. "It's on me," Dynah said before Joe could take it.

"Why don't I follow you back to your place?" Joe said, pulling back her chair and helping her shrug into her jacket. "You can leave your car, and we can take a drive around town. You can show me where you work, where you go to church, where you hang out."

Dynah laughed, wondering what he would make of "her place."

"Cozy," he said when she ushered him in. No leaks or water stains on the ceiling. A good lock on the door. The motel room was clean and simply furnished, with a queen-size bed, a dresser, two side tables, a television in the corner, and a table by the sliding-glass windows. The bed was made, the drapes were open to allow the sun to stream in, and a worn Bible was open on the side table. He noticed a hot plate on the vanity counter. Cans of Campbell's soup were stacked beneath the mirror, along with a box of saltine crackers, two Red Delicious apples, a small jar of peanut butter, a banana, and a bottle of multiple vitamins.

"The manager has been very kind to me," she said as they went back out and she locked the door. "I help with the laundry, and he keeps my rent at winter rates."

They drove to Maryann's first. Charlie's sister was working and greeted her with a warm smile.

"Hey, Dynah!" Harvey called from the counter, where he was sitting with two of his friends, both of whom had become regulars over the past week. "Who's the gent?"

"A friend," she said and made introductions all around. She took Joe back into the kitchen to meet Charlie.

Leaving Maryann's, they walked along Main Street. Dynah told him the history of the town. Sitting on a bench, they watched the Skunk Train come in from Willits, disgorging its tourists.

They walked up to North Franklin and the antique stores and stopped in at Schats for coffee and a fresh baked apple fritter. "What are you going to do about your parents?" Joe said finally, knowing they had to talk about it. "You want me to call them?"

"I'll call, Joe. I don't want to put you in the middle of all this."

"You can't make it here alone."

"Why not?

"For one thing, you haven't got the money for proper medical care. For another, what are you going to do when the baby comes? You won't be able to work."

She turned her head away. "I haven't looked that far ahead."

"It's not that far, Dynah. Only three more months."

"Then I guess I'll have to think about it pretty soon." She didn't want to talk about it now. Time enough tomorrow when he was gone. God would take care of her.

Joe wasn't going to leave things as they were. "There's a free clinic in Berkeley."

"Berkeley's a long way off."

"I have a two-room apartment."

She looked at him in surprise. "What're you suggesting? I move in with you?"

"Yes."

"Joe . . ."

"You can have the bedroom. I'll bunk down in the living room."

"Joe."

"Hear me out. I am *not* leaving you here on your own. Like it or not, we need to settle this. Today. I'm not going to let you have the baby all by yourself in that motel room. I'd live up here if I could, but my classes started, and the job I have lined up is connected to my attendance at the university."

"Joe . . ."

"It's Berkeley with me or San Francisco with your parents."

She winced as she thought of facing them again.

Joe took her hand and held it firmly in both of his. "You came up here because you didn't know what to do, right? Now you know. You're going to have the baby. You needed time alone before the Lord. You've had that. You can have it any-where you go. You know what he wants of you now, Dynah. You don't need to hide anymore."

He was right, but her heart trembled at the thought of going home.

"Oh, God," she said softly, closing her eyes. She had more choices to make than he knew. He was assuming she would keep the child. But should she? Could she be the parent the child needed? And what of *her* life? *Her* plans? She had never thought she'd be a single parent, or a parent at all for years to come. How could she provide for the child and herself? One problem seemed to roll into a dozen others.

"Be not anxious about tomorrow," the Lord said. *I will not be anxious. I will take things day by day. I will. I will!*

"Which is it going to be, Dynah?"

"I'd rather live with you than go home," she said with a weak smile and then shook her head. "But it wouldn't be right."

"What'd be wrong with it?"

"People would assume I'm having your child, Joe."

"So what? It's no skin off my nose."

She blushed. "We're Christians. We have to care what people

think. The appearance of wrongdoing, remember? I'm not going to move in with you and have people think we're living in sin. What sort of witness would that be?"

"Believe me, Dynah, nobody cares, especially in Berkeley. I could walk down University Avenue in a dress with my hair dyed blue, and no one would blink twice."

She gave a soft laugh and fell silent, solemn. "What about my parents?"

"You know them better than I do."

"They'd mind, Joe. They'd make assumptions. I wouldn't want them thinking ill of you."

"OK. Then it's San Francisco."

"Oh, Joe . . ."

"Don't 'oh, Joe' me."

"Give me a week to think about it."

"No way. Two minutes after I leave, you'll take off again."

"No, I won't."

"Yeah, right," he said glumly. He'd probably be combing the Oregon coast for her in a week. Or maybe she'd head for the woods this time. The high Sierras, the Grand Tetons, or the misty Olympics. *Lord, is this the way you're answering my prayer to see the country?* he asked wryly. *Having me chase after Dynah?*

"I promise, Joe."

He looked at her and watched the endearing smile light her face. "Don't soft-soap me."

"You can take my rotor with you, if you like."

His mouth tipped ruefully. "Don't think I won't."

■　■　■

Joe checked into the motel where Dynah was living. He figured he could stay another day before heading back to the Bay Area. By then, he hoped Dynah would make up her mind.

Dynah rang his room at six. "I'm going to be working this evening. Maria has the flu, and Concepción finishes her shift in half an hour. She can't work late. . . . She has a family waiting for her."

"I'll help out."

She laughed. "OK. I'll meet you in the laundry room." She told him where to find it.

Joe spent the evening shuffling bath towels and sheets from washing machine to dryer. By ten, they were folding and stacking linens on the cart for Maria's rounds the next morning. It was eleven before the work was done.

Pale with exhaustion, Dynah wished him good night. Joe knew she had to be up and at Maryann's by eight.

Neither slept well. Joe prayed far into the night, while Dynah tossed and turned with troubled dreams. She knew Joe wanted to take care of her, and she was half willing to allow him to do so. Yet she also knew God had something else in mind. Like Joshua, the Lord was telling Dynah to go forth into the Promised Land, and still she stood on the desert side, afraid to put her feet in the water.

It would be so easy to move in with Joe and allow him to take care of her. It was what he wanted to do. She wouldn't have to face her parents. They wouldn't even have to know. She could lick her wounds in private, have the child, and give it up for adoption. She could have her life back. She could forget the past and start over.

Haven't I suffered enough, Lord? The world has crushed me. I'm going to have the child, isn't that enough? Oh, God, what more do you want of me?

EVERYTHING. OBEY ME, AND I WILL ESTABLISH YOUR FAMILY IN THE PROMISED LAND. I WILL SET YOUR FEET UPON THE ROCK. I WILL BLESS YOU FOR GENERATIONS TO COME.

I felt so happy yesterday. I felt close to you again. I'm happy where I am. I can get by.

I WILL GIVE YOU LIFE ABUNDANT.

I don't want to go home, Lord. Can't you understand? I don't want to hear them fighting over what I should or shouldn't do. I don't want to know about what my mother did or my grandmother did. It was their life, their decision, their sin. Why should I feel the weight of it? I don't want the burden of their pain. I've enough of my own.

YOU CAN DO ALL THINGS IN ME, BELOVED. TRUST AND OBEY.

What purpose does it serve, Lord? Tell me and maybe then I'll do what you want.

TRUST AND OBEY.

It's not that easy. What about Charlie? How can I quit after three weeks and leave him in the lurch? What'll he do for a waitress now that Susan is settled in San Francisco? Hire Harvey?

Plagued, she arose before dawn and showered. She glanced at Joe's car as she went out, half wishing he hadn't found her. Just when she had come to terms with having the baby, he had to arrive and remind her of all the other things she needed to consider.

Charlie was always at Maryann's by six, getting everything ready for the new day. She tapped on the window, and he let her in. "You early."

"I couldn't sleep," she said, looking for something to do. Charlie's sister had refilled all the salt-and-pepper shakers, the ketchup, soy sauce, and mustard. The tables were set with napkins and silverware. The floor was washed and polished.

"You sit on stool." Charlie pointed. "I fix you bacon and eggs and some hash browns. My wife not sleep too good when this far along with our son."

"I didn't know you were married, Charlie."

"Long time ago in Vietnam. My wife work for American soldiers in Hue. Cook, clean up, like you."

She waited quietly, watching him, hoping he would tell her more.

"Vietcong took city. Shot my wife. I never know what happen to my son." He eased her eggs over so as not to break the yolks. He didn't look at her. "I search for long time and find nothing. When Americans leave, my family flee to Cambodia. We live five years in camps before we come to America. Too late now to go back and start again. My son be grown man. If he alive."

Her chest ached. "I'm sorry, Charlie."

He looked at her. "Why you be sorry? You not there. You do nothing wrong." He scooped her eggs onto a plate, adding bacon, hash browns, a twist of orange and a sprig of parsley. "I am here. I am free. I have work. I have my brother and sister. I am a rich man. Come. Eat." He carried her plate into the dining room and put it on a table by a front window. "Sit. I bring you juice."

Tears pricked her eyes. "Thank you, Charlie."

He patted her shoulder and walked away.

Staring down at the meal, she thanked God for his mercy.

Oh, Lord, in the face of others' suffering, how do you stand my constant whining?

Harvey came and brought three friends with him. He ordered his usual coffee while the others had breakfast. All four launched into a political debate. Two families stopped in at eight-forty-five and were followed by three more within the next ten minutes. Maryann came in at nine and sat at the counter. Showing her deference, Charlie served her himself, leaving the cooking to his brother Ng. Charlie and Maryann talked like old friends.

"She want to work," Charlie said after Maryann left. "She tell me she misses this place. She has nothing to do. She say she sick of talk shows and soap opera."

Dynah knew there wasn't enough work or money to keep both of them busy full time. God was giving her more than a nudge: He was giving her the boot.

Joe came in at nine-fifteen.

"You look like you need a cup of coffee," Dynah said, pot poised as she set a mug before him "What would you like for breakfast?"

"Surprise me," he said, hanging over his mug, food the last thing on his mind. He'd been praying most of the night, asking God for the desire of his heart.

"Charlie makes great pancakes."

"Sounds fine."

She put in the order. Joe had drained his mug by the time she turned around. She refilled it. "I'll go home the end of the week, Joe."

San Francisco instead of Berkeley. *So be it, Lord*. Joe raised his head and looked at her. "I'll go with you when you talk to your parents."

"I appreciate the offer, Joe, but I have to go alone. I'm not sure what to expect."

"All the more reason I should be with you."

"I'll call first and test the waters."

"And if they're still cold and stormy?"

Her mouth tipped ruefully. "Trust me, Joe. I'm not going to change my mind about having the baby."

Joe pushed his coffee cup aside. "Promise me something. Call me whatever you do. Make it a once-a-week thing. I'm not good at guessing what's happening, and I care about you." He couldn't say more than that without adding to her burdens. He held his hand out, palm up for a high five.

Dynah took his hand in both of hers. "Once a week. I promise. Only, one thing, Joe."

"Anything."

Her blue eyes lightened with amusement. "I need your number."

■ ■ ■

Hannah heard the quiet whir of the garage door going up and then closing. Doug was home from the deacons meeting. She had expected him by nine-thirty. It was almost eleven. Under normal circumstances she wouldn't have waited up, but Dynah had called. Hannah needed to tell him what was coming, prepare him and herself for the future. She needed to pave the way for Dynah.

God, soften his heart. Give me the words so he will hear. Open his eyes to the pain he could cause.

Her heart thumped as the back door opened. She breathed in deeply through her nose and slowly exhaled through pursed lips, hoping the technique would calm her.

Doug entered the family room and saw Hannah sitting in her swivel rocker, one of his shirts on her lap. She was sewing on a button. He looked at her face and something down deep inside tightened.

"The meeting went long tonight," she said quietly.

"The meeting was over by nine," he said, dropping his jacket onto the arm of the sofa. "I stayed and talked with Dan."

"About Dynah?"

He sat down and rubbed his face. Raking his hands back through his graying hair, he leaned back in his chair, let out his breath, and looked at her. "She called tonight, didn't she?"

Hannah nodded, her eyes filling with tears. *God, I can hardly breathe, let alone tell him what she's decided. Help me, Jesus. Help us.*

Doug raised his head slightly. "And?"

"She wants to come home."

"Thank God."

Hannah swallowed. "She wants to have the baby."

He shut his eyes. He had just spent two hours talking with his pastor. He had spilled his guts about Dynah and his part in sending her on the run. Within an hour, Dan had pried the rest out of him. The pain of twenty-seven years had boiled over, and he had wept like a child.

Opening his eyes, he looked at his wife. "Dan wants to talk with you."

"About what?"

He paused. "About everything."

Her hands whitened on the shirt she was mending. "What *everything?*" When he didn't say anything, she knew. She could see it in his face. She dropped the shirt into the basket. He could sew his own buttons on. He could wash his own dirty laundry. "So that's why this evening went so long," she said quietly. "You were busy confessing my sins and absolving yourself."

Doug heard the bitterness in her voice and understood it for the first time. "I'm sorry," he said simply. "I'm sorry, Hannah."

"Sorry about what? Sorry you married me? Sorry I gave you a daughter who got herself raped?" Her mouth trembled, and the tears came hot. "I'm sorry, too, Doug. Sorry I ever trusted you. I knew the day I told you what I did nothing would ever be the way I hoped. I gave you the club, and you've beaten me with it ever since. I'm sorry I ever trusted you with my love and my life."

She saw her words strike deep, and she was glad. She wanted to hurt him. She wanted to annihilate him just as he had annihilated her countless times with a look or a careless toss of angry words. How long had she lived under the mountain of stones?

"The one good thing I have from you is Dynah. I thank God for her every day of my life. She's the *only* thing that makes it worth living. And I'll tell you something else, Doug. I will never—do you hear me?—*never*, take her into another abortion clinic! Rant and rave all you want at me. I don't care. Divorce me. *Please*. Put an end to the hypocrisy. Tell Dan and the whole congregation what a whore you married and what a mistake you made from the beginning. I don't care what you say or do anymore. The *only* thing I care about is Dynah." She stood. "One more thing. If you say one word to her about getting rid of this child, I swear before God, I'll pack and leave you and never forgive you!" She walked out of the room.

Doug turned the light out and sat in the dark far into the night. He prayed. He prayed as he had never prayed before. His ears were open, and the sounds of mourning vibrated in the silence. His eyes could see the shattered pieces of the two people he loved most in the world. And his heart was broken.

Oh, God, why do we always hurt the ones we love?

When the clock chimed three, he went upstairs to an empty bed. Hannah had moved into the guest room.

■   ■   ■

Dynah took the Boonville Road to Cloverdale. She stopped at a Frosty Freeze and had an ice-cream cone dipped in chocolate. It brought back fond memories of her childhood and trips north with her parents. She drove through town rather than back-track to the freeway.

I'll be home before I'm ready, Lord. Make me ready.

She had dreamed about Dr. Wyatt the night before, a disturbing dream she couldn't quite remember. It was on the edge of her mind niggling, nudging.

His sister died from an illegal abortion.

Had he said that in the restaurant, or was she imagining it?

She kept remembering the look on his face as he spoke with her. Why did it hurt so much?

Lord, he's an abortionist. I don't want to go anywhere near him again. . . . Help me protect my child.

James Michael Wyatt.

She couldn't exorcise him.

She drove past Healdsburg and Windsor. Traffic was slow going through Santa Rosa, speeding up through Rohnert Park and Cotati. After that, she felt as though she were flying toward disaster. What was waiting for her in San Francisco?

San Rafael lay up ahead, five lanes of traffic narrowing into three. Why did she have this sick feeling in her stomach? Why was her head pounding so hard her vision was blurry at times? Maybe she was hungry. Maybe she should stop and have something to eat.

A high green freeway sign read East Blightdale.

"Cynthia and I have a place in Mill Valley."

Dynah took the off ramp. The gas tank was half empty, and she needed to use a rest room anyway. This seemed as good a place as any to stop. Pulling into a Chevron station, she chose the full-serve lane. Her back ached as she got out of the car. An attendant approached.

"Could you direct me to your telephone?"

"Inside, near the back. Before you get to the rest room."

"Thanks."

She used the ladies' room first. Her ankles were swollen, and her backache worsened.

Paging through the telephone book, she looked for James Michael Wyatt, M.D. He wasn't listed.

C. Wyatt was.

"Cynthia and I have a place in Mill Valley."

Jotting down the street address, she went back outside and asked the station attendant for directions.

As she got into her car, she grimaced.

The attendant leaned down and looked at her. "You OK, miss?"

Forcing a smile, she started the car. "I'm fine, thanks."

She found the house without trouble. It was a two-story gabled house in yellow and white. A high, decorative, black iron fence surrounded it with small steel notices warning intruders that a security system was in place. The lawn and shrubbery behind the fence were perfectly manicured. Marigolds, alyssum, and Royal Salvia were planted in neat rows along the curving walkway to a carved oak door, which boasted stained-glass panels.

A large terra-cotta pot with a neatly pruned miniature Japanese maple stood on the cobbled front steps.

Dynah found the button for the intercom by the gate and pressed it. She expected to wait for someone to ask what her business was. Instead, the lock clicked, and the gate popped open. Surprised to be admitted so easily, she opened it and went through. As she approached the front door, she could hear the ferocious barking of a big dog somewhere in the house.

A little girl opened the front door.

"Hello," Dynah said and smiled at the adorable child in designer coveralls, a pink T-shirt, and long red pigtails.

The little girl smiled back. "Hello."

"Cricket, where are you? Don't open the door, honey! Wait for Mommy!"

"Close the door like your mother says, sweetheart," Dynah said. "I'll wait." She glimpsed a lovely woman dressed in Levi's and a tank top in the corridor just as the child did as she told her. At the woman's side was a large black Rottweiler.

Waiting on the doorstep, Dynah could hear the mother speaking firmly to the child behind the door. She sounded distressed and was reprimanding the child for disobedience. A moment later, the door opened again, this time with the woman standing before her, the dog standing guard beside her.

"I'm sorry, but if you're a solicitor, I'm not buying anything."

"I'm not," Dynah assured her. "Does Dr. James Wyatt live here?"

"My daddy's a doctor," Cricket piped up, "but he's not home now. He will—"

"Go to your room, Patricia."

"—be here in—"

"*Now,* Patricia."

Patricia's lower lip protruded, but she obeyed.

Cynthia Wyatt looked at her, and Dynah smiled. She felt so tired, and she could feel perspiration dotting her forehead. "My name's Dynah Carey. I met Dr. Wyatt at . . ." She hesitated, unsure whether this lady would know her husband worked in an abortion clinic. If not, Dynah didn't feel it her place to inform her. ". . . in San Francisco. He and my mother went to college together."

The woman hesitated, clearly unsure what to do.

"Will he be home soon?" Dynah asked, faced with the lady's reticence. She seemed uneasy. Knowing the fire abortionists had come under in the last few years, Dynah wondered if there wasn't good reason for Mrs. Wyatt's caution.

"What business have you with Dr. Wyatt?"

"None, really. I just wanted to talk to him for a few minutes."

"He's not here right now, and I'm not sure when he'll be back."

Dynah stood perplexed. "Well, thank you anyway." She turned away. *Lord, why did you bring me here?*

■　　■　　■

Cynthia watched as the young woman turned away. She had looked so sad . . . and ill. She knew she was being less than welcoming, but with the threats James had been receiving, who could blame her? Still, the girl didn't seem at all threatening. . . .

"Wait," she said on impulse, opening the door wider. "Don't go. Come in and sit down." Despite what she'd said earlier, she knew Jim should be home soon. He'd called her a few minutes ago to tell her he was on his way. Hopefully the girl's business with him wouldn't take long. As she turned and came back to the door, the Rottweiler barked twice, taking a stance to prevent entrance to the house. "Arnold, release!" The dog relaxed but remained watchful as he circled the young woman when she entered the foyer. He sniffed at her skirt. When she extended her hand, Cynthia started to warn her not to touch him, but before she could speak, the young woman bent slightly and began scratching him behind the ears. Arnold's stub tail wagged, and he moved closer.

"Arnold doesn't usually take to people," Cynthia said, surprised that he was treating this young lady like a member of the family.

"I like animals. I think they sense that."

"So it seems," Cynthia said, smiling, all her anxieties evaporating. "Why don't you come into the family room? Would you like something to drink? A cup of herbal tea?"

"A glass of water, please," Dynah said, looking around her at the lovely surroundings. The living room revealed a couch, a love seat, and two high-backed wing chairs that made a comfortable grouping around a large polished mahogany coffee table with a flower arrangement. A baby grand piano stood near a wall of plate-glass windows, a large potted palm to the left. The drapes were a gorgeous deep rose-and-green paisley with hints of gold. Everything looked new and had the stamp of professional decorating.

The family room was another matter. The room was furnished with an overstuffed, slightly worn sofa with four needle-point pillows and a crocheted afghan. Nearby was a recliner. Beside it was a table piled high with medical journals. One wall was covered with family pictures. Another was all bookcases and cabinets. A television was mounted in the center. Big Bird was singing with Cookie Monster. On the floor in the middle of the room was a large circle of denim strewn with Legos.

"Arnold, place," Cynthia commanded.

The Rottweiler trotted over and lay down near the cabinets. Lowering his head to his paws, he watched Dynah.

"Sit down, please," Cynthia said, going over to the sliding doors to the backyard. "Todd, come inside and clean up your Legos!"

"I'm swimming!"

"Dry off and put your things away. Then you can get back in your wading pool." She left the door open as she turned. "Make yourself comfortable, Miss Carey."

"Please call me Dynah."

"Only if you call me Cynthia." She felt drawn to the girl. Entering the kitchen, she opened a cabinet and took down a glass. "Would you like ice?"

"No, thank you." Dynah sat on the sofa.

Just then Cynthia's son, Todd, came in, wet hair plastered to his head, a towel wrapped around him. Disgruntled as only a young boy can be, he marched across the family room, leaving wet footprints on the carpet. Taking hold of the knotted ends of two strings, he lifted the circle of denim. With a crash of plastic pieces, it swallowed the Legos and hung like an oversized purse on his arm. He dragged it to the cabinets, opened one, and shoved the plump denim pouch inside. A portion hung out. Nudging it in with his foot, Todd pushed the door closed. Without a glance in either his mother's or their guest's direction, he ran back outside again, forgetting to close the sliding screen door behind him.

Cynthia laughed and shook her head. "That was Todd." She handed the glass of water to Dynah. "You look pale. Are you feeling all right?"

"I have a headache."

"Would you like something for it?"

"I don't know if I should take anything," Dynah said, putting her hands over the bulge of her abdomen.

Cynthia understood the protective gesture. "I'll get you a cool cloth."

Surprise and simple gratitude touched the young woman's features. She thanked Cynthia quietly as Cynthia went to get the cloth. When she returned to the room, Cynthia saw that the girl had finished the water and set the glass carefully on the side table. Cynthia brought the damp cloth to her, watching as Dynah dabbed her forehead and held the cloth over her eyes. "I'm sorry to be a bother," she said in a faint voice.

"No bother."

"I shouldn't stay long," she said, looking up at Cynthia again, uncertainty in her eyes. "I'm on my way home."

"Jim should be here soon," Cynthia said. "Why don't you lie down and rest until he gets here?" The young lady looked tired, so terribly tired. "I need to start dinner anyway." Hunkering down, she untied the girl's ankle boots and helped her slip them off. She noticed how swollen her feet and ankles were, so swollen she doubted the girl would be able to put her boots back on again. "Lie down now," she said gently, taking a pillow and putting it beneath Dynah's feet to elevate them as much as possible. Taking up the afghan, she draped it over the girl. "Try to sleep if you can." On impulse, she stroked the damp strands of blonde hair back from the girl's forehead.

"You're very kind to strangers," Dynah said softly.

"Not usually," Cynthia responded frankly. In fact, under

normal circumstances the door would not have been opened, let alone anyone invited into the house. Jim said looks could be deceiving, and he didn't want to take any chances.

"Mommy!" Patricia called. "Can I come out now?"

Cynthia went down the hallway and shushed her. "Yes, you may come out, but the young lady is resting on the sofa. I want you to play outside. Take Arnold with you."

I hope you get home soon, Jim, she thought as she watched her daughter skip away. *And I hope you can help that poor girl.*

■ ■ ■

Jim pulled into the garage and punched the remote, closing the door behind him. As he came in the side door, Cynthia met him. She kissed him in greeting and took his medical bag. "You look tired."

"I am." He could feel himself sinking into his Wednesday depression. "I'll take a shower and be down in a while."

"We have company."

"Who?" He didn't feel like entertaining anyone for any reason.

"Dynah Carey."

"Dynah Carey?" The name sounded familiar, though he couldn't place it.

"She said she met you in San Francisco. Her mother went to college with you."

He remembered and dread filled him. Was she here to ask him to perform a late-term abortion?

"What's the matter, Jim?"

"Nothing." He'd do it if the girl asked. Considering the circumstances of her pregnancy, how could he refuse? He would arrange to perform it at the hospital. It would be safer there.

Entering the family room, he saw Dynah Carey asleep on his

sofa, his dog, Arnold, lying in guard close by, his children playing quiet games in the middle of the room. They came to him in greeting. "Dynah's sleeping," Cricket whispered, a finger to her lips. Even Todd was cooperative.

"Her ankles are swollen," Cynthia whispered, "and she was perspiring."

"Did she complain of cramping?" Maybe she'd be lucky and miscarry.

"No, but she had a headache."

"Did you give her anything?"

"I offered, but she said she wasn't sure she should take anything. I think she's worried about her baby."

Frowning, he nodded. If she was worried about her baby, why had she come to him? He approached the girl as Cynthia told the children to play in their rooms for a while so Daddy could talk to the young lady. Leaning down, he put his hand lightly on her shoulder. "Dynah?"

She roused. Opening her eyes, she focused on his face. "Oh," she said groggily, pushing herself up. She was so tired. "I'm sorry. I didn't mean to fall asleep."

"That's all right. What can I do for you?" The sooner she was on her way, the better he would feel about it.

She rubbed her forehead, trying to think clearly. She had just had the strangest, strongest dream. Raising her head, she looked at him again, sensing his impatience. Clearly, he wished she wasn't there.

"I know I'm intruding, Dr. Wyatt, but I have to talk with you."

"About what?"

"Me."

Frowning, he waited, tense. "How'd you find out where I lived?"

"C. Wyatt. The address was in the telephone book."

Odd. He knew they weren't listed, but why would the girl lie? Glancing at Cynthia, he saw her shrug. She was as perplexed as he.

Closing her eyes, Dynah prayed. *Lord, I need to know if this is you working here. Say through me whatever you have to say to this man. Then let me go. Let me get out of this place and away from this man. My mom and dad are waiting.*

Watching her face, Jim pulled the hassock close and sat down in front of her. "Are you in pain?"

She opened her eyes. Like his wife, he was concerned. She saw it in his eyes just as she had the first time she met him. "No. Not the way you mean." She studied his face for a moment and, with startling clarity, she knew what she had to say. Would he listen? Would he heed? Would he submit to the word of the Lord? Or would he think she was crazy?

It didn't matter. She knew only one thing: She had to obey God, even when he didn't seem to make sense.

"Dr. Wyatt, you said you began doing what you do because of what happened to your sister." She saw the anguish fill his eyes. She saw, too, how his wife moved closer in quick defense, a look of horrified pain filling her face. They were both expecting an attack.

"Miss Carey," Cynthia said stiffly, hoping to stop her.

Dynah reached out impulsively and took Jim Wyatt's hands. "Think of me as your sister. James Michael Wyatt, brother of Carolyn Cosma Wyatt, the Lord forgives you. The Lord loves you."

"How did you know her full name? How did you know?"

Her eyes widened, startled and yet filled with understanding. "I didn't know. God did."

Gooseflesh rose over Jim's entire body, pricking the hair to the top of his head. He felt a presence he couldn't deny. Dynah Carey's hands were warm and strong, and there was a light in her eyes that offered the promise of hope. How long had it been since he had felt hope about anything?

Her hands tightened. *"Please.* I think God sent me here to tell you he wants you to turn back to him. He wants you to be the doctor he meant you to be. I believe you want to help women. And so I'm asking you. I'm pleading. Help me. Please, Dr. Wyatt. Help me have this baby."

Pierced, he couldn't breathe.

The message delivered, her appeal made, Dynah felt at peace. She saw in Jim Wyatt's eyes that God's plea had been received, and joy grew inside her until she felt filled with it. "'He has removed our rebellious acts as far away from us as the east is from the west,'" she whispered.

"Yes," he said softly. *Oh, God, yes! Please!* came the anguished cry within him. And in that instant, James Michael Wyatt felt the burden of years of sin lift, like a dense fog evaporating.

Above shone blue heaven.

■ ■ ■

"Is she all right?" Hannah said, her voice trembling, full of pain.

"She's at risk right now," Jim said, trying to be reassuring and firm at the same time. "She's going to stay with us for a few days. She needs bed rest and a special diet. We'll see to everything, Hannah. I don't want you to worry."

How could she not? "Does she still want the baby?"

"Oh, yes," he said with a soft laugh. How long since he had felt so light he could fly? He knew it came from being a part of bringing life into the world rather than taking it. "She wants the baby very much. That's why we're taking these precautions."

"You're the last person I would've expected her to ask for

help," Hannah said, and he heard the loss and rejection in her tone.

"Considering where you found me a few weeks ago, I can understand that. I swear to you, I swear on my life, I won't do anything to harm Dynah or her child. I'll do everything I can to safeguard her and the baby. And there won't be any expense. Whatever comes, I'll take care of it."

"What happened to you, Jim?"

"Redemption." He couldn't speak for a moment. "Dynah brought me a message—one I've been waiting to hear since I lost my sister."

There was a pause, then, "May I talk to my daughter?"

"She'll call tomorrow morning. Right now, I've ordered her to bed. Cynthia's bringing her dinner. Dynah said she wasn't sure you and her dad agreed with her decision, and I don't want her upset about anything."

"You can tell Dynah I support her completely in her decision to have the baby."

"And Doug?"

"Her father will stay out of it." The response was firm—and cold. "What about the clinic, Jim? Are you still working there?"

He wondered if she meant for the sarcasm to seep through. "I've made two calls this evening. One to Elizabeth Chambers tendering my resignation, the second, to you."

"I'm sorry. It's just that—"

She broke off, but the implication was clear. She had sinned less than he. She had killed only her baby; he'd killed hundreds. Thousands . . .

He has removed our rebellious acts as far away from us as the east is from the west.

He closed his eyes in gratitude. *Thank you, God. Thank you.*

"I understand," Jim said quietly. "Believe me, Hannah, I understand." His life had made a complete about-face in the last hour. He was free. After so many years, he could scarcely take it in. He gave her the address and telephone number. "If you and Doug want to come up, feel welcome. Our house is open to both of you. Anytime."

■　■　■

Hannah hung up the telephone, her fingers trembling.

"*Redemption*," Jim had said. Hannah wanted to be happy for him but found herself feeling jealous instead. If he could find redemption, why couldn't she? And why was Dynah with him instead of her parents? The irony of the situation struck Hannah's heart. She supposed she couldn't blame Jim for his suspicions. After all, she was the one who had brought Dynah to the abortion clinic.

She turned and saw Doug standing in the archway between the family room and the kitchen.

"Stay out of what?" he asked, watching her carefully.

"Nothing," she said rigidly, letting her anger show clearly in her eyes. "Your briefcase is in the family room where you left it last night."

His eyes narrowed slightly, whether from pain or anger, she didn't know. Nor did she care. She was past caring what he thought about anything.

"Was that about Dynah?"

"Yes." She looked at him, her mouth tipping in a bitter smile. "She's staying with Jim Wyatt."

"Who is Jim Wyatt?"

"An old friend from college days." Her eyes were hot, challenging. "Go ahead, Doug. Ask me if he was one of my lovers. Wasn't I supposed to have had a drove of them?"

He let it pass. "How does she know him?"

"He's a doctor. We ran into him at the clinic where you sent us. The abortion clinic. Funny, isn't it, Doug? Our daughter wants to save her baby, and where does she go for help? To *him*. She couldn't come home to us, could she? Not knowing how you feel about the *thing* she carries."

Turning away, Hannah went into the family room. She stood with her arms around herself, fighting for control. She felt as though she were drowning in a storm-tossed sea.

Doug went to the notepad near the telephone and tore off the top sheet. Stuffing it into his pocket, he went for his briefcase. "I might be home late."

"Take your time." Turning slightly, she glared at him. "In fact, I don't care if you take the rest of your life."

Doug walked through the family room and out the back door.

■ ■ ■

"Joe?"

Joe's heart jumped at the sound of Dynah's voice. "Hey, kiddo. How ya doing?"

"Better. I'm not home yet, but I'll be there soon."

"Are you still in Fort Bragg?"

"No, I'm staying with friends in Mill Valley." She gave him the telephone number and address. "Jim's a doctor. So you don't have to wonder if I'm getting proper care."

"Do your folks know where you are?" She was quiet so long, he was afraid he'd lost the connection. "Dynah?"

"They know. Daddy called this morning."

"And?"

"I need you to pray for them, Joe. I don't know if they're going to make it through this."

■ ■ ■

Evie returned from an afternoon Bible study to find a message on her answering machine. "Mom, Dynah called. She's coming home in a few days. Right now, she's under the care of a doctor. She's decided to have the baby."

Sitting down in her swivel rocker, Evie wept in relief. She sat for a long time, hands covering her face, allowing the news to sink in and revive her spirit. She had been so afraid for Dynah, so afraid for Hannah and Doug and all the rest who didn't understand the destructive effects of a single decision.

Oh, God, only you are faithful. Hannah gave Dynah to you before she was born, as did I. Bring her through, Lord. Bring her through for all of us. Give us a handhold. Draw us up out of the pit we have dug for ourselves. Oh, God, help us climb toward the light above and not fall into the darkness below.

The telephone rang.

Scrubbing the tears from her face, Evie rose and answered, disgruntled at the interruption.

"Is everything all right?"

Nosy old coot. "Everything's fine, Glad. Why are you calling me again?"

"I don't know."

"We talked this morning."

"So what? We can't talk now?"

"You're turning into a pest."

"Don't be such an old crab."

"Look who's talking."

"What's up?"

"I'm going to be heading south again."

"You're turning into a yo-yo, Evie."

"Well, when I bob back up, I hope I'll have Dynah with me."

"She's home?"

"On her way. She's going to have the baby."

"Good for her," Gladys said with a lilt in her voice, then more solemnly, "You OK?"

"I think I will be." She was shaking inside, her throat tight. "Finally."

"What do you say we get the girls together?"

"They don't know the whole story."

"Maybe it's time they did."

■　■　■

Pastor Dan Michaelson stepped from his car and breathed a quick prayer for wisdom. He knew the conversation he was about to have wouldn't be an easy one . . . but he was ready for it. And not just because of his recent talks with Doug Carey. It seemed he'd been preparing for this for the past few years.

He knew the emotions Hannah Carey was feeling. They were the same emotions he'd felt from so many others who suffered as she was suffering. Several women in his congregation had approached him for counseling over the past few years. But he was a preacher, not a counselor. And so, feeling ill-equipped and time-pressed, he had recommended a professional—a Christian counselor he knew well and trusted.

Several of those he'd referred had been helped greatly. They'd come to him, gratitude shining in their eyes, thankful that he had directed them to someone who could understand their turmoil in light of God's Word, someone who had helped them begin to deal with the pain and find God's healing. With such successes, it only made sense to continue referring women who struggled as Hannah did to others who had the training to help them. Then his counselor friend called to tell him he couldn't take any more new patients, so Dan decided to call area counseling centers for a list of Christian counselors. He'd felt a tinge of unease at sending his charges to someone he didn't know, but he pushed the concerns aside. These people were Christians, after all, and professionals. They knew what they were doing.

Then, four days ago, one of his deacons called. In a broken voice the man explained that his wife was in the hospital after attempting suicide. Shock ran through Dan as he realized she was one of the women he had sent to a counselor on the list. When Dan visited the woman in the hospital, he asked what had brought on such despair. She said she had tried to come to the point where she would feel no guilt or remorse. She had tried to justify what she had done. She had tried to see that she wasn't to blame. Failing, she wanted to die.

Stunned, he called his friend, who gave him a list of questions to ask Marsha's psychologist: Did she use Scripture? Had she prayed with Marsha? Had she come alongside Marsha and tried to guide her back into obedience to God? Dan contacted the counselor—and within moments learned Scripture had no place in her therapeutic sessions, nor did prayer. As for coming alongside her patient, the woman said Marsha needed to learn to stand alone.

Dan shook his head. "Without God, who can stand?"

"Religion is part of her problem, Dan. Marsha needs to love herself more. She needs to realize her full potential and value. The goal is to *remove* her guilt, not increase it."

Remove God and the guilt is gone? How do you remove the Almighty?

He chose his words carefully. "But she feels the guilt for a reason. She *is* guilty."

"In your opinion, perhaps," the woman said in a patient tone. "But Dan, she did nothing illegal, nothing that our society doesn't condone."

"God doesn't condone sin."

"Your view of God, you mean. I see God as tolerant, merciful, loving. He wouldn't condemn Marsha for doing something she felt she had to do. Her circumstances were difficult, Dan. Perhaps you don't understand how difficult."

"Financial difficulties."

"Yes, financial and emotional. She couldn't cope with a crisis pregnancy, so she took the avenue open to her. God loves her anyway. Isn't that what you preach on Sundays? She need not make any sacrifices. Jesus has already done it. Isn't that so?"

"You've left no room for God to bring healing," Dan replied. "No room for confession, forgiveness, restoration. The path to healing is clear. 'If we confess our sins to him, he is faithful and just to forgive us and to cleanse us from every wrong.'"

"Yes, I know the verse, Dan," she said, her tones indulgent, as though she were talking to an obtuse child. "And the Bible can be very helpful in its place, in church. But I'm sure you can understand my caution about bringing it into a patient's session. My place is to listen and help patients focus, not lay even more guilt on them with words of condemnation, especially from something as influential as the Bible. Now, if you don't mind, I have patients waiting."

She hung up, and Dan was left floundering, appalled that he had sent Marsha into the mire and left her to drown. How could a woman who had an abortion not feel guilt or some sense of remorse? How could she justify what she'd done? Whom else could she blame when everyone was telling her it's her choice? Without facing the truth and confessing it, how could she be forgiven? How could she be restored? How could she be free?

He had listened and heard the counselor's gentle, seemingly compassionate words and recognized them for what they were: words that ripped life to pieces. With such a foundation, it was little wonder some closed themselves in behind walls or lashed out at one another or chose death. Families crumbled. Communities writhed in turmoil. An entire nation was collapsing, and everyone was asking why.

CAN YOU NOT HEAR? CAN YOU NOT SEE?

Dan closed his eyes, filled with sorrow. *I hear, Lord. I see.*

Oh, God, there is an answer. There always has been. Only the world doesn't want to listen. It doesn't want to see. It plays deaf and blind and seeks its own end. And where does that lead us? To death. Of our children—and ultimately of ourselves.

God, forgive me. I believed Satan. Jesus, I sent your wounded lambs to the wolves for healing. Forgive me, Lord. I have sinned against you. I heeded Satan's battle cry and not your still, small voice of love and peace. I trusted those I didn't know. I didn't think there was anything I could do to help. I forgot who you are. Creator, Wonderful Counselor, Mighty God, Eternal Father, Prince of Peace. Oh, Lord, I forgot you have equipped me for battle. You have given me all things necessary for victory. I forgot that through you, all things are possible.

He had the tool to break down the walls that imprisoned his people. He had the tool to rip away the veil to the Holy of Holies so that his flock could come before the Lord and be cleansed, made whole, transformed, and have a personal, loving relationship with their Creator. That very tool sat on Hannah's bookshelf right now, gathering dust until Sunday morning. Her Savior was there, waiting to speak to her and show her the way home again, the way back to love.

Your Word is life!

Why didn't more people understand that?

Why hadn't he?

Oh, God, if I believe Scripture is inspired by you, it's time I put it all to practice. It's time I put my feet in the water, ford the river, and break down the walls. It's time I used your principles and precepts for the purpose you laid out since the foundation of the world. Lord, you are God! You made us. Who better to know how to fix us when we've gone wrong? Who better to set us to rights again? Who better to love us through the fire and refine us into something beautiful and useful despite our wrongs?

Now, as Dan readied himself to talk with Hannah Carey, he was struck again at the remarkable ways God worked. *Jesus, could your timing be any more perfect?*

The very day before Doug Carey came to him in desperation and despair, Dan had made a decision. He would not run away anymore. He would not close his eyes and ears. He would not pass the buck to someone outside the church, someone he didn't know and trust.

Lord, help me never to turn my back again. Help me bring your people to the cleansing stream. Use me, Father, as you will.

■　■　■

Irritated, Hannah ignored the second ring of the doorbell and continued to remove things one by one from the china hutch. Dusting a candy dish, she set it carefully on the dining table and reached for a cake plate. When the doorbell rang again, she tossed down her dust rag and headed for the door. If it was a solicitor, he was going to wish he had skipped this house. Not bothering to look through the peephole, Hannah yanked the door open, ready to send the intruder packing.

Pastor Dan Michaelson stood on the front step. "Hannah," he said with a nod of greeting. "Can we talk?"

All the pain from the night before swelled up inside her. She felt the prick of tears and resurgence of betrayal. "That depends on what you have to say."

"I've come to listen."

"Really? Aren't you here on my husband's behalf?"

"I love you both, Hannah. May I come in?"

She wanted to tell him no, she didn't feel like having company, but that would be impolite. Resigned to suffer through the interview, she stepped back, opening the door a little wider. The sooner she let him in, the sooner he would say what he had come to say. Then he would leave, and she'd be alone again.

Cursing Doug, Hannah ushered her pastor into the family room and invited him to sit on the family sofa. "Would you like some coffee?"

"Please."

Gritting her teeth, she went to make some. She made no attempt at conversation.

"Have you heard from Dynah?"

Hannah opened a cabinet and took down two cups and saucers. They rattled as she set them on the counter. "Didn't Doug tell you? She's coming home in a few days." She faced him, loaded and cocked. "By the way, she's pregnant. Did Doug tell you that? She was raped in Illinois. She had lots of support. The dean asked her to leave college. Her fiancé felt she was defiled and didn't want her anymore. So she came home to us for help. Doug told me to take her straight to an abortion clinic and get rid of the problem. He said I had the experience. Did he tell you that in his little meeting last night?"

Dan sat quiet, allowing her to vent, hoping enough steam would escape that she could accept help.

Getting no response, Hannah fell silent, ashamed, furious, and fighting tears. Why had he come? Why couldn't he mind his own business and leave her alone? She stood in the kitchen waiting for the coffeemaker to finish dispensing brew. Filling the cup, she put it on a tray and carried it into the family room. As she set the tray down before him, she realized she had forgotten cream and sugar. She knew Dan liked both. Well, he could do without today. Maybe the bitter brew would send him on the run.

"Thank you," Dan said, leaning forward. "Why don't we pray?"

"You go ahead. Just don't do it out loud." She stood up and moved away, going to stand at the windows, arms crossed, staring out at the small vegetable garden. It needed digging under, mulching, and replanting. Maybe she'd start this afternoon. She felt like getting down and dirty.

Dan's appeal to the Lord was brief and heartfelt. Hands clasped loosely between his knees, he raised his head and looked at Hannah Carey where she stood near the windows, arms wrapped protectively around herself. "I am not here to cast blame or condemn or judge. I've come as your brother in Christ. I want to help, Hannah. I want to come alongside you and Doug. I see two people I love very much coming apart, and it grieves me."

"Thanks for the thought." She tossed the words over her shoulder. "It's too late."

"I can't help unless we can get your anger out of the way."

She faced him again. "That's rich. Was that what the two of you decided last night in your little meeting? Maybe you should counsel *him* about *his* anger. Help *him* get rid of it."

"Doug will be coming in for counseling once a week starting this evening."

His words took the wind from her sails. Doug in counseling? When she'd suggested it before, he'd always said no. He'd insisted they could work out their own problems.

"I want you to come in as well."

There was always a kicker. "No, thank you. I don't want to be in the same room with him. I'm sick to death of recriminations."

"What will your anger accomplish, Hannah?"

She knew, and the tears came, swelling hot. "I don't care anymore."

"I think you do."

"Right," she said bitterly. "You know better than I do what I'm feeling. Or is the bottom line something else entirely?" She smiled cynically. "What would people say if couples in the church started falling apart? We want to look good for the world, don't we? God forbid they find out we're just like everyone else." Glaring at him, she waited for a reaction. None came.

Feeling ashamed, she looked away.

What was the use? "You can't understand, Dan. You haven't a clue how I feel, and neither does Doug."

"God knows, Hannah. There isn't anything new under the sun. He understands the very heart of you."

"That's what I'm afraid of."

"You don't have to be."

"Easy for you to say." If God was even remotely like any of the people she had known in her life, she didn't have a chance. She'd committed the unforgivable sin. She'd taken the life of her own child. And why? Embarrassment. Shame. Fear. All of that and more. Yet no reason, no excuse, could suffice. Nothing could seem to still the voices crying out deep within her that she was guilty . . . of murder.

And she had encouraged her daughter to follow in her footsteps.

"The Lord loves you, Hannah."

She turned away again, staring out the window into the backyard, bereft. "I wonder how many times I've heard that before. It doesn't mean anything. Doug said he loved me. Words, that's all they are, just empty words."

He heard the hopelessness in her voice and wanted to reach her. "You gave your life to Jesus more than twenty years ago, Hannah. You were cleansed of all your sin on that day."

She turned to him, her eyes burning with a fierce light. "If that's true, why don't I *feel* clean?"

"You have to lay your burdens down and leave them at the Cross."

His words angered her. "I've tried," she said softly, fighting tears. "It's not that easy." Not when you have someone to remind you.

"Others have done it."

"Yeah, right. I suppose now you're going to tell me about the apostle Paul and Mary Magdalene and a dozen others who lived two thousand or more years ago."

Dan met her defiant gaze, feeling her fear and sadness. He took in her angry, hurt expression, her protective stance. Silently, he rose and went to Hannah. He came alongside her at the windows. "I'm not talking about people who lived two thousand years ago, Hannah. I'm talking about now. There are others in our congregation who've been through what you have."

She turned slightly and looked at him, surprised, half hopeful.

"You're not the only woman in our church who's had an abortion."

"Are there many?" Misery loves company.

"Six that I know of. I'm going to put prayer baskets out on Sunday, and we may have a better idea of how many more. I contacted a Pregnancy Counseling Center this morning and spoke to one of the directors. She has materials on Postabortion Syndrome, as well as a Bible study. She's offered to teach it."

"At the church?" Hannah grimaced inwardly at the thought, knowing she wouldn't attend. Her life had been difficult enough with Doug knowing what she had done. How much worse if a few loose-tongued men and women in the congregation got wind of her past? They would blow her apart like a tornado.

"No," Dan said, seeing the look in her eyes. It confirmed everything the PCC director had told him. "Donna suggested we meet somewhere other than the church. We'll protect the women's anonymity and privacy. They have to know up front that everything will be held confidential." Perhaps in time, after healing and restoration, they would have the courage to stand and strip away the lies the world taught.

"Where do you plan to have the study?" Hannah said, hoping it was close.

"The PCC is too far away, and my house is next door to the church. I'm still thinking over possibilities."

"You can have it here."

He smiled. "I was hoping you'd say that. You'll have to discuss it with Doug, of course."

"He won't mind." And if he did, he could leave. He could take a boat to China for all she cared.

Dan suspected her feelings and decided to call Doug himself and discuss it with him. After the conversation last night, he didn't think Doug would stand in the way. More likely, he'd be standing on the sidelines cheering.

They decided to hold the first meeting on a Wednesday evening. Dan said he would be attending. He planned to review all the materials beforehand to make sure they were Scripture-based and didn't veer in any way from the path of God's Word. He would be calling the other women and encouraging them to attend too.

"I won't tell them it's here unless they commit to it," he said, offering her no names to protect their confidentiality as well as her own. "Pray for open hearts, Hannah."

"And if no one will come?"

He smiled gently. "We'll begin with you."

9

Cynthia peeled potatoes at the kitchen sink while Dynah read to Cricket and Todd. Feeling oddly melancholy, she paid no attention to the humorous poem, nor to the children's laughter. Something was plaguing her, something that wanted to come up into the open. She knew it was something she wasn't going to like.

Birds fluttered around the feeder on the lawn, finches mostly, scattered by an arrogant blue jay. The smaller birds fluttered to the ground, intent on feeding on the seeds tossed about by the proud jay. She would have to refill the feeder tomorrow as the birds had been feasting the last three days. Since Dynah's arrival, the children had played little in the backyard, giving the birds free access.

Cynthia missed watching her children through the glass as they raced around the backyard playing soccer or tag. Lately, they stayed indoors with Dynah. Right now, Todd was glued to her right side, and Cricket was plastered to her left; both listened raptly to words written by Robert Louis Stevenson. Dynah's voice was gentle and fluid, with just the right lilt of drama. They were eating it up.

Picking up another potato, Cynthia remembered her own mother reading to her from that same book. When she had been old enough to read for herself, she had taken the worn, red Childcraft volume outside with her. Mustard flowers grew as tall as she in the family walnut grove. She had made hiding places among the yellow blooms and dreamed of living in a butter-bean tent and having a calico cat and chocolate dog. Sometimes she'd lain back and stared up at the blue sky and wondered what it would be like to eat warm animal crackers and drink hot chocolate in a cozy English kitchen.

Todd left the couch and sat among his Legos, an architect with a vision. Yesterday, he had invited Dynah to join him. Rather than decline, she sat down beside him cross-legged and began putting red and blue plastic pieces together. Cricket left her beloved crayons and tried to join them, but Todd, ever territorial, ordered her away. It only took a few tender words from Dynah to have him enlisting his sister's help in an expanded project.

Cynthia liked the young woman. She felt drawn to Dynah's easy, loving manner, which seemed to bring out the best in both children. Even Arnold had fallen in love with Dynah. The old dog was lying with his head on her feet right now.

Cutting the potatoes, she dropped them into a pot and added water. Putting them on the stove, she turned the burner to high. The leg of lamb was browning nicely. The peach cobbler was cooling. The salad was tossed and covered with clear wrap in the refrigerator, and the dressing was made. She'd change her clothes, freshen up, and then set the table.

Rinsing her hands, Cynthia dried them and hung the towel on the oven handle. The children laughed again. Dynah was laughing also. She was so young and pretty, her blue eyes bright and clear, unshadowed by her situation. Cynthia marveled.

How would I feel if I were carrying the child of a man who raped me? A man I couldn't even identify?

Dynah looked so at peace. And she had brought that peace to Jim as well.

What was it about Dynah Carey that had broken down the wall that had surrounded her husband for so long? Cynthia felt as much in awe of her as her children did. The girl had come to Jim for help and brought with her redemption. Cynthia would ever be thankful for that. So why did she feel so . . . detached?

Jim would be home soon. She wondered how his meeting with Elizabeth Chambers had gone this afternoon and why he had decided the telephone call hadn't been enough.

"Dynah, would you please keep an eye on the potatoes while I freshen up? Jim should be home soon."

Dynah smiled in quick response and closed the book. "I'll set the table for you."

"Oh, would you? That would be nice. There are some linen table cloths in the china hutch. Cricket, show Dynah the good china. We'll use that and the crystal glasses this evening. The silver is in the middle drawer."

Todd glanced up from the hospital he was building. "Is it your birthday, Dynah?"

"No . . ."

"Dynah's going home tomorrow," Cynthia said. They had to know sooner rather than later.

Both children put up an immediate protest. "Why can't you live with us, Dynah?" Cricket said.

"My mom and dad are expecting me home, sweetheart."

"They can come visit."

"I'm sure her mommy and daddy miss her every bit as much as I'd miss you," Cynthia told her daughter. "And Dynah will come back and see us. Won't you?"

"I'd love to."

Cynthia walked down the hallway to the master bedroom. Distracted and depressed, she sat at her vanity table and loosened and brushed her hair. She tried to analyze what was bothering her. In the past three days, their lives had been turned upside down and inside out. Yet, on thinking about it, she didn't care about the outward changes that would come from the decisions Jim was making. It was the change of heart that made her anxious.

Something chewed at her sense of security, some niggling apprehension. And guilt.

"Hi," Jim said from the doorway.

She glanced up sharply, relieved to see him. He still made her heart jump. She rose as he entered, and he took her in his arms and kissed her. It wasn't the usual casual peck of greeting but one of hunger and promise. She leaned into him, clinging, relishing the moment. Seldom in the past few years had he come home in such a mood. After a long moment, he drew back, his fingers lightly combing through her hair. "I love you," he said, eyes warm, expression clear of tension. She hadn't realized how much the stress had affected him until it was gone.

Those three words still had the power to reduce her to tears. How had she ever been so lucky as to have won a man like Jim Wyatt? Reaching up, she touched his face, loving him with every particle of her being. She couldn't speak.

"You look a little down," Jim said. "You OK?"

She lifted her shoulders slightly, unable to explain, not sure she wanted to diagnose her feelings. Perhaps it was best not to examine some things too closely. You might find corruption. She went back into his arms, her head resting against his chest so she could hear the steady, solid beat of his heart.

Oh, God, have I been wrong? Have I been wrong all along?

She withdrew, crushing the traitorous thought, afraid of where it might lead. "Dinner should be ready."

Jim knew something was wrong, but he didn't press her. "I could smell the leg of lamb when I came in. And peach cobbler, too, I hear. Dynah said you've been busy all afternoon." He loosened his tie and headed for the walk-in closet.

She followed him. "You like her, don't you, Jim?"

"Very much. Don't you?"

"She's like a little sister," she said truthfully, gripped by a terrible sadness. She knew she could talk to Dynah, and yet she had refrained. Why? She had seen proof that this young woman would cast no stones and bear no grudges. She was like a sweet fragrance in the house, an open window that brought in fresh air and sunlight.

And she's leaving tomorrow.

Cynthia's throat closed at the thought.

Dinner turned out to be a quiet, glum affair. Neither Todd nor Cricket was very hungry, both obsessing about losing their newfound playmate. Even the peach cobbler with a dab of whipped cream failed to raise their spirits. Usually Cynthia had to tell them to slow down and not be in such a hurry to rush back to their play. Tonight, Jim had to ask them to leave the table. When they still resisted, he bribed them.

"There's half an hour of sunlight left before you two have to get ready for bed. What do you say I challenge you both to a game of soccer?"

It was an offer neither could refuse. To have their father play with them was a delight beyond anything.

Grinning, Dynah rose and began gathering dishes.

"I'll do them," Cynthia said quickly. "You go rest."

"You cooked. It's only fair I clean up."

Cynthia busied herself with finding containers for the leftovers. She glanced out the window several times, smiling as she watched Jim and the children competing for the black-and-white ball.

Dynah finished putting the rinsed dishes into the washer and turned to her. "Cynthia, thank you for taking me in."

"Nonsense. It was Jim who helped you."

"You opened the way for him."

Cynthia didn't know what to say to that. She had opened the door to this girl, and her life was never going to be the same. Because of Dynah, Jim had made a decision that would change everything, most of all him. Was she happy about it? Part of her rejoiced, while another part was afraid. It was the fear she didn't want to dissect.

Dynah sensed there was something troubling Cynthia Wyatt. The last thing she wanted to do was add to the woman's distress, but she knew some things had to be addressed before she left. "You have more influence than you realize," she said, fully aware how quickly things could change if Cynthia wanted it so. A woman could be the wind beneath a man's sails or a gale to send him into uncharted waters. She could be an anchor in stormy seas, or she could let him drift onto the rocks.

"Jim has always done what he felt he had to do." Cynthia turned away, hoping Dynah would leave it at that.

She didn't. She couldn't. "It's easy to see how much you both love each other. Jim said the other evening you've supported him in everything."

In everything. Cynthia closed her eyes tightly, her stomach tightening. "It was never my idea that he perform abortions. He did it because of what happened to his sister."

"Were you against it?"

"I didn't think about it." She hadn't dared. Wasn't a wife's job to support her husband and not fight against him? Turning, she looked at Dynah, resenting the question. "I was for Jim. That's all."

Dynah looked into Cynthia's eyes and wanted to weep for her. Cynthia turned away again, stacking containers and opening the refrigerator. She shoved them in heedlessly and let the door swing shut as she straightened. She faced Dynah again, anger stirring. "I find it rather amazing that you would dare stand in judgment after all we've done for you."

Dynah shook her head, her eyes filling with tears. "I'm not judging you, Cynthia."

"But you think I was wrong, don't you? You think I should have spoken up." Stepping past her, she reached for the dish-cloth. "Well, I think you should pack." She began wiping down the counter Dynah had already wiped down. Clutching the cloth, she found herself alone in the kitchen. Leaning on the counter, she shut her eyes, ashamed.

The truth was, she had never allowed herself to think too deeply on the issue of abortion. She had always been against it until Jim had explained another side. Then she had been for it for his sake. She had chosen to close her eyes and ears and mind to all sides but his. It was too complex an issue, too volatile, too sensitive to discuss. And after all, wasn't it a matter of personal choice? Everyone said so, didn't they? The newspapers, magazines, television. From the president of the United States on down the line.

She hadn't wanted to think about it too much or look too closely, not when the love of her life was so intimately involved. She couldn't bear to think he might be wrong. It had been easier to follow his lead rather than try to pull him in another direction. He had been so convinced he was doing right. She had chosen not to question him.

Oh, God, why didn't I? Was I afraid he wouldn't love me anymore?

She had only seen the smallest measure of anguish he had suffered in taking the course he had. She hadn't guessed the depth of it, had never dreamed of the battle going on inside him, the sense of shame and despair he had lived with for the past four years. And then the dam had broken three nights ago. She had never seen her husband weep as he had then.

Now he had made a complete U-turn in his thinking and his life.

And she was falling into step again, saying nothing, accepting.

Cynthia went into the living room, away from the windows looking into the backyard, and sat down. Her chest was so tight she could hardly breathe.

Maybe if she had said something in the beginning, maybe if she had given even the smallest hint of warning, she could have saved him all the suffering. Maybe if she had reminded him of why he had worked so hard to become a doctor in the first place. Maybe if she had suggested other ways to help women facing crisis pregnancies besides aborting their babies.

Oh, God, oh, God, I shared in it.

It was too late now. They would both have to live with their sins; Jim for his actions, her for her inaction, her silence and omission.

The sliding glass door banged open as the children came inside and charged down the hall for their baths. Todd was old enough to manage for himself, but Cynthia could hear her daughter calling for Dynah. She was glad for it. She wanted to sit here in the solitude of the living room and nurse the wounds that were opening with every thought.

"Honey?"

She tried to smile at her husband, but her mouth trembled as he entered the room. He studied her for a moment. When she couldn't hold his gaze, he sat down in the chair facing her and leaned forward, hands loosely clasped between his knees.

"Are you sorry we'll have to give all this up?"

Cynthia looked around the elegantly decorated living room. Nothing she was looking at was irreplaceable. She didn't care if they gave up country-club membership. She had seldom had the time to enjoy it anyway. She didn't care if they sold the house and moved. None of the neighbors had ever been particularly friendly. Perhaps that was her own fault, living in fear behind the high iron gate. Or had shame kept her hidden away?

"It doesn't matter to me," she said. "None of it. These are just things." Only Jim mattered, Jim and the children—and she'd failed them all.

She looked at him, aching inside, and shook her head, struggling to contain the turbulent emotions twisting and churning inside her. "I'm sorry, Jim. I'm so sorry."

Jim sensed what was bothering her and loved her all the more for it. "You're not to blame for the choices I've made."

"No, but I'm to blame for not talking to you about my reservations. I'm to blame for not asking the hard questions that might have helped you look at things in a different way. I knew you were suffering." Tears coursed down her cheeks. "I knew, but I convinced myself I shouldn't interfere." She touched his cheek. "You know, you never had to tell me which days you worked at the clinic. I knew by how depressed you were the morning you left. I knew because you were angry when you came home. I knew when you spent the entire evening in your den going over cases from your office. I thought keeping silent would make it easier for you. I was wrong."

"You did it because you loved me."

"Yes. I loved you. I do love you. I love you so much, I'd die for you. So why couldn't I love you enough to be completely honest?"

His eyes moistened as they searched hers. "I never knew you had any reservations."

"I was afraid to tell you."

"Why?"

"I don't know." Another lie. She tried again. "I knew by the way you talked about Carolyn how much your sister meant to you. I didn't want to add to your hurt." An excuse. And yet again, she tried. "I think the truth is I was afraid it would tear us apart." Saying it hurt. She was getting closer. "My parents disagreed on a lot of things, and they fought constantly. I swore I'd never live like that." Even that sounded like an excuse to her. "There's no good reason for not dealing with things. I should've said something." Who better qualified to hold up a yellow flag? Or a red one?

Jim came and sat beside her, drawing her into his arms. "It probably wouldn't have made a difference."

This from the man who had chosen to go to medical school in San Francisco because she'd always loved the West Coast. This from the man who had moved her to Mill Valley because she was concerned about rearing the children in the city. This from the man who had bought this house because she had loved it at first sight.

It would have made a difference.

It would have made all the difference in the world.

■ ■ ■

Dynah awakened in the night, needing to use the bathroom. Glancing at the small digital clock on her bedside table, she saw it was two-fifteen in the morning. Sighing wearily, she flipped the covers back and pushed herself up into a sitting position. She felt the baby move strongly, feet down on her bladder. Leaning over, she felt for her robe. It was lying across the foot of her bed within easy reach, convenient for her nightly visits to the bathroom across the hall. Smiling faintly, she shrugged into the robe as she rose, one hand beneath the bulge of her abdomen.

On her way back to bed, she noticed a light was on in the living room. Curious, she drew the sides of her terry-cloth robe more snugly around her and went to see who was up at such a late hour.

Cynthia was sitting in one of the swivel rockers, barefoot. She was wearing a pink-and-white flannel nightgown and looked more like a girl of twenty than a woman in her late thirties. A young girl anxious about something.

"Are you feeling all right, Cynthia?"

"I should be asking you that."

Dynah rested her hand lightly on her abdomen. "The baby's tap-dancing."

Cynthia smiled. "I remember. At the end, I couldn't fit behind the steering wheel of our car." Her expression grew solemn again. "I heard you get up. I was hoping, if you weren't too tired, we could talk awhile."

"I'd like that." Dynah came into the living room and sat in the matching rocker nearest her. Her expression was open and sweet, almost thankful. Cynthia's anxiety evaporated.

"I didn't mean to come at you the way I did earlier," she said. "I was feeling defensive."

"I understood."

Cynthia saw she did. "Jim and I talked about it. He doesn't really understand what I'm feeling. Men seem to see things in black and white rather than shades of gray." Her mouth curved ruefully. "That's where I've been living for a long time. In the gray area."

"Sometimes it feels safe there." Dynah said. Hadn't she gone along for months without making any kind of decision or stand? She'd like to think now she did it to protect her baby, but in truth, she hadn't. She had wanted to deny its very existence. She had wanted to wish it away.

"Unfortunately, life has a way of slapping you in the face with reality," Cynthia said quietly.

Dynah knew that only too well. She also knew that after the sting of awakening came the blessing of dawn.

"You were right, Dynah. I did support Jim in his work. It's a damning word, isn't it? Support. I upheld him in it. He'd like to absolve me. As much as I'd like to let him, he can't. Inaction is an action in itself, and silence can speak louder than words." She smiled weakly. "Trite, but true. I just wanted you to know that before you leave tomorrow."

Leaning forward, Dynah took Cynthia's hand. "I came because God sent me, and you opened the door. I needed help, and you took me in."

"You said that once before," Cynthia said, touched by her concern.

"I'll say it again. Others weren't so kind." Ethan. Dean Abernathy. Even her own parents.

Oh, God, who are the infidels? These people who took in a stranger off the street? Ethan and Dean Abernathy are saved. So, too, are Mom and Dad. None of us deserve it, but you cover us with your grace and mercy. Oh, but, Lord, what of these two people I've come to love? What of their children? Oh, Jesus, please. I beseech you on their behalf. You've opened their eyes. Open their hearts as well so that their names are written in the Book of Life.

"I've been very glad of your company," Cynthia said, squeezing Dynah's hand gently in return.

"We haven't talked very much." Not enough. "Not about the important things." Christ. The gospel.

"No, but I've watched you."

"I want you to have the peace God's given me."

"I know, but I don't think I'm ready for it. Not like Jim was." He was ripe for the harvest. She was still standing grain. "You've made me hunger and thirst, Dynah, but I'll have to find my own way to the well."

God, may it be so. When Cynthia withdrew her hand and leaned back slightly, Dynah understood that the spiritual side of their conversation had been closed.

"What of the young man who's been calling you?"

"Joe? He's been a wonderful friend."

"Are you sure it isn't more?"

"He was my fiancé's best friend. When my relationship with Ethan disintegrated because of . . . well, difficult circumstances, I think Joe felt someone had to shoulder responsibility for me."

Cynthia raised her brows. "So he moved all the way to California to do that?"

"He's been talking about going to UC Berkeley since I met him. He said it'd be a great place for testing a person's faith."

"Well, he's probably right about that. Does he plan to become a minister?"

"I don't know," Dynah said, frowning slightly, wondering. "I've never really nailed Joe down about anything." All she knew for certain was that he loved the Lord wholeheartedly. That had been enough to cement her respect and admiration from the beginning. As to the rest, Joe had never been quick to share his hopes and dreams or his plans. Not the way Ethan had.

They talked for over an hour, about the children mostly and some about Cynthia's college years and her dreams of being an interior decorator. Both grew drowsy. They walked down the hall together. Cynthia touched Dynah's arm lightly. "I'll miss you."

Dynah embraced her. "May God bless you and your family."

Cynthia watched the door close behind her. She felt a strange ache in her heart, a pang of loneliness.

■ ■ ■

"Is one of the children sick?" Jim said groggily when Cynthia slipped back into bed.

"No. Dynah got up to go to the bathroom. I thought I'd visit with her for a while."

"Hmmmm. Good."

"Sorry I awakened you."

He was snoring again within two minutes. Cynthia curled onto her side and tucked herself against him. Doctors learned early to sleep whenever they had the opportunity.

"May God bless you and your family."

Maybe the blessing of a girl like Dynah was enough to assuage the guilt. She hoped so. Her own faith was lacking.

Closing her eyes, Cynthia Wyatt willed herself to sleep.

■   ■   ■

Tense, heart pounding, Evie sat silently in the wing chair near the sliding glass doors that led out to Gladys's deck. The door was open, allowing the warm breeze to carry in the scent of the pine forest and the sweet sound of birdsong. The calm atmos-phere did nothing to ease Evie's turbulent spirit.

Virginia Hart, Doris Fulton, and Marva Novak chattered gaily, delighted with Gladys's flavored coffee, cookies, and cupcakes, totally oblivious to Evie's wretched state of mind. Gladys had called the women together for an afternoon "tea."

Gladys surveyed the gathering, heart drumming. On the surface, all looked grand and congenial. Gladys liked to "put on the Ritz" as she called it. Hailing from Queens, she said she was born to put on airs. True to form, she had brought out her best, the delicate bone china from Victoria, the silver tea service from London, and the crystal platters from Ireland. She was dressed in a pretty turquoise sweat suit that probably had never been out-of-doors.

"I should've laced your coffee with Valium," Gladys said *sotto voce*, standing over Evie with one of her plates of goodies. "You've got that pinched look."

"What do you expect? I'm facing the gallows."

"You underestimate your friends. We won't desert you. Now have a tea cake."

"I'm not hungry."

"Have one anyway. It might sweeten that look on your face."

Evie took one just to shut her up.

"And don't you dare sneak out that door," Gladys said in parting.

Disgruntled, Evie ignored the remark and looked at her friends. She had known Virginia, Doris, and Marva as long as she had known Gladys McGill. Over the past eighteen years, they had all shared triumph and tragedy. Doris, the first to lose her husband, had served with Evie as church deaconess. Evie had been with Marva at the hospital when her husband died after open heart surgery. Virginia Hart had coaxed Evie into taking over the presidency of the women's auxiliary when her husband had been in the last stages of Parkinson's disease. Gladys was the only one not a widow in deed. Her husband had Alzheimer's.

Over the past four years, every Sunday after church, Evie had met these women at one of the local eateries to share lunch, sorrow, and joy. They jokingly called themselves the Widows' Brigade. In all seriousness, they had been through wars together—grieving over spouses who died, children who divorced, grandchildren on drugs, deaths of siblings, living alone, paring down households, and moving into "assisted-care retirement facilities."

She loved these women like family, and they loved her. Or had. Would they still feel the same when she was finished baring her heart and soul and confessing her sin? Even as close as she was to these women, she had withheld part of herself from them. She wanted them to know the best of her, not the worst. Never the worst. So she had kept some of her struggles secret, buried with the dead. Only Gladys knew the whole of it, and Evie wondered what sorry weakness in herself had made her spill the beans to even one soul under heaven.

God, I wouldn't be in this mess if I had kept my mouth shut!

Gladys was looking at her, waiting.

Evie looked back at her. *I'm not ready.*

"Ladies," Gladys said, drawing everyone's attention. "I called you all here for a purpose. We have some trouble that needs addressing."

Evie felt the heat come up into her cheeks. She glared at Gladys, annoyed. Gladys looked back at her unintimidated, her expression clearly encouraging. The old coot was all but sending telepathic messages: *I know all about you, Evie Daniels, and I love you anyway. Trust us.*

Evie was most worried about Virginia and how she would take the news. Virginia was a staunch advocate and financial supporter of a pro-life organization. In the beginning of her involvement, she had been lividly verbal about her revulsion of babies being killed. If anyone was going to throw stones, it would be her.

"What's happened?" Marva said, looking around the room for enlightenment.

"Evie has something she needs to discuss with us," Gladys said, and all eyes swung to her, pinning her back against the wing chair.

Evie rolled her eyes heavenward and then looked around at Virginia, Doris, and Marva. "My granddaughter Dynah was raped, and she's pregnant."

"Oh, my heavens," Doris said, always the first to shed tears for others. She had reached the ripe old age of eighty-one and still had a difficult time believing people could do awful things to one another.

"I swear," Marva said, the one ready to do battle in any crisis, "our world is going to hell in a handbasket! Did they catch the man?"

"No. Dynah couldn't identify him."

"Why not?"

"Because it was dark, Marva. Very dark. And she never saw his face."

Virginia remained silent, assessing Evie's expression, seemingly not drawing any conclusions, making no remarks.

"Since the rape and learning she's pregnant, her fiancé has dumped her, and she was asked politely to withdraw from school. Things got even worse when she came home. Doug and Hannah both tried to pressure her into having an abortion. She ran away seven weeks ago. No one knew where she was. She called several times, just to let us know she was all right. A few days ago, she called to say she's coming home."

"Poor girl," Doris said.

Evie looked at Gladys and then the others. "I want to go and get her and bring her up here to live with me so she can have that baby."

Virginia seemed to breathe again. She leaned back slightly and sipped her Cappuccino.

"Is that what Dynah wants?" Doris said.

"That was the impression she gave Hannah, but as I see it, nothing's changed. She's walking right back into the same situation she faced when she left. Doug was dead set against Dynah's having the baby. He despises the thought of it and is convinced Dynah will ruin her life by having it. And Hannah is so confused, she'll go along with him."

"Maybe they're right," Doris said. "I mean, if any girl has a good reason for an abortion, it's Dynah." When the others fell silent, she looked around, her eyes fixing on Virginia. "Would you want to have the child of a rapist?"

"I don't think that's the issue," Virginia said quietly, a troubled expression in her eyes.

"Maybe not, but I can certainly see Doug and Hannah's point of view."

"So can I," Virginia said, surprising everyone, "but adding abortion to rape won't lessen Dynah's trauma. It'll add to it."

"You can't get involved without alienating your daughter and son-in-law," Marva said to Evie. "She's their daughter. I'm sure they have her best interests at heart."

Best interests. Killing words. Anger stirred within Evie, an anger that had been sparked decades before.

Here we go, like it or not.

"Let me back up and explain why I feel so strongly about Dynah's having this child," she said. With a steadying breath, she told them her own story—every painful, shameful detail.

No one said a word when she was finished. They all sat stunned, unsure what to say or do after such a confession. Virginia sat pale and still, eyes closed.

Evie let out her breath slowly and drew it in again. "Frank had my best interests at heart, Marva, and so did that doctor. Or I'd like to think so. The problem is, I think I would've made it. But I didn't take the risk. I gave in and let them take my child's life, and there hasn't been a week during the last forty-six years that I haven't regretted it and wondered what my son might have grown up to be."

She leaned forward, setting the rattling cup and saucer on the coffee table. It was done. They knew everything about her. If they decided to stand in judgment, so be it. She looked at her friends, chin up slightly, waiting for the blow. It hurt to stand alone.

"What about Frank?" Virginia said quietly. "Did he get over it?"

"No." She struggled against the tears building. "We agreed never to talk about it, and we didn't. Then he mentioned it the week before he died. He looked at me and said he was sorry. So sorry. I knew what he meant." Her hand trembled as she smoothed a wrinkle in her skirt. "I don't want Dynah to live with the guilt and anguish I've lived with all these years. I don't want her growing old with an abortion on her conscience."

Only Virginia looked her in the eyes, her own filling with tears as she did so. Evie searched for condemnation and saw none. The tight ball of fear in her stomach uncoiled, relaxed. She wasn't forsaken after all. Oddly, it broke her heart all the more. Had she met opposition, she could have been strong. Seeing compassion and love, she felt herself crumble inside as the walls of self-defense came down and grief and tears were free to rise.

"Oh, Evie," Virginia said softly. "It must hurt so much. I miscarried years ago, and there are still times when I feel guilty about it and wonder if I lost that child because of something I did or didn't do." Tears slipped down her cheeks. "I hurt for you. . . ."

No one said anything for a long moment, but Evie felt only compassion in the room. Until this meeting, she hadn't realized how afraid she'd been that her friends would turn away from her.

"Tell them the rest," Gladys said quietly.

Sniffling into her Kleenex, Evie glowered at her. "The rest doesn't matter."

"Oh, yes, it does. Tell them, or I will."

Evie pressed her lips together and glared at her, refusing to be bullied.

"Evie has breast cancer."

"Oh, Evie!" Doris said. "Not you, too." Her sister had succumbed to cancer the year before. "Has it metastasized?"

"It's gone into the sternum and spine," Gladys said. "And there are a few hot spots in her right leg. She's in pain, but she's too stubborn to admit it."

"Aspirin takes care of it," Evie said, embarrassed.

"Aspirin, my foot," Gladys muttered.

Doris dug in her purse for a handkerchief.

Pale, Virginia set her cup and saucer down carefully. "Howard told me once that there may be a connection between breast cancer and abortion. When a natural process like pregnancy is disrupted, it has long-term repercussions to the body. Some friends of his were doing research on it."

"Oh dear! I'm sure that can't be true," Doris said. "I've never seen anything about that in any of the women's magazines." She subscribed to half a dozen and bought others in the supermarket.

"I've read about it, too," Evie said, struggling to keep her voice even. "Hormonal changes permanently alter the breast's structure. And when a pregnancy is terminated through abortion, the process is interrupted, which leaves cells in a state of transition. And they say cells in this state have a very high risk of becoming cancerous. So the woman's chances of developing breast cancer later in life may be greatly increased."

"Actually," Virginia added, "I'm not surprised you haven't read about it in the magazines, Doris. Howard and his colleagues had little success getting their results published, and funding was a never ending problem. Can you believe they actually had to find private sources because the government didn't seem to want to know the adverse effects of abortion on women?"

"Well, good gracious, think about it," Marva said. "What women's magazine would even open the question? They wouldn't dare for fear of the protest letters they'd receive."

"Why would women protest?" Doris said. "Young women are very astute these days. I've listened to my granddaughters talk. They want to know all the facts."

"Perhaps, but those selling abortion don't want them to have them," Virginia said heatedly. "Besides, the Supreme Court doesn't agree with you. The judges seem to think we poor women would fall apart if we knew the facts, so they decided women don't have the right to know the full truth." She shook her head. "They've made it legal to withhold vital information, even when a woman requests it, for heaven's sake."

"That doesn't make sense!" Doris looked at the others wide-eyed.

"It makes absolute sense when you're trying to protect a billion-dollar business," Marva responded firmly. "The less a woman knows about what's being done to her body and what her baby looks like as it develops, the more likely she is to buy an abortion. When you're told the fetus is nothing but tissue, a quick fix to a long-term problem seems appropriate."

"It sounds so—so *cold,*" Doris said.

"It is cold, but they'd like you to think they're acting out of mercy and compassion." Virginia's eyes snapped. "And do you know the argument used for withholding information? They say it spares the woman trauma. I wonder how those judges would feel if we told them the sad truth is that they betrayed the million and a half women each year who go into an abortion clinic and aren't given the truth. It doesn't take two minutes on an examining table for a girl to know that abortion is painful and destructive and it'll have far-reaching effects on her life. Besides the emotional trauma of going through something so violent, there are the physical aspects, the aftereffects. Unfortunately, by the time she's gone that far, it's too late to change her mind."

"You sound as though you know firsthand," Gladys said, casting Virginia a curious glance. "Have you had an abortion?"

"No, but one of my granddaughters did. Tracy went to a reputable clinic. When they didn't inform her of the risks, she didn't think there were any. They told her it was a simple procedure. She believed them. Unfortunately, it wasn't simple enough. The doctor didn't get everything. He was probably rushed. She said the waiting room was full that day. All it takes is a tiny piece of the fetus left in the womb to cause serious infection and complications. And that's what happened. Now she can't have children."

Virginia looked at Evie, her eyes glinting with tears. "The awful part is that Tracy wanted that baby as much as you wanted yours, Evie, but her husband said no. It wasn't health in her case; it was money. They'd made a budget early in their marriage, and Tom wanted to stick to it. He insisted they shouldn't have a baby unless they could provide a proper home for it, and to him, that meant a house in the right neighborhood. He told her if she quit her job to have the baby, they wouldn't have enough money to move out of their condo for another six months. Six months, for Lord's sakes! Six months! They sacrificed their child for a budget."

"How are they doing now?" Evie asked with quiet compassion.

"As the world sees it, I guess they're fine. They bought a house, a nice big house with four bedrooms. It's in a cul-de-sac in a very nice neighborhood. It has a big backyard. There's even a swing set left from the previous owners. There's a paseo at the end of the block so children can walk to school without ever crossing a street. A school is less than three blocks away, and there's a nice park. Everything was all carefully planned. The perfect setting for an all-American family. Unfortunately, that plan has blown up in their faces." She shook her head, her mouth trembling. "They're two very unhappy people. It breaks my heart."

No one said anything for a long moment.

"It reminds me of what we were reading about in Bible study on Wednesday," Marva said, holding her coffee cup between both hands. "When the Israelites turned away from God, they sacrificed their children to the god Molech. Remember what Pastor said? The babies were laid in the arms of that stone god so they'd roll down into the fire."

"What an awful thought," Doris said, shuddering.

"And children were sacrificed on the walls of the city because the people thought it would help them win a war," Gladys said, her horror clear in her voice.

"Pastor said people in Ephesus buried babies in the foundations of their homes in hopes of having good luck," Marva said. "Can you imagine believing a dead child can bring prosperity?"

"It's easy to believe when you base your happiness on money and material possessions," Virginia said flatly. "It does cost money to have a baby. It costs money to raise children. Money. All anyone seems to think about these days is money. I would've given them the money to buy that house. So would my son. Tom was too proud to ask. He wanted them to do it all by themselves. He wouldn't bend his timetable by even six months. And now they're going to live the rest of their lives in a big empty house."

"'Children are a gift from the Lord,'" Gladys recited quietly, "'they are a reward from him. Children born to a young man are like sharp arrows in a warrior's hands. How happy is the man whose quiver is full of them!'"

"This generation seems to see children as a financial burden and responsibility to be avoided," Marva said. "My grand-daughter just got her master's degree in business. She and her husband have no plans to have children at all."

"I remember my son going through a period in the seventies when he said he didn't want to bring children into such an awful world," Evie said. "I told him people who cared that much about children should be the ones having them."

Virginia's face crumpled. "It makes me so angry!" She drew a ragged breath, tears coming. She pressed her hand over her heart. "I miss my great-grandchild. I know that doesn't make much sense, but I do. I ache for that baby, and I ache for my son and daughter-in-law, and I ache for Tom and Tracy because we're all living with the loss, Tom and Tracy most of all."

She looked at Evie, her eyes brimming with tears. "They always wanted children. I remember them talking about it at family gatherings when they were just newlyweds. They looked forward to the day they would begin having babies. They even had names picked out. I wish I knew how they got so caught up in the foolish notion that all the circumstances had to be perfect before they could have them."

Evie felt her anguish and couldn't speak.

Gladys sat down beside Virginia and laid her hand gently on hers. "That's why you became so involved in the pro-life group, isn't it?"

She took a deep breath, calming herself. "Yes, initially, but I'm going to withdraw my support."

"Why?" Doris said, surprised. "It's a good cause."

"Yes, it is, but this group's focus is so fixed on saving the child, they have no compassion whatsoever for the mother thinking about having an abortion." She fixed her gaze on Evie again. "You'll have to be very careful about that."

"I love Dynah. I want what's best for her."

"I'm sure you do, Evie. Just be sure you're not interfering in order to atone for the child you aborted."

That was direct. And painful. Yet, Evie saw Virginia hadn't meant to sting with cruel words but make her think about her motivations.

She could be as honest.

"Yes, there's that, but mainly, I don't want to see Dynah herded into a clinic against her will."

Marva put her plate aside. "It makes me wonder what's coming."

Gladys glanced at her. "What do you mean?"

"Well, how can we expect to raise up new generations to value life when all around them they're seeing it as a matter of convenience? I mean, does anyone see what I'm seeing, or am I just a foolish old woman? America's 'quality of life' is beginning to sound like Germany's 'Final Solution,'" she said bleakly.

"You're overreacting, as usual," Doris said, taking a cookie from the plate.

"Maybe so, but it reminds me of things my father said to me when I was a little girl. He was German. He immigrated to this country shortly after World War I, but he had lots of relatives still in the old country. He and my mother corresponded with them over the years. When Hitler came on the scene, those German relatives thought he was the second coming of Christ. Papa and Mama wrote and tried to warn them what was happening, but they couldn't see it. They were utterly blind to it."

"What's Germany got to do with abortion?" Doris said, lost.

Marva folded her napkin in half and then crumpled it in her hand. "The Holocaust didn't start in concentration camps, Doris. I remember Papa talking about Hegel, a German philosopher. Papa subscribed to periodicals from the old country and read about the new ethic in the 1920s, before Hitler was even on the scene."

"New ethic?" Gladys said. "What sort of new ethic?"

"Whatever solves a problem on a practical level must be considered moral," Marva said. She looked around the room. "Sound familiar?"

"Abortion," Virginia said grimly.

Doris looked between them, disturbed.

Marva tossed her napkin onto the coffee table. "The first to be killed weren't the Jews. They started with anyone who cost the state money. They were exterminating the aged, the infirm, the senile, and mentally retarded, defective children. With World War II on the horizon, more undesirables were added. Epileptics, amputees from the First World War, Gypsies, children with minor deformities, even bed wetters, for heaven's sake. It was only later they went after the Jews and Christians and anyone else who didn't agree with those in power. I guess nowadays, we'd say they were politically incorrect."

"That sort of thing could never happen here," Doris said. "There are too many checks and balances in our government."

"Really?" Marva said. "How many times have I heard that? 'It could never happen here.' It could. I think it's going to happen."

"Well, you're wrong," Doris said.

"Am I? There was a euthanasia bill on the California ballot a few years ago. I never thought I'd see that happen in my lifetime. Did you? It still chills me when I think about it because I'm afraid of what's coming. They cloak death with talk of dignity and mercy, but it all boils down to saving the government money. How much does it cost to keep an AIDS patient alive? How much to take care of the elderly in convalescent homes? How about terminal patients in VA hospitals?"

"It costs three thousand dollars a month to take care of George," Gladys said quietly.

"We're not talking about George," Doris said.

"Aren't we?" Marva said. "I imagine there are probably a lot of people who think taking care of him is a waste of money."

Doris turned, shocked. "What an awful thing to say!"

"It's all right, Doris," Gladys said, patting her hand. "And it's true." A flicker of pain crossed her face. "One of the nurses said to me last visit that it was a pity George has such a strong heart. I couldn't believe someone thinking that way would be working at the home, but there she was, head nurse on the ward." She looked at Marva. "It does make me wonder."

"We're eliminating all our opportunities to show compassion," Virginia said. "How do you learn something when you can't apply it?"

"You don't, and without compassion, you destroy your humanity," Marva said grimly.

Gladys looked between them. "Do you think things could really go that far?"

"No," Doris said firmly and set her cup and saucer on the coffee table. "I don't believe it."

"Because you don't want to believe it," Marva said.

"Just because things happened the way they did in Germany doesn't mean it's going to happen that way here."

"And it doesn't mean it won't."

Virginia leaned forward. "The more you think about all of it, the more horrible it is. There's no end of ramifications. You mentioned our Bible study, Marva. Well, firstborn children belong to the Lord, don't they? Doesn't it say that somewhere in Scripture? How many firstborn are being aborted across our nation? Do we think God doesn't see what we do? Do we think there won't be consequences?"

"I've had forty-six years to think about ramifications and consequences," Evie said. "Forty-six long years to see what's happening around me. Sometimes I feel as though I was at the beginning of a chain of events and somehow it's up to me to put things right again." She had done it first, then Hannah, and now Dynah faced the same decision.

She clenched her hand. "This is Dynah's first child, regardless of the circumstances of its conception! I know her. I know the love she's always had for the Lord. She wants to do right, and she's decided to have this child. By God's strength, I swear I'm going to stand beside her so she can." Tears welled. "Even if it means I have to go against Hannah and Doug to do it."

Virginia smiled at her. "They may thank you in the long run."

Gladys looked at Evie, and tears filled her eyes. Would Evie live that long?

Evie knew what she was thinking. "I don't have a long run," she said wearily, her hand relaxing. "I have about a year."

"Don't talk that way!" Doris said. "You sound as though you've already given up."

"I'm not giving up. I'm facing facts."

"You could go through chemotherapy."

"It's not an option. I'm seventy-eight years old, Doris. I'm close enough to the grave as it is without pushing it with drugs."

Doris looked from one to another. "I don't like this conversation. I don't like it one bit."

"It's not exactly my cup of tea either," Evie said drolly. "Blame Gladys."

Gladys smiled at her tenderly, unruffled. "You're not hanging from a gallows, are you?"

"No," Evie said with a faint smile. "I'm not."

"Does your family know you have cancer, Evie?" Marva said.

"I told my son. We've talked on the telephone almost every night the last few weeks. I'm driving down to San Francisco tomorrow to tell Hannah. It's going to be hard in the face of everything else that's happening, even harder when I ask Dynah to come live with me. I'm going to need help in the months to come, and I hope my request will offer her the way out she needs."

"Do you think she'll want to keep the baby?" Doris said.

"Considering how it was conceived, I doubt it," Evie said. Dear Doris, ever the optimist. "I'd think the baby would be a constant reminder that she was raped."

"What if she does decide to keep it?" Gladys said.

Evie hadn't even thought of that possibility. "I'll cross that bridge if I come to it."

Virginia smiled. "I'm assuming Gladys invited us here because you need some kind of help. What can we do?"

"I need you to pray," Evie said simply. "Pray Doug has a change of heart. Pray Dynah stands firm in her decision to have this baby. Pray Hannah forgives me for butting in again. Right now, our family's torn apart over this situation, and I'm probably going to throw more fuel on the fire. I seem to have a talent for that. Right now, I imagine Doug sees me as an intruding mother-in-law. I need you all to pray that the words that come out of my mouth will be from the Lord and not from me. I have to speak from love." She looked at Virginia. "I want that to be my motivation."

Virginia nodded.

"How about praying the cancer goes into remission?" Doris said. "Couldn't we pray for that, too?"

"That'd be nice," Evie said.

Gladys stood up and came around the coffee table. Crossing the room, she held out her hand. Evie took it and stood up.

Virginia, Doris, and Marva rose and joined them. As they each laid hands on Evie, Gladys smiled at her. Evie recognized that look: *Didn't I tell you they wouldn't let you down?* She smiled back, her throat closing in thanksgiving.

And then the Widows' Brigade did all Evie asked of them.

Five old saints called upon their Commander-in-Chief and went to war against the enemy.

10

Joe closed his notebook and shoved it into his backpack. Zipping it shut, he slung it over his shoulder and joined the exodus from the lecture hall. He couldn't say he had learned anything. His mind hadn't been focused. Or rather it had been, but not on the subject at hand.

Dynah was on his mind.

It had been nine days since she had called. He wanted to get in his car and drive across the bay and find out how she was doing. Clenching his jaw, he kept walking, knowing he couldn't do that. She had to make her own decisions. He didn't have the right to butt in again.

Unless she asked.

Which didn't seem likely after the long silence.

She had called to tell him her parents' marriage was on the rocks and she was staying with a doctor and his family in Mill Valley. She called again a few days later and said she'd arrived home safely and he wasn't to worry.

Yeah, right.

Taking a break, he purchased an espresso at the student union. Maybe a jolt of caffeine would pick up his spirits. Outside, on the steps of Bolt Hall, a young man dressed in a T-shirt, sports jacket, new blue Silver Tabs, and hiking boots was giving a speech about the tyranny of a consumer-based society. Amused, Joe listened for a few minutes. The young man never would have made the grade in a homiletics class. His points were vague, and he rambled. He didn't like people putting in their two bits either. Someone called out for him to give up his Seiko watch, and the speaker didn't even give him the time of day.

Other students lounged around or passed through on their way to the student union or classes. There was a sameness to everyone, though no two people dressed alike. The atmosphere hummed despite the tranquil parklike setting. There was a lot going on here, but not a lot of it had to do with truth.

Joe shook his head. The way he saw it, the thousands of students who thronged the campus were being molded by the values of secularization. Love was libido; judgment, politics; religion, fantasy. Ah, but they all had their gods, though they didn't recognize them for what they were. Education in and of itself had become a god. He'd seen it too often to doubt it. And then there were the other idols: career, money, position, sex. Oh, they were here learning all right. They were drinking in the poison of a decaying society and getting drunk with the pride of their achievements.

What a dead-end place.

It was laughable and tragic how highly reputable professors would come so close to the truth and then veer away from it. On a college campus, admitting there was a God was secular blasphemy. Two days ago, a professor had cited research from a Harvard professor who proposed that humans are engineered for religious faith. Joe had sat forward in his seat after that statement, waiting for the rest to come. Unfortunately, the conclusion was that evolution had equipped mankind to ponder mortality in order to find a way to dissolve the fear of death. Neat reasoning.

Joe had stood and asked if it was possible God created mankind for a personal relationship with him? What he got in answer was a pained air, some soft snickers, and attacks from those who seemed threatened at the mere hint of Christianity.

Glancing at his watch, Joe saw it was one-forty-five. He was expected to meet a group of eleven undergrads near the steps of the Bancroft Library at two for a Bible study. Eleven curious out of thirty-plus thousand. Odd that so few made him feel hopeful, but then Jesus had started with twelve. Twelve against thousands, but the odds had been stacked in God's favor.

Finishing his espresso, Joe crumpled the Styrofoam cup and tossed it into a garbage bin.

Only eight showed up. Maybe his homiletics weren't that great either.

Joe suggested they sit on an expanse of lawn not far away. He started on time with a prayer and then picked up the discussion of the Gospel of John where they had left off at their last meeting. A few minutes later, the missing students arrived with three friends. Joe welcomed them with a broad grin. Things were looking up.

It was a mixed group, with only two other born-again Christians, a girl from Iowa and a foreign student from Hong Kong. Several came out of curiosity, one to debate. Two of the young men seemed more interested in the girl from Iowa than in Scripture. And one of the girls was looking at Joe with a decided gleam in her eyes. He hoped it was his teaching that kept her so focused. *Lord, be merciful. I'm only flesh and blood.*

He kept the study to an hour and a half, then ended it with prayer. He had found it was better to have parameters than to let the discussion wander. He asked them to read the next chapter and gave them several questions to think about before their next meeting. Then he dismissed them and tucked his Bible back into his backpack.

The girl who had been studying him rose when he did. When he headed toward University Avenue, she fell into step beside him. Paige was her name, and she came from Tennessee. She asked him questions about what they had been discussing, but he had the feeling she wasn't concentrating on his answers.

"It's all very interesting, but I'm still not clear about several things you said." She looked up at him. "Maybe we could talk about it more at your place. I'd ask you to mine; but I have two roommates, and the place is always a mess."

Uh-oh.

She smiled. "I could bring some wine."

"I don't think that'd be a good idea."

"The wine or coming to your apartment?"

"Both."

She widened her eyes. "Why not?"

"Conflict of interest."

She gave a soft laugh. "Are you afraid I might seduce you?"

He stopped and faced her. "You'd try," he said bluntly. It wasn't the first time a girl had come on to him under the guise of being interested in God.

She reached out and ran a finger playfully down his sleeve. "That sounds like a challenge."

"It wasn't meant to be."

"No? Well, you know what I think, Joe? I think you'd enjoy yourself." She looked him in the eye. "In fact, I'm sure of it."

The old Joe rose inside him, stirred by her invitation and the pictures suddenly playing in his mind. Time was he would have taken her up on the offer with little thought of consequences or conscience. She was pretty. She had a very nice body. And she was willing. What else mattered?

God mattered. And God knew what was going on inside and outside. God even knew his struggle.

The spark that had flickered briefly died. He recognized

this girl. He would have had a lot in common with her six years ago. That was another lifetime, another person. Now, he saw her as he saw his old self: carried away by carnality, eager for a partner, physically attracted to someone. A lost soul. She was looking for love, but not the kind he had to offer.

Joe decided to give it one last try. "Everything you're looking for is in that book you're holding."

Her chin tilted slightly. "What if I told you I was more interested in you than anything this Bible has to offer?"

He could see she meant it as a compliment. "I'd say you were wasting your time."

She looked surprised and bemused. He figured she hadn't been turned down very often.

"That's blunt. I thought Christians were supposed to be kind."

"I am being kind."

"You're being rude."

"Because I said no?"

Blushing, she glared up at him and called him a foul name. "You know what I hate about Christians? You can't stop preaching, and you think you're better than everybody else." Adding a hair-raising adjective to the name she had called him, she turned on her heel and walked away. As she passed a garbage can, she tossed the Bible into it.

Lord, I give her into your hands. It's a cinch I didn't get anywhere with her. He retrieved the Bible and took out his handkerchief to wipe off a stain of catsup from a castaway bag of french fries.

When he entered his small apartment, he pressed the button on the answering machine and shrugged out of his backpack.

"Hi, Joe."

His heart jumped at the sound of Dynah's voice.

"Just thought I'd call and check in. You must be out evangelizing. Granny got here last night. Mom moved back in with Dad so she could have the guest room." She didn't say anything for a long moment. "I wish I'd come to Berkeley, Joe."

Click.

Picking up the telephone, he punched in a number. It rang four times before it was answered. "Hello?"

"It's Joe, Mrs. Carey. May I speak to Dynah?"

"Just a minute, Joe. I'll tell her you're on the line."

He let out his breath in a hard puff and sat on the worn couch. He could hear Mrs. Carey calling to Dynah. A moment later, another line clicked open.

"Joe?"

"Hi, kid."

Mrs. Carey's end hung up, and they were alone in silence, his heart hammering. "The offer's still good." He tried to keep his tone light.

"I wasn't thinking, Joe. I shouldn't have said what I did. I just wanted to run away and hide before everything blew up again."

"Has it?"

"No. They're talking. They've been talking all afternoon."

"That's good."

"Maybe."

"What are they talking about?"

She gave a soft laugh. "What to do with me and the baby. They're assuming I don't want to keep it."

"Do you?"

"I don't know."

He put his feet up and leaned back. "Want to talk about it?"

"Oh, Joe, all I ever do is dump my troubles on you."

"What are friends for?"

"You've got better things to do. How's the Bible study going?"

His mouth tipped. "One of the girls propositioned me about an hour ago," he said dryly.

"Oh? And?"

"I resisted temptation and was crowned with a couple of names I won't repeat."

"It must be tough being a sex symbol." Her voice brimmed with laughter. It was good to hear that instead of the restrained pain.

He laughed. "Well, I guess fighting off women is part of a pastor's lot in life."

"Is that what you're planning to do, Joe? Be a pastor?"

"Someday. Maybe. Probably. I don't know."

"You sound as decisive as I've been."

"Let's put it this way. I don't see myself in front of a congregation." He lacked Ethan's charisma and talent for making fine speeches.

"You'd make a wonderful minister, Joe."

"We're all ministers. Some of us just have smaller congregations, that's all."

"Whatever we do, may we do it as for the Lord."

Joe smiled, thankful that after the months of wandering in the wilderness her faith was growing stronger. She was ministering to her family without even knowing it. One person standing on the Rock can throw a lifeline to others drowning in the sea.

He heard her sigh. There was a rustling sound as though she was turning over on her bed. "I feel like a beached whale," she said, and he could picture her with her hand moving down over the baby.

"You're supposed to get big."

"In a few weeks I won't be able to get behind the wheel of my car."

"Planning on going somewhere?"

"I'm not going to run away again, if that's what you mean," came the wry response. "Not that I wouldn't like to."

Joe waited for her to say more, but she was quiet. He wanted to see her. He wanted to make sure she was all right. Maybe she would open up to him if they were sitting across a table from one another. "You sound like you need an evening out. What do you say I come over and take you out to dinner?"

"I say yes."

Joe took his feet off the coffee table and planted them on the floor as he leaned forward. "I'll see you in about ninety minutes," he said and hung up. Getting up, he headed for the shower.

■   ■   ■

Dynah put the telephone back on the receiver and relaxed. Smiling, she put her hands lightly on her abdomen as the baby moved. "We're going out tonight," she said, rubbing gently over the place where she felt a foot pressing. It was an odd sensation, part of her and yet separate. Boy or girl?

Pushing herself up, Dynah took her robe from the closet and went across the hall to the bathroom for a shower. She took her time, relishing the warm stream of water and the droning sound that seemed to rinse away stress. When she opened the door and stepped out, she got a full-length view of herself in the mirror. Averting her glance quickly, she dried herself.

"You look good, Dynah. Real good," Joe had said in Mendocino.

Taking the towel away, she looked at the mirror again and studied herself. She had gained twenty-four pounds. It all seemed to sit in the front. She didn't feel beautiful, but neither did she feel ugly. She was all curves now, no plains. Turning to the sink, she looked at the profile of her body. Shaking her head, she smiled sadly. Gone were the slender days of a virginal youth. She had stretch marks. Her body would never be the same. Perhaps if she had conceived this baby in marriage to someone she loved and who loved her, she would feel beautiful.

BELOVED, YOU ARE MINE. YOU ARE BEAUTIFUL TO ME.

Was it the barest whisper she heard in the cloud-filled bathroom or remembered verses? She felt surrounded by love, engulfed in it, protected by it. Closing her eyes, she reminded herself that this child belonged to the Father.

I love you, too, Lord. You are life to me.

Life. What greater blessing was there for a woman than to take part in God's creative power and bear a child for him? She felt the baby move and smiled. Affirmation.

Joe. Joe was the only one who seemed to understand. And she was going to spend an evening with him.

Smiling, she picked up her hair dryer and began brushing her hair.

"You look lovely," her grandmother said when she came downstairs.

Dynah smiled and thanked her. She had taken special care with her appearance. She hadn't worn makeup in months but had put on a touch of blush and lipstick and some Shalimar perfume. "Joe's coming over in a little while," she said. "We're going to go out for something to eat. Where's Daddy?"

"He went to the movies," her mother said.

Hannah studied her daughter. She was beautiful. There was a glow about her that hadn't been there before, even when she had brought Ethan Turner home from the airport. "He didn't want to be in the way of our meeting tonight. Pastor Dan's coming over, you know."

"I forgot. Did you want me to stay?"

"No, you go out, honey. You've been cooped up in this house for the last two weeks. It'll be good for you to go out."

There was an odd atmosphere in the room, a stillness that

was disquieting. "Is everything all right?" Dynah said, looking between her mother and grandmother.

Hannah looked at her mother, unable to answer. She knew if she said one word, she'd start to cry. Dynah would know soon enough that her grandmother had terminal cancer.

Evie smiled. "Nothing for you to worry about, Dynah. We'll talk tomorrow morning."

Dynah knew better. "I love you both," she said, looking from one woman to the other. "And I love Daddy, too."

Hannah nodded, understanding her daughter's need to make a declaration. She wouldn't be drawn into battle. She wouldn't take sides.

Oh, Lord, I've made such a sorry mess of my life, and still you've blessed me with a daughter like Dynah.

It never ceased to amaze her and fill her with a sense of responsibility. How much more hurt could Dynah take? The rape had turned her life upside down. Divorce would shatter her.

Who was going to win the war she had declared? Certainly not her, nor Doug, who had withdrawn from the battlefield. Then who?

They'd argued again last night in the privacy of their bedroom. She knew she had baited Doug over and over again before her mother had come. She wanted to fight it out and have it done with, but he refused to follow her rules. She had suspended hostilities with her mother's arrival. She could pretend for a little while longer.

Her mother hadn't been fooled. After a quiet evening, she had excused herself early and gone upstairs to bed. "Mom knows something's wrong," Hannah remarked. Doug said nothing, but she could feel his anger. It filled her with a sick sense of satisfaction—and despair. "I suppose I could tell her. Maybe she'd understand." It was just about over. A few more pushes would do it. "She already knows my sordid history, so it won't come as too much of a surprise."

She hadn't reckoned with his stubborn will.

Doug stood up. "If you're willing to throw twenty-seven years of our lives away, you file for a divorce," he said, dark eyes hot and filled with pain. "You've always seen your life as half empty instead of half full. I'll tell you something, Hannah. In all the years I've shared with you, I remember more of joy than sorrow. Those are the times that I'm holding on to with everything I've got in me. I love you, but if you're not willing to fight for our marriage instead of trying to rip us apart, there's not a lot I can do about trying to help you put things back together."

"The only reason I'm still here is because God hasn't released me. Yet."

"Considering what he did for us, don't expect him to say you can quit!" He walked out of the room and went upstairs to bed.

She had spent the night on the couch, weeping and thinking about what he had said. She resented every word because she knew Doug was right. God wouldn't release her from their marriage. It galled her, but Scripture was very clear. God hates divorce. "Love one another as I have loved you," he said. Unconditionally. Sacrificially. Completely. Be willing to die for Doug.

The doorbell rang, bringing Hannah back to the present.

"That must be Joe," Dynah said, giving a quick kiss to her grandmother. "We won't be very late."

Hannah got up and walked with her to the door. "I hope you and Joe have a good time," she said, feeling bleak inside. "Get a jacket, honey. It's supposed to get cool this evening."

While Dynah went to the hall closet, Hannah opened the door. "Hi, Joe."

"Mrs. Carey," he said with a smile and nod of respect. "How are you?"

"We're all fine." What a laugh! She opened the door wide so he could come in, but Dynah came around her and went out the door instead. Hannah watched Joe's expression as he looked at her daughter. Oh, my.

"We won't be too late, Mom," Dynah said, kissing her mother's cheek. She smiled up at him as he put his hand beneath her elbow, giving her support as she went down the steps. Hannah watched them go down the stairs, then quietly, thoughtfully, closed the door.

■ ■ ■

"Thanks, Joe. I can't see my feet anymore. Where are we going?"

"The Wharf."

"I love the Wharf," Dynah said, feeling the tension flowing from her as they walked to his car. Joe opened the door for her and helped her in. Shutting the door, he went around the front of the car. She was still fumbling with the seat belt when he slid in behind the wheel.

"Here. Let me." Joe leaned across to loosen the buckle and slide more strap through it so it would fit around her. He grinned at her as he clicked it into place. "My, you've grown."

She laughed. "By leaps and bounds."

Joe drove up Ocean Avenue and turned onto Nineteenth Avenue. As they drove north, passing through the west end of Golden Gate Park, she asked him questions about his life in Berkeley and his progress with the Bible study.

"I'll be finishing the courses in a few weeks," Joe said, "and then I'm considering a break."

"Will you be moving again?"

He glanced at her and saw she was troubled at the idea. "No. I'm going to stay in the bay area." She didn't say anything but sat pensively, looking out the window. Joe took the turn off

Nineteenth to Highway 101. "Have you started Lamaze classes yet?"

"I started Monday evening. Mom went with me."

"How long is your grandmother going to stay?"

"She never stays longer than a couple of days."

He took the turn for the marina. "Your mom looked tired."

"She slept on the couch last night." She glanced at him. "I think she and Daddy are going to get a divorce."

"People go through rough times, Dynah. Don't give up on them yet."

"The anger's so thick it's like a cloud around my mother." She closed her eyes. "Oh, Joe, I don't know how much I can tell you." She didn't want him to think less of her parents.

"Anything you tell me stops with me, and it won't change how I feel about them or you."

She was touched by his reassurance but thankful he didn't press her.

Joe parked the car at Ghirardelli Square. "Walking's supposed to be good for an expectant mother." He took her hand as he helped her out. "And it's a nice evening."

They walked down the hill, turning away from the Maritime Museum and wandering by the sidewalk merchants selling jewelry and knickknacks. A crowd of tourists was waiting for a ride up the San Francisco hills on the famous trolley cars. She and Joe walked around them and down the hill toward the piers.

Joe drew her close as people walked toward them and around them. So many tourists. He wished he had taken her somewhere else, somewhere quiet, away from the confusion of high summer at Fisherman's Wharf. He heard a dozen languages spoken by passersby, most armed with cameras. Maybe if he had taken Dynah someplace quiet she'd feel more like talking.

They stopped at the rails overlooking the small boats docked behind Alioto's #8. Dynah touched his arm. "Thanks for bringing me here, Joe. I've always loved coming to the Wharf. It was so exciting to me as a child. The smells, the sounds, all the people from so many places around the world. I wanted to sit on a bench along the way and watch them, but Daddy doesn't like crowds." She laughed. "He'd usually plow a path for us to one of the restaurants. Once there, he'd ask for a table by the windows so I could look out. That was as close as he wanted to get to the multitude."

Her smile dimmed as she looked down at the railing. She picked at the peeling white paint. "I don't know what to do to help them, Joe. It's my fault things are falling apart."

"It's not your fault."

"In a way, it is. My pregnancy stirred up the past for them. And then I ran away, and that made everything worse for them." She raised her head and looked at him bleakly. She knew she could trust him. He had given her wise counsel on other things. Maybe he could advise her now. "Mom had an abortion before she met Daddy. I'm not even sure they know I know. I don't think Mom ever intended to tell me, but they got into this terrible argument a few months ago, and I overheard everything."

"Was that before or after she took you to the clinic?"

She grimaced. "Before," she said quietly.

Oh, Jesus, no wonder Dynah felt betrayed. What do I say, Lord? What a muddle we make of our lives.

"It was so hard for me to understand after all the things I remembered her saying against abortion," Dynah said, "but I think she did it to appease Dad. He was so convinced it was the only way to deal with my pregnancy. And I wasn't any help. I didn't know what I felt or what to do. I agreed to go, and then I couldn't go through with it."

"Thank God."

"Yes, thank God," she said quietly, putting her hand over her unborn child. She stood silent for a long time, eyes closed. "Tell me what to do, Joe. Tell me how to help them."

"Love 'em."

"I do love them, but I have to do more than that."

"If you step in the middle, you may be getting in God's way."

"What if they decide to get a divorce?"

"They may not."

"What if they do?"

"They can always change their minds." He brushed a tear from her cheek. "You're borrowing trouble, Dynah. You're worrying about what might happen. Deal with now."

"It's so hard to watch what they're doing to each other."

"Emotions are powerful, but they also change as quick as the wind. That's why the Lord says to renew your mind. Don't base decisions on what you feel. Your parents know the Lord. From what you've told me about them, they've been in the Word a long time. They'll remember. If they don't, let God remind them."

"I'd like to spare them the pain."

"Pain has its own rewards. It keeps you out of the fire." He took her hand. "Come on. Let's walk a little."

Around the corner was a covered walkway lined with seafood merchants. Red boiled Dungeness crabs lay arranged on tables of cracked ice. Glass cases held displays of crabmeat in small red-and-white cardboard bowls. Sourdough French bread was bagged and stacked high on the counters.

A man carrying a round of French bread filled with clam chowder bumped Dynah. He apologized and moved on. Joe moved in front of her to keep her from getting jarred again.

"That smelled so good."

"I'm taking you someplace swanky, not buying you a piece of bread with soup in it."

"We'll have to wait an hour or more to get a table, Joe, and then wait thirty minutes more to get our food."

Looking back at her, Joe grinned. "Are you trying to tell me you're hungry?"

She grinned back. "I'm starving."

He bought a sourdough round filled with clam chowder for each of them. *"Bon appetit,"* he said dryly, but enjoyed watching her savor every bite.

The sun went down, and the breeze off the bay turned chilly. The stars were out by the time they returned to Ghirardelli Square. Joe was in no hurry to take Dynah home, and she didn't appear in any great hurry to return. They talked of all manner of things—all except the baby and Dynah's plans for it.

A string quartet was playing in the courtyard. They sat at a small round table near the brick wall. Joe ordered espresso, Dynah decaf and a piece of German chocolate cake. He leaned his elbows on the table and watched her. She made a science of eating dessert. One small bite at a time. At the rate she was going, they'd take up residence before she finished the hefty slice. He grinned. "I've never seen anyone enjoy a piece of cake the way you do."

She forked off a full bite-sized piece and held it toward him. "Have a taste of heaven."

Leaning closer, he let her feed it to him. Raising his brows slightly, he made a sound of approval. Laughing, she pushed the plate toward him. "You finish it. I've eaten all I can." Amused, she watched him enjoy the rest.

After a few bites, he sucked his cheeks into a pucker and drained his black coffee. "Sweet," he said. "Very sweet."

Dynah found herself studying Joe as he turned his attention to the musicians. Odd how a man's appearance could be deceiving. This gentle, caring man looked street tough with his black hair growing past his shirt collar. He was under no obligation to cut it short anymore and was letting it grow. His earlobe was pierced, and on his hand he had a small tattoo of a cross with a diamond in it. She had asked him about it once, and he said the diamond was for a robbery he had committed. When he became a Christian, he had the cross tattooed over it.

Dynah saw how the young women noticed him. He was handsome. She had never thought much about it before, perhaps because she had been so fixed on Ethan. And the two men were so different.

"Are you interested in anyone in Berkeley, Joe?"

Joe looked at her. He saw nothing in her expression to give reason to her question. Just casual interest. "I'm interested in a lot of people."

"I mean girls."

"I look, but that's about as far as it goes."

"You like redheads, don't you?" she said, remembering a student nurse he had dated at NLC.

"I like blondes," he said, making a point of looking at her hair.

She laughed, not taking him seriously. "And brunettes. You were mush over Carole."

"I wasn't mush. I was . . . well, never mind what I was."

"She liked you."

His mouth tipped up on one side. "She liked a lot of guys."

Dynah frowned at that remark and looked him in the eye.

"Don't worry," he said, catching her meaning. "I haven't backslid into that particular sin. Not that I haven't had trouble with some others."

"What others?"

He hesitated. "Envy," he said, glossing over it quickly. "And anger. That's a big one. I had quite a few daydreams about what I'd do if I ever got my hands on the guy who raped you."

She lowered her gaze. "Ethan felt the same way."

Joe didn't argue. Ethan had done a lot of ranting and raving. Unfortunately, he had gotten things twisted. His anger had focused and poured onto Dynah's head when she wouldn't "submit to his authority" and have an abortion. *God, how do people get so screwed up in their thinking?*

"Who did you envy, Joe?"

Joe realized she was listening closely to everything he said. He figured he had better be a little more careful from here on. "A lot of people before I became a Christian. Only one since."

"Who?"

He looked at her but didn't answer.

Dynah stared back at him, wondering. His dark eyes were so intent, she felt warmth flooding her cheeks. "Joe?"

Lord, he thought, *what if I told her the truth? What if I cut the nonchalance and got down to basics?* Weighing the possibilities, he grimaced. "Maybe someday I'll tell you." *Admit it, Joe. You're chicken.*

The musicians were dispersing.

Joe glanced at his watch, and his stomach dropped. "I'd better get you home. You told your mother you wouldn't be out late, and it's already midnight."

On the way down the stairs to the garage, Joe took her hand again. He didn't let go until he opened his car door for her.

She leaned her head back as he drove out of the garage and up the hill. "Thank you for a wonderful evening, Joe."

"My pleasure."

A relaxed silence settled between them as Joe drove across town and turned south on Nineteenth Avenue.

"You know something, Joe? You've turned out to be my best friend." When he said nothing, Dynah blushed, sure she had embarrassed him. "I hope you don't mind my saying that. I mean, I'm not trying to change our relationship or anything."

"Don't ruin it," he said roughly.

Neither spoke for the rest of the drive to Ocean Avenue.

Joe pulled up in front of her house and shut off the engine. When he turned slightly and looked at her, his heart galloped at the tension in her body. What'd she think he was going to do? Kiss her?

"You've always been close when I needed you, Joe," she said without looking at him.

"That's what friends are for."

Tears gathered, tightening her throat. She put her head back against the car seat, trying to relax. "I don't know what's wrong with me. My emotions are always in such an uproar."

He brushed his knuckles against her cheek. "I'd say there's good cause."

She turned her head and looked at him. "We've talked about everything this evening—everything but the baby."

"I figured you'd talk about her when you were ready."

She smiled, eyes brightening. "Her?"

"Or him."

"Her," she murmured, bowing her head and looking down at her body. Her hands moved tenderly over her abdomen. "A little girl," she said in wonder.

"Or boy."

Her hands stopped their gentle caress and rested lightly on her unborn child.

Joe saw her frown slightly. He waited for her to talk about what was worrying her.

"What do you think about adoption, Joe?"

"It's not what I think. It's what you think that matters."

"I want your opinion."

Joe wondered how she'd be able to live with giving her baby up. Two months ago, she had wanted desperately to deny the child's existence. Now, she treasured the life growing inside her. It was evident in the way she touched her growing child, in her expression when she talked about the baby. "It's a noble thing, but so is raising a child."

She looked at him, stricken. "I don't see how I could. I mean, I've no way to support myself, and with a child, it'll be even more difficult. I don't even know where to begin. Any which way I look, I feel torn." Her mouth trembled. "There's no way through this without pain, is there?" Her mouth tipped. "Aside from physical, I feel my heart being torn from me."

He ached for her. "The Lord has a plan for you, and it's not a plan for your destruction."

"I know that in my head, Joe, but sometimes I can't see where this is all going. I felt so close to the Lord in Mendocino." She let out her breath softly. "That day when you found me, I'd sought the Lord, and he opened the door again. I felt such peace. I knew everything would be fine, that this child belongs to him. And then I came home. . . ."

"Are things that bad?"

She hesitated, thinking it over. "Not like they were, I guess. Maybe Mom and Dad are finally dealing with things they should've dealt with years ago and buried instead. I don't know. It's not them so much anymore, Joe. It's me. I'm the one who can't seem to decide anything." She closed her eyes for a moment. "And there's so little time left."

Joe could tell her the exact date the baby was expected. He knew how little time was left for her to make a decision.

"I know it would be best to give up the baby, Joe, but I don't know if I can do it."

"Then don't."

She looked at him, tears shimmering. "How can I not, Joe? How can I raise this baby? I can't rely on my parents forever, depending on them for financial and emotional support. I have to get a job. I have to stand on my own. And when I do, I'd have to find someone to take care of the baby. I can't ask my mother to give up her life to raise my child. And my father . . . He was so set on my having an abortion, I can't imagine him welcoming the idea of me keeping the baby."

"Have you asked him how he feels?"

She looked away. "No, but he made his feelings clear a long time ago."

He felt her grief and confusion. "Women aren't the only ones who change their minds, Dynah." Hadn't he changed his?

"Everything's changing so fast. Maybe he's changed, too. I don't know. I . . . oh . . ." She felt the child move strongly within her.

"What's wrong?" A bubble of panic popped inside Joe at the look on her face. Was she starting labor?

"Nothing," she said and smiled. She reached over and took his hand and placed it on her abdomen.

He felt movement. "Oh, Lord," he said in awe, his hand spreading. "Does it hurt?"

"Not at all." She covered his hand with both of hers as the child pressed and stretched. Giving a soft laugh, she leaned back further as she felt the pressure against her ribs. "She's running out of room."

Joe leaned closer. Was that a tiny foot he felt against his palm or his own overcharged imagination? His heart was racing. He moved his hand gently, in awe of what was happening. It was the closest he could get to being part of the miracle taking place within Dynah.

"I wonder if you know how lucky you are," he said without thinking of the circumstances that had brought this child into being. The jarring memory came swiftly enough, and he looked at her, appalled at his insensitivity.

But she shared the wonder of it. "It is a miracle, isn't it?" Looking into her radiant eyes, Joe almost gave in and did what he had thought about doing from the moment he laid eyes on

Dynah Carey. Catching himself, he drew back slightly. "I'd better get you in."

He walked her to the door. Taking her key, he unlocked it and pushed it open for her. "I'll call you in a few days." He turned away, going down the first two steps.

"Joe?"

When he turned toward her in question, Dynah's heart squeezed tight at the cool look on his face. His mind was already elsewhere.

Oh, Lord, what would have become of me had you not sent this man to pull me back from destruction? Not once, but countless times.

She came back out onto the front step. Putting her hand on his shoulder, she leaned toward him and kissed his cheek. "Thank you."

She saw she had surprised him. He looked back at her, his eyes searching hers briefly. She wondered at the bleakness that came into his expression just before he turned away.

Somehow she had hurt him deeply, and she didn't know how or why.

■　■　■

Evie heard the front door open and knew Dynah was home. *Here we go, Lord. Give me your words. Don't let me tell her the news in a way to cause more pain.* She smiled as Dynah came into the family room. She noticed her troubled expression. "Everything all right?"

"I don't know." Dynah unlooped her small shoulder bag and put it on the side table as she sat down. "I think I hurt Joe's feelings."

"How?"

"I'm not sure." She glanced at the television. "It must be something good to keep you up this late, Granny."

"I haven't been paying much attention." Evie pressed the remote, and the television went black. "Just passing time. I was waiting for you. I wanted to talk with you."

"Does it have to do with whatever you and Mom were discussing earlier?"

"Yes."

"And Daddy?"

"I talked with your dad a little while ago." She could see Dynah was already worrying, and was sorry for it. There was no easy way to break bad news. "I have cancer, honey." She saw the shock spread across Dynah's face as her color ebbed. Her eyes filled. *Oh, dear.* "Now, don't start crying or you'll get me started. Your mom and I have done enough of that."

"What kind of cancer?"

"Breast cancer, but it's spread."

"Oh, Granny," Dynah said in a choked voice. "How far?"

Evie just looked at her granddaughter, hesitant to go into details at this time. The cancer had gone far enough for her to know the outcome. Six months to a year, the doctor had said. Longer, God willing.

Dynah got up and came to her. Sinking down onto the carpet, she rested her head in her grandmother's lap. "I love you so much," she said in a choked voice. "Why does life have to be so unfair?"

Evie stroked her hair. "I've asked myself that question a few times. Why did it have to be you in the park that night? Why me with cancer? And the answer is always the same. Why not?"

"I'm glad you'll be with us."

"I'm going home on Friday."

Dynah raised her head. "But how can you?"

"I've got a car. I can drive."

"You have to have chemotherapy or radiation or something, don't you?"

"If I was thirty and had children to raise, I'd fight with everything I have. I'm seventy-eight, honey. I'm tired and set in my ways. I want to be in my own home, not among strangers in some hospital."

"You can't give up, Granny."

"I'm not giving up. I'm taking medication. I'm following my doctor's instructions. Extensive chemotherapy isn't an option. It makes no sense. Why would an old lady like me want to be sick for weeks on end in an effort to prolong my life one more year or two?"

"But it'll get worse if you don't."

"It's going to get worse anyway, sweetheart." Evie touched her cheek tenderly. "It's the way of all flesh. I can't live forever, you know." She smiled, at peace. "At least, not here."

Dynah rested her head on her grandmother's lap again and wept. "You'll be so far away from us."

Evie's eyes grew hot with tears. "That's why I want you with me. I'll need someone to help me in the months ahead and someone to take care of me down the road as the cancer runs its course. I'd like it to be someone I love and who loves me."

"You're asking me to watch you die?"

"No, I'm asking you to live with me. I see the months ahead as being very precious. I intend to live them to the fullest and make the best use of them I can." Her hand rested on her granddaughter's head. "The Lord has always had his hand upon you, Dynah, from the instant of your conception and before that. I believe he has his hand in everything that's happening right now."

She patted Dynah's shoulder. "Look at me, honey." When she did, Evie smoothed away the tears from her granddaughter's cheeks. "I know you have a lot of things to decide over the next few weeks, hard decisions to make." Hannah had already told her they had an appointment with an adoption agency. She couldn't imagine how difficult that would be. "When all this is passed and behind you, you'll need to get away. You'll need to be active so you won't think about what's happened every minute." She cupped her cheek tenderly. "I want you to know you have a home waiting for you in Oregon. You'll have work to keep you occupied. You'll have time to heal and decide what you want to do with your life. And you'll have an income so you'll be independent when you do know. I'll pay you the going rate for a live-in nurse."

Dynah shook her head. "I won't take any money, Granny."

"Oh, yes, you will. It's the one condition I'm attaching to this. Don't argue with your elders, Dynah. God is good. He makes provisions for those who love him. And you have loved him since you could walk and talk." She gently stroked the fine silken tendrils of blonde hair back from her granddaughter's temple with a trembling hand. "Let him provide for you."

■　■　■

Several weeks after her grandmother went home, Dynah took a long walk along Ocean Avenue. She'd needed to get out of the house, away from the tension between her mother and father. They spoke no harsh words to one another, but neither did a tender one pass their lips. They moved around one another cautiously, as though one brush of contact would ignite the final battle and obliterate them both.

Oh, Lord, why do people retreat to their private citadels? Why do they shoot their cannons from a distance rather than sit at the peace table and speak the truth of what's in their hearts? They love each other and hurt one another with every breath they take.

It was cool this morning, a light fog rolling back as the sun burned through. San Francisco's weather had improved over the past few years. Global warming.

As she walked down the street, Dynah thought about the baby, weighing alternatives while trying to test her feelings. Everyone assumed she was going to give the baby up for adoption. True, she had spoken with an attorney who specialized in adoptions. Vera Adams seemed sensitive to her situation. Within a week, she had several families applying to adopt the baby. Dynah had already received several letters and an album of family pictures from two, each doing their best to reassure her of the good home they could provide her child.

The baby moved within her. Heart aching, she laid her hand over the spot, feeling the prick of tears. It shouldn't matter so much, should it? This child had been forced on her against her will. Why should she be so encumbered?

Oh, Lord, how long must I wrestle with my thoughts and every day have sorrow in my heart?

She could smell the sea and realized how far she had walked. Her mother would be worried.

On the way back, Dynah thought of Joe. She wished she could talk to him again. He always had such a cool presence of mind, but he hadn't called for six days. Was he annoyed with her or just busy? She wondered what he was doing at that moment. Conducting another Bible study near the student union? Working? Classes were over, so he should have more time on his hands. Maybe he was looking for a full-time job.

Craving his companionship, she had almost called him last night but decided against it. Joe was kind and tenderhearted. He had also proven himself a faithful friend. She had to remind herself that there were limits to what one could ask in the name of friendship. Joe had a life of his own, and she had intruded upon it long enough.

An odd twinge gripped Dynah's abdomen. She stopped, alarmed. This was something different from the false labor she had endured over the past two weeks. The tightening increased until she moaned.

This is it! Oh, God, this is it! It's early! I'm not ready! And she was still a mile from home.

Calm down! For goodness' sake. Did she think the baby was going to fall out on the pavement? Not likely. She giggled, remembering some of the humorous remarks her Lamaze instructor had made over the course of weeks.

She panted softly as she continued to walk at a leisurely pace. After a moment, she let out her breath. Odd that she should feel so calm now. All the waiting was over. Ready or not, here she comes! Ten minutes later, another contraction started. Dynah paused this time, pretending interest in the garden of one of the neighbors. Panting softly, she glanced at her watch.

Like menstrual cramps, her mother had said. Not quite.

Why on earth had she walked so far?

Four contractions later, she reached home. She was hot and perspiring. "Mom!"

No answer.

"Mommy!"

A note was on the kitchen counter. Panting through another contraction, Dynah picked it up with a shaking hand and read, "Gone shopping. Back in two hours. Love, Mom."

Dynah punched in a number and asked for Dr. Wyatt. "He's in surgery this morning, Dynah," the nurse told her. "I don't expect him back until two."

"I'm in labor," Dynah said, glancing at the kitchen clock when another contraction started. "The contractions are seven minutes apart."

"I'll notify the hospital you're on your way."

On her way? How could she get there? She'd have to take a taxi. Money. Oh, Lord. She didn't have any money. She dialed Joe and then put the telephone down on the third ring. Why did she always think of Joe when a crisis came? What was she going to say? Drop everything, Joe, and come drive me to the hospital? He was an hour away, and he had his own life. It was time she got on with hers.

She moaned and began pacing nervously. She needed a shower. She needed to pack. She needed to calm down!

As she rinsed out her hair beneath the warm spray, the portable telephone rang on the sink counter. It had stopped by the time she finished rinsing off. Shutting off the water, she opened the glass door and reached for a beach towel with bright tropical fish designs. Bath towels weren't big enough anymore.

The telephone rang again. Picking it up, she punched the button. "Hello?"

"Did you call me a while ago?"

Joe. Oh, thank you, Jesus. Thank you. Thank you! "Yes."

"Three rings and you hang up? What gives?"

"I wanted to talk to you and then thought better of it."

"Thought better of it?"

"Don't be miffed. I just thought better of running to you with every little thing that happens."

"You hear me complaining?"

"No, but . . ." She sighed.

"Why didn't you pick up a minute ago?"

"I was wet." *Oh, Lord, it was starting again.*

"Wet?"

"In the shower," she said tersely.

There was a pause. "What little thing is happening?"

She gave a laugh. "Oh, nothing much." The contraction built and intensified.

"Are you panting?"

"Hang on a minute, Joe." She slapped her hand over the receiver and concentrated on her breathing. *Oh, Lord, oh, Lord, oh, Lord . . .*

"Dynah!" She heard him utter a short, foul word, and there was a thud.

She paced the bathroom, puffing. After a long moment, she let her breath out and lifted the receiver. "Sorry, Joe."

"You're in labor, aren't you? What're you doing home?"

"Calm down, Joe." She giggled. She couldn't help herself. She started to laugh at the ludicrous picture of her marching back and forth in the bathroom with a fish-covered beach towel around herself.

"Stop laughing and get to the hospital!"

"As soon as Mom gets home from shopping."

"Shopping? Why is she shopping?"

"I think we needed groceries." She laughed again. She couldn't seem to stop. Maybe her mother was out buying baby booties and diapers. Seemed appropriate. Perfect timing.

"She doesn't know, does she?"

She giggled. "Nope."

He uttered a short, succinct word and hung up.

"Joe?" She stared at the receiver and then punched his number quickly, knowing if she didn't, he'd be on his way out the door. "For Pete's sake!" One . . . Two . . . Three . . . Four . . . "Pick it up! Pick it up!"

"Hang on. I'm on my way."

"I'm not a baby, Joe!"

"No, you're having one!" He slammed the receiver down.

He didn't answer this time. Frustrated, Dynah held the portable in both hands and shook it, growling under her breath. She dressed and packed and carried her overnight case downstairs.

The back door from the garage opened, and her mother came in, arms loaded with groceries.

Hannah smiled. "Hi, honey. Have a nice walk?" She noticed the overnight case and stopped. Looking from it to Dynah's face, her body went cold. "Oh!" Hurrying into the kitchen, she dumped the bags onto the counter. "Two more bags to unload, and we'll be on our way," she said, rushing out to the car. "How long ago did it start?" she called back.

"Four hours."

"Four hours? Oh, Lord! How far apart now?"

"Five minutes."

"Lord . . . Lord . . . Lord . . . Lord . . ." Hannah raced past, dumping two more bags on the counter. A carton of eggs spilled out onto the floor. "Oh, blast!"

"I have to put this note on the front door for Joe," Dynah said. "He's on his way over. Unless he's been stopped for a ticket."

"Did you call your dad?"

Dynah blushed. Truth was, she hadn't even thought of calling her father. "I'll do it right now."

"Never mind. I'll call him later." Hannah picked up the soggy carton of smashed eggs and dumped it into the sink. "Here. Give me the note for Joe. You go get in the car."

Dynah watched her mother darting hither and yon, clearly getting more nervous by the minute. She was always testy when she was stressed. "Maybe I should drive."

"Very funny. You can't even fit behind the wheel."

The hospital staff was ready with a wheelchair and admission papers. As she was rolled down the antiseptic corridor, the accompanying attendant asked questions and made notations on the form on her clipboard. Recent fluid and food intake? Onset of labor? Bleeding? Exposure to infectious disease? Progress and character of contractions?

As soon as she was in a room, undressed and in a hospital gown, her vital signs were checked, as were her eyes, ears, nose, throat, lymph nodes, and breasts.

"Things are moving right along," the nurse said, glancing at her watch as another contraction started.

Dr. Wyatt entered the room smiling. "D day," he said, coming up alongside the bed. He saw by Dynah's face that she was in the midst of a contraction. He glanced at the nurse.

"Four minutes apart. One minute duration. Typical."

He nodded. As Dynah relaxed, he leaned down and placed his stethoscope on her abdomen, listening carefully. "The baby's heartbeat is strong and fast," he said with a smile. Hannah moved closer, standing guard on the opposite side of the bed while he palpated the fundus and identified the fetal presenting part. The baby's head was engaged in perfect position for normal birth. He gave the nurse instructions to start an IV infusion.

"You're doing fine, Dynah. When the next contraction comes, I'm going to do a pelvic examination to determine cervical dilation and effacement. Try to relax. All right?"

Relax? Was he kidding?

When it was over, Jim removed the plastic gloves and smiled down at her. "You're about halfway there."

Hannah looked noticeably relieved.

Jim lingered, talking with Dynah between contractions while observing her carefully. He cared about this baby with an intensity he hadn't felt since his own children were born. Over the past few months, since Dynah had come to his home in Mill Valley, he had spent every spare minute boning up on obstetrical procedures and speaking with medical colleagues to whom he had referred pregnant patients in the past.

Two weeks ago, on Cynthia's suggestion, he had spent a day in a birthing center. The relaxed atmosphere had been a startling contrast to this bustling hospital setting. One of the things he had noted was the constant reassuring and encouraging presence of the birth facilitator. He intended to play that role for Dynah. "Try to rest as much as you can," he said, patting her arm.

Looking across the bed, he smiled at Hannah. "You're about to become a grandmother."

Hannah smiled back at him, though she felt far from happy about it. Under other circumstances, she would have rejoiced, but how could she when this child was the product of an act of violence upon her daughter? She brushed tendrils of hair back from Dynah's face. "Would you like some water, honey?"

"I'm fine, Mom. Really."

Fine. What an innocuous word. She saw the uncertainty. Dynah didn't know what to do. The day had come, and no decision had been made. She wanted to reassure her and tell her she didn't even have to lay eyes on the child if she didn't want. She could make sure the baby was whisked away by a nurse. The attorney could see it was given to loving parents.

It could be taken care of so easily. So why this pain inside her? Why this ache in her breast?

She remembered the day she had given birth to Dynah. Oh, the joy she had felt. It was indescribable. Tears pricked and she swallowed convulsively. What would Dynah think if she started to blubber all over her?

Oh, God, help me get through this. Give me strength so I can give her strength.

But her insides were shaking like Jell-O. How strange that her voice should sound so calm in her own ears when everything inside her was crying out loud.

"Pant, honey. That's it, sweetheart. You're doing great." She panted with her daughter as another contraction built, stronger and quicker than the last. "Ride it out."

Hour after hour passed as Dynah made a slow climb and then a sharper one through transition.

"It won't be long now," Jim said, removing another pair of plastic gloves and depositing them in the wastebasket.

Dynah moaned. "Have you called Daddy yet?"

"I'll do it as soon as—"

"Call him now."

"I don't want to leave you."

"Now, Mom."

Hannah saw Dynah wouldn't relax until the chore was done. She hurried down the hallway and asked to use the telephone at the nurse's station. Holding the receiver, she punched in his number and gave his secretary the message. She asked if everything was all right, and Hannah gave a hasty yes.

"Did you get him?" Dynah said when she came back in the room.

"He knows."

Dynah looked at her, and Hannah forced a smile. She saw the sorrow creep into Dynah's eyes and was ashamed to be the cause of it. How much pain would her stubbornness cost? But there was no time now for repentance. The steel railings were being pulled up and locked as the bed was being moved from the labor room to the delivery room.

"He'll come, Dynah." In all fairness, she knew Doug would have been here hours ago had she told him his daughter was in labor. He might not care a whit about the baby, but he loved Dynah more than his own life.

Dynah puffed soft, quick breaths as the contraction built and crested. She was making noise now, no quietly heroic ladylike silences. Tears came, along with a rising bubble of panic as the bed was wheeled into a brightly lit room. She couldn't see her mother and asked for her.

"She's putting on a sterile gown," Jim said. "Try to relax."

"I don't think I can do this. . . ." As if she had any choice.

"You're doing fine."

Hannah heard the fear in her daughter's voice and hurriedly pulled on the gown. "I'm right here, honey."

"Eight centimeters," Jim said. "It'll be soon now, Dynah."

Not soon enough, Dynah wanted to say as another contraction came. She moved her hands very lightly over her taut abdomen, trying to relax, trying to breathe, trying to be brave. Her heart was thumping wildly.

"Don't push, Dynah," Jim said.

Easy for him to say! Her body was doing it for her.

Everyone was in masks and paper gowns, even her mother. People were talking, whether to her or one another, she didn't know or care. Soft music was playing. She wanted to ask for something loud and fast but hadn't the breath as another contraction came rolling over the last. *Oh, God, oh, God, oh, God . . .*

I AM THE LORD, YOUR GOD, WHO TAKES HOLD OF YOUR RIGHT HAND. DO NOT BE AFRAID. I WILL HELP YOU. I HAVE DONE THIS SO THAT PEOPLE MAY SEE AND KNOW, MAY CONSIDER AND UNDERSTAND THAT THE HAND OF THE LORD HAS DONE THIS, THAT THE HOLY ONE OF ISRAEL HAS CREATED THIS CHILD.

"That's it, honey. Pant. Remember what you know."

I AM HE, BELOVED. I AM HE WHO WILL SUSTAIN YOU. I HAVE MADE YOU, AND I WILL CARRY YOU.

"It's almost time, Dynah."

Two nurses covered her with sterile drapes and painted her with antiseptic.

"Turn the lights down a little," Jim said.

YOUR MAKER IS YOUR HUSBAND, THE LORD ALMIGHTY IS HIS NAME, THE HOLY ONE IS YOUR REDEEMER, THE GOD OF ALL THE EARTH.

"Everything's going fine, honey."

Dynah looked up and saw the fear in her mother's eyes.

I WILL TURN THE DARKNESS INTO LIGHT BEFORE THEM AND MAKE THE ROUGH PLACES SMOOTH. THESE ARE THE THINGS I WILL DO, BELOVED. I WILL NOT FOR-

SAKE YOU. I AM HE WHO BLOTS OUT TRANSGRESSIONS AND REMEMBERS SIN NO MORE.

Dynah was perspiring and trembling. Groaning, she bore down, her hands tightening.

"Jim!"

"It's OK. We're ready," he said, the table tilting slightly.

Dynah looked at Jim and saw by his eyes he was smiling as he told her it was all right to push now. Not that she needed to be told. She had been waiting for this moment for months. "Oh, Lord . . ." She clenched the handholds tighter.

"That's it, honey," Hannah said. "It'll be over soon. . . ."

Dynah heard herself groaning and couldn't stop.

"The baby's crowning," Jim said. "Don't clench your teeth, Dynah. Do your breathing. That's it. Gentle now. Let your body do the work. Don't press it. Easy, easy."

"Keep breathing," her mother said.

One of the nurses touched her leg. "You're doing great."

Why wouldn't these people shut up? She didn't need them telling her to push or not to push, to breathe and to pant. She couldn't have stopped the process if her life had depended on it. A force beyond herself was in control now. God was bringing her baby into the world with a baptism of water and blood. Her body shook with the awesome act. She felt the ring of fire and gasped in pain.

"Your water just broke, Dynah. Pant now," Jim said firmly.

"That's it, honey."

"Gently now. Keep breathing. The head's coming."

As the head was born, Jim cleared the baby's mouth. Dynah heard the mewling cry and instinctively reached down to touch her baby. Tears burned as she caught a glimpse of her child. *Oh, God . . .*

Jim placed his hand briefly over hers. "I'm going to rotate the baby slightly. The shoulder's coming now. Gentle pushes. That's it. Easy . . ."

She let out her breath as she felt her child slip out in a wet rush.

WHEN YOU PASS THROUGH THE WATERS, I WILL BE WITH YOU. . . .

Jim gave a joyful laugh as he held the squalling child in his hands. Perfect in every detail. Exhilaration filled him. He hadn't felt this good in years. Choking up, he didn't relinquish the infant when the nurse reached out for her. He knew it was against procedure, but he held the baby girl closer to him and savored this moment.

Oh, God, forgive me. How many have I helped sacrifice on altars of fear and selfishness? Sons and daughters of an entire generation.

And even as his heart cried out in anguish, a feeling of forgiveness and redemption swept through him as the darkness fled before the Word of God.

I HAVE MADE YOU A NEW CREATION IN CHRIST JESUS. YOU ARE BORN AGAIN THROUGH THE POWER AND LOVE OF MY BLOOD. I HAVE SET YOUR FEET UPON THE ROCK OF MY SALVATION SO THAT YOU WILL STAND. YOU WILL STAND. YOU WILL STAND.

"Doctor?" the nurse said. "Is everything all right?"

"More than all right," he said hoarsely. "You have a daughter, Dynah," Jim said gruffly and placed the infant on Dynah's abdomen.

"Ohhh . . ." Dynah said, her throat closing with tenderness as she brushed her baby's palm and tiny fingers clamped around her little finger.

"I'll take her," a nurse said, aware of the circumstances.

"Not yet," Jim said and looked up at Hannah. "Do you want to do the honors?" He nodded for another nurse to give her the scissors as he set the clamps.

Hannah took them without a word and cut the cord. Her hand was shaking as she handed the scissors back to the nurse and returned her full attention to her daughter holding the wailing infant close against her breast.

Dynah started to cry. Her feelings were in such a muddle, and she didn't know why. She held her baby closer, distressed at the pitiful wail and trembling limbs. Her daughter turned her head and nuzzled, finding what she sought, and a piercing sense of surprise and connection gripped Dynah.

Hannah saw and understood. Her own child was becoming a woman before her eyes. It had happened in the barest few seconds. A shifting, a subtle change in her demeanor. Tenderness smoothed away the shadows of pain and hours of labor. Dynah smiled at her daughter and spoke softly. "Hello, little one. Welcome to the world."

Hannah looked at the baby then, carefully, fully.

Oh, Lord, what did I expect? That because of the circumstances of her conception, she might be some kind of monster? She's beautiful. So perfect.

Over the past three weeks, she and Dynah had spoken a number of times with the lady at the adoption service. There were families waiting for this baby, families who promised her a secure future. She shouldn't have let Dynah touch her. She shouldn't have looked at the baby herself.

This is my granddaughter, Hannah thought, *my own flesh and blood.*

Another contraction brought forth the placenta. Jim examined it carefully to be sure it was fully intact while a nurse tended Dynah. Another took the baby from her.

"Mom?" Dynah said, her voice husky.

Hannah glanced at the nurse and saw her expression. It was clearly a warning: Don't make things more difficult.

With trembling fingers, Hannah combed the damp tendrils

of hair back from Dynah's forehead. "They're bathing her and putting her under a warm lamp."

Dynah could hear her daughter screaming. *Oh, Lord, must I give her up so soon?* She felt a bubble of panic and fought it down.

"She's fine, honey. They'll take good care of her," Hannah said in a choked voice, unable to look and see that they were.

Washed and draped with a lightweight warm blanket, Dynah was wheeled into the corridor. "You did beautifully, honey," Hannah said, walking alongside her to the recovery room. She was unable to say more than that. Glancing back, she saw the baby bundled in a clear plastic basin heading toward the nursery. Her heart did a sick flop. Her granddaughter.

"You rest here. I'll be back to check on you in a few minutes," the nurse said, leaving them in a quiet, antiseptic recovery room.

As the door closed behind the nurse, Dynah started to cry, deep wrenching sobs of relief mingled with grief. "Oh, Mom. Did you see her? Did you see how perfect she was?"

"Yes, honey. I did." And her heart was breaking.

11

Leaning down, Hannah kissed her drowsy daughter. "I'm going home to get some sleep, honey. I'll be back tomorrow." Dynah was already asleep, exhausted from the hours of labor. Hannah stood a moment longer at the bedside, gazing at the blonde tendrils of hair curling against her daughter's temples. She looked so young and untouched by the tragedies of life.

How is it possible you gave me such a daughter, Lord? I am so undeserving. She's brave and true, and she stood firm. God, forgive me. I tried to convince her to follow in my footsteps. I remember all those years of emptiness and separateness from you, and yet, you redeemed me. You brought me up out of the pit. And you gave me this atonement child. I was like Rachel of old, mourning for my child, refusing to be consoled because my baby was no more. And then I returned to you, and you said to me, "Cease your cries of mourning. Wipe the tears from your eyes. The sorrow you have shown shall have its reward. There is a hope for your future." And now you've shown me, Father. Thanks be to you, Jesus, Dynah followed you and not me.

She took Dynah's limp hand and studied the slender fingers and short clipped nails, remembering how her granddaughter had clasped one and clung before being taken away. Her throat closed tight.

Oh, Lord, Lord, whatever you say, I'll do it. Whatever. Only tell me soon. Please.

Though it was past eleven, the lights in the corridor outside Dynah's room were fully on. A nurse passed by and smiled. Two others were at the nurses' station discussing a chart. Hannah hesitated, standing in the cross of two intersecting corridors.

One last look, Lord. Just one last look . . .

She hadn't expected to find Doug standing at the nursery window, but there he was, staring in, one hand against the glass. Sensing someone staring at him, he turned his head and saw her. Lowering his hand, he stepped back slightly.

As Hannah came closer, she saw a nurse had brought the baby over so he could get a good look at her. She looked up at him and then back at her granddaughter being carried back to the clear plastic bed. She was afraid to look at Doug again, afraid what she would see in his eyes, afraid he would see the anguish in her own.

"Dynah?" he said gruffly.

"Sleeping."

"How is she?"

"Fine." She swallowed convulsively and let out her breath softly, regaining control of her emotions. "When did you get here?"

"A little past five."

She shut her eyes, ashamed. He had arrived before the baby was born and had waited hours for word from her. She had cut him out deliberately, punishing him for past hurts. She bit her lip, waiting for his accusation and retaliation. He was silent, pensive. She remembered his telling her she viewed life as a half-empty cup rather than one half full, and she knew he was right. She had built her life on that habit and brought pain on herself and others for her unrelenting self-centeredness.

God, forgive me.

"How'd she do?" he said quietly, not looking at her, his eyes still fixed on the baby.

"Beautifully."

"I'm not surprised."

She waited for him to ask why she hadn't called him before leaving the house for the hospital. He didn't. He didn't ask her anything. He didn't accuse. He didn't berate. She had cut him out of the second most important event in their lives, the birth of their granddaughter, and he said nothing of the hurt he must feel. "Joe kept me company," he said. "He'll come back and see her tomorrow."

Joe. Ever faithful Joe. "That's nice."

They stood in silence, both hurting, staring in through the glass at the sleeping baby in bin #7 with *Carey* printed in clear black letters.

"I remember the day our daughter was born like it was yesterday," Doug said finally. "She looks just like Dynah."

Hannah heard the tears in his voice and understood perfectly. Hadn't she been afraid? Hadn't she expected the worst? Odd that it had never occurred even to her that despite all circumstances God had brought this child into being. God had created her. How could she be anything less than wonderful?

Sing, O heavens, for the Lord has done this wondrous thing.

And she knew as well what God wanted of her. It was no less than what she wanted for herself. Restoration.

She surrendered. Simply. Completely. And as she did, all the tension went from her with a soft sigh. She could breathe again and inhale the fresh air of God's sweet grace. All the years she had struggled and fought to attain peace for herself, and it came as a free gift with her obedience.

Filled to overflowing with love, Hannah slipped her hand into Doug's and wove her fingers with his. "Let's go home."

His fingers tightened around hers, telling her more than words ever could.

■ ■ ■

Dynah awakened feeling empty and alone. The other bed was empty, the patient having been discharged shortly after Dynah arrived. "You're lucky to have a room to yourself," the nurse had said as she put Dynah's dinner on the rolling tray. "You'll be able to sleep."

Glancing at the clock on the wall, she saw it was two-thirty in the morning. A crack of light shone beneath her doorway. Someone was talking in the corridor.

She needed to use the bathroom. Rather than ring for a nurse, she pushed the covers back and eased her legs over the side. She sat for a moment waiting for the light-headedness to pass. The last thing she wanted to do was faint on the floor and bring everyone running.

Rather than return to bed, she pulled on the robe her mother had left out for her and sat in the chair near the windows. She let out her breath slowly, surrendering the ache in her heart. "Abba Father, surely this suffering has been for my benefit. You've kept me in your love, and I am not destroyed." Her eyes pricked with tears. "Your will be done."

I WILL LEAD THE BLIND BY WAYS THEY HAVE NOT KNOWN, ALONG UNFAMILIAR PATHS I WILL GUIDE THEM.

Tears trickled down her cheeks and spotted her white hospital gown.

AND A LITTLE CHILD WILL LEAD THEM ALL. . . .

"Lord," she whispered, "she is born. She is wonderful. All I have done, you have done for me. What now?"

And God told her.

Dynah did not hesitate.

Standing shakily, she returned to bed and pressed the call button. The door opened a moment later and a nurse entered.

"Would you please bring me my baby?"

The nurse hesitated. "Under the circumstances, it might be best if you didn't hold the baby."

"The circumstances have changed. I'm keeping her."

The nurse was aware of the difficulties surrounding this child as well as the circumstances of its conception. "It might be better if you spoke to someone about this."

Dynah smiled, radiant. "I already have."

■　■　■

Evie received two calls on the morning of September 25. The first was from Hannah informing her that Dynah had given birth to a baby girl. Mother and child were both in perfect health. The second was from Dynah. The conversation was brief.

"Granny, I'm going to keep my baby."

"Praise God," Evie said, feeling the weight of decades lift as a new road was forged ahead. "When can I expect the two of you?"

■　■　■

Dynah watched her daughter suckle and marveled at how perfect she was. Her head and body, her arms and legs, her tiny hands and feet were all combined to make a work of art. The small mouth stopped tugging as she fell asleep, replete and content. Dynah smiled, pressing her little finger lightly against her breast to break the suction.

Covering herself, Dynah lifted her daughter against her shoulder and rubbed her back gently. The baby was a melting softness against her heart. She loved the smell of her child, the feel of her silky smooth flawless skin, the soft sounds she made.

Laying the baby down between her thighs, Dynah opened the blanket and studied her perfect little body again. She was in awe of her.

Oh, Lord, you formed my baby's inward parts; you wove her in my womb. I give thanks to you, for she is fearfully and wonderfully made. Oh, Father, how wonderful are your words, my soul knows it well. Her frame was never hidden from you. You saw her unformed substance and wrote her name in your Book of Life. You even knew the days ordained for her when as yet there was not one. She is beautiful as you are beautiful, perfect in every way.

I WILL POUR OUT MY SPIRIT AND MY BLESSINGS ON YOUR CHILDREN. THEY WILL THRIVE LIKE WATERED GRASS, LIKE WILLOWS ON A RIVERBANK. SOME WILL PROUDLY CLAIM, 'I BELONG TO THE LORD.'

Leaning down, Dynah kissed the soles of her daughter's feet and felt the tiny toes curl against her lips.

"Hi, kid."

Dynah's heart leaped at the sound of Joe's voice. Lifting her head, she saw him leaning casually against the doorjamb, watching her. Her heart turned over as he smiled. She smiled back. "I made it to the hospital on time."

"I figured that when I found the note taped to the front door," he said, entering the room and pushing the curtain back farther.

"I'm sorry, Joe."

"About what? Not waiting around? I'd have been ready to strangle you if you had."

"Mom said you were here the whole time."

"In the waiting room with a bunch of nervous dads."

"Including mine."

"Have you seen him?"

"This morning. He stopped by the nursery last night to see

her," she said, looking down at her daughter. She looked up at Joe again and smiled. "He and Mom went home together." She laughed. "Mom forgot she drove her car."

Joe's eyes twinkled. "I take it things are looking up."

"You could say that. They were here together this morning." She cocked her head in a teasing manner. "And you were right, Joe."

"About what?"

She grinned. "She's a girl."

He came around the bed, smiling down at the baby. "And a beauty, just like her mother. May I?"

"Of course," she said, watching him.

Joe lifted the baby carefully, cradling her tenderly in his arms. He walked around the room, gazing down at her in wonder. "Hello, princess," he murmured softly, and the baby awakened, gazing up at him. Stopping at the foot of the bed, Joe looked at Dynah. "You did good."

Dynah blushed and lowered her head. She felt how he looked her over. She wished she had taken the time to brush and French-braid her hair and put on a little makeup. She must look a fright in her hospital gown with her hair in disarray.

Joe thought she had never looked more beautiful. He cleared his throat. "What are you gonna call her?"

"Deborah," she said, "Deborah Anne Carey." Deborah for Israel's judge who led her people into battle, Anne for the prophetess who knew the Word of the Lord.

"Welcome to the world, Deborah Anne Carey," Joe said, stroking the soft cheek with the back of his knuckles. He had never felt anything so soft or beheld anything so untainted and perfect. He brushed her palm and felt the tiny fingers clasp his finger. He swallowed hard, struck by the depth of God's mercy.

"We'll be moving to Oregon in a few weeks."

Joe glanced up. "What'd you say?" He felt as though Dynah had kicked the wind out of him.

Just like that, Lord? Here one day and gone tomorrow?

"Deborah and I. We're moving to Oregon," she said again. Joe didn't look pleased. She explained about her grandmother's condition and offer as well as the welcome mat laid out by Granny that morning.

"That's great," Joe said flatly. *Oregon, huh? OK, Lord. If that's the way you want it. Oregon, it is. I've always wanted to see the Northwest.* "I've heard it's a great place to live."

"Maybe you'll come visit sometime," Dynah said. She felt like one of the Israelites after forty years in the desert. She was stepping into the Jordan. Would God hold back the water and let her get to the Promised Land?

Joe looked at her, dark eyes clear and direct. "Just give me the address."

She blinked. And if that wasn't confirmation enough . . .

THIS IS THE MAN I HAVE CHOSEN FOR YOU, BELOVED.

As she stared into Joe's eyes, her heart soared. *Oh, Lord, Lord. I am so undeserving.*

As Joe returned his attention to her baby, Dynah watched him, her heart softening and warming. Every doubt and hesitation melted away, and she felt the wonder of God's love for her. *Oh, Jesus, I love you. I love you so much.*

"Oh, Joe . . ." she said softly, seeing him fully for the first time. He had always been there, right beside her, exactly where the Lord had placed him.

Joe raised his head and looked at her, bemused by what he saw in her eyes. He had waited so long he didn't recognize it for what it was. "Sorry," he said. "Didn't mean to monopolize her." He brought the baby around the bed and laid her gently on Dynah's thighs.

"Joe . . ." Cupping his cheek, she turned his face toward her.

"My sweet, sweet Joe . . ." Leaning forward, she kissed him full on the mouth.

Joe caught his breath and drew back slightly, searching her eyes. When she smiled, heaven opened. "Oh," he said, that hushed word the beginning of a psalm. Raking his fingers lightly into her hair, he let the wonder of it flood him. "It's about time."

She laughed softly. "Will you marry me?"

His mouth curved wryly, eyes shining. "I thought you'd never ask."

Leaning down again, Joe kissed her the way he had dreamed of doing since the moment he saw her walk into the gymnasium at NLC.

Epilogue

A young girl sat in the full waiting room of the clinic, her heart hammering, her stomach so tense she felt sick. One girl sat crying silently while an older, narrow-eyed, tight-lipped woman sat beside her. A woman in her late thirties sat with her slender legs crossed reading Fortune. Another girl, in her early teens, in a pair of baggy black Levi's and a scoop-necked white T-shirt sat forward, knees and toes together, beside her friend in a short black skirt and tight red sweater.

No one spoke. No one met the gaze of another. They stared down at their hands or a magazine or off into space.

The young girl closed her eyes tightly, praying for strength.

I AM HERE, BELOVED. I AM THE LORD YOUR GOD, WHO LOVES YOU.

The door opened, and a woman in white stood looking at her clipboard. "Number nine."

The waiting room emptied of one.

The young girl hunched in her chair. *Oh, God, oh, God, I'm so scared. I want to go home.*

COME OUT FROM THEM, BELOVED, AND BE SEPARATE, AND I WILL LEAD YOU IN THE WAY EVERLASTING.

Shaking, she got up.

Her boyfriend clamped his hand around her wrist. "Where're you going?" he said in a hushed, taut voice.

She leaned down and whispered. "I don't want to do this."

He pulled her down beside him again. "Do you think I do?"

"Then let's leave."

"And do what?" He leaned closer, speaking so only she could hear. "Look, this isn't easy for me, either. Don't make it any harder. We've been over this a hundred times. There's nothing else we can do."

She tried not to cry. Crying only upset him more. She didn't want him to get mad at her. "I don't think I can go through it."

"You said your parents would disown you."

THOUGH YOUR FATHER AND MOTHER FORSAKE YOU, I WILL NEVER LEAVE YOU.

"And what about school?"

"There must be another way."

"What other way? You tell me what other way."

She looked up at him pleadingly. "We could get married."

"Yeah, right," he said *sotto voce*. "And live on what? Love?"

"I'd work. . . ."

"Give me a break. At that fast-food place? Making minimum wage? And what about after the baby comes? Kiss my future good-bye. I want to go to college. Remember?"

Her eyes burned with tears at his tone. He had been so sweet and tender before they had sex. After the first time, that was all he ever wanted. And now that she was pregnant, he was angry with her most of the time. It wasn't all her fault she was in this condition. She'd only forgotten to take her pill that one day, and he'd never once taken precautions.

"I'm scared," she said in a soft shaky voice.

TRUST ME. I AM YOUR ROCK AND YOUR FORTRESS. I AM YOUR DELIVERER, BELOVED. TAKE REFUGE IN ME, FOR I AM YOUR SHIELD AND THE HORN OF YOUR SALVA-

TION. CALL TO ME AND I WILL RESCUE YOU FROM YOUR ENEMIES. THE CORDS OF DEATH WILL NOT ENTANGLE YOU. . . .

"I'm scared, too," he said, surprising her.

"I want to leave."

He took her hand and held it tightly. She could feel the perspiration on his palms. "I've heard it's not so bad," he said bleakly.

SEEK ME, BELOVED, AND I WILL ANSWER YOU. I WILL DELIVER YOU. I WILL BE YOUR HIDING PLACE. I WILL PROTECT YOU AND SURROUND YOU WITH SONGS OF DELIVERANCE.

"It's only supposed to take a few minutes. By tomorrow, it'll all be behind us."

She looked at her boyfriend and saw how uncomfortable he was. He didn't want to talk about it anymore. He just wanted to get it over and get out of here.

Oh, God, I don't want to lose him.

I AM THE LORD YOUR GOD AND THERE IS NO OTHER.

Her heart jumped as the door opened again.

TURN TO ME IN YOUR HOUR OF NEED AND I WILL . . .

Her number was called.

. . . LOVE YOU WITH A LOVE THAT WILL LAST FOREVER.

She hesitated.

"Go," her boyfriend said, looking at her imploringly.

DO NOT HIDE YOUR FACE FROM ME, BELOVED. I LOVE YOU WITH AN EVERLASTING LOVE. I WILL PROVIDE FOR YOU. HEED MY VOICE.

Her number was called again. She wanted to jump up and run screaming from the room.

CALL OUT TO ME AND I WILL BRING YOU UP OUT OF THIS PIT OF DESPAIR AND SET YOUR FEET UPON THE ROCK. I WILL PROTECT YOU. I WILL PROVIDE FOR YOU:

OH, MY BELOVED CHILD, YOU ARE SO VERY PRECIOUS TO ME, SO PRECIOUS I DIED FOR YOU AND ROSE AGAIN THAT YOU MIGHT LIVE IN ME. TRUST ME. OH, MY BELOVED, TRUST ME.

Her boyfriend took her hand and stood. Heart hammering, she stood with him.

He didn't take her out of the clinic. He handed her over to the woman in the doorway with the clipboard in her hand. The woman smiled and said everything would be all right. Letting go of her, the boy stepped back and turned away. As the girl went forward, she looked back and knew she was alone. When the door closed, death surrounded her.

And into the silence and separation that followed could be heard the weeping of God's only begotten Son, the Atonement Child.

Beloved,

If this story has opened old wounds, please know that Jesus is waiting with open arms to welcome and comfort you as his own. There is nothing, absolutely nothing, that the Lord won't forgive—and forget. He promises that as far as the east is from the west, so far has he removed your transgressions from you. He died for you and rose again so that you can have new life in him. All you have to do is accept him. His love is not earned but given as a free gift. That's my prayer for you: that you will know and accept Jesus Christ as your Savior and Lord and learn who you are in him.

In Christ, you are his child. You are raised up with him. You are forgiven. In Christ, you are a new creation, the very temple of the Holy Spirit. You are delivered from the power of darkness. You are redeemed, blessed, holy, and sanctified. Even now, God is holding your child close. And in Christ, you will be reunited in love.

You are victorious and set free from sin and death. You are more than a conqueror. You are strong in the Lord, able to withstand any storm through him.

You are sealed with the Holy Spirit of promise. You are accepted. You are complete in him. You are crucified with him, free from condemnation, and reconciled to God Almighty—

and reunited with your children. Through Jesus, you are qualified to share in his inheritance. You are a fellow citizen with the saints and the household of God. You are built upon the foundation of the apostles and prophets, and Jesus Christ is your Cornerstone, your High Priest, your Husband.

You are born of God, and the evil one cannot touch you.

You are overtaken with blessings.

You are called by God.

You are chosen!

You are an ambassador for Christ, a messenger of the Good News. You are healed by the stripes of Jesus, and you are being transformed into his likeness.

You are loved.

You are one in Christ.

You have everlasting life.

You can do all things in Christ Jesus.

His grace and mercy are beyond anything I can explain in words. The Bible is filled with his love for you, and his promises. Please allow yourself to experience this love and forgiveness, to live in it, to walk with him. Let go of yourself, and cry out to the Lord, and he will hear and answer. He knows all about you. He knows everything you've done, where you've been, what you've said, how you've felt, and he loves you with a love everlasting.

The Holy One, Jesus Christ, the most mighty God, holds out his hand to you right now. All you have to do is open the door of your heart and invite him in.

May it be so.

Francine Rivers

Support Groups

The following national organizations have information and referrals for postabortion counseling and support groups in your area:

American Rights Coalition
P.O. Box 487
Chattanooga, TN 37401
(423) 698-7960
Please call 1-800-634-2224
   for referrals for medical,
   legal, and emotional
   assistance.

Care Net
109 Carpenter Dr.
Suite 100
Sterling, VA 20164
(703) 478-5661
Please call 1-800-395-HELP
   for a referral to the closest
   Care Net Crisis Pregnancy
   Center in your area.

Heartbeat International
7870 Olentangy River Rd.
Suite 304
Colombus, OH 43235-1319
(614) 885-7577
WWWeb: http://www.qn.net/
   /heartbeat/
E-mail: heartbeat@qn.net

National Office of Post-
   Abortion Reconciliation
   and Healing
P.O. Box 07477
Milwaukee, WI 53207-0477
1-800-5WE-CARE
(Will give referrals to Project
   Rachel programs in
   Catholic dioceses)

Open Arms
P.O. Box 9292
Colorado Springs, CO 80932
(719) 573-5790

Victims of Choice, Inc.
P.O. Box 815
Naperville, IL 60566-0815
(630) 378-1680
(Offers guidebook for
one-on-one abortion-
recovery counseling)

Life After Assault League, Inc.
Kay Zibolsky
1336 W. Lindbergh
Appleton, WI 54914
Phone (920) 739-4489
FAX (920) 739-1990

Other titles by best-selling author Francine Rivers

MARK OF THE LION
#1: *A Voice in the Wind*   0-8423-7750-6
#2: *An Echo in the Darkness*   0-8423-1307-9
#3: *As Sure as the Dawn*   0-8423-3976-0

A Voice in the Wind Discussion Guide   0-8423-1638-8

The Scarlet Thread   0-8423-3568-4
The Scarlet Thread Audio   0-8423-3564-1